RONAN
THE BARBARIAN

RONAN
THE BARBARIAN

----

translated from the Original Gibberish by
James Bibby

MILLENNIUM
An Orion Book
LONDON

First published in 1995 by
Millennium
An imprint of Orion Books Ltd
Orion House, 5 Upper St Martin's Lane
London WC2H 9EA

A CIP catalogue record for this book is available
from the British Library

ISBN: (Csd) 1 85798 282 7
(Ppr) 1 85798 432 3

Typeset at The Spartan Press Ltd,
Lymington, Hants
Printed and bound in Great Britain by
Clays Ltd, St Ives plc.

FOR MY MOTHER

Acknowledgements

Grateful thanks are due to Tony Peake, Alan Brodie and Anneka for their help and encouragement. Thanks also to everyone who has tried to bring Ronan to the attention of the Powers That Be in television (and most especially to Humphrey Barclay). And thanks also to L.H. and C.T. for their help and advice over the years.

Special thanks are due to Richard Ball (of Richard Ball Publishing) for office and computing facilities, copious red wine, several foul hangovers, and That Holiday. Thanks, Rikko. Buy his A-level aids, guys.

Finally, thanks and love to Collette. For everything.

'Many are the myths and legends woven around the deeds of Ronan Mage-bane, greatest of warriors. Only here, in the The Pink Book of Ulay, can the real truth be reliably told . . .'

The Pink Book of Ulay

'The Pink Book of Ulay is about as reliable and truthful as a sales-rep describing his recent sex-life to another sales-rep.'

The Good Chronical Guide

'Hey – must be some book, yeah?'

Mav Mavson (Chief Sales Executive for the Orcbane Sword Corporation)

BOOK ONE

SWORD

. . . but the first to recognise the true value of Spellstone was Vataan, the Elven Mage of B'Ibaq. An avid collector of gemstones, he was examining some examples of an unfamiliar green crystal that he had collected during a holidiay in South Behan when a hornet buzzing around the window began to irritate him. Carelessly flinging a minor fireball at it he was amazed to find that for some reason the power of his spell was increased a hundredfold, and the fireball took out the entire wall, the house next door, and half the corner shop.

When he had at last shaken off the resulting lynch mob, Vataan settled down to do some serious research into this new crystal. To his amazement, he found that it acted like a magnifying lens to magic, vastly increasing his powers. Wishing always to have the crystal on his person, and being a skilled lapidary, he set it in the centre of a torque of gold, bound about with filaments of silver and platinum and imbued with all his magic guile, and this he wore around his neck. So did he become a powerful and renowned mage within the city where he lived, and thus did this magical jewel become known as the Torque of Vataan . . .

The Pink Book of Ulay

The lizard scuttled across the stone-flagged floor and then froze like a lime-green statue, alerted by a sudden movement on the other side of the room. It waited, head on one side, senses analysing the currents of air, the vibrations of the floor, the curious gasps and moans emanating from the pile of furs heaped in front of the dying log fire. It listened uncomprehendingly as the sounds quickly reached a crescendo before fading, and then hugged the floor as a large threatening figure hauled itself upright and lurched through the door into the next room. Silence descended, and the lizard scuttled forward again. And then a hand poked out from the furs, a hand that was slender, feminine, and trembling with suppressed annoyance. The lizard froze once more as every sense screamed a warning of danger, and then blue light blasted from the finger-tips and hammered into it. There was a small explosion and a tiny puff of lime-green smoke, and the lizard was instantly transformed into a very surprised-looking cheeseburger (with extra cheese). The hand beckoned impatiently and the cheeseburger floated across the floor and settled reluctantly into its palm.

Shikara took a huge bite of the burger and then snuggled back sulkily into the warmth of the furs. Well, what a disappointment tonight had been! Normally there was a lot to be said for being a sorceress, particularly when it came to love-making. For starters, you could usually forget all the age-old problems associated with having to make love to such a self-centred species as man. No more let-downs. No 'not-tonight-love-I've-got-a-jousting-tournament-tomorrow'. No 'that's-me-satisfied-tough-luck-darling-I'm-going-to-sleep'. Whatever the potential problem, you could isolate it and cure it, sometimes before it had even come into existence. For the wine-wasted, a quick Spell of Rigidity. For the inexperienced or selfish, a Charm of Delayed Ecstasy. For the under-endowed, a Potion of Enlargement.

She snorted sarcastically and reached out for the wine goblet on the edge of the hearth. God, how unimaginative men were! Offer them a choice, and it was always the Potion of Enlargement they went for. And always for the same part of the body. Why wouldn't they experiment? Mind you, maybe they did know best. She remembered that young warrior she'd had the crush on, a few decades ago. She'd given him a two-foot tongue. It was great at first, until he started catching flies with it. She'd found that most off-putting. Especially in the middle of making love. Still, it hadn't been all bad . . .

Shikara flexed her body, enjoying the feel of the furs against her skin, and luxuriated in memories of past lovers. There had been that young Prince . . . what-was-his-name? He'd been a sweet boy. Inexperienced, upright, moral . . . he'd refused to make love once, as it was a holy day, and when she'd tried to coerce him, he'd locked himself in the bathroom. Amused, she'd cast a spell of Invisible Lip-love through the keyhole. The noises that had emerged over the next hour! It sounded as though the Prince was being sucked to death by a giant leech. When he eventually emerged, he was about a stone lighter and shaking like a leaf. Mind you, he'd been no use to her after that. He was a spent force. Eventually, she heard that he'd retired from public life and sought peace and tranquillity in a monastery. In a fit of nostalgia, she'd cast a spell unbeknown to him, granting him one hour of Invisible Lip-love every year on his birthday. It must have come as one hell of a shock to him on the first birthday after that. One hell of a shock to the other monks, too.

The sound of footsteps in the next room brought her sharply back to the present, and she scowled with annoyance. Some lover this Nekros had turned out to be! Two weeks ago, when she'd first seen him, striding into Drenai Dreams ('Unch Haven's Premier Nightclub'), she had been immediately struck by his swarthy, muscular good looks. And when he'd carelessly decapitated the barman with his own sword for serving someone else out of turn, she had been smitten. She had always found the combination of macho beauty and casual butchery a bit of a turn-on. But on their first night together the scales had fallen from her eyes like an *apatodon*[1] falling from a cliff. She had rather hoped that Nekros would be something of a sexual athlete . . . and, it had to be admitted, in his own way he was. Unfortunately, he specialised in the sprint. Since then she had used every spell in her book to try and introduce a little stamina into his repertoire. At first she had met with some success, but lately it seemed that her magic wasn't doing a single klatting bit of good at all. Like most world-class sprinters, Nekros appeared to be trying to break the ten-second barrier every time he performed.

With a frustrated sigh she drained the goblet, and then scowled at the doorway as Nekros sauntered back through it, his six-foot-plus muscled frame seeming faintly ridiculous wrapped in the woman's robe he'd donned against the chill of the other room. The sarcastic barb she had prepared froze on her lips, and an angry glint lit her eyes as she saw that he was leafing through an ancient leather-bound book. Her Minutiae Carmenorum! Her

[1] For information on *Apatodons* and other Midworldian oddities, see Appendix 1.

own personal book of spells! Not that she needed to refer to it these days . . . and not that it would be of any use to someone without the Power . . . but still! How dare he! Didn't he realise that a woman's spell-book was more private than her diary? This felt worse than the time she'd spent three days inveigling the legendary Tobylt Dragonslayer back to her place, only to find him standing in front of the mirror in her bedroom, trying on some of her most feminine underwear.

Furious, she flicked a quick Mind-string at Nekros, then fell back in amazement as he deflected it straight back at her. That hurt! How the hell . . .? For some reason she couldn't move, couldn't seem to think . . . The wine! Her thoughts turned inward as she sought the contents of her bloodstream, analysing, evaluating. Drugged! But even so, she should be able to mindblast Nekros with one hand tied behind her back. How had he got the Power to contain her? Puzzled, she stared up at him, and then her guts twisted with horror as she saw the glint of gold nestling about his throat. By the five Great Demons! The Torque of Vataan! How had he found it? She could have sworn it was safe, bound about by spells and incantations and stuffed in the bottom of her underwear drawer. He must have had it for days . . . no wonder the Spell of Delayed Ecstasy hadn't been working. He must have been casting a counter-spell! Well, that explained why she had suddenly run out of Grated Bull's Pizzle. The sly bastard!

With a satisfied grunt Nekros found the page for which he had been searching. He gazed down at Shikara and she was horrified to see that his eyes were empty of all emotions except for satisfaction and . . . surely not! Yes, hatred! God, what a prat she'd been! She sank back into the furs, stunned and vulnerable, unable to think, and lay there helpless as Nekros began to chant. His voice seemed to fill the room like a melon filling an egg-cup, and the words seemed to be crushing her as she tried to cudgel her brain into action. The combination of drug and spell had robbed her of the ability to harm him, but she knew she had to do something. The Torque and the spell-book gave Nekros the potential for a vast amount of power, but it was a power which he would be unable to control. Even though he did possess some latent ability he was, quite simply, a magical maladroit. The one time that Shikara had tried to show him how to do a basic spell, he had accidentally turned the kitchen stove into a pool of molten metal. Letting him loose on the world with both Torque and book would be like letting a five-year-old loose in a pet shop with a chain-saw.

Desperation gave her one last surge of magical strength. Her eyes flared briefly, and the book erupted in a sheet of green flame, turning to ashes in an instant. Nekros roared with pain and fury, stared for a second at his singed finger-tips, and then hurled the final words of the incantation at her. Shikara had one brief moment to realise that this time she really was in bottomless do-do, and then everything imploded in white light and the four walls of the room seemed to slam in and crush her.

TRIBE

Came there a time in the second age when evil spread its thrall throughout the land. Men walked in fear, as trolls and orcs multiplied, goblins took up long division, and dragons dealt with fractions. Many a once-noble tribe forsook the ploughshare for the sword, and mighty were they, for they had studied the Black Arts, and knew of anabolic steroids. And chief amongst them was the Tribe of Fallon. None could withstand their might, and at their leader's name grown men would bow their heads in fear. Nekros the Black was he, for black was his horse, and black his helm and shield, and he cared naught for personal hygiene. Some said that he had sold his soul to the Demon Lord, Asgarbad, others that he had swapped it for some curling-tongs. Fell was he, and where he rode death and destruction followed . . .

The Pink Book of Ulay

The Nevacom Plains stretched for mile upon mile between the Northern Mountains and the Forest of Dreams. Once a thriving area of arable farmlands in the east of Frundor, the plains had been savagely affected by climatic changes. Earthquakes had diverted the two main rivers away from the area. Lack of rainfall had turned the topsoil to dust, and searing north winds had blown the dust away. Successful farming became an impossibility, and the people began to leave, gradually at first, and then in droves. Eventually, the plains became a virtually uninhabited wasteland. You could still grow things there . . . lonely, for example. Bored. Hungry and thirsty. But crops? Tricky. The few remaining folk who tried to scratch a living in the barren wastes were one of three things. Poor, extremely poor, or dead.

Right in the middle of the most desolate part of the plains stood a primitive shack that looked as though it had been built by somebody who had no tools, no ability, and quite probably no hands. The biting wind whistled around the matted filth of the thatched roof and blew grit and gravel under a door that was more hole than wood. In the lee of the wattle-and-daub walls, where the wind was merely uncomfortable rather than painful, huddled an underfed, under-sized donkey. The donkey was extremely pissed off. It had spent most of the day looking for food, and the rest of the day thinking about food. So far it had managed to eat a few straggly leaves of *pata* grass, some earth, a bit of one of its own hooves that had come off, and a paper bag. The paper bag had been something of a highlight. Now as night fell it was standing there in the encroaching gloom, stomach rumbling, chewing on a stone which it was trying to pretend was a piece of turnip, and staring pessimistically up at the thatch.

Bloody typical! it thought, as the aroma of rotting straw wafted tantalisingly down. The best meal for miles around, and they've stuck it on top of the shack. Keep me going for weeks, that would! It had spent ages trying to think of a way of getting up to the roof, and was currently working on mutating and growing wings – not with a lot of success, it had to be said.

Suddenly, the donkey pricked up its ears. What was that in the distance? It sounded like approaching hooves. Could this possibly herald the advent of food? Maybe some donkey-loving charity had got wind of his plight, and was speeding to his rescue! Straw for the Poor, perhaps, or Hay on the Way. Yeah, that must be it! With optimistic heart and rumbling stomach, the donkey waited patiently as nemesis approached.

Like crows seeking carrion, the Tribe of Fallon came out of the east. They rode like the wind, black shadows on a blacker plain. Their horses' hooves were muffled by cloths, to deaden the sound of their coming. Surprise was their weapon, as was terror, and all men were their foe. No man would they spare, nor woman, nor child. These were seriously bad bastards.

As they flowed past like some polluted tide, the two leading riders peeled off from the group and cantered their horses towards the shack. The larger of the two stared at it for a moment and then spoke.

'Go with the tribe, Angnail. There is only enough sport here for one. I will join you later.'

Angnail spurred his horse in pursuit of the rest and merged silently with the night. His leader dismounted, leaving his huge coal-black horse to paw restlessly at the bare ground, and then paused to sniff the air. Ye gods! The stench was enough to make an orc vomit! How anyone could be so stupid as to construct their cess-pit so close upwind from their house! Nekros shook his head despairingly, and the golden torque at his throat glinted in the moonlight. Then holding his cloak bunched over his nose, he stalked purposefully towards the shack, a gleam of happy anticipation in his watering eyes.

Inside, Varg the Slender was concentrating on dinner, while his wife watched with tremulous admiration. For the record, calling him 'Varg the Slender' was something of a misnomer. In fact, even calling him 'Varg the Painfully Thin' would have been doing his skeletal frame an injustice. But as Varg liked to say, you don't get anywhere by being pessimistic. It was his irrepressible optimism that led him to call his wife 'Elen the Not-too-ugly'. The same optimism had led him to stick it out in the plains when all his neighbours had given up.

'Never mind,' he'd say, when the harvest had failed again, and everyone was facing starvation. 'Worse things happen at sea!' But the neighbours just threw a few bricks at him and moved away to the south.

'Quitters!' he'd said. 'This place is on the up.' For a brief while this year, it had looked as though he'd be proved right. It had actually rained one afternoon a few months back, and by mid-summer, the wheat had rocketed up to six inches tall. But since then, nothing. Once again, it had been a poor harvest. And tonight, the last few grains of wheat had been ground down to make the minuscule bread roll that sat on their only plate. But Varg was not discouraged. Varg had a plan.

Varg was very proud of his little plans. Without them, they would probably have starved to death by now. It had been his idea to site the cess-pit where they had, and to stop putting quick-lime into it. He called it his F-plan diet: F for flies. They came in their thousands, and Varg and Elen spent a lot of time developing interesting recipes based around this unusual source of protein. There was Blow-fly Pâté, Crunchy Blue-bottle Surprise, and of course his favourite, Crushed Maggot Terrine. It was at about this time that their neighbours stopped coming round for dinner. As Varg was forced to admit, the F-plan diet may have been pretty sound nutritionally, but the main problem came with actually keeping the food down.

However, if all went well his latest plan would result in their first proper meal for weeks. Yesterday, Elen had discovered that they had a rat living in a hole beneath the indoor shed that Varg insisted was a wardrobe. A real, live, plump, juicy rat. For the past two hours, Varg had laboriously and painstakingly been painting the index finger of his left hand until it was an exact representation of a piece of stale cheese. Then Elen had told him that she thought rats went as much by scent as by sight, and so he'd wrapped it in his underpants for an hour. He wasn't sure whether his finger smelled of cheese, but it sure smelled of something, and it looked the part. Now he was lying on the floor, index finger extended in front of the rat-hole, a rock poised in his other hand.

Behind him his wife stood in front of the table, watching nervously, while behind her, their baby joggled up and down on the table-top in his home-made baby bouncer. (Varg was very proud of the baby-bouncer he'd fashioned out of *festa* vines and old elastic and hung from the roof. He was less proud of their baby, Glob, and even in his most optimistic moments couldn't come up with a better name than Glob the Revolting. For this was not a bonny baby. This was a baby so ugly that even the best parents in the world would have been tempted to put a nappy on over his face.)

And so Varg watched the rat-hole, Elen watched her husband, and Glob bounced up and down and made a noise like someone sucking a slug. And behind him, Nekros sauntered into the hut. At first, no one noticed him, for as he entered, the short-sighted rat stuck its head out of the hole and grabbed Varg's finger, and Varg, with a yell half of pain and half of triumph, brought the rock smashing down on its head. Then holding up the tiny corpse, he grabbed his wife, and the two of them hugged each other in exhilaration.

Behind them, Nekros watched impatiently. He wasn't used to being ignored. He liked to Make an Entrance, and see the fear in people's eyes. For a moment he looked round, then his eyes lit upon Glob. Grabbing the bottom of the baby-bouncer, he stretched it diagonally down past the table-edge almost to the floor, and then let go. There was a twang like a gigantic catapult, the sound of something large crashing through the thatched roof, and the wail of a baby fading into the distance. For a horrified moment Varg and Elen stood like statues, staring up at the baby-shaped hole in the roof, then their gaze switched to the menacing figure advancing towards them with raised sword. At once, Varg's natural optimism took over, and he held up the rat.

'Care for a spot of dinner?' he asked.

Outside, the donkey was just trying to work out some way of conning this large, black, and bone-headed horse out of the wonderful bagful of hay that was strapped to its saddle when the big human came striding out of the hut. Pausing only to wipe his blood-stained sword on the donkey's mane, he leapt into the saddle and spurred his horse off at a gallop into the darkness.

Typical, thought the donkey. Use you as a dish-cloth, then bugger off without so much as a hint of a carrot. Then, vaguely wondering whether the human had left something edible indoors, it ambled towards the entrance of the hut.

Inside, however, it found no food. Just its master and mistress lying on the floor, rather still. In fact, very still. And there seemed to be an awful lot of sticky red liquid splashed around them both . . . and on the floor . . . and the walls . . . and even on the ceiling. It ambled across to where most of its master was lying, and sniffed him carefully. The red liquid was steaming gently, and had a sickly, cloying smell that was oddly attractive. A strange idea crossed the donkey's mind.

I wonder what he tastes like, it thought.

VILLAGE

Yet even as evil stalked the world, still were there havens of peace beyond the turmoil. Within one corner of the world yet overlooked lay the land of Tak, which in the Elder Tongue means 'Haven of peace beyond the turmoil, within one corner of the world yet overlooked'. Here was there a village small in size, where lived a youth called Ronan. Son of the Smith was he, and so the villagers called him Ronan Cook-son, for they were simple folk, and most were downright cretinous . . .

The Pink Book of Ulay

The blacksmith's forge roared as the bellows pumped air through the burning charcoal. The long flat blade of steel glowed a fiery orange as the Smith pulled it from the furnace and rested it on the anvil. Once again he set about the sword with a huge metal hammer. Deafening clangs reverberated around the walls until even the very shadows seemed to vibrate, and red-hot sparks skittered down to the ground like drunken fireflies. His muscles bulged with effort and his black skin gleamed in the eerie light as the sweat flowed down his face and arms. And then he paused, and turned to the skinny youth working the bellows.

'OK, Ronan. That's fine, son.'

Thankfully, Ronan dropped the bellows on to their rack and sat down on an old anvil in the shadows. He winced as the Smith set to work with the hammer again, and shoved his fingers in his ears. He desperately wanted to please his father, but the roasting heat made him feel sick, the acrid smoke stung his eyes, and the reverberating clangs had given him a headache. He sighed, and moodily traced patterns in the metallic dust on the floor with his toe. He wasn't going to find it easy, following the family business.

Again the Smith paused, and looked across at Ronan with concern. One of the main problems in this world, he had often thought, was that trades were passed down from father to son, just like haemophilia or baldness. It made no difference how unsuited your son was to the trade. It made no difference if he was a six-foot-bean-pole with less muscle than a malnourished earthworm. It made no difference if he was an intelligent and sensitive romantic who wanted to roam the world in search of adventure. If you were a Smith, and your father before you, then your son was supposed to forget all about being a Poet, or a Story-teller, or a Warrior. Tradition dictated that he was destined to spend the rest of his life banging bits of red-hot metal about. And somehow Ronan had never seemed able to raise any enthusiasm for this prospect.

Oh, he'd tried, the Smith had to admit that. The boy had waded through all the books he had given him, but titles such as *The Big Boy's Bumper Book of Blast Furnaces* or *A Hundred and One Things To Do With Ferruginous Clinker* had for some reason failed to grip him. He'd sat and listened as his father had expounded on the mysteries of metal malleability and tensile strength, but the Smith could always sense his attention wandering. And, quite frankly, the Smith had to agree that the thought of spending the next fifty years knocking together ploughshares and pan lids in this tiny village miles from anywhere was enough to drive anyone out of their mind.

The problem was that Ronan just didn't fit in. In fact, the whole family had never fitted in, not since the Smith's father had settled there thirty years before. It wasn't because they were black, while the local tribe, the Edmak, were white-skinned. (In Midworld, the hue of a person's skin was immaterial, and Race Relations simply meant that you could have relations with anyone who you could out-race. It was always easy to tell the fleet of foot by the fact that they usually wore a lazy, satisfied smile . . . and little else, half the time. The terminally slow usually had a squint and a sore wrist.) No, it was the difference in intellect that set them apart from the rest.

In such an isolated village, in-breeding had become something of a problem over the years. Not that the locals saw it that way. To them, it was just a delightful way of passing the long winter nights. Love thy neighbour . . . and thy other neighbour . . . and how about thy cousin . . . and gosh, thy sister is looking rather damn attractive these days ... As a result, by the time the Smith's father moved in the average villager was about as rational as a duck but with only half the I.Q. And in a society where anyone who could count up to four without having to have a lie down afterwards was regarded as being positively rapier-brained, the Smith's family shone out like a beacon.

The Smith had been proud of the fact that Ronan had always come top of his class at school. Mind you, this hadn't been difficult. The final maths exam had consisted of one question. I have three potatoes. How many potatoes have I got? Ronan had been the only scholar to get it right. But he had always been a bit of a loner. The other lads were friendly enough, but he seemed to get no enjoyment from games such as Gravity, where you toppled out of a tree and hit the ground head first, or North-south-east-west, where you belted a little kid on the back of the skull with a rock and tried to guess which way he'd fall. So while the other boys were all happily running around with concussion, Ronan could usually be found curled up with a book. And not books on Smith-craft, either. No, it was always books on myths and legends, epic battles and heroes. As a result he had developed an extremely highly coloured and romantic view of the world. He had also developed a damn-fool idea of what he wanted to do with his life. He wanted to be a Warrior, and have Adventures. The Smith sighed. If the news that he was getting from every traveller who passed through the village was correct, then pretty soon the boy would have more adventures than he could cope with ...

The Smith's train of thought was interrupted as the door of the workshop swung open and one of the villagers entered. It was Thom, not the brightest person in the village, but a genius compared to some of his neighbours. He was dressed in a soil-coloured jerkin and breeches, and had soil-coloured sandals on his feet and a soil-coloured hood slung over his head. They'd probably all been really bright and interesting colours initially, but Thom had this thing about soil. He liked to do things with it. Hold it, throw it, talk to it, roll in it ... the Smith winced. He had spent one awful night at Thom's house, looking at his soil collection. Please God this wasn't another dinner invitation.

Thom advanced, grinning. 'Hello!'

'Hi, Thom,' replied the Smith. 'How ya doing, guy?'

'Fine. Fine, fine. Fine, fine, fine . . .' Thom's voice died away as his brain searched in vain for a conversational gambit that wasn't too soil-related. He'd begun to suspect lately that perhaps other people didn't share in his fascination.

'So. What can I do for you?'

'Ermm . . .' Thom thought for a while, then remembered. 'Oh, yeah. I know. I want to buy some of them . . . oh, what are they called . . . you know the things. Round, and as hard as iron . . .'

'Horse-shoes?' the Smith suggested, without much hope. 'Shields?'

'No . . . pork pies, that's it. I want to buy some of them pork pies!'

'This is the smithy, Thom.' The Smith's voice was patient. He'd got used to all this after thirty years. 'The pie-shop is three doors away. You can't miss it. It's the one with the large picture of a pie hanging over the door.'

'Really?' Thom was delighted. 'That's a bit of a lucky coincidence, isn't it? They sell pies, and they have a picture of a pie hanging over the door! Here, just wait until I tell my soil about this. It'll never believe me!'

He turned and wandered through the door, burbling happily. The Smith raised the newly forged, still-glowing sword from the anvil and plunged it into a barrel of cold water. Steam hissed up like an ethereal snake, and he lifted the sword and studied its blade for a moment. Then handing it to Ronan he crossed to the door that Thom had gone through and jerked it open. Grabbing him by the arm, the Smith pulled Thom out of the store-room and propelled him across the forge and out through the door to the street.

Thom ambled happily off in the wrong direction, and the Smith leaned against the door-post and took a deep breath. Evening was falling, and a steady drizzle had set in, adding to the general dankness that always seemed to pervade the village. On the other side of the muddy, dung-covered track that they laughingly called the main street, Warty Baker was attempting to repair a gaping hole in the roof of the filthy rat-infested hovel that served as the village bakery. The Smith watched as Warty laboriously hammered the slate tiles into place. He seemed to be having a great deal of trouble getting them to stay there, but this was probably because it was a thatched roof. Several tiles slid down to the eaves and fell off, and Warty appeared to lose his temper and stamped on the remainder. They splintered, and with a surprised yell and a loud crash he disappeared through the roof. Flour fountained out through the hole along with a few of the smaller rats, and then with a tired creaking sound the rest of the roof gave way.

The Smith shook his head and turned to go back inside. He could tell from the muffled cursing that the baker was all right, and anyway he knew from years of experience that it took more than a roof falling on top of him to stop Warty. He would be up and baking next morning, although tomorrow's bread would probably be full of pieces of rotting thatch. Still, it would make a nice change from rat droppings.

He shut the door behind him and smiled at the sight that met his eyes. Ronan, lost in some fantasy of his own, was waggling and stabbing the sword about, and was giving some imaginary opponent a really hard time. The Smith watched tolerantly as his son parried, riposted, and then fluently tripped over. Leaping up, he banged his shin on the anvil, and then raising the sword he delivered a slashing cut that would have been quite impressive if the blade had not flown off the handle. The Smith ducked, and the blade whizzed over his head and stuck quivering in the door-post behind him.

Ronan stared in horror, but his father seemed more resigned than annoyed. Taking the handle from Ronan he forced it back on to the blade, and then twisted the sword free and rested it next to the others he'd recently made. Ronan gazed round the forge curiously. There was something he'd been meaning to ask for a while. Piled in the shadows against the walls were items made by his father . . . ploughshares, railings, cauldrons, stacks of horse-shoes . . . all made months ago, and all gathering dust. And in front of them were piled his father's recent preoccupations. Stacks of swords (mostly with handles, many of which were loose), piles of arrow-heads and lance-tips, large flat shields, and a host of irregularly-shaped objects that looked like distorted buckets with eye-holes, and were apparently called 'helms'. (The Smith freely admitted that he hadn't quite mastered helms yet.) Ronan watched as his father moodily picked up and examined one bulging and misshapen specimen that would have been a perfect fit for an elephant.

'Father?'

'Hmm?'

'Why do we make nothing but weapons these days? No one in our village is interested in them. The only thing we've sold was a helm to Thom, and he just uses it to carry soil round in.'

'These are evil times, Ronan.' Wearily the Smith dropped the helm back on the pile and laid his arm about his son's shoulders. 'Every traveller who has visited our village in the past few months has told the same tale, the tale of a tribe of savage horsemen riding out of the east and falling upon quiet villages like ours. A tribe led by an invincible warrior with dark powers, who burn and loot and kill without mercy. The Tribe of Fallon.'

Ronan shook his head in disbelief. 'No one in the village has said anything about this!'

'Of course they haven't!' The Smith began pacing up and down, and Ronan stared. He'd never seen his father so agitated. 'They don't know! They never talk to travellers. Not about what's going on in the real world, anyway. Oh, they'll happily chat for hours about soil, or whether you can stand on one leg and eat fish at the same time. But they don't realise what's going on out there!' The Smith looked up, and Ronan was horrified to see the depth of sadness in his eyes. 'I've talked of this with Brenno the Shaman. He's been having visions again. He says that you and I are bound to this invincible warrior in death.'

Ronan felt dizzy and a little sick. It was almost as though someone had chosen him as a target during North-south-east-west.

'You always said that Brenno Goat-bane is at least three incantations short of a charm!' he stammered.

'Oh, he's as bad as the rest,' answered his father. 'But he was having one of his lucid moments. His magic is pretty damn' effective when he's like that. Remember how he got his name?'

Ronan nodded. Two years ago, one of the village goats had charged and butted Brenno, and in a fit of anger the Shaman had managed to cast a spell that should have been well beyond his capabilities and had transformed the entire herd into tulips. The Smith had been furious, but most of the other villagers had been pleased, as firstly the goats didn't wander off and get lost any more, secondly they smelt one hell of a lot better, and thirdly it wasn't anything like as messy when you cut their heads off and stuck them in a vase. Admittedly, the milk yield had gone right down, but then you couldn't have everything.

'Is this why you've called the meeting in the village hall tonight?' Ronan asked.

'That's right. We've got to get through to our folk. We've got to teach them how to defend themselves.' The Smith pushed open the door. Outside it was nearly dark. Muffled curses could still be heard coming from the bakery. 'We'd better get moving. Help me carry a few samples across. We're going to give a little demonstration tonight.'

With arms full of weapons, the Smith and his son staggered out into the street. At first, as they emerged, everything was quiet, and the cool dung-scented air came almost as a relief after the heat of the forge. And then all at once the air was rent by the sound of crowing, as the village cocks heralded the arrival of night. Inbreeding hadn't done much for the intellect of the local chicken population, either.

An hour later they were set up in the village hall. Calling it a hall was a little on the optimistic side. It was more like a village shed . . . and a shed built hastily by a very bad D-I-Y enthusiast using a cut-price wattle-and-daub flat-pack bought in a very cheap home improvements warehouse. But it was all they had. It might be cold, draughty, and with a roof that had more holes than Ronan's underwear, but holding a meeting here gave them some vestige of authority.

The Smith had pinned a large map to one wall. It showed the whole of the Ancient Realm of Frundor, from the Northern Mountains down to the Great River Leno, and from the Nevacom Plains in the east to the coastal ports of the west. Forbidding black arrows had been inked on, sweeping across from the east to show the reported raids of the Tribe of Fallon. Some of them reached almost as far as Tak.

In front of the map was a small table, on which were various examples of home-forged weaponry, and beside this was a series of flip-charts on an easel, demonstrating how the weapons were

21

to be used. The flip-chart was a new idea of the Smith's. The only way to guarantee holding the undivided attention of the average villager for more than a few seconds was to grip him by the neck with one hand and shake him forcibly, while gently but firmly clutching his testicles with the other. As this wasn't feasible with a crowd, the Smith had vague hopes that his new flip-charts might be some help. Now he was standing at the door, desperately hoping that not too many villagers would forget about the meeting, or go to the wrong place, or get distracted on the way by interesting bits of soil . . .

Ronan was staring at the map wistfully. Tak was merely a speck in the middle of Frundor, and wherever he looked, there were place-names redolent of adventure and romance. Port Raid, on the west coast, the nearest city to Tak. The Great River Leno, with its twin ports of Unch Haven and Dol Dupp, where corsairs and pirates mingled with warriors, elves, and dwarves, and life was as cheap as a flagon of Isle B'Ibaq wine. And far upriver, the city of Minas Tryk, gateway to the east, which, generations before, had been nearly destroyed when the great dragon Flarg had held his legendary stag-night there. Ronan felt a sudden urge to travel to far-off lands, to drink with fellow travellers in rough hostelries, to swap jests with warrior and merchant, elf and man . . . With a sigh, he tore his eyes away. He was enough of a realist to know he'd probably be mugged before he'd gone fifty paces.

At the door, people were starting to arrive. His father was greeting them as they entered, shaking hands, ushering them in.

'Good evening . . . thanks for coming . . . hi there! Glad you could make it . . . Tobold! Nice to see you . . . why, Thom, thank you! That's very kind of you!'

The Smith stood there with a resigned expression on his face, holding the large clump of grass and earth that Thom had pressed into his hands. Thom grinned, embarrassed, and shuffled his feet.

'Aw, well, I knows you like chicken,' he said.

Carefully, the Smith placed the clump on the table, then wiped his hands on his breeches. They're good people at heart, he reminded himself. They need protecting. Secretly he was quite pleased. Thom didn't often give soil away – it was quite a mark of respect. And he'd got quite a good turn-out here. Already there were thirty people crammed into the hall. He decided he'd better start, before they got fed up and began drifting away, and so standing on a small dais, he addressed the expectant faces before him.

'My friends! For weeks I have been hearing rumours that give me reason to believe we are in mortal danger! The Tribe of Fallon are rampaging through the eastern lands, killing all that stand in their way! I know that you have heard nothing of this but I want you to trust me. I've talked with Brenno Goat-bane, our Shaman, and from his prognostications I think that we . . .' He paused. Damn! He'd used a five-syllable word. Most of his audience had instantly gone glassy-eyed, and Rangvald Mud-maker had fainted. He'd better move on quickly.

'We need to learn to fight, if we want to stay alive. For months now I've been forging weapons for the defence of our village. Tonight I want to show you these weapons, and explain their use. This one, for instance, is called a sword . . .'

Drawing it from the scabbard, he brandished the newly forged blade aloft, and winced as it flew off the handle, shot past the ears of two startled villagers, and disappeared through the window. From outside came a shout of pain.

'You throw that at people, do you?' asked Tobold. He was the miller, and one of the brightest villagers.

'Not intentionally, no. That's just a minor design flaw. We're working on it. You're meant to hold it by the handle, so . . .' The Smith took another sword, and gingerly demonstrated how to lunge and parry. This time, the blade stayed firmly in place. 'When the enemy come, they will all have swords and shields. You must practise . . .'

'Here, this is good!' Thom had taken a bow and arrow from the table, and was examining it with an eagerness hitherto reserved solely for more telluric-related objects.

'Ah, the bow and arrow!' the Smith said, pleased. 'This is something you can make yourselves. I can supply the arrowheads.'

'Boa narra. Hm.' Thom was fascinated. Experimentally he flexed the bow-string, and turned to the other villagers. 'It's got a long bit of wood, and this string thing going all the way from the top to the bottom, and another bit of wood with a pointy end and

23

feathers, that goes . . .'

There was a loud twang. Thom stared down.

'. . . right through my foot.'

'No, no, not like that!' Angrily the Smith grabbed the weapon off the bemused villager, and a hum of excited murmuring started. Ronan watched, nervously. His father seemed close to losing his temper, and Ronan was well aware of the spectacular results on the few times this had occurred. There had been that time when one of the Mad Monks . . . Ronan mentally apologised to whatever deities were listening, and hastily corrected himself . . . one of the Religious Brotherhood, rather, had threatened him with eternal damnation. The Smith had picked him up bodily and thrown him out. Through the wall. Admittedly, it was only a wattle-and-daub wall, but it had been a lot harder than the monk's face.

Suddenly, the door swung open. 'What manner of meeting is this?' hissed a sleazy voice. The Smith cursed, and Ronan turned and gasped in dismay. Apparently you couldn't even think about the Brotherhood now without them turning up!

For there in the doorway stood two members of the Most Holy Brotherhood of the Truly Humble – Prior Onion and Brother Turnip. The latter was large and fat, and when by himself could be quite a nice, friendly guy. But the Prior! Small and skinny, with a pale face sporting the sort of precisely clipped moustache that only total bastards wear, sneering eyes that never seemed quite to meet your gaze, and hair that looked as though it had half a tub of lard on it. He delighted in scaring the shit out of the less intelligent with sermons of hellfire and damnation, and only his lack of imagination had prevented him and his order from frightening the villagers out of their few remaining wits. That, and the rather odd nature of the Brotherhood's Holy Book – the Gospels of Saint Tim the Insipid.

Prior Onion gazed round, enjoying the sudden silence, embarrassed foot-shuffling, and clearing of throats that greeted his appearance. He was always most at ease amid the discomfort of others.

'I said,' he continued in a voice like goose-grease dripping off a wheel-shaft, 'what manner of meeting is this?'

The Smith knew he could not afford to alienate the Prior, who had such a hold over the villagers that he could undo everything the Smith was trying to accomplish with just one word.

'Holy Father,' he said, 'I am merely warning our people of the dangers that threaten us all. The fell tribe that is sweeping the land draws ever nearer, and we must prepare ourselves . . .'

'Prepare ourselves, yes!' The Prior's voice sliced through the Smith's like a scalpel through butter. 'But not with such profane weapons! Do you not see in this the hand of the Lord? We of the Brotherhood are prepared, for is it not foretold in the Divine Writings of Saint Tim? Know ye not the Seven Holy Plagues?'

He raised one hand, and the sleeve of his voluminous habit fell back to reveal a book in his grasp . . . a leather-bound book, embossed on the cover with a golden question-mark. The Smith had opened his mouth to argue, but the gasp of reverential fear from the assembled villagers warned him that he'd lost them. Prior Onion continued, voice raised in religious fervour, and a self-satisfied smirk playing around his lips.

'Hear ye the words of Saint Tim the Insipid!' He opened the book, and began to read. 'And it shall come to pass that the Children of the Lord shall turn away from the Lord, and shall not behave themselves. And the Lord shall be a little put out, saying unto himself, I suppose I'd better do something about this. And behold, the skies shall move, the heavens shall open, and there shall be minor local showers, so that the people get wet, coming home from the pub! And there shall be slight overnight frost, so their tomato plants, they shall not flourish! But still the people shall not turn to the Lord, and he shall be rather put out. And then shall there be a plague of cheap cigarette-lighters, and the people shall incinerate their eyebrows. And then shall there be a plague of greenfly, and other garden pests, and the people shall cry out, saying, "Lo! the leaves have fallen off me chrysanths, and the birds have been at me strawberries again!" But still they shall not repent. And his vexation shall be rather disconcerting to behold! And he shall visit upon them a plague of dung, a plague of salesmen, and a plague of chesty coughs!'

The Prior slammed the book shut with satisfaction, and looked round at the villagers to make sure that they had got the message. 'A plague of salesmen, you see! Thus is it written!'

The Smith was staring at him as though he was stark staring

mad. Unfortunately, Ronan realised, everyone else was staring at him as though he was God. Somebody muttered, 'A plague of chesty coughs! Rabid Dan was coughing only yesterday!' and suddenly all the villagers were on their knees, hands clasped in supplication. Except, that is, for Thom, who suddenly discovered how difficult it is to kneel when one foot is pinned to the floor by an arrow. The Smith stared round him in desperation, and had one last try.

'But a plague of salesmen!' he cried. 'Surely you're not suggesting that Nekros and the Tribe of Fallon are rampaging through the land selling thatch extensions?'

'Only repent and ye shall be saved.' The Prior smiled at him like a lizard that had woken to find itself knee-deep in succulent flies, then raised his voice to address the villagers. 'My people! It is not too late! Join with me in prayer! Brother Turnip shall lead us in selected hymns of the Blessed Saint Tim, while I shall take up the Sacred Collection!' Quickly, he whipped a large collection-box out from under his habit. 'And remember, money is the root of all evil. So lighten your pockets, and be pure in the eyes of the Lord!'

He started to move among the villagers, who were all feverishly scrabbling in their pockets for money. Brother Turnip produced an ancient *kaladion*, which he desperately tried to pump into action. It gave a couple of choking sounds, then suddenly screeched into life, sounding like an elderly soprano sheep having its legs pulled off. The resulting 'tune' was almost impossible to recognise, but could have been 'Oh Lord, we've really been quite naughty', one of Saint Tim's more interesting hymns.

The Smith knew when he was beaten. Taking Ronan by the shoulder, he led him through the door into the cool night air. Outside, it was nearly as noisy as inside the hall. The death-throes of the *kaladion* had woken every dog in the village. Most were barking, some were miaouing, and at least one was clucking. Ronan looked at his father, worriedly.

'Shouldn't we do something? I mean . . .' His voice died away as he saw the desperation in his father's eyes.

'We will, but now is not the time. Damn those Mad Monks to hell!' The Smith stood there glowering for a moment, then slapped his son on the shoulder and smiled raggedly.

'Come on, back to the forge. We have work to do. There will be other nights. We have little time, but we can still save our people.'

Unfortunately for the Smith, he had no idea just how little time they had . . .

Four nights later, Ronan was lying in his bed on one side of the single large room that was their hut, watching the smoke curl up from the dying embers in the central fireplace towards the small smoke-hole in the roof, and waiting for his father to come home. He'd nipped out to the village's tiny alehouse, the Headless Chicken, for a celebratory drink, as that evening they'd held their first proper weapons-training session. Uninterrupted by the Religious Brotherhood, they had successfully demonstrated all of the weapons and several of the villagers had begun to get the idea. There had only been two minor accidents. Gael Bark-eater had insisted on holding his sword by the wrong end and now had no fingers left, and Thom had shot an arrow through his other foot, although he said this was no problem, as he hadn't removed the first arrow yet and it gave him a matching pair. Still, Ronan's father had been really pleased with their progress and for the first time in weeks seemed almost happy.

Ronan was just about to reach out and extinguish the oil-lamp, when Pratt, their guard-dog, began a loud and agitated clucking. Suddenly all hell broke loose outside . . . yelling, screaming, neighing of horses, clashing of swords, and above everything, his father's voice, shouting commands. Fearfully, Ronan got out of bed and then, clutching the sword and helm that his father had recently presented to him, and the teddy-bear that his mother had given him the year she died, he crept to the door and peered out. The sight that met his eyes was enough to freeze him to the spot with horror.

Dark-clad horsemen seemed to be everywhere, galloping through the village square, setting fire to huts, and slashing at the panicking villagers with swords. In the eerie silver light of the two moons and the smoke from the burning buildings they looked like some phantom force from hell. One or two villagers were desperately running from hut to hut, seeking non-existent shelter, but many were lying very still in unlikely positions on the ground, their blood soaking into the dry earth.

In front of the forge a small group led by the Smith were fighting back. Most had little idea of how to use their weapons, and were swinging their swords in wild arcs. Some had absolutely no idea, and were as much of a threat to their comrades as they were to the enemy. Ronan saw Thom fire arrow after arrow – but he was holding the bow the wrong way round, and all the arrows were shooting backwards over his shoulder. One thudded into his brother's arm, another just missed Tobold and buried itself up to the flights in a dark horseman's eye-socket. Tobold himself managed to maim a dismounted rider with a round-house sweep of his sword that sheared through the neck and took the head clean off. Ronan noticed that Tobold was wearing two helms. One on each foot.

However, bravely as the villagers were fighting, they would have had no hope without the Smith. He was standing to the fore, yelling encouragement, and his smith's hammer was a whirl of death in his hand. Seven of the enemy were lying dead before him, and as Ronan watched he dispatched two more with fearsome blows that crushed helm, skull, and brain as though they were paper. Behind him Brenno Goat-bane was crouched, hurling whatever incantations and spells he could muster. Unfortunately he was incapable of major magic these days, having peaked two years earlier with his goat transformation, but several of the enemy were coming up in rather nasty boils, and at least two had started sneezing.

Slowly, foot by foot, the little knot of villagers pressed forwards, but just as Ronan thought they might somehow prevail, the dark warriors lowered their swords and stepped back. An expectant hush fell over them, so that the only sounds were the crackling of the burning huts and the whimpers of the wounded. And then a tall and menacing figure stepped out from the shadows at the edge of the square. Imposing and powerful, with swarthy bearded face and evil eyes, he was dressed all in black. As he strode towards the Smith, reflected flames writhed and twisted about his jet-black helm, and blood dripped slowly from his massive sword. He raised the sword and licked the point clean with evident enjoyment, and Ronan shuddered. This just *had* to be Nekros. Then the silence was broken by the Smith's voice.

'You want to watch it. You could catch hepatitis, doing that.'

Nekros lifted his ice-cold eyes and studied the Smith with

interest. 'You fight well for a mere peasant, blacksmith,' he hissed. 'Such bravery could I use.'

'Side with you? Ha!' The Smith laughed in the amused manner of someone who has just had a scorpion dropped down their neck. 'I'd rather die!'

'That's rather what I had in mind.'

'So be it. But I shall take you with me to the very bowels of hell!' The Smith paused, aware that he was sounding a bit pompous. 'So stick your sword up your ass and swivel on it, *katimo*!' he added.

In his doorway Ronan gaped in amazement. He had never heard his father use such a rude word before. He watched wide-eyed as his father and Nekros warily circled each other, but before either could move there was a commotion off to one side of the square. The door of a hut flew open and Prior Onion popped out like a weasel from a burrow. He was followed by one of the riders, who was waving a sword and grinning.

'Nekros!' called the rider. 'There's more gold in this one hut than in the whole of the rest of this stinking village!'

'That is the Lord's gold!' As soon as the words were out of his mouth, you could see that the Prior was regretting them. Then, as he had only one card in his hand, he decided he might as well play it. He held up his leather-bound Holy Book, and started on his sacred spiel. 'Hear ye the words of Saint Tim . . .'

Nekros drew a dagger from his belt, and raised it so that it was pointing directly at the Prior, who suddenly found that his voice-box had gone on strike. A beam of red light stabbed out from Nekros's hand straight at the Holy Book, and the dagger flew along the beam as though shot from a gun, smashing through the book to lodge in the Prior's forehead. His eyes rolled up to stare in horror at this unfamiliar object protruding from his skull, and he had just enough breath to gasp 'You bastard' before breathing became a thing of the past and he slumped to the ground.

The Smith tensed himself to attack, but then a restraining hand was laid on his arm and Brenno Goat-bane stepped past him. The Shaman's eyes were glowing red, and his mouth was twisting and writhing with a life of its own. He looked like a psychotic scarecrow. Raising a clawed hand, he began to chant an incoherent incantation, and little runnels of white light began to eddy about his finger-tips and chase up and down his scrawny arms.

The Smith stared in amazement. He'd never seen Brenno get it quite this right before. It was almost as though for the past two years the Shaman had been hoarding his powers for one spell that was way beyond his usual ability. He paused dramatically and then stabbed his hand towards Nekros, and the light coalesced into a glowing ball that hurtled from his finger-tips towards the dark warrior. But as it hit him, the golden torque at Nekros's throat seemed to flash with fire, and the ball of light rebounded and fizzed straight back at its creator. Brenno screamed, and then there was a rather squelchy explosion, and the horrified villagers were showered with small sticky fragments of Shaman.

The Smith stared in horror at a gobbet of gently steaming flesh that clung to his fore-arm, and then he was suddenly aware of a huge gleaming sword arcing towards his face. Desperately he flung up his hammer to ward off the blow, but Nekros's sword sliced through the hammer's head as though it were some form of delicate pastry. There was a loud crunching sound, and the last sensation the Smith was aware of was the agonising pain as the iron blade smashed through the bridge of his nose and deep into his skull.

In the hut doorway, Ronan stared in disbelief as his father's lifeless body slumped at Nekros's feet, his head almost sliced in half. For a moment he felt as though he was going to pass out, but then a red mist of hatred seemed to grab hold of him, and jamming on the helm he flung down his teddy-bear and charged forward, sword upraised. It was as he reached his father's assassin and struck that he realised he'd made one of those awful mistakes that are still toe-curlingly embarrassing to think about years later. Somehow he'd got confused, and instead of throwing down his teddy he'd thrown down his sword. Nekros, however, had sensed the coming attack, and turning leisurely to meet it, raised his weapon to ward off the blow. The descending teddy-bear connected with the blade and its head sheared off and hit Nekros on the nose. He blinked in surprise, then stared in amusement at the bean-pole of a youth now cowering in front of him.

As suddenly as it had come, the fit of anger that had taken Ronan had vanished, to be replaced by absolute terror. He realised he was about to die, probably horribly, and behind him, blood-curdling screams gave him a good idea of what was happening to the rest of the village. Nevertheless, he stood his ground. If he had to die, he was determined to do so in a way that would have made his father proud of him. But instead of following up, Nekros bent down and picked up the headless corpse of the teddy-bear. Then he held up the bear in front of Ronan's face and gently ran his blood-stained sword down its chest. The material parted and the bear's woolly guts spilled out in a torrent of fluff.

This blatant sadism was too much for Ronan. Weaponless, hopeless, he lowered his head and blindly charged at Nekros. Deftly, the warrior side-stepped, and as Ronan careered past him he delivered a sweeping back-hand cut with his sword that smashed into the back of the youth's helm. Ronan nose-dived into the ground like an *apatodon* coming to rest, and lay there motionless. Nekros looked down at him, and smiled with pleasure as blood began to flow out from underneath the helm. Good! That would teach the idiot to attack people with cuddly toys! Leering with satisfaction, Nekros turned on his heel and stalked off in search of someone else to massacre.

Ronan woke up with the headache of a lifetime and lay there with his eyes tightly shut, vaguely wondering why his bed felt so hard and uncomfortable. Various memories flitted round his badly dazed brain. The headache reminded him of the time he'd drunk a whole bottle of Stumpy's Fart Fermenter, a dwarfish barley wine, when he was ten. There was a strange clamped sensation about his skull that was reminiscent of the time he got his head stuck in a pan when he was eight. And the air seemed permeated with the stench of badly burned flesh, which reminded him of that disastrous time his father had tried to do a barbecue. His father! Oh God! With a suddenness that overwhelmed him, full memory came flooding back, and he sat up and dragged off the badly dented helm that had saved his life. The back of his head felt as though some incredibly powerful smith was beating flat a red-hot sword on it, and his face and chest were covered in the encrusted blood that had poured from his nose when he smashed into the ground. Aghast, he stared about him.

It was morning, and the Tribe of Fallon were long gone. There was little sign that they had even been there – save for the fact that most of the village had been burned down and the ground was littered with bodies. A haze of pungent smoke drifted upwards from a few still-smouldering huts, and hordes of sated crows hopped heavily about from corpse to corpse, their beaks and feathers soaked in blood, half-heartedly searching for the odd delicacy that might have been overlooked. Ronan hauled himself upright and staggered across the square, desperately searching for survivors. As he stared at the charred remains of once-welcoming homes and stumbled over the lifeless bodies of friend after friend, the enormity of what had happened was almost too much for his mind to cope with. He felt emotionally numb. Coming to his father's corpse, he stopped. He just couldn't believe that this was real. Never again to lie in bed and hear his father's hearty greeting as he strode in from the ale-house? Never to stand together in the unbearable heat of the forge, side by side as his father hammered out another sword? A lot of use they'd been, though. The handles always came off . . .

Suddenly Ronan was on his knees, clutching his father's ice-cold hand, the tears streaming down his face. For what seemed an age grief overwhelmed him, until eventually the pain abated and he found he was left with a cold implacable hatred. He had no idea how he was going to do it, but he was going to track down Nekros and kill the bastard. Then, as he rose, he realised that the hush of death that hung over the village was being gently broken. Someone somewhere was humming.

Ronan finally tracked the sound down to Water Street, where he found Old Palin slumped against the well, a black-feathered arrow sticking out of his groin. Palin had often been referred to as the wisest man in the village (which is rather like referring to the roughest billiard ball, or the most attractive tapeworm). Now he was sitting there in a pool of blood, with a shield in one hand, a broken sword in the other, and a battered helm on his head, softly humming to himself.

'Old Palin!' Ronan gasped. 'You're alive! But . . . you're wounded!'

'Not much gets past you, eh, lad! Nay, don't fuss. 'Tis naught but a scratch.'

'A scratch?' Ronan stared at the wicked-looking arrow doubtfully.

'I was lucky, boy. Bound for my heart, it was, 'til I deflected it with this shield-thing your father gave me. Pity I deflected it downwards, though. It's gone straight through my wedding-tackle. What a way to go, eh? Pinned to the ground by your privates!' He started to laugh, then coughed, a dry hacking cough that racked his whole body. Ronan watched fascinated as the tip of the arrow jerked up and down with every spasm.

'You must be in agony!' he said.

'No, no.' Old Palin waved a deprecatory hand. 'In a strange kind of way it's almost enjoyable.' His breathing was slowly becoming more laboured. Ronan stepped past him to the well and drew up a bucketful of water. Then he gently removed the helm from Palin's head, tapped it a couple of times on the well's brickwork to dislodge the numerous unpleasant little creatures that had moved into it from Palin's scalp, and filled it with water. He handed it to the wounded man, who gratefully drank from it.

'Ah! Thanks, Ronan. You're a good lad. Take after your father, you do.' He sighed. 'He was right, your dad. Said we should watch out for Nekros and his tribe. We should have listened.'

At the mere mention of the name Nekros, Ronan was nearly sick with hatred. He found himself wanting to do horrid things to someone with sharpened poles. 'Good Master Palin,' he ground out, 'I swear to you that I will not rest until I have sought out Nekros and consigned his foul soul to the dark chasm that spawned him!'

Palin chuckled painfully. 'Where do you get these phrases from? The dark chasm that spawned him, indeed! You've been reading too many Chronicles!' Suddenly serious, Palin reached out and grabbed Ronan's sleeve, pulling him closer. 'Listen, son. You're no match for a hard bastard like Nekros. Not yet, anyway, though your dad had hopes for you. You need to learn to fight. Go to Warrior School. Port Raid is the place, on the west coast. Learn the trade . . .' His voice died away, and his hand loosened and slipped to the ground.

'Old Palin! Don't leave me!' But as Ronan looked down at the glazed eyes and the slack jaw, he knew it was no use. Sadly, he stood up and looked round. Yesterday, he had a home, family, friends . . . Now all of a sudden he was totally alone. There was nothing left to live for.

Except revenge.

TOWN

So were Ronan's tribe, the Edmak, destroyed. Nekros the
Black was their bane, and thus was he known in the land of
Tak as the Edmak Bane . . .
*   . . . and so in his sixteenth year did Ronan come to Port*
Raid, on the west coast of Frundor. A rough and dangerous
town was this, where mingled the three free races, dwarves,
elves and men. Sailors from countless ships thronged the
Old Town, and many was the elf touched up in a dark
alley . . .

The Pink Book of Ulay

Ronan wandered along the teeming street, gazing in awe at the
unfamiliar sights of the city of Port Raid. Although he'd already
been here three days, he still couldn't quite get used to it. He felt
hemmed in by the ancient red-stone buildings that towered above
him, three or even four storeys high, for street after street. He felt
intimidated by the throngs of people who jostled and pushed past
him, but didn't even seem to notice that he was there. He felt
deafened by the continuous noise. And yet he found it all totally
and wonderfully exhilarating. The place was so alive!

People leant out of windows, yelling to each other. They stood
in doorways, yelling to each other. They thronged the street,
yelling to each other. Greetings were called, news passed on,
wares were advertised, deals were struck, and all at maximum
volume. Shop-owners, stall-holders, and street vendors plied
their trade, warriors strutted importantly about, and harlots and
holy men touted for business. The scent of the exotic spices and
fruits from the stalls at the side of the road mixed with the
incense from a burner above a temple door, and the mouth-
watering aroma of a dozen different cuisines drifted out from the
doorways of countless bars and eating-houses.

Ronan watched as a couple of monks from the Order of the

Seventh Day Hedonists stopped a sauntering prostitute and began to negotiate terms for their next party. Then suddenly there was the sound of a window opening and a muffled cry from above, and Ronan and everyone around him dived for shelter. There was an unpleasant spattering sound in the centre of the suddenly vacant street, and then people picked themselves up as if nothing had happened, and the hubbub began again. Ronan smiled to himself, and continued to stroll along. He was definitely starting to get the hang of the place now. He'd learnt the hard way that if you heard a cry of 'Wezlops!' from a window above you, you dived to one side quickly, or else you were likely to receive the contents of someone's chamber-pot over your head. He'd also learnt that in the big city you don't trust *anyone*.

On the day that he arrived, he hadn't gone more than twenty paces past the city gate before he had been relieved of his money, his back-pack, and his boots by three separate and totally plausible strangers. He would probably also have been relieved of the cartload of weapons forged by his father if the next guy he met hadn't got over-confident and tried to talk him into handing over the clothes he stood up in as well. Luckily, common sense had prevailed. He'd hung on to the cart and pushed it up Eastgate Street until he found a shop called 'Honest Elric's Sword-Store and Arms Emporium'. Elric (a white-haired old warrior with one arm missing, and breath that could have stripped wall-paper) had taken a liking to him, and had warned him of the pitfalls waiting in the city for a young innocent boy fresh from the countryside. Then he'd examined and offered Ronan the very generous price of sixty silver *tablons* for the lot. It was only the next day, when he'd passed Honest Elric's and seen that just one of the thirty swords he'd sold was in the window priced at ten *tablons* that Ronan had realised that maybe it wasn't too generous a price after all. Still, sixty *tablons* was a small fortune. Ronan was sure he could enrol in Warrior School for less than that.

Then he'd gone down to the Old Town and fixed up lodgings at a quayside tavern. The owner had asked him if he wanted a harlot for the night. Ronan, unsure what a harlot was, but thinking it might be some kind of small onion, had declined. A short while later, he had been standing at the bar with a flagon of Imp Ale shandy when the landlord brought in the harlot ordered by the

36

warrior who had just checked in. Ronan had stood. And stared. And then stared some more. A harlot was a woman! Soft brown skin, almost as dark as his own, long jet-black hair that fell to her waist, lips that looked as though they'd been inflated, and eyes that could have set fire to snow. And her figure! Ronan had never realised women could be shaped like that. She had cast a quick glance in his direction, and smiled at him. Ronan had thought his loins were going to explode. He'd had to leave quickly.

For a while, as evening crept on, he'd wandered along the quay, looking at the ships. The place had been alive with rough sea-faring folk of every description, quite a lot of whom had sidled up to him and muttered odd suggestions. Ronan hadn't been quite sure exactly what those suggestions meant, but he had a feeling that his father wouldn't have approved. At first, they'd tended to pester him, but he'd quickly discovered that laying his hand on the hilt of his sword and snarling discouraged them, and they'd left him alone.

He'd been standing admiring a particularly wicked-looking ship (the *Profane Dreamer*, a slaver out of Unch Haven), when the sound of breaking glass behind him had caught his attention. He'd turned round to see a small group of people sitting slumped in the doorway of a chandler's store. Elves! But not as Ronan has always imagined them to be from the stories he'd read. Elves were supposed to be the Beautiful People — fair of face, always laughing and singing — but this little group had been anything but beautiful. With filthy stained clothes and distorted features, they had been mumbling and swearing to themselves and swigging some clear liquid from bottles wrapped in dirty brown paper. One, with the fragments of the bottle he had dropped strewn at his feet, had lurched over to a midden and poked around until he found a filthy old flagon. Then he'd staggered past Ronan and down the harbour steps and filled it with sea-water. Raising it to his lips, he'd drunk deeply, at which point his legs had given way, and he'd sat down heavily on the steps with his feet in the water. Ronan had felt shocked and disap-pointed. This had been worse than the time he'd walked into Brother Purity's hut and found him doing rude things with one of the goats. It was only when he had got talking with the landlord back at the tavern that he'd discovered the truth about elves[1].

Suddenly, Ronan was dragged back to the present by the clanging of the temple bell. High up on the roof, two of the brothers of the Order of Seventh Day Hedonists could be seen tugging at the rope. Ronan blushed and turned away. He'd never before seen a bell that was quite such an obscene shape. Then he realised that they were chiming the hour. Nine o'clock. He was going to be late – and on his very first day at Warrior School!

He strode off purposefully up the street to confront his future, thrusting his way confidently through the crowds, hand resting on sword-hilt like a true warrior. In his mind he already was a warrior, proud, noble and fearsome, Ronan the Terrible, Vanquisher of Evil and Slayer of Thousands. And suddenly there it was, his future, in the middle of a row of shops. On one side was a necromancer's supplies – 'El Spells'. On the other side, 'Just Slaves'. And between them, the finest fighting academy on the whole of the north-west coast (or so the landlord had assured him) – 'Blades'.

Striding through the front door, Ronan found himself in a reception area that was like no other room he'd ever seen. The walls were decorated in really welcoming shades of grey and peach, and on them hung beautiful tapestries depicting the exploits of some of the school's more notable and blood-thirsty graduates. The floor was covered in the thickest carpet Ronan had ever stood on, and plants of every description cascaded from hanging-baskets and pots. A massive desk stood to one side, next to a filing cabinet. On the desk was a quill pen in an ink-pot, and an in-tray full of important-looking documents and parchments. Behind the desk a beautiful but (to Ronan's eyes) emaciated girl was studiously ignoring the documents and concentrating on painting some strange blue liquid on to her nails.

She looked up and flashed him a totally insincere smile. 'Hi, I'm Lenya, your receptionist, how may I help you?' Her voice sounded as though it hadn't changed since she was eight years old.

'I want to enrol. In Warrior School.'

[1] See Appendix 2.

'Uh-huh.' From under the desk she produced a form, which she started to fill in. 'Name?'

'Ronan.'

'Second name?'

'What? Oh . . . er, Smith. Ronan Smith.'

She looked at him with narrowed eyes. 'Smith, eh? On the run, are we?'

'What?' Ronan was confused.

'Never mind.' She carried on writing. 'Warrior Course. What level entry? Beginner, greenhorn, novice, experienced, hardened, murderous, or total bastard?'

Ronan could feel his confidence disappearing like rainwater down a grid. 'Beginner,' he mumbled.

'Day student or live-in?'

'Live-in, please.'

'Right. That will be thirty *tablons* initial fee, please. That covers the first term's tuition, plus accommodation and full board. It will be extra for books, armour, weapons, and any battle-field trips that may be necessary. Sign here.' She held out the pen and parchment, and Ronan handed her the money and signed. 'If you'd like to go through.' She indicated a door behind her. 'Along the corridor, third room on the right. Tazmir Fastblade will be taking today's class. He likes to talk to new students first. Says he can't stand maiming people he doesn't know personally.'

The last remnants of Ronan's confidence swirled away with an almost audible gurgle, and he had a sudden urge to curl up on the floor with his thumb in his mouth. As he went to open the door his hand was shaking like a leaf. Ronan the Terrible, Vanquisher of Evil, was in imminent danger of becoming Ronan the Terrified, Dampener of Trousers.

The warrior with the scarred face ducked, and his opponent's sword whistled over his head. Swiftly he swung his own massive blade in a scything blow, but his opponent's recovery was as fast as the strike of a snake, and the two swords clashed together. For a moment both men struggled, each seeking to force the other back by sheer muscle-power, and the only sound in the room was the harsh gasping of their breath. Then they leapt apart and the scarred warrior, sensing an opening, slashed back-handed at his opponent's side. But again, the other warrior was ready. With one fluid movement he parried the blow and then struck, and his sword flashed towards the scarred warriors unprotected neck . . . and stopped a hair's-breadth away. For a moment they stood motionless, and then the scarred warrior laughed, and stepped back.

'You're right!' he said. 'That's a pretty impressive sword!'

'Yeah,' replied his opponent proudly. He held it up, and the light glinted off the black and silver patterns etched into the blade. 'It's the new Orcbane Headcleaver. She's a little beauty. Light, manoeuvrable, fast. I tell you, it's a pleasure to drive her into someone's guts!'

'Really evil looks, too!'

'Mmm! The blade's engraved with runes of power. Not just for decoration, either. See the way they're etched in? All those little runnels help the air-flow. When you're dragging the sword out of someone's entrails the air can get in, so your blade doesn't get stuck. She just slides out! And she's easy to clean, too. You know the mess someone's lower bowel can make of a blade . . .'

The warrior paused and looked across to the doorway of the practice-room. In the corridor outside, the tall skinny black youth who had been watching them practise with a look of horror on his face was noisily throwing up the remains of his breakfast.

It was ten minutes before Ronan had recovered enough to brave whatever horrors the third room on the right held. He pushed open the door and found himself in a long, brightly lit room. The floor was of yellow wood-blocks, polished to a brilliant shine. On the right-hand wall a full-length mirror ran from one end of the room to the other. At the far end was a set of lockers, some chairs, and a low table. Behind them, an open doorway led through to a white-tiled wash-room. Pots of fresh flowers were stationed at regular intervals against the wall, but their scent couldn't quite mask a pervasive odour of male sweat. There was more testosterone in the air than you could shake a stick at.

Several warriors were already here, changing by the lockers or doing warm-up exercises in front of the mirror. With two exceptions, they were all large, powerful, and terrifying. The two exceptions were dwarves. They were short, powerful, and terrifying. Both wore iron helms with horns protruding from the top, and had long forked beards hanging in plaits. One was sharpening a battle-axe, producing a high-pitched scraping sound that made Ronan's teeth curl up.

Ronan staggered to a chair, feeling sick again. He didn't dare look at anyone and so picked up one of the glossy magazines that were strewn carelessly across the table. It was called *Maim!* He quickly dropped it, then curiosity got the better of him and he picked up another one, entitled *Stab!* On the front cover was a ridiculously handsome male model, dressed in stylish warrior gear and holding out a severed head. Ronan winced, then scanned the list of contents. 'Decapitation – how to get a head!' . . . 'Berserkers – still crazy after all these years!' . . . 'Garotting – the choke's on you!'

At that moment, the door at the far end of the room opened and a huge figure stalked in, with the receptionist fluttering beside him like a moth next to a vulture. It was Tazmir. His muscles bulged beneath his ebony skin like a sackful of melons, his eyes burned red like the coals in the Smith's forge, and killer was written on his face (literally, in a tattoo across his forehead). Slung behind his back was a sword at least five foot in length. The terrifyingly macho effect was slightly marred by the soft felt dancing-pumps and leg-warmers he was wearing. He strode down the room, reading a parchment that the receptionist had thrust into his hands, then stopped and turned to her.

'No way do we take this guy on as an instructor,' he said, slapping the parchment with the back of one hand. 'Look here . . . under Previous Employment. Berserker, see?' He thrust the parchment back at her. 'The last berserker we took on wiped out an entire class one afternoon. Sodding lunatic! Said he got these headaches . . . Find me someone else. Now, where's the new boy?'

Ronan stood up shakily, painfully aware that his chest measurement was probably less than one of Tazmir's biceps. The warrior looked at him with something approaching pity in his eyes.

'By the gods,' he said. 'They're sending them to us in nappies now!' He walked across and studied Ronan, who stared back.

41

Frightening as Tazmir was, he didn't generate the same sense of evil that Ronan had experienced with Nekros. He gave the impression that, although he might kill you as soon as look at you, he'd do it in an honest, clean, and straightforward way. To his surprise, Ronan found himself liking the man. Even more surprisingly, it seemed to be mutual, for Tazmir suddenly grinned and slapped Ronan on the back (nearly dislocating his spine). 'Welcome to Warrior School, lad!' he roared. All at once, Ronan felt accepted. This was the beginning. This was his new home. In three years, he'd be a warrior!

That is, if he managed to survive three years closeted with this gang of psychopaths.

INTERSTICE

Many were the famous warriors who learnt their trade at the school of Tazmir Fastblade in Old Port Raid. Orgon the Terrible, who rode at the right hand of the Elven Prince, Evelyn, throughout the long campaign against the Eastern Orcs, now known as the Evelyn War . . . Drax the Strange, who drank the great dragon Faud under the table one legendary night in an Orcville wine-bar . . . but mightiest of all by far was Ronan Mage-bane, son of a Smith. Strong was his arm, sharp his sword, and great was his street credibility! Vengeance did he bring to those who lived by lies and by deceit, and many was the tabloid journalist who went in fear for his life . . .

The Pink Book of Ulay

Ronan sat in the barber's chair, studying his reflection in the mirror, while behind him Vosene the Camp, the Elven Hair-stylist of Lothl'Oreal, fiddled and twittered busily. It was amazing what a difference four years could make. Four years of rigorous training. Four years of high-protein diets and pumping iron. Idly, he flexed biceps the size of a man's head. His own father wouldn't have recognised him now. He would have been proud of him, though. Winner of the Orgon the Terrible Memorial Trophy . . . the only student ever to beat Tazmir himself in single combat . . .

Behind him, Vosene stopped fiddling, and stepped back proudly. 'There! Is sir not deliriously happy?' Ronan dragged his thoughts back to the present, and switched his attention to his hair. For a moment he stared, then an amazed grin spread over his face. Yo! Style, or what!

For months, Vosene had been going on and on about 'dreadlocks'. Ronan had no idea what these were, but had supposed that it was some style which would fill one's enemies with dread. But this was something else! He moved his head, and the long plaits jostled round his shoulders like a score of angry snakes. Oh yes!

'Yo, Vosene! Gimme five!' Ronan held out his hand.

Vosene looked at him, and raised an arch eyebrow. 'I think if I gave sir just one, I'd come over all faint.'

Ronan grinned, then stood up and flicked him a silver *tablon*. He liked the outrageous stylist. It took guts for an elf to stick it out in Port Raid, having to stay indoors with the windows tightly shuttered whenever the slightest sea-breeze blew. But Vosene had his own way of getting drunk on sea-water. As he put it, 'The merest sniff of a sailor's hair and I'm gone, love.'

Strapping on his sword in its shoulder-harness, Ronan walked out into the teeming streets. He now bore a warrior's sword (five foot plus of gleaming steel that was so heavy, Vosene couldn't even lift it) which he wore slung southern fashion, down his back. The tooth-pick of a sword that he'd brought with him to Port Raid had long since gone. Now, he wore just the one reminder of his past . . . a severed teddy-bear head hanging from a leather thong round his neck. Absently, he fondled one of the bear's ears as he walked. Tomorrow was graduation day, the culmination of four years of effort. (More information on Ronan's years at Warrior School can be found in *Ronan – the Acne Years*, by Maxon the Small, or *Ronan Mage-bane – from Pimples to Paladin*, by the Scribe of Welbug.) And then, the real purpose of his life could begin. Somewhere in the world was a scumbag called Nekros. And someday, Ronan would track him down, even if it took him the rest of his life.

BOOK TWO

QUEST

... and many famous taverns were there in those days. Finest, so folk say, was the Lost Dwarfish Pub of Legend, but that famous inn was long hidden from the ken of mortal folk. Strangest, surely, was the Wooden House of Troy, built during the siege of this fair town by the attacking army. It was their plan to leave this inn-on-wheels outside the gates, with many well-armed warriors hid inside, and feign withdrawal. Then, when the Wooden House was wheeled within the walls of Troy, the warriors would wait for night, and fall on the defenders as they slept. Alas, this plan came to naught, for by the time night fell, the warriors inside were all too pissed by far for fighting, but sat there in the taproom, loudly singing ... oldest and most isolated tavern at this time was probably the Tavern at the Edge of Darkness, on the northern edge of the Forest of Dreams ...

The Pink Book of Ulay

The Tavern at the Edge of Darkness stood in the tiny hamlet of Bol on the southern rim of the Nevacom Plains, where the Great East Road and the Southern Highway met. Once, long ago, it had been a thriving place, offering fine ale and a bed for the night to travellers of all descriptions. These days, however, business was bad. Few people went north into the Nevacom Plains any more, and the danger from roving tribes or bands of orcs discouraged people from going east. Now, there might be the odd dwarf heading from his homeland to the Northern Mountains, or a group of elves travelling from the Forest of Dreams to the coast for a stag-party, but that was about it.

However, the landlord, Watal Stoneface, wasn't too bothered. He was getting on a bit now and, as he frequently told his few regulars, his back wasn't what it had been. A load of fussy customers demanding drinks, food and fresh bedding every day would be more than he could cope with. Local trade and the few passing travellers kept him and his wife in the necessities of life. True, the tavern could do with a little renovation, but it would last longer than he would. Moodily, he eyed the dust-covered cobweb-strewn row of fine spirit bottles on the top shelf behind his bar. At the current rate of trade, most of his stock would outlast him, too.

He started to wipe the top of the bar with a cloth that was even dirtier than the spirit bottles. The bar didn't need wiping, but Wiping Down Bar-tops was the first thing they taught you in this trade and it was a reflex action now. As he did so, he studied tonight's customers. There was a single itinerant dwarf clad in a chain-mail shirt and an iron helm, who was sitting by the blazing fire reading one of the more scurrilous dwarf newspapers, *Small Talk*. There were a couple of elves on their way home from Port Raid who were slumped in a corner nursing king-size hang-overs. And sitting at a table on the other side of the room was a man, a sword salesman on some sort of business trip. He appeared to be waiting for someone and was in a bit of a state. His clothes were stained with some horrid-looking white encrustation, and his face and hair were liberally streaked with the same stuff. Every time he moved, fine white dust drifted off him, leaving a trail.

Watal gave the bar another wipe, just in case any of the white dust had landed there. You couldn't be too careful. He was just wondering whether he ought to go and give all the table-tops a bit of a wipe when the door opened, and the wind whipped in, causing the fire to roar in the grate and sending a small cloud of white dust billowing round the salesman. Watal tut-tutted, then his eyebrows rose at the sight of the figure who had just entered. It was a warrior, large, dark-skinned, with braids of hair hanging like black snakes round his head and the most enormous sword slung down his back.

A warrior of the old school, thought Watal. Don't get many of them in here these days. He looks a bit pissed off.

In fact, Ronan was no more pissed off than any other guy who had spent the past two years searching for his father's killer without even a sniff of success. He'd had a number of minor triumphs while fighting for the cause of good against evil, and was getting a bit of a reputation amongst the nastier elements of the

50

Western Lands as A Guy Not To Be Messed With, but no one seemed to have seen Nekros for several years. Now he was heading east on the advice of a soothsayer he'd consulted. She had told him he'd find his destiny beyond the source of the Great River Leno. She'd also told him that he was a window-cleaner by profession, that his real name was Muriel, and that his father was a badger. Not for nothing was the soothsayer known as Manya the Screw-loose. Still, he'd decided to follow her suggestion. It had cost him a bronze *tablon*, and he had nothing else to go on.

Ronan stood for a moment looking round the inn before moving to the bar. Despite the roaring fire the place was cold and gloomy, with a pervasive smell of damp dust. However, to judge from the impressive array of pump handles on the bar, at least they had a pretty good selection of ales.

'A tankard of Manticore, please, landlord.'

'Sorry. We don't stock it any more. Well, there's no call for it round here.' The landlord gave the bar an extra wipe, by way of making amends.

'Oh. Well, a tankard of Old Organs, then.' Ronan had got quite fond of this orcish brew during a couple of weeks he'd spent in High Meneal, hunting down a group of mountain-trolls that had been terrorising the town.

'Old Organs! I used to be rather partial to that one myself!' Watal sighed in fond memory. 'Problem is, they won't deliver this side of the mountains any more . . .'

Five minutes later, Ronan was standing looking suspiciously at a tankard of Whitebeard's Flagon, the only beer that the tavern actually stocked. Renowned as the worst beer in the west, Flagon was usually gassy and tasteless. Gingerly, Ronan took a mouthful. Well, there was a surprise! It was even more gassy than ever, but actually tasted of something! He tried not to grimace. New vinegar flavour, eh? Still, it was the only beer for twenty miles . . .

Watal had taken up his favourite gossiping-to-the-customer position, and was polishing an already sparkling glass. (Glass-polishing was the second thing they taught you.)

'Nice evening, sir.' Ronan thought of the bitter wind, and the rain that had driven him to seek refuge, and let that one pass. The landlord carried on, 'So, what brings you to these parts? On a quest, are you?'

'Yeah, as it happens.' Despite himself, Ronan was quite impressed. The old guy was showing a bit of insight. 'How can you tell?'

'Ah, a lot of the warrior-types we get in here are on quests. They always have the same expression on their face. Noble, but pissed off.'

There was a moment's silence as Ronan considered this. Thoughtfully, he sipped his beer, then wished he hadn't. The flavour wasn't improving. Over by the fire, the dwarf turned a page of his paper and started to read about 'Lovely Lenya's Night of Passion with Thorin Oakenshield'. In the corner, one of the elves groaned gently and held his head in his hands. The other one had fallen asleep. Behind Ronan, the salesman was studying him with intense concentration.

'Did any of them ever tell you how . . . er . . . how they actually managed to, well . . . fulfil their quest?' Ronan asked, nonchalantly.

The landlord held the glass up to the light. It sparkled like a diamond. Not a speck of dust to be seen. Just in case, he gave it another polish. 'No, but then they wouldn't, would they? None of them had ever done it.'

'What?'

'It beats me why you fighting types choose such difficult ones. A Quest for the Holy Wine-bottle of Saint Tim . . . or a Quest for the Singing Sword . . . I mean, it takes a lifetime, and you still don't accomplish it.' He put down the glass, and leant on the bar. 'Now, if it was me, I'd choose something a bit easier. A Quest for a New Shirt, perhaps, or a Quest for the Tin-opener. That way, you could get up in the morning, have a bit of breakfast, do your quest, and still have half the day left.'

Mentally, Ronan counted to ten. The world was full of smart-arses, and he'd often thought that the problem with being a good guy was that you only got to slice up the really evil ones. However, something in his expression warned the landlord he might be on shaky ground, and he carried on hurriedly.

'So . . . what are you questing for?'

'Vengeance. I seek Nekros the Black. Do you know him? Big guy. Nasty. Leaves a lot of dead bodies behind him.' Ronan tensed slightly. Behind him he could feel the salesman's eyes boring into his back.

The landlord thought for a moment. 'Hm. Don't think I do . . .' He went to the cellar door and called down the steps. 'Ethel! Do we know a Nekros the Black?'

'Is he the one who's moved in to number seven?' a shrill voice suggested.

'No, that's Dakros the Thick.'

'Don't know him then. Oh, bugger!'

The sound of an enormous crash reverberated up from the cellar. The landlord crossed to a little list of 'Things To Do' that he kept pinned to the wall, wrote down 'More replacement glasses', and came back to the bar, shaking his head.

'No, sorry. Can't help you there.'

'Maybe I can,' came a voice from behind Ronan, and he turned to find the white-streaked salesman approaching him, hand extended.

'Hi,' the man said, 'I'm Belladon.' He glanced admiringly at Ronan's sword. 'Hey! Nice sword! I'm in swords myself, actually. I'm Sales Executive (South Frundor Region) for the Orcbane Sword Corporation.' They shook hands, and white particles fell in a shower to the floor. 'Just got back this evening from a convention in Unch Haven. Left there on Friday morning. Now I know what you're gonna say!' He held up both hands to stem a non-existent argument, and Ronan's heart began to sink. 'It takes more than three days to get here from Unch Haven. Sure it does, if you take the West Road then come up the Southern Highway like most people do. But I cut straight through the mountains to Carn Betw, and Bob's your uncle!' He looked down at his white-stained clothes a touch ruefully. 'Yeah, I know what you're gonna say. There are drawbacks. It takes you straight through the Forest of a Million Pigeons. But if you're ever pushed for time, it's a life-saver!'

Ronan sighed. He had met salesmen before, and he thought he knew exactly how the conversation was going to go. Firstly Belladon would tell him how his horse had come all the way from Unch Haven on only half a bale of hay, then there'd be a couple of hobbit jokes, then an enquiry after his sex-life, and then he'd try to sell Ronan a sword. He turned away and stared moodily at his Whitebeard Flagon as Belladon's voice droned on.

'And you'll never believe this, but my horse came all that way on just half a bale . . .'

There was a faint sound behind him, no more than a whisper of metal on leather, but a sound that might be made by a sword being drawn ever so quietly. Ronan reacted instinctively. He swung round like lightning, and the point of his dagger came to rest against Belladon's throat. The salesman froze, his sword half out of its scabbard, and his face went the colour of fresh pigeon crap. Ronan stared unblinkingly into his eyes.

'Hey!' The sound came out like a strangled croak, and Belladon tried to swallow. His throat was suddenly bone-dry, and it felt as though he was swallowing a football-sized lump of chalk. He tried again. 'I only wanted to show you my sword! I mean, it's a beauty, it's our latest model, the Orcbane Mucromatic, you'd love it, and I'm a klatting sword salesman, for Trann's sake!' Fear caused his voice to rise through several octaves, until even a bat would have had difficulty in picking up the last couple of words.

There was a pause while Ronan stared at Belladon and the salesman's bowels turned to iced water. But Ronan wasn't pausing for effect. He was faced with something of a dilemma. Quite simply, he wasn't sure what to do.

When Ronan started out in Warrior School, he had thought that things would be pretty straightforward. You helped good people, and killed evil people. The problem was, there was this massive grey area in the middle that no one had warned him about. Take Belladon, for example. Anyone who quietly tries to draw their sword behind your back is probably up to no good, but the guy was apparently a sword salesman, and Ronan couldn't think of a reason why he would want to assassinate him. Instinct said that he was up to no good and would probably benefit from a quick decollation, and yet Ronan was stuck with a moral code created by his father and by the romantic literature he had absorbed as a child. As a result, he just couldn't bring himself to kill someone who might possibly be innocent.

Deciding to give Belladon the benefit of the doubt he sheathed his dagger, and then thinking that it would be a friendly gesture to talk shop with the guy for a moment, he drew his massive sword. But the mere sight of five foot of razor-sharp blade had a strange effect on Belladon. Shaking like an elf the morning after a sea voyage, he bared his teeth in that rictus of a smile people use when they want to look terribly, terribly friendly and began to babble desperately.

'Don't! No, don't! I can help! Look, you want to know about Nekros? He was the leader of the Tribe of Fallon, right, the ones who went on the rampage a few years ago. Well, I heard that they came from the north-east, somewhere between Setel and Goblin City, on the other side of the plains. You could try there.'

Ronan stared at the terrified salesman. There was something a little odd about this, but it was the first sniff of a hint of a breath of a clue that he had found all year, and the guy's voice held the desperate ring of truth. He might as well act on it. He sheathed his sword, and Belladon sagged with relief and fell back into a chair. His legs were shaking so much that you couldn't see them through the resulting cloud of dust.

Ronan reached out for his beer, but then he thought better of it. The night was still young and he could cover a good few miles before sleeping. The alternative was to stand here, drinking Whitebeard's Flagon, and talking to a highly dubious sales rep covered in pigeon crap. Quickly he strode to the door and was gone.

Behind him, the landlord called out, 'Goodnight, sir. Walk safely now,' then started to wipe down the bar, which had got a little smeary. In the corner one of the elves was suddenly sick. But Belladon said nothing. He just sat staring blankly into space.

In a darkened room in a southern city, six smartly dressed men were seated at an expensive table, watching a flickering image that moved on the wall in front of them. It was a view of the Tavern at the Edge of Darkness, seen through Belladon's eyes. As the door shut behind Ronan the scene seemed to freeze, and then the lights of the room came on and the six men looked at one another.

'So that is the warrior who could destroy us,' said one. 'Are we sure of this?'

'Anthrax was quite definite in his prediction,' replied another.

'Then we must take steps. Can he not be bought?'

'No. Acquisitions are testing this, but again Anthrax was quite definite.'

55

'A pity. He would have been most useful.' The first man thought for a moment. 'We had best warn Nekros. And I think we could give him Belladon. The man is of no further use.'

He gestured to the wizened old woman who was fussing over a small cauldron that bubbled on top of a fire in the grate. She muttered something and sprinkled a foul-smelling purple powder into the cauldron, and the image on the wall vanished as if turned off by a switch.

Belladon sat up and rubbed his eyes, and then.stared round at the tavern. He couldn't seem to remember anything that had happened since he walked through the door. He must have blacked out again. He shook his head to clear the fuzzy feeling. It was a bit worrying – he'd been having these attacks quite often recently, ever since the sales conference last year. Still, no point in fretting. He had more important things to worry him, such as what to do about his poor sales figures for the month.

And there, right at the front of his brain, was the answer to this problem. Of course! Nekros! The guy was rumoured to be the leader of a tribe of rampaging psychopaths. Leaders make decisions, and rampaging psychopaths need swords. He was exactly the sort of person an enterprising sales rep should be targeting.

With a smile on his lips and pigeon crap all over his clothes, Belladon (Sales Executive, South Frundor Region) set off to meet his doom.

MEETING

We have heard already of the wasteland known as the Nevacom Plains. By the time Ronan entered manhood, this was a barren, tortured place. No longer were men able to scratch a living in the arid soil, and few were the creatures that could survive the burning sun. Thus was it fit only for Holiday Village developments, and few who entered this wild and savage place returned to tell of the horrors of Time-sharing Flatlets . . .

The Pink Book of Ulay

In a hollow in one of the most desolate parts of the Nevacom Plains, a small and rather scared man sat by a camp-fire, staring nervously into the night. His name was Tarl (unless you happened to be a debt-collector, an irate husband, or the police), and he was wondering whether it might be a good idea to get pissed. He was staring nervously because he felt about as at home out here as a fish would in a brick. His natural environment was the city – and preferably a noisy, dirty, crowded city with an awful lot of booze, women, casinos, and illicit substances.

When he'd set up camp at dusk, there had been no sign of life anywhere – just an awful lot of broken, jagged rocks, as far as the eye could see. Then, as darkness fell, a dank, creeping mist that smelt of decay had settled gently around him, and all sorts of strange noises had started up. Snuffling noises, howling noises, snarling noises, and screeching noises. The sort of noises made by Things That Eat Tarls. And some of them were getting closer.

Quickly, he grabbed a handful of the dead wood that he'd painstakingly gathered and flung it on the fire. A few more hesitant flames staggered into life. In the distance a demented braying started up – the sort of noise that might be made by the Donkey from Hell. Tarl, deciding that if there were going to be a lot of noises, they might as well be noises he was familiar with, started to chat out loud to himself.

'You must be mad. Sitting out here in the middle of the wilderness, miles from anywhere, surrounded by things you wouldn't even play cards with. Well, it's your own fault. You knew what would happen if those orcs caught you with your hand in the till.' He jumped as something screeched loudly almost overhead, and small coruscating sparks began to skitter around his finger-tips. Damn! That always happened at moments of extreme stress, and he hated it. The only way to stop it quickly was to have a few drinks. He sighed and reached out for the wine-skin that was lying on the ground beside his back-pack. At that moment, the distant braying reached a crescendo, and was answered by the low whinny of a horse. A low whinny that was close. Very close.

Slowly, quietly, Tarl drew himself up to his full five feet, and rested his hand on the sword-hilt. Horses don't go wandering round in the wilderness by themselves. They've got too much sense. That meant a rider. And whoever it was wouldn't pass by a fire without investigating. A friendly traveller would be glad of the company, and an unfriendly traveller would . . . Tarl gritted his teeth, and then nearly stopped breathing. It had suddenly gone very quiet. Every single animal noise had stopped.

'OK, who's there?' Tarl's voice filled the silence like a rain-drop filling a swimming-pool. Red and green sparks seeped from his finger-tips and fell crackling to the ground. 'Come on, I know you're there . . . Say something.' He listened again. Not a sound – then the clink of one stone against another as someone moved. 'Come on, whoever you are! Say something, otherwise there's going to be a nasty accident! I'm not joking . . . my bowels scare easily!'

There was a moment's silence, and then a massive and rather frightening warrior strolled out of the darkness. He was leading a large horse and holding the biggest sword that Tarl had ever seen. Around his neck he wore a leather thong, from which dangled a teddy-bear's head. For some reason, this childish object made him seem more threatening. He paused, and then challenged Tarl. 'I am Ronan, Vanquisher of Evil. Will you aid me or thwart me? Choose quickly!'

Tarl didn't need more than an instant to make up his mind. Vanquishers of Evil tend to be good guys, and this bozo had 'good' written in every noble line of his face. And good guys don't usually stick swords in you if you're nice to them. Tarl held up a welcoming hand, and grinned from ear to ear.

'Oh, aid you! Definitely, aid you! By the gods, you scared me then! I thought you might have been something malevolent and vicious creeping up on me. The police or something. Here, pull up a rock and warm yourself by the fire!'

Ronan stuck his sword point-first into the dry soil, and sat down, leaving his horse standing untethered in the shadows. (Warrior horses seldom need to be tethered. When you belong to a warrior, you quickly learn to behave, or you end up as a burger in some seedy orc take-away.) Tarl, rigorously following his policy of being nice, carried on babbling away.

'I'm Tarl, by the way. Ronan, Vanquisher of Evil, eh? Good name! Says it all, really. I've always fancied something like that for myself. Something with a bit of style. Tarl the Mixer of Cocktails, maybe. Or Tarl the Thrower of Parties.'

Ronan looked at him quizzically. 'How about Tarl the Crasher of Gates?' he suggested.

Tarl stared in surprise. 'Here, have we met before?' he asked, worriedly. Ronan smiled and shook his head, and Tarl picked up the wine-skin and unstoppered it thoughtfully. Despite the fact that he had a teddy-bear head hanging round his neck, this guy was no idiot. Tarl took a long gulp of wine, then remembered his Nice Guy policy and offered the skin to Ronan, who took it and raised it to his lips. He swallowed, and his eyebrows met in the middle of his forehead with an audible thump. Ye gods! He'd expected the wine to be a little on the rough side, but it felt as though someone had sand-papered his throat and blow-torched his stomach! And the aftertaste! He'd drunk a fair bit of wine in the past two years, and become quite knowledgeable, but this was like nothing he'd ever experienced.

Tarl, who firmly believed that you could tell the quality of a wine by the size of the lumps in it, grinned proudly. 'Good, eh? That'll put hairs on your chest! My pet rat used to go round beating up cats after a glass of this stuff!'

'You have a pet rat?' Ronan smiled to himself as he handed the wine-skin back. Tarl looked more likely to *be* a pet rat than to own one.

'Yeah. He's called William . . . well, I don't actually own him, we shared a cellar together. He was great, I'd taught him all sorts of tricks. I taught him to play dead, and to sit up and beg, and to fetch, and to carry . . .'

'That's pretty clever. What does he carry?'

'Bubonic plague, mostly.' Tarl smiled at the memory of his pet, then a frown crossed his face. 'I hope he's all right. I had to leave him behind when I slipped out of Orcville. I was in a bit of a hurry. Didn't have time to say goodbye.'

'Orcville? That's one dangerous town!'

'You're telling me! I was a Gambling Chip for three weeks when I first went there. I was pretty desperate, I can tell you. Then I got a safer job, working in the Blue Balrog Club. I used to take the money at the door.'

'Why did you leave?'

'They caught me doing it. So I thought I'd better get out before I ended up in a casserole. You know what orcs are like. One minute it's "We must do lunch sometime", the next moment you *are* lunch. Here, have some more wine.' He handed the skin over to Ronan, who looked at it for a moment, then took a deep breath, and had another drink. It was probably the bravest thing he'd done for many a long year.

Orcville, in the Northern Mountains, is a city famed for its relaxed attitude to life. (In fact, most people there have a very relaxed attitude indeed, especially when it comes to other people's lives.) Orcville is also famous for its casinos. It was the birth-place of legalised gambling. For many years, people happily gambled with money, but after a while, the excitement began to pall. So you'd won a small fortune, or you'd lost one. So what? It was only money.

As business slumped, the casinos tried gambling with other commodities in an attempt to reintroduce the old excitement and bring the punters back. And of course what provides more excitement than gambling with your life? For a while, the Life and Death Stud Poker Game at Gashnik's Palace was the biggest game in town. And then people began to realise that maybe it was a bit *too* dangerous. It was fine if you won. You'd had a real evening's excitement. But what if you lost? That was it. Finito.

You lost your life. End of story – and end of you.

Then someone hit on the idea of gambling with other people's lives. Anyone who was foolhardy or desperate enough could hire themselves out as a Gambling Chip. If your employer won, he paid you a sizeable fee. If he lost . . . well, that was life. Or rather, death. Your death, of course, not your employer's.

Habitually lucky gamblers would usually find a host of Gambling Chips clamouring for employment at the casino door. Notoriously bad gamblers had an unfortunate way of ending up with a knife in their back down some dark alley on the way to the casino. Well, the odds were stacked against the Gambling Chips, so it wasn't surprising if they wanted to increase their chances of survival slightly . . .

In the hollow on the Nevacom Plains, the fire was dying down. Ronan and Tarl had swapped a lot of stories, and drunk a lot of wine. Ronan, bathed in that rosy glow of well-being that comes after a few drinks, had decided that Tarl was a Good Guy. A bit lacking in the Ethics and Morals Department, perhaps. Well, OK, completely lacking. But otherwise, a Good Guy. Slowly, he raised the nearly empty wine-skin to his mouth. He'd almost got used to the taste now, and you had to admit it gave you a lovely warm glow in the stomach. Just the thing for cold nights in the middle of nowhere.

On the other side of the fire, Tarl was slumped against a rock, with a silly grin on his face. Spending a night in the middle of the wilderness miles from the pleasures of civilisation was not his idea of a good time – but if he had to do so, to do it with a skinful of wine in the company of a guy who liked him, and who could have kicked sand in a dragon's face with impunity, was definitely the best way. Happily, he watched Ronan swig from the wine-skin.

'Great wine, isn't it?' he said proudly. 'Wonderful vintage.'

Vintage? Ronan found that surprising. 'What vintage is it?'

'Thursday.'

'What?'

'I made it last Thursday, the day before I ran off.'

'I wouldn't have thought you could get grapes that far north.'

'Oh, you don't need grapes! My gran taught me how to make wine. Elderberries, dandelions, nettles . . . you can use just about anything you find lying around in the countryside.'

'So what's this one made out of?' Ronan took another swig, savouring the flavour and trying to decide what it could have come from.

'Sheep shit.'

Tarl sat up in concern as a spray of wine jetted from Ronan's mouth. It hit the embers of the fire and ignited with a loud 'whuff', burning with a weird blue flame. Tarl went to speak, and then stopped. Something a little strange was happening. The blue flame grew to a height of three feet, burning brightly, yet seeming to suck in heat rather than throw it out. Deep within it something was moving. Something dark but tenuous, which slowly coalesced into a recognisable human shape, a moving image barely two foot high.

Ronan was staring in disbelief. 'Father!' he gasped. In the flame, an image of the Smith seemed to be arguing with someone out of vision. As Ronan spoke it turned and looked out at him with pride, and he was shocked to see his father's face disfigured by a livid, half-healed slash where Nekros's sword had struck.

'Listen, my son. I haven't got much time!' The voice was faint, not whispered, but like something speaking normally fifty yards away. 'Your path lies through the city of Welbug, but beware! Your enemies are everywhere! Trust no man.'

Ronan looked across at Tarl with suspicious eyes. The image of the Smith turned to follow his gaze, and peered at Tarl for a moment. 'Oh, don't worry about him!' it said, dismissively. 'He's harmless.' For a moment, it reconsidered. 'Well, relatively harmless. Just don't go to any parties with him. Now listen.' The image searched its pockets and produced a scrap of paper. It took a deep breath, then turned and snapped 'All right, all right!' at someone unseen, before starting to read from the paper.

Dwarfish chart and magic potion,
Sword of Myth shall Sing again.
No man's hand shall aid the son
Who would destroy his father's bane.

The image looked up, and seemed to be rather embarrassed.

62

'I'm sorry about the crappy verse. I had to write it myself. There aren't any professional writers up here. They're all down in the other place.'

'But what does it mean?' Ronan asked.

'I can't tell you that. Apparently it's against the rules.' The image of the Smith looked daggers at the unseen person. 'You wouldn't believe how many stupid bloody rules the DHSS have.'

'The what?'

'The DHSS. Department of Haunting, Spirits and Spectres. I've done nothing but fill in forms for two years, just for this one short appearance.' Suddenly the image began to fade. It yelled, 'That was never two minutes, you bastard!' at the unseen person, before turning back to Ronan with a look that was half desperation, half love. 'Go to Welbug, Ronan. You can succeed, but don't forget the rhyme!' It was very faint now. 'Love you, son! Goodbye!' Then it was gone, and the blue flame died as suddenly as it had arisen, leaving just the red glow of the dying camp-fire.

Ronan sat staring into the embers as a wave of sadness and home-sickness washed over him. Memories and feelings that he had carefully buried five years ago had suddenly erupted and were sloshing about in his mind. Tarl, respecting his mood, kept silent. He hadn't followed much of what had been said, but he realised that they had just seen an image of Ronan's father. Not that he really understood this father/son relationship thing – his own dad had buggered off while Tarl was still a spermatozoon – but everyone seemed to place great importance on it. And so, quietly, respectfully, he drained the wine-skin.

After about ten minutes, Ronan stirred. 'So,' he sighed. 'My path lies through Welbug. The Ancient City of the Elves.'

'What?' laughed Tarl. 'Elves? Where have you been the past thousand years? They call it the Pleasure City of the East these days. The place is a right den of iniquity. Harlots, booze, gambling, drugs . . . everything that makes life worthwhile! As a matter of fact, I'm on my way there now. I'm planning a few weeks R and R.'

'It's a pity you're on foot,' said Ronan. 'Our paths could have merged, and I could do with a companion I can trust.' Tarl blinked at this. He wasn't used to people who thought he was trustworthy. 'But I have need of speed,' Ronan continued, 'and I doubt if my horse could carry us both as far as Welbug.'

His horse whinnied, as if in agreement, and out of the darkness once again came the demented braying of the Donkey from Hell. Only this time, it sounded mere yards away. Tarl and Ronan stared in surprise as a small, unkempt creature ambled painfully out of the shadows and stood looking at them. It was a donkey, thin and dirty with matted light brown hair, that looked as though it had been wandering round the wastelands for at least five years. Suddenly, it threw back its head and brayed again. Close to, there was a strident screeching edge to the bray that chilled the blood. Tarl shivered.

'I think it's hungry,' said Ronan. Rising, he crossed to his horse and unstrapped its fodder-bag from the saddle. Tossing it to Tarl, he said, 'Here. Give him some food. If he's tameable, he could be the answer to our problem. We could ride to Welbug together.'

Tarl took some hay from the bag and held it nervously on his outstretched hand. 'Come on, ace,' he called encouragingly. The donkey's nostrils twitched hungrily and it ambled across. Lovely! it thought. Food! And it reached out, nudged the irritating grassy stuff aside, and attempted to take a large chunk of nice tasty flesh out of Tarl's arm.

An hour later, the donkey was lying beside Ronan's horse, listening to Ronan and Tarl reminisce. It had a full stomach for the first time in ages, having eaten four pounds of dried meat from Ronan's supply bag, and had decided that it would be worth sticking with these two if they could provide a decent dinner each night, even if it meant having the little smelly one riding round on its back all day long. After all, he didn't look as though he weighed much, and he would be handy if the food ran out. And there was something rather touching about him . . .

Tarl was wrapped up in his blanket, a filthy brown object that looked and smelt as though it had been used as a nappy by a succession of incontinent *apatodons*. 'I always wanted a pet when I was tiny,' he said to Ronan, 'but I soon learned not to get too attached to things. Any animal unlucky enough to come into our house wasn't around long. Two days at the most and it would end up in bits on a plate, fried to a crisp and swimming in some foul-tasting muddy stuff that my old gran claimed was called gravy. Even the hamster I borrowed from the boy next door. When I gave it back to him he beat me up. And I'd spent ages gluing the bones together!'

He looked fondly across at the donkey. He'd got over the initial shock of being attacked now. After all, why shouldn't a starving donkey fancy a mouthful of Tarl? He'd often eaten donkey-meat. And there was definitely something rather touching about the little creature . . .

'Goodnight, boy,' he called, and then turned back to Ronan. 'We'd better give him a name.'

The donkey pricked up its ears. It had always longed for a name of its very own, but no one had ever before thought it important enough to merit one. It had always just been 'the donkey'. Accurate enough, as names go, and descriptive, but a shade lacking in imagination. Now, all of a sudden, someone was going to give it a real live name of its very own. It sat up in anticipation. What would the small human choose? Something with a bit of a bite, hopefully. Killer. Or Genghis, perhaps. Or maybe Beelzebub.

'I think I'll call him Puss,' said Tarl. 'I always wanted a little kitten.'

The donkey swore quietly to itself. Typical! it thought. There must be hundreds of travellers wandering around in the north, and I latch on to one with the brain of a duck. It sighed and lay down with its back pointedly towards Tarl. Still, it thought as it drifted off to sleep, it could have been worse. At least it isn't Tibbles.

AMBUSH

Orcs . . . a right shower of bastards.

The Pink Book of Ulay

Orcs are about as elegant and sympathetic as a tapeworm, but with absolutely none of the good points. Even worse, they never buy a round.

Tarl's World-Wide Guide to Free Booze

A beer-glass flew across the room and smashed into the wall, showering Kalik the barman with fragments. Seconds later, the orc who had thrown it flew across the room and smashed into the wall, showering Kalik the barman with fragments. The rest of the orcs gave a loud and extremely drunken cheer, and then launched into an old orcish drinking-song, *'Zuluh Brachgag Mizgag Ul'* ('If You Haven't Bought a Round, You're Going to Die').

Kalik wiped himself down with a cloth and sighed. He was close to exhaustion now. It was a house rule that whichever members of staff were on duty when an orc party arrived in the pub had to stay on duty until it left. That way, the landlord wouldn't have too many staff wiped out during one drinking session. There were compensations, of course. A week in lieu, danger money, and free health and accident insurance. But Kalik had been stuck here for thirty-six hours now without a break, and he knew he couldn't last out much longer[1].

He looked across at Andros, the other barman, and shook his head admiringly. What a hero! Four hours ago they had nearly run out of glasses, and Andros had volunteered to go out into the room and collect the empties. It was a suicide mission, but he'd nearly made it. He was on his way back to the bar with his third trayful

---

[1] For details of orcs and their drinking habits, see Appendix Three.

when the orcs grabbed him and hustled him across to the spearboard alley that ran along one wall of the room. Now he was stapled to the board, and a group of laughing orcs stood at the oche, forty feet away, hurling razor sharp spears at him and trying to see how close they could get without actually hitting him. So far Andros was unhurt, but it probably wouldn't be long now. The orcs were getting pretty drunk . . .

Kalik ducked as another glass flew over his head. Klatting orcs! He could remember when they weren't even allowed through the city gates. Now Welbug was full of them, and even members of the Town Council consorted with them. He looked across to the corner of the room where the orc sergeant was deep in conversation with the smarmy figure of Councilman Ritta. As he watched, Ritta handed over a heavy leather purse and the orc nodded and stood up.

'Right, lads,' he snarled, 'the party's over. We've got a job on.'

Instantly the room was silent. The sergeant strolled over and inspected the other orcs, most of whom were trying to stand to attention. He stopped in front of one who was slumped across a table, dead to the world.

'Can't take your ale, eh, Shagger?' he snarled, and pulling the comatose orc's head back by its lank greasy hair, he sliced its throat open with his dagger. Black blood fountained across the table and the sergeant let the head fall back and turned to the remainder of the orcs. 'No room for wimps in this outfit!' he growled, then after wiping the dagger on the dead orc's hair he spat copiously and accurately on the back of its neck and swaggered out, followed raggedly by the other orcs.

Ritta stared at the dead orc with an expression of distaste on his podgy features and then sidled out of the door. Andros sagged against the spearboard, weak with relief. The last spear thrown had grazed his side, but he was otherwise unhurt. He looked across to the bar, expecting Kalik to come and set him free. But Kalik's head was resting on his arms, which in turn were resting on the bar-top, and his eyes were closed. Kalik was sleeping the sleep of the deeply relieved.

Tarl was feeling deeply uneasy. It wasn't just the oppression of the gloomy dank forest they were riding through. It wasn't just

the mist that curled about their legs or the water that dripped
endlessly from the forest canopy high above. It wasn't just that he
was seated on a donkey who seemed to view him as a prospective
lunch. No, there was something else. A threatening feeling, a
sense of imminent danger. He remembered the vision of the
Smith saying 'Your enemies are everywhere'. Tarl shifted uncomfortably on the donkey's bony back. Far from being a useful
companion and protector, this Ronan could turn out to be a
definite liability. Still, they were no more than an hour's ride
from Welbug. Once they reached the city he would quietly slide
off. Ronan could go charging about on his quest and get himself
killed, but Tarl would be safely engaged in his own quest. A Quest
for the Most Lethal Cocktail in Town.

As Tarl dreamt of Alcoholic Refreshments Beyond the Ken of
Mortal Man, Ronan was still puzzling over his father's message.
He had been thinking about it for three days now and still hadn't
got anywhere. A Sword that Sings . . . well, yes, there were rather
a lot of those in legend. But which one? And what potion? What
dwarfish chart? Ronan was hoping for a few answers in Welbug,
but he was beginning to wonder how he was going to find them.
Welbug was a big place, apparently. And you can't just walk up to
people in the street and ask them if they have the odd dwarfish
chart they don't want, or if they have any swords with interesting
vocal capabilities.

He was just mulling this over when suddenly his horse tossed
its head uneasily and whinnied gently, and Tarl's donkey stopped
dead and stared along the path ahead. Its nostrils whiffled slightly
and then a strange gleam came into its eyes, and it licked its lips.
Tarl himself was peering nervously around, and little sparks were
fizzing out of his fingertips and drifting down to fizzle out in the
mud. He turned to Ronan.

'Someone's coming. Someone dangerous. I can feel it.'

The two of them sat listening. At first, the only sound that
could be heard was the steady drip of water from the branches, but
then in the distance they could just make out the rhythmic tramp
of feet and the clink of armour.

'Whoever they are, they're coming this way,' said Ronan. 'I
think maybe we should hide.'

'Good idea!' said Tarl. At last! he thought. I'm getting through

68

to him. For the past few days, Ronan had been expounding his method of dealing with threats or dangers – meet them head-on, stare them down, and belt them with a sword if they so much as blink at you. Tarl had spent the whole time desperately advocating a more softly-softly approach. At the first sniff of danger, run like buggery, was his motto, although he'd managed to couch it in terms more acceptable to a guy like Ronan.

He was greatly relieved when Ronan dismounted and led his horse away from the track, brushing through the damp ferns into the deeper gloom of the forest. He wasn't so happy when Ronan stopped behind a large boulder, still in sight of the glade, and whispered, 'I want to see who it is.' However, Tarl didn't fancy wandering further into the trees all by himself and so, after shushing the donkey (which was contentedly chewing on a dead squirrel it had found), he crouched down in the ferns next to the warrior and waited.

As the tramping of feet approached, it began to sound less rhythmic and more disorganised. They could hear a voice snarling 'left, right, left, right!' though for all the good it was doing, it might as well have saved its breath. There was the occasional 'clunk' that sounded like someone being hit on the helmet with the flat of a sword, and a number of muttered curses and groans. Tarl was only too familiar with voices like that. Orcs! he thought. I hope it's no one I know.

The orcs marched raggedly into the clearing and then, at a command from their leader, came to a halt. There were eight of them, all armed to the hilt. Their leader carried a short brutal sword and a large metal hammer studded with nails, while the rest carried slim-headed spears with backward-pointing barbs down the length of the shaft. A couple had bows slung round their necks.

Tarl knew that these were not the sort of people you would ask to a dinner-party if you wanted to impress the neighbours. He'd lived among orcs for a while, and could even pass for a half-orc if he had to (although his skin was not naturally dark grey, it had merely gone that colour after a lifetime spent avoiding baths and getting up at five in the afternoon, just as the sun was going down). He knew they were a nasty, vicious, cruel race.

'OK, this looks like a good place for the ambush,' shouted the orc leader. 'Bleb, Vomit, you two scout round, look for the best place for the bows to set up. Sputum, you sort out some food. We'd better eat before he gets here. Ringworm, get up to where the track disappears and keep guard. We don't want him surprising us.'

One of the orcs started rummaging in the filthy sack he had been carrying slung over his shoulder. A second one slouched off up the path, and the two with bows began to wander off the path into the forest, but to Tarl's relief they stopped short of where he and Ronan were crouched, and stared up into a tree.

'Here, Vomit, isn't that a bird's nest up there?' said one.

'Yeah,' snarled the other, peering up into the foliage. 'I think it is. Let's shake it down.' Gleefully they grabbed the thin bole of the tree and began to shake it from side to side. In the clearing, one of the other orcs started to complain in an irritatingly whiny voice. The leader turned on him.

'For Grak's sake, Knob-rot, don't you ever shut up! We're here because the boss told us to be here. I don't know how he knew the target would be coming this way . . . he just knew.' The leader turned and took one of the foul-looking pieces of dried flesh that Sputum had produced from his sack, and bit into it hungrily. Knob-rot took the piece that was handed to him, and looked at it scornfully.

'And why we're eating this crap, when there's a human about to stumble into our ambush . . .'

'We are not eating the human!' the leader cut in. 'We are not eating him because the boss wants to see his body, as proof that we've done the job. And if he doesn't get the proof, it will be us going into the pot instead. Comprenez, dung-brain?'

At the side of the clearing, Bleb and Vomit were still violently shaking the tree, until Vomit suddenly yelled, 'It's coming!' He stood back, staring up at the falling nest with an evil grin on his face, and then after a moment, his grin began to falter. The nest seemed to have been falling for quite a while without getting much nearer. Perspective wasn't a thing he knew much about, but he suddenly realised that something a long way off that looked very small could actually be pretty damn' big. Such as that nest . . .

Bleb desperately leapt to one side, but Vomit remained rooted to the spot. His mouth opened, but nothing came out, and then an eight-foot nest weighing a quarter of a ton smashed down on top of him. Out of it bounced an egg that was a good three feet in diameter. It ricocheted off a boulder and landed a couple of yards away from where Tarl was crouched in the ferns. For a moment, the forest seemed to reverberate, and then there was a stunned silence, which was broken by Bleb.

'Here, chief, come and look at the size of this nest that's fallen on top of Vomit,' he called. The leader ran over, followed by the other orcs, and stared at the huge tangled mess of dead branches and *festa* vines.

'Grak's blood!' he swore. 'You've only shaken down a *pakas* nest, that's all! Vomit?' He bent down, grabbed hold of the only bit of Vomit that could still be seen (half a leg), and pulled. 'Ah, it's no good, we'll never get him out from under all that. Pity. I could have done with a bit of fresh meat for tea. We won't get much off his foot.'

'He had mange as well, chief,' said Bleb. 'We could have got some lovely orc scratchings off him. Tell you what, though. There was a klatting big egg in the nest.'

'What? A *pakas* egg? Bloody lovely, man! Where did it go?'

Bleb pointed towards Tarl's boulder. 'Over there somewhere, behind that rock.'

Tarl was horrified to hear the sound of the orcs pushing their way through the ferns towards him. He buried his head in his arms and tried to squirm even deeper into the leaf-mould that carpeted the forest floor. For a moment, he thought that he might not be seen, and then a voice spoke directly above his head.

'Well, well, what have we here?' It was the leader of the orcs. 'What are you up to, sonny boy?'

Tarl leapt up, yelling, 'Klat! They've found us, Ronan!' and stared around wildly. In front of him in a rather unpleasant semi-circle stood the orcs, grinning horribly in anticipation. And beside him stood . . . no one! 'Ronan?' he said in a voice so small it was invisible. But there was no reply. Ronan, his horse, and the donkey had vanished as though the earth had opened up and swallowed them.

It was one of those moments when your whole life flashes before

71

your eyes. Normally, Tarl would have enjoyed this, as his life included some pretty interesting moments. However, when you're all alone apart from a group of orcs who have just suggested shoving a large spear up a very private part of your anatomy and spit-roasting you, you have other things on your mind.

Quickly, he weighed up the options. Running like buggery was out. He knew from previous experience that talking your way round a hungry orc is next to impossible. It was unlikely that all seven were going to drop dead from heart-attacks. There was only one thing left. He was going to have to try fighting his way out.

Mentally cursing the fact that, after a lifetime of cowardice, mixing with some nutty warrior had brought him to such a state of affairs, he drew his sword. Although he'd bought it years ago, he'd never before needed to take it out of its scabbard. There had always been another way. Not this time, though.

'OK, you scumbags!' he snarled. Whoops! That sounded a little shrill. We don't want them thinking we're scared. He grabbed hold of his voice and dragged it down a couple of octaves. 'If you want trouble, you can have it. All at once, or one at a time. I don't mind.'

Fired by desperation, he took a couple of steps forward and brandished his sword. To his horror, the blade fell off the handle. For a brief moment, hope flickered in his mind, as it looked as though a couple of the orcs might die of laughter. But then the leader's face hardened. He stepped forward and placed one foot on Tarl's blade.

'Right, lads. Looks as though we'll be able to have a bit of fun with this one. Any suggestions?'

'We could disembowel him and roast his entrails over a fire.'

'We could cut his eyes and his balls out and play marbles with them.'

'We could stick our spears up our little bums and let him go.'

This last suggestion came in a deep and frightening voice from behind the orcs. There was a moment's stunned silence, then they all turned round and stared. Tarl was nearly sick with relief. For there in the clearing stood salvation in the form of Ronan. His sword was drawn and he was holding it two-handed, in the casually relaxed way of someone who is totally at home with it. To his left stood Puss the donkey, eyes ablaze with excitement. It opened its mouth and brayed threateningly, and the forest echoed to its strident cry.

Despite this unexpected development, the orc leader wasn't too worried. Seven on to three isn't normally an overwhelming advantage, but when one of the three is a wimp with a novelty sword and the second is a small brown donkey, things are looking a little better.

'OK, boys,' he said, calmly. 'Let's get the big black one. Standard pattern. Go!'

The orcs may have been a little shambolic when they were marching, but they'd been together a good while and they were professional killers. They knew how to fight. Five of them charged Ronan, fanning out to come at him in a broad front, while a sixth dodged to one side and fitted an arrow to his bow.

Ronan moved rapidly to the right away from the archer, so that the charging orcs had to veer to come after him. Now, instead of attacking him in line abreast, they came one after the other, scrambling over the rough ground and snarling with excitement. But as Ronan suddenly stopped and turned, his mind was as clear and cold as a mountain lake. As always, warrior training had taken over, and events seemed to move in slow motion as thoughts flashed through his brain like knives.

Firm footing here, turn and cut two-handed, sword perfectly balanced as it hisses through the air, stupid look of surprise on the head of the first orc as it topples from the shoulders, step over the body, black blood spurting from the neck, could be slippery, careful, a backhand cut to the stomach of the second orc, watch it, those entrails definitely *will* be slippery, a couple of steps back, two of them coming at once, dodge that spear, sword arcing down, don't know my own strength sometimes, it's wedged in his chest cavity, let go with one hand and grab that spear, ouch, damn orcs putting spikes down the shaft, like needles in the palm, bugger, blank off the pain, pull sword free, yes, tug him forward by his own spear, smash pommel of sword into his face, ha, that nasty invention of Tazmir's, the needle-sharp pommel, always sur- prises them, straight through the eye into the brain, mustn't forget the archer, didn't expect that, need a shield, fifth orc will do, he's stabbing, a look of terror on his face, easy to dodge, grab him, wallop! out cold, don't think I 've killed him, check archer,

73

he hasn't got a clear shot, check orc leader, klat! he's after Tarl, have to be a thrown dagger, klat! I haven't enough time, he's going to get him . . .

Tarl had been standing staring open-mouthed as Ronan blurred into action and blood, guts, and bits of orc sprayed everywhere. This was exactly the sort of thing he'd always wanted to happen to people who were being nasty to him, yet he had to admit that the reality was a little on the gruesome side. Poor bastards. But then a snarled curse brought him sharply back to his own situation, and he turned to find the orc leader leaping at him. Yelping with fear, Tarl sprang backwards and fell over a tree root. The orc raised its sword to strike and Tarl, terror-stricken, lifted his arms to protect himself. A huge wash of fear seemed to sweep from his brain along his arms, and a surge of blue flame shot out of his hands and enveloped the orc. For a couple of seconds it stood there, rooted to the spot with surprise and smoking gently, and then one of its charred eyebrows fell off. Snarling, it raised its sword again, but before it could move there was a loud 'thock' and the tip of Ronan's dagger was poking out through its throat. Hot sticky blood spurted out over Tarl's upraised arms, and then the orc crashed to the ground beside him and Tarl gasped with relief.

Ronan's brain was still ticking over. Nice throw, got the bastard, Tarl's OK, interesting trick with the blue flame, klat I needed that dagger for the archer, grab an orc spear, throw that, klat! he's behind that tree, can't get him, and you know how good orc archers are, put an arrow in a moving eye-socket at fifty paces, some of them, we're sitting ducks, klat! we've had it, he's lining up on Tarl . . .

Ringworm, the orc archer, was feeling pretty confident. He knew exactly how good he was with a bow. Shame about the other lads, but then they wouldn't be needing their share of the fee any more. Leering to himself, he decided to take out the small snivelling human first, and he was just swinging his bow towards Tarl when a screeching braying noise seemed to freeze every muscle in his body. Something like a sledgehammer with teeth slammed into him from behind and he went sprawling over the roots of the tree. Looking up he found he was staring into the glazed red eyes of the small brown donkey from a range of about six inches. It felt like about twenty miles too close. Before he could move it struck like a snake, bared teeth slashing like knives, and Ringworm was screaming and writhing on the ground with blood spurting from the stump of his severed arm.

Tarl dragged himself upright. He couldn't believe how quickly all this had happened. Thirty seconds ago, he had been in imminent danger of a horrible death. Now, the people who had threatened him were scattered in bloody bits all over the forest. He watched in horrified fascination as Ronan hung the unconscious survivor from a handy branch by its belt before walking across to the screaming orc and dispatching it with a quick stab of the sword. Tarl turned away, unwilling to watch, and found himself face to face with the donkey. It was holding the severed arm in its jaws and seemed fairly happy with life.

'Yeuch! Puss! What are you doing with that in your mouth?' asked the revolted Tarl.

The donkey just stared at him pityingly. I thought you might want to shake hands, it thought. What do you think I'm doing? It's my dinner for tonight. One orc arm, to go. It looked at Tarl disparagingly. I've known glaciers that moved faster than your brain, mate, it thought, and turned away.

Tarl sat down on a rock. He found he was shaking. Normally, when he shook like this, it meant he'd had a pretty good time the night before. But to be shaking for no decent reason whatsoever, that was no fun. No fun at all. If this is adventure, he thought, you can stuff it. Suddenly, Ronan spoke from about two foot behind him, and Tarl fell off the rock.

'Don't do that!' he said, as he picked himself up.

'Sorry,' Ronan apologised. 'I'm used to moving silently. That's what Warrior School does for you.' He bent down and wiped his blood-stained sword on the orc leader's back. 'You took him by surprise with that fireball,' he added. 'How did you . . .'

'I don't want to talk about it!'

Ronan looked at him with interest, then noticed the sword handle in his hand. It looked strangely familiar. 'That was brave,' he added casually. 'Trying to take on eight orcs with a broken sword.'

'Bloody thing!' swore Tarl. 'Just wait until I go back to Port Raid.'

'What?' Ronan was suddenly very still.

'I'm going to get my money back from Elric if it's the last thing I do. Honest Elric, indeed! I should have known better. One *tablon*, he charged me! You don't get a decent sword for that sort of price, even in a sale.' Tarl paused, and looked at Ronan as he re-sheathed his sword. Funny, he thought. He looks really embarrassed. He must think I'm a right pranny, owning a weapon like that!

Ronan was embarrassed all right. He was wondering how many more of his father's duff swords had fallen apart just at the wrong time for other poor innocents. Not that 'innocent' was the first word that sprang to mind when you looked at Tarl. Thoughtfully, Ronan pulled his dagger out of the orc leader's neck and crossed to where the last pitiful survivor was dangling from a tree. It was clearly regaining consciousness and was beginning to kick and squirm. Tarl followed him, trying not to look at the remnants of the others.

'Strange to find mountain-orcs in the middle of the forest,' he said. 'What do you think they were after?'

Ronan carefully wiped his dagger on the orc's filthy jerkin, and it stopped wriggling and went very, very still. Tarl had seen livelier statues. Ronan looked it carefully in the eye, and held up the dagger. 'I'm hoping to persuade this creature to tell us,' he growled. The orc went even stiller. Tarl felt sick.

However, he needn't have worried. Although Ronan had the look of someone whose greatest pleasure in life is removing people's kidneys via their rectum with a sharp knife, inside he too was feeling queasy. For Ronan had this problem with guilt. Even three years in Warrior School hadn't been enough to shake off his scruples. Every time he killed someone, no matter how deserving or how fair a fight, he was left wondering whether he had done the right thing, or whether his mother would have approved. He was currently fretting over having had to put that wounded orc out of its misery. The idea of torturing the terrified orc hanging in front of him made him feel ill. He had totally flunked the Interrogation and Torture module of his Warrior Course. However, he had learned that quite often you don't need to torture a prisoner. You just need him to believe you are going to.

Ronan smiled cruelly at the orc, and gently touched the tip of its nose with the dagger. 'I am Ronan, Vanquisher of Evil,' he drawled. 'And this is Tarl. We are going to ask you some questions. If you lie, you die. Understand?'

The orc's eyes were squinting horribly as it stared at the dagger. Somehow it managed to nod its head vigorously up and down without moving its nose a fraction. 'Fine by me, guv!' it gasped. 'Fine! Fine-fine-fine-fine-fine!'

'OK then,' Ronan continued. 'Name?'

'Ronan, Vanquisher of Evil.'

'Not my name, idiot!'

'Oh, er, Tarl then,' replied the orc, apologetically.

'No, no, no, not me either!' muttered Tarl. He was seriously concerned that another thirty foot of orc intestine was about to join that already on the forest floor, and he'd seen enough to last him a lifetime. 'Your name, you plank! What is it?'

'It's the title I use to distinguish me from other people,' gabbled the orc.

'But what is this title!' yelled Tarl.

Light dawned for the orc. 'Oh! It's Bleb!'

Ronan smiled mirthlessly. 'Now we're getting somewhere. Well, Bleb, what are you doing here?'

'Messing my trousers,' came the truthful reply.

Ronan wrinkled up his nose in distaste. 'No, I meant what is your band of orcs doing here?'

Bleb's eyes revolved rapidly, taking in the scene. 'Well, most of them are lying round without any heads on,' he muttered.

Tarl laid a restraining hand on Ronan's arm. 'Let me,' he said confidently, and turned to the terrified orc. 'Look,' he continued, '*why* are you here?'

'Coo, don't ask me, guv, existentialist philosophy is a closed book to me.'

Tarl thought this one through for a few moments and then turned back to Ronan. 'I don't think he's quite as dumb as he looks,' he said.

Ronan decided to up the stakes slightly and exerted the slightest pressure on the dagger. A small droplet of black blood trickled from the tip of Bleb's nose, and Ronan ruthlessly suppressed the thought that his father would definitely not have approved. 'Listen, dragon-breath,' he said in a low growl, 'your band of orcs had a special reason for coming here, into this forest. Tell me what it is.'

'It's a big place with lots of trees.'

Ronan's eyes bulged, and Tarl looked away. Bleb, sensing that maybe this wasn't the required answer, babbled on. 'But if you want to know what the *reason* is, it's because that man in the pub paid us to come out here and kill you.'

'Kill *me*?'

'That's what he said. You'll find a black-skinned warrior with a little bear head hanging round his neck, he said. Ambush him and bring back the body.'

'Which pub was that?'

'The Dragon's Claw, I think. Rough place. In Welbug. Lot of vomit on the floor, and broken glasses and things. Well, there was when we left.'

Ronan turned to Tarl. 'Do you know this tavern?'

'I think I've heard of it . . . the roughest in the whole of Welbug, if I'm right.'

Ronan nodded. 'Then that's where we start,' he said, and lowered his dagger to the orc's throat.

Tarl turned away, unable to watch, but the sight behind him made him want to retch. Flies the size of small birds were already whanging through the trees and homing in on the stickier bits of dead orc. The corpses were a mass of jostling, buzzing, swearing insects. He turned back.

'Listen,' he began, but then he saw the look on Ronan's face. He was staring at the orc with a sickly expression and the dagger in his hand was shaking. A wave of realisation swept over Tarl. The guy couldn't bring himself to kill the creature in cold blood! The great softie! Tarl felt a sudden affection for the big warrior. Trying not to smile, he stepped forward and confronted the orc.

'Listen,' he said. 'We're not going to kill you. But we're going to Welbug and we don't want anyone to know. So we have two choices. One, you promise not to say anything, and head west as fast and as far as you can. Just disappear, OK? Or two, we take you with us to Welbug.'

'Take me with you?' repeated the orc, suspiciously.

'Yeah,' said Tarl innocently, and then dropped his little bombshell. 'In a boat.'

The orc's jaw dropped open, and sweat broke out on its face. Its skin had turned the colour of month-old milk.

'No! Lemmego! Please, I won't say a word, honest I won't, go on, honest-honest-honest-honest-honest, just don't take me inna boat, OK?'

Smiling, Tarl stepped forward, took the knife from Ronan and sliced through the creature's belt. It fell to the ground in a heap, then picking itself up it dashed off through the trees towards the west, gibbering with panic.

'He won't stop till he gets to the Forest of Dreams,' grinned Tarl. 'Trust me,' he continued, as Ronan looked at him doubtfully. 'I've lived with orcs. I understand them. It's common knowledge that they hate water, but what few people know is that they hate boats even more. They get seasick just looking at pictures of boats. Orc galley-slaves have literally thrown their guts up during rough weather. The worse thing you can do to an orc is threaten to take him for a boat trip. Mind you, don't ever carry out the threat. Orcs are bad enough at the best of times, but one which has just regurgitated the entire contents of its stomach all over your shoes is about as unpleasant as you can get.'

Ronan nodded. 'Well, OK,' he said. 'I guess it's better than having to kill him.' Then taking his horse's reins, he began to lead it back to the path.

Tarl hopped nimbly to one side as the donkey pushed past him and trotted after Ronan, the orc arm still hanging from its mouth. Just the companions you need for a nice safe journey, he thought to himself. A psycho-killer with a guilt complex, and the Donkey from Hell. Still, when we get to Welbug you can slide out quick. We're only a couple of hours away, and now the orcs are dead, no one knows where we are. You should be safe until then!

And with this thought in mind he set out after them on foot.

Anthrax the Wizard watched the tiny figure of Tarl scampering after Ronan, then muttered a command and the crystal ball turned abruptly opaque.

'So they got away,' he mused. 'Hm. Nekros seems to be losing his grip. This might turn out to be more enjoyable than I thought. Better let him know, I suppose. It might be more fun to tell Ritta and let him pass on the news.' And with a smile hovering about his mouth he snapped his fingers, and the crystal ball flared with white light once more.

WELBUG

In the First Age, the City of Welbug was a place of great beauty. Here lived elves who were noble. Fair were they to look upon, and so fit and full of good health that they became legendary for their vigour. And in other towns, should any child be weak and sickly, his parents would look upon him and sigh, saying, 'Alas, he is not a Welbugger.'

But then did the renegade Wizard, Amplex the Foulmouthed, turn his attention to the city, assuming friendly guise. And the elves saw through him not, for they were innocent, and legion were the drinks he bought. And so did he introduce them to Tupperware, and to labour-saving artifacts of rare device! And then, as they grew worldly-wise, did he teach them of contact magazines and bondage, and so were the elves of Welbug debased! And many was the elf in need of penicillin . . .

The Pink Book of Ulay

From a distance, Welbug still looked like the beautiful elven city it once was. Built upon a spit of land at the confluence of three rivers, it was enclosed by ancient walls that had never been breached in battle. Slender stone towers and elegant marble turrets reached towards the sky, and the reds and pinks of the myriad roof-tiles glittered in the evening light like a million sunstones.

However, close to it was a different story. No sooner had Ronan and Tarl passed through the main gate into the city than a small ugly man was attempting to sell them his sister. When they showed no interest, he attempted to sell her to the donkey, and it was only when Ronan laid his hand on the hilt of his sword that the man slunk away, muttering curses.

As they passed up Wolfpole, the road that led from the gate to the city centre, Tarl was shocked at the changes in the few years since he had last been here. He stared around sadly. The houses were rundown and unpainted, with grimy walls and overgrown gardens, and many windows were cracked and broken. A number of shops were closed and boarded up. The remainder had all moved sharply downmarket, and seemed to be mainly concentrating on the seedy and the squalid. The streets were dirty and unswept, and litter and filth was gathering in the gutters. And where once the pervading smell had been of gardens full of flowers and blossom, now there was the stench of blocked drains and rotting waste.

And the people! There was a fair ration of fun-seekers, tourists and hedonists strolling round with laughing faces, looking for the pleasures that could obviously still be had. But they were leavened with an equal number of the flotsam of life. Surly Easterlings, lounging in unfriendly groups on street corners, swarthy Southrons jostling the passers-by, and orcs gazing round with unfriendly eyes and snarling to each other in their barbaric tongue. Half the under-life of the world seemed to have ended up on the streets of Welbug. Tarl was saddened. The atmosphere reminded him of Goblin City in the Northern Mountains, and he had always firmly believed that if Midworld ever suffered from haemorrhoids, you would stick the suppositories up Goblin City.

As they reached the top of Wolfpole, he was even more saddened to find that Jalapeno's Bistro had closed, and been replaced by a nasty little shop selling pornographic pamphlets. He'd had a great night at Jalapeno's last time he'd visited Welbug. Got very drunk indeed on Pol Perot wine with a group of tinkers from Far Tibreth. So drunk, he'd ordered two plates of the hottest *mulampos* in the house. Klat! He'd spent nine hours on the toilet and lost half a stone in weight the next day! Happy times!

The huge market square, however, had hardly changed at all. Gaily coloured stalls stretched from one end to the other, and even though it was almost evening, people of every race still jostled and pushed between them. All round the edge of the square, street-vendors, barrow-boys, entertainers, and tricksters were plying their trade. Tarl watched with a smile on his face as a shell-game operator separated a baffled country boy from his money. Close by, a group of yelling soldiers were betting heavily on a slug-race. Next to them, a street-mage was taking coins from passers-by and making them vanish before their very eyes. Tarl grinned wryly. He'd often thought of trying that as a career. If only he had some control over his little problem . . .

Suddenly, his arms were nearly yanked out of their sockets. Puss, whom Tarl was leading on the end of a tether, had spotted a butcher's shop and had taken off like a rocket. Tarl hauled it back.

'Listen, Puss!' he said. 'We don't go charging into shops and pinching whatever we feel like. Round here, you're expected to pay for things. Savvy? Otherwise they're likely to throw you into jail. And you wouldn't like Welbug jails. They're filthy, smelly, and boring.'

Look who's talking, thought the donkey, but it came back and stood quietly beside him.

In front of them, Ronan had been standing watching the interplay of the crowd with a pensive frown on his face. 'This isn't what I'd expected,' he said to Tarl. 'There's a much greater feeling of evil in this town than there should be.'

'It's changed,' replied Tarl. 'It's going downhill. Getting shabby. Or maybe it's just me. Maybe I just built the place up too much in my memory . . . maybe I need a drink. Or several.'

'Maybe.' Ronan didn't sound convinced. 'So, where's the Dragon's Claw?'

'I dunno. I've heard of the place, but I've never been there,' Tarl answered. 'But it should be easy to find. We just need a copy of the party-goer's Bible . . .'

He walked over to a book-stall, and bought the latest edition of *Welbug Weekly*. As he strolled back to Ronan he opened the paper, turned to the Listings pages, and started to thumb his way through them. Klat, this really took him back! Adverts for places he'd known and loved . . . 'Pilgrims! Travellers! For the hottest babes in town, try the Club Gargantua, just off Eastgate!' . . . 'Oubliette's – for a night that you'll never forget, but you sure as hell won't remember!' . . . 'Dastard's Troll Bar, on the corner of Wolfpole and Maim' . . . It had been in Dastard's that he had got so pissed one night that he had tried to pick a fight with an eight-foot cave-troll. Luckily the troll had been kissing drunk, and they'd ended up staggering off to the Dragonbone Rib-house together. Great days!

Happily he worked his way through the listings like a

gourmand working his way through a menu, until half-way down the third page, he found what he was looking for.

'Here we are! This is it: "Gentlemen! For a different class of entertainment, try the Dragon's Claw, Rue Battue." Hmm . . . that's over in the elven quarter.'

'Then let's get moving.' Ronan looked at the donkey, which was standing staring at the butcher's shop with its tongue hanging out. A small pool of saliva was forming on the ground underneath. 'We'd better get the animals fed and watered, too. Any tavern will have stabling for horses . . . but will they have anything this creature will eat?'

Tarl laughed. 'Ronan,' he said, as they started to thread their way through the market-place, 'the roughest dives in this town serve meat of every description . . . and I mean *every* description. Orcs and Southrons eat here. If you've ever wanted to try cannibalism, this will be your chance.'

'Charming!' said Ronan.

'Yeah,' said Tarl.

Yum! thought the donkey.

Councilman Ritta sat in a darkened room at the top of one of the tallest towers in Welbug. He was fidgeting and sweating slightly, and his piggy little eyes were flickering uneasily as he stared into a crystal ball the size of a man's fist which sat on the table in front of him. It rested on a jet-black stand, on which were ten numbered buttons, and from it issued a dull, faintly shimmering white light. All at once the light changed to a red glow, and Ritta swallowed nervously, and then spoke.

'They failed,' he said, and then winced.

From the depths of the crystal an evil voice spoke. 'Then you must try again. And this time, do not fail. Understand?'

Ritta nodded. He seemed to be having difficulty in speaking. The sweat was beginning to trickle into the folds of his neck.

'He is trouble. He must be stopped. And he must be stopped before he meets Tyson.' The evil voice paused, and then continued in a tone which could have frozen water. 'If you do not succeed this time . . .'

'I will!' Ritta cut in. 'I'll send Karth. He's the best assassin in Welbug!'

'Report when it is done,' said the voice, and the red glow changed back to dull white light.

Ritta let out a great gasp of relief. Thanks be to Grak! Another chance! He stood up, held one hand out in front of him, and looked at it. It was shaking badly. His bowels felt as though they'd turned to iced water. Thank Grak I didn't have that plate of *mulampos* for lunch, he thought, and went out to brief Karth.

Evening had fallen by the time Tarl and Ronan found the Rue Battue, which was dark and deserted. It was lined with tall, elegant houses built in the elven style, set back from the road with pleasant tree-lined gardens in front of them. The night air was heavy with the fragrance of *taboghee* blossom, and there was little sound save for the clip-clop of horse and donkey hooves. A gently swinging sign with a rather stylised dragon's foot on it was the only hint as to which house was the Dragon's Claw. They tethered the horse and the donkey to a rail outside and studied the heavy oak door. All was quiet.

'Popular place,' said Ronan.

'Well, what do you expect?' replied Tarl. 'This is supposed to be the roughest dive in Welbug!' He looked round doubtfully at the neatly kept garden. 'Half the regular clientele have probably been murdered by now! And it's only six o'clock . . . the rest probably aren't out of bed yet. Come on.'

He strode forward, followed by the warrior, and pushed open the door. It opened on a small stone-flagged vestibule. Ahead of them was another door. They could just make out the low hum of conversation beyond it. 'Here we go,' said Tarl, as the second door opened in front of them. 'Welcome to the roughest, vilest . . .' his voice slowed as he looked round '. . . most danger . . . er . . . plushest . . .' His voice died completely.

They had entered a room some forty feet long, with a high ceiling, walls panelled in finely carved satinwood and decorated with exotic tapestries, and a floor covered in red carpeting that had a pile so deep that you nearly had to stand on tiptoe to see over it. Along one side were a few alcoves with plumply cushioned semi-circular couches and low marble tables, and halfway along was a magnificent life-size marble statue of a warrior, naked save for a helmet. At the far end was a bar, behind which a barman in a crisp white shirt was mixing cocktails from a few of the hundred or so bottles that lined the shelves behind him. The room was brightly lit by a chandelier of fifty candles which fired off countless shafts of diamond light from the shimmering crystal ornaments that hung underneath, and the musky aroma of exotic Southern Isles perfumes hung in the air.

There were maybe twenty people in the room, seven or eight of whom were wealthy-looking merchant types, and the rest of whom were expensively dressed beautiful women. As Tarl watched, one of the women took a couple of cocktails from the barman and undulated across to an alcove where a merchant sat. She put the drinks down in front of him, then sat beside him, draped one long elegant leg across his, and started to play with his hair. Two other women who were chatting near the bar looked across to Tarl and Ronan, smiled, and winked. Both were blonde and tanned, with the sort of figures that you normally only see on the front covers of slimming magazines.

'By the balls of Amrod!' exclaimed Tarl, slapping his forehead with one hand. 'I don't believe it! The roughest pub in Welbug only turns out to be a high-class cat-house! Your orc was feeding you porkies . . . they'd never let a band of orcs in here!'

Ronan was gazing round, bewildered. 'It can't be right!' he muttered. 'He wouldn't have dared. This can't be . . .'

'It's a cat-house, all right,' said Tarl. 'I can tell. See those two girls who are eyeing us up? One winked at you, and the other winked at me! Look, she's still giving me the come-on!' He paused, and flashed her back one of his best leers. 'Now, I don't want to sell myself short . . . there are plenty of women who think I'm pretty cool. But when two girls like that look at us, what do they see? Mr Universe, and Slug of the Week here . . .' He tapped himself on the chest. 'And if one of them wants to make it with me, it ain't for my boyish good looks. Right?'

'Well . . .' Ronan sighed. 'I guess you're right.'

'Oh, thanks!' Tarl sounded hurt. 'You might at least have argued a bit!' He turned away, and found himself confronted by someone who could only be the doorman. He was wearing a smart dark blue coat and a peaked cap, both of which were edged with gold braid. This neat ensemble was a little spoiled by the three-inch fangs that jutted up from his lower lip. He bowed to Ronan, and started to speak.

'Kazad, nik grechik bee blollong.'

Ronan flashed him a hopeful smile. 'What?' he said.

The doorman began to look agitated. 'Kazad,' he repeated. 'Kazad!'

'Tarl, I can't understand a thing this guy is saying!'

'It's OK, Ronan, don't worry,' said Tarl, confidently. 'It's the Eastling tongue. I've picked a bit of it up over the years. Let me.' He smiled at the doorman. 'Kazad Tarl,' he hazarded, pointing at himself. 'Y kazad Ronan.'

'Ah!' said the doorman. 'Kazad Grimbal!'

'Grimbal.' Tarl was confident now. 'Kazad du-long. Gron zintal dee wangeh. Wangeh ti kak.'

'Wangeh?' The doorman looked surprised. He stared at Tarl, then shook his head and retreated to rummage in the bottom drawer of a desk in an alcove behind the front door.

'Hey, very good,' said Ronan, impressed. 'What was he saying?'

'Well, he asked who we are, and what we want. I think. I told him we only wanted a quick drink.'

'Oh. Listen, ask him if they've had any orcs in lately?'

'OK.' Tarl turned back, but before he could say anything, the doorman walked back up to him, handed him a box of tissues and a picture of a very rampant stallion, and walked away, shaking his head disgustedly. Ronan tried not to laugh.

'Speak it fluently, do you?' he said. 'Hello . . . what's this?'

The two girls who had been watching them were sauntering over, accompanied by a smartly dressed man. He was wearing black trousers and tuxedo, a stiff white shirt, wing collar, and bow tie. He had a small neatly clipped moustache, and his oiled hair was parted in the middle and clung tightly to his head as though it was scared of falling off. He nodded politely to Tarl, and flashed a set of perfect teeth at Ronan. 'Good evening, sir,' he drawled. 'Welcome to our establishment. Allow me to present Serena . . .' at which the smaller of the two girls pouted at Tarl '. . . and Attali.' The larger girl moved next to Ronan and purred up at him.

'You are the owner of this . . . place?' Ronan asked, with a wave of his hand.

'Merely the manager. You may call me Posner. No, the

Dragon's Claw is owned by Tyson.' He stopped, obviously expecting Ronan to know the name.

'Tyson?'

'Ah, you gentlemen must be strangers in town. Tyson is a warrior, the most feared in Welbug, upholder of right and the Champion of our fair city.'

'Then we're in the wrong place,' said Ronan. 'I thought we must be. We'd heard that the Dragon's Claw was the roughest tavern in town, and we hunt one who might be found in such a place.'

'I think you may be mistaking us for the Dragon's Gizzard on Quayside,' smiled Posner. 'Haunt of the dregs of the city. But if you have business there, could we not . . . entertain you, before you leave?'

Attali began to rub herself against Ronan's side. He swallowed. He was beginning to find it difficult to concentrate. 'Sorry,' he said, 'we have to go. Tarl? TARL?'

Tarl was staring at Serena, who was standing with one hand on Posner's shoulder, the other on her hip, and was returning his gaze beneath lowered lashes. For some few seconds she had been very gently gyrating her hips and making little moues at him, and his eyes were riveted on her like a starving rabbit eyeing a large juicy carrot. Ronan realised his friend was vibrating gently and making a low growling noise.

'Tarl!' he repeated, shaking his arm. 'Time to go.'

'What?' Tarl was jerked out of his reverie. 'Must we? Surely we can stay for an hour. Or four.'

'We must go now! Time is important. Every hour we waste, the trail gets colder.'

'OK. I guess you're right,' Tarl said reluctantly. 'Let's go.'

'If you must, gentlemen,' said Posner. 'But perhaps we may see you again.' He bowed, and then made his way back to the bar, with Serena wriggling after him. Attali smiled sadly at Ronan, leant forward, and touched his chest with the very tip of her tongue. Then she stretched up and whispered in his ear. A look of surprise crossed his face. She smiled, and whispered some more. Ronan looked shell-shocked.

'With ice-cubes?' he said. 'You're joking!'

'Hey – let's go,' repeated Tarl.

'No, listen,' said Ronan, suddenly reluctant. 'There's no real hurry. We could stay an hour . . .'

Tarl put his hands between Attali and Ronan, and detached her. It was like prising a limpet off a rock. 'Come on, lover boy,' he said, and hustled Ronan through the door.

Outside in the garden, the chill of the evening air hit them like a cold shower. Ronan stood blinking in the darkness. His thoughts were on Attali and he completely failed to notice the doorman whispering to a shadowy figure that slipped away into the darkness. Tarl, however, did, and he was just about to comment on it when it was unfortunately driven from his mind by a voice that spoke beside him.

'Hey, you!' it said. 'Help me do something about this moth-eaten donkey, will you?' The speaker was an unpleasant-looking warrior clad in full armour. He was hopping about on one leg and waving his arms around in an attempt to keep his balance. Standing in front of him, with its teeth firmly clamped around the armour on the man's second shin, was Puss. It was determinedly chewing away in an attempt to get at the leg inside.

'Sorry about this,' said Tarl. 'He's only playing.'

Am I bollocks! thought the donkey. My ma always told me not to play with my dinner.

Tarl grabbed its halter and tried to pull it away. 'It's a bit hungry,' he continued. 'I recognise the signs.'

Absolutely amazing, thought the donkey. You'd almost think intelligence was at work.

With a slight rending sound the metal greaves of the armour gave a little, and the warrior began to look worried. Tarl yanked at the halter again. 'Come on, Puss,' he said. 'We're going to go and get you some real food. How about a few nice juicy steaks, eh?'

Ah, now you're talking, thought the donkey, and let go of the warrior's leg. Anyway, I hate tinned food, it thought, staring disparagingly at the buckled armour.

The warrior glared at Puss with a look of fury on his swarthy face, and was just dragging his sword loose when Ronan stepped forward and laid one hand on the donkey's neck. He stared coolly at the warrior for a moment, then the other's eyes slid away and, slamming his sword back into its scabbard, he pushed roughly past Tarl and into the Dragon's Claw.

Tarl exhaled thankfully. 'Nice one, Puss!' he muttered. 'Next time you want a quick snack, try and pick on someone a bit more suitable. Preferably someone small and weedy who can't fight back.'

I would have done, thought Puss, but you'd gone inside.

Tarl turned to Ronan who was staring after the swarthy warrior with a thoughtful expression on his face. 'Come on,' he said. 'Let's go and find the Dragon's Gizzard before Puss decides to take on the entire City Guard.'

Ronan nodded and untethered his horse, and the two men walked off down the street, completely unaware of the stealthy figure that followed them at a distance, gliding from shadow to shadow like a malignant ghost.

ASSASSIN

... Of all inns, most dangerous to the unwary traveller was probably the Grave Mistake in Orcville, a tavern run by Cecil the Pink, a nine-foot mountain-troll with a very short fuse. Almost as dangerous was the Dragon's Gizzard in Welbug Town. It was the haunt of wild and savage folk, and many was the dwarf found face-down in the toilets, singing ...

The Pink Book of Ulay

... Whatever you do avoid the Dragon's Gizzard. They have their own judicial system operating in the pub. Crimes (and punishments) include Spilling Someone's Beer (fine of all your money, or be kicked unconscious), Drinking Someone Else's Beer (fine of all your money and be kicked unconscious), and Failure to Buy Your Round (they cut your hand off). And don't drink with any guys who only have one hand ...

Tarl's World-Wide Guide to Free Booze

Ronan slung his saddle-bag over his shoulder and dragged shut the broken stable door. Inside, his horse was chomping resignedly on some mildewed hay, while in the next stall the donkey had its muzzle happily buried in a double helping of some unidentifiable meat stew. Ronan crossed the cluttered stable-yard and emerged on the quayside. Above him the town walls stretched up into the night sky, blocking off the northern stars. In front of him the Great River Leno flowed slowly past the old stone jetties, and the battered wooden skiffs and wherries jostled tiredly at their moorings. On the far side of the river he could just make out the few lights that marked the huddle of houses about the ferry-point. Beyond lay the wide plains and fields of Behan and the road to Far Tibreth.

He paused for a moment, breathing in the cool night air and listening to the sounds emerging from the shabby tavern behind him, yells, snarls, and raucous laughter, punctuated regularly by the sound of breaking glass. He was still puzzling over his father's message and over how the orcs had known where to find him, but his thoughts kept getting interrupted by little day-dreams of beautiful women who stick their tongue on your chest. He felt tired and drained. For two years now he had been busily Seeking Vengeance and Righting Wrongs, and he was beginning to wonder whether there wasn't a little more to be had from life. He looked across to where Tarl sat on a bollard, moodily throwing stones at the large bats that skimmed the river. Now there was a guy who really enjoyed life.

But at that particular moment Tarl wasn't feeling too happy, for a most unusual thing was happening. His conscience was bothering him. Tarl had a very simple philosophy of life: Do unto others before they do you. He'd learnt the hard way not to place his trust too easily in people, and as a result he looked on friendship in the same way as he looked on money. Other people had it, but he seldom did, and when he did get his hands on some it usually wasn't around for long. It certainly wasn't something he was used to.

But in the past four days, that hulking great warrior had become his friend. This in itself was no problem, but the guy was dangerous. Boy, was he dangerous! People were trying to kill him! Normally, Tarl would have slid off as soon as Ronan had got him safely through the gates of the town. But the guy liked him, trusted him, and genuinely seemed to want him around. Not that it made too much difference. Tarl knew Ronan would soon be charging off into the wilds again, and no way was he going with him. But he actually felt guilty about this! What the hell was wrong with him?

Angrily he flung one last stone at a moth the size of a large vulture that was wandering past, and then stomped across to where Ronan was waiting under the revolting inn-sign that depicted the Dragon's Gizzard. Light flooded out from the doorway of the tavern as they entered, and the dark figure that had followed them from the Dragon's Claw paused and waited in the shadows for a few moments before following them inside . . . and was itself followed moments later by a second, smaller shadow.

The bar of the Dragon's Gizzard was a large, crowded, stone-flagged room. The floor was covered in sawdust, old food, and bits of broken furniture. To one side was a huge carved fireplace, in which a blazing log fire radiated a heat level that reminded Ronan of his days in the forge. The occasional down-draught in the chimney sent the odd cloud of smoke billowing out into the room, adding to the general fug from numerous pipes. Tarl was sure that he could smell the distinctive aromatic scent of elfweed. Along the right-hand wall ran a brightly lit spearboard alley, in which a number of shouting, jostling men were engaged in competition.

Ronan and Tarl pushed their way through the crowd to the bar. Although Tarl looked as though he belonged here, Ronan stuck out like a sore nose, and many of the drinkers paused and watched him suspicously. Tarl leant on the bar, feeling rather nervous, and studied the list of cocktails pinned on the wall. Normally, he was secure in his anonymity. He fitted in with the crowd in places like this, and so people didn't notice him and he was safe. But entering with Ronan, every eye in the inn had been on them and Tarl found it a little disconcerting. Thinking that it might be a good idea to keep a fairly clear head, he regretfully decided against the delights of an exotic cocktail such as an Orc's Balls, a Gutwrencher, or a Dagger Up The Rectum, and ordered two tankards of Footrot, an orchish beer. Then he turned to Ronan, who had picked up a menu card and was studying it with a frown on his face.

'I can't believe how far down-market this town has gone,' he muttered. 'Southrons, orcs and such you could make allowances for. But look over there, by the spearboard. A couple of the Undead! Not nice, that. Definitely not nice.'

Ronan followed his gaze and saw two zombies standing by the man in charge of the spearboard competition. Both had all the typical characteristics – the grey-white skin mottled with rotting black patches, the staring eyes, and jaws that hung slackly open, from which dark liquid drooled. They were heckling the competitors, and Ronan could smell the sickly-sweet scent of decay from where he stood. As he watched in horror, a finger fell off one of them, hitting the floor with an audible squelch. He turned away, disgusted.

'This is a foul place!' he hissed to Tarl.

'Oh, I don't know. The beer's not so bad.' Tarl was watching a group of dwarves who were playing cards with an elven pack near the fire. He was wondering if he could find a way of being invited to join them. He loved playing cards with dwarves, as they normally had loads of money and played really badly. One good session of Cydorian Sweat and he might end up with enough cash to go back to the Claw.

'And have you seen the menu?' continued the enraged warrior. 'What sort of food is this meant to be? Bread and Buttock Pudding?'

'That's the orc menu,' said the barman, who was pouring Tarl another beer. He was a half-orc himself, with a spine so curved that it looked as though his neck had melted, causing his head to slide down his chest until the top of his skull was level with his shoulders. 'Bread and Buttock Pudding is one of our most popular dishes. Layers of fresh bread and sliced human buttock with mushrooms and giblet gravy, all baked under a pastry crust.'

'That's what I've ordered,' snarled an orc that was leaning on the bar next to Ronan. 'Er . . . could you pass the finger-bowl?'

The barman picked up an earthenware bowl full of cooked fingers and slammed it down in front of the orc, who took one and started to gnaw on it with a horrid crunching sound.

'Looks like someone didn't buy a round yesterday,' muttered Tarl.

Ronan felt sick. 'Is there no food fit for a man to eat?' he snarled, reading down the menu. 'What about this one? Irish soup.'

'That's a Broth of a Boy, sir.'

'Gamey Shepherd's Pie?'

'Made with a real shepherd, that is.'

'Why gamey?' asked Tarl.

'He was well hung, sir,' replied the barman. 'Or so the barmaid told us.'

The orc picked a fragment from between his fangs with a clawed finger then leant over and pointed at an item at the bottom of the menu. 'If you're looking for an absolutely yummy pudding,' he volunteered, 'I can thoroughly recommend the Adam's Apple

Pie with Eyes Cream . . .'

His voice died away as he saw the look in Ronan's eyes. Tarl tried to take the menu from Ronan with the intention of finding out more about these unusual items, but found that the warrior's hand was gripping it like a vice. Looking up into his face, he found such an expression of rage there that he took an involuntary step backwards. Ronan's other hand crept towards the hilt of the sword hanging down his back, and Tarl grabbed it hastily and hung on with all his might.

'We'll eat later,' he said to the barman, before turning back to the warrior. 'Ronan! No!' he hissed. 'Look, orcs think no more of eating human flesh than you do of eating a lamb chop! It's not their fault, it's just the way things are! And if you throw a wobbler in here and massacre half the clientele, we'll never find a lead to whoever's after you!'

For a moment, Ronan's hand continued to creep upwards and Tarl was dragged on to tip-toe, but then it stopped, and the fire in his eyes died a little. 'You're right,' he said. 'But I feel so . . . so . . . angry! I've got to kill someone!'

Again, he reached for his sword. Tarl clung desperately to his arm. 'Look!' he said. 'If you want to take it out on something, have a go at the spearboard. It will make you feel better, and we might win some money!' Ronan looked across to the spearboard alley, then angrily shook off Tarl's restraining hand and pushed his way through to the organiser, who looked up at him with interest.

'Going to have a go, sir? Only a *tablon* a throw. Sixty per cent of the takings to the winner. Leading score is sixty-five at the moment. That was Graal over there.' He indicated a burly local, who was leaning confidently against the wall. Ronan looked coldly at him, then flicked a *tablon* to the organiser, took the three large spears, and stalked to the throwing line.

He hefted the spear in his hand. For a moment his gaze ran round the watchers, and then it settled on the zombies. Ronan knew that all the positive emotions got left behind in the grave. The only feelings a zombie retained were bitter and malevolent. How could two such evil creatures be allowed into any city? Anger again flared up within him, and he hurled the first spear with such rage that it buried itself to the end of the blade in the twenty segment.

'Temper, temper!' admonished one of the zombies in a croaking, slurred voice. Ronan glared at him, but it was no use. You can't kill someone with a look when they're already stone dead. He weighed the second spear for a moment, then an icy calm seemed to settle on him, and he hurled it with unerring accuracy into the double twenty. A gasp went up. Now he only needed six for the lead, and so rather than risk an unlucky deflection off the two spears that were stuck in the twenty segment, he hurled the third one smack into the nineteen, inches away from the double.

A roar of appreciation went up as the organiser called 'Seventy-nine!' and Ronan noticed that even Graal was applauding. Smiling, he made his way back to the bar and leant on it beside the grinning Tarl.

'Nice spears!' said Tarl. 'No one will beat that!' He was about to remind Ronan that it was his round, when a sudden commotion broke out over near the fire, and they turned to watch.

Two Southrons had started to fight and were rolling round on the floor, knives in hands, each trying to stab the other. For a moment one seemed to gain the upper hand, but then his opponent managed to hurl him backwards and he went crashing into the dwarves' table. Beer-mugs and playing cards flew everywhere, and the Southron lay there stunned. His opponent picked himself up and rushed forward, knife raised, but then he slipped on the seven of hearts (elven packs of cards have four suits; Hearts, Flowers, Ribbons, and Little-furry-animals. This says an awful lot about elves.) As he crashed into another table, stunning himself, the first man staggered up, only to trip over a dwarf who was scrabbling round on the floor trying to recover his winning hand (a flush of gerbils – very difficult to beat in five-card stud).

Ronan was watching all this with the tolerant amusement of a professional watching a couple of rank amateurs. He totally failed to notice the thin hooded man just behind him who quietly brought a dagger tipped with green liquid out from under his cloak. Which was a shame, because the man was Karth, Master of Assassins, and Ronan was his target.

Karth had sized up the situation within seconds of slipping into the tavern behind Ronan. He'd followed him all the way from the

Dragon's Claw, where Grimbal the doorman had pointed him out, but had held off in the street. One thing you learn as a professional assassin is who you can safely deal with face to face, and who you have to creep up on very quietly. But this tavern was ideal. Half the clientele were hooded or cloaked and were conducting shady little deals whilst staring suspiciously round, and he fitted in perfectly. He had slipped the two Southrons a bronze *tablon* each to start a diversion at his signal, and then worked his way unnoticed along the bar until he was right behind the big warrior. And now, a quick strike with a dagger tipped with the traditional poison and another commission would be safely fulfilled. The warrior's gimpy little friend wasn't likely to give him much trouble, and no one else would care about the death of the big stranger. It was a quiet night indeed when no one got killed in the Dragon's Gizzard.

Silent, quick, and lethal as a snake, Karth the Assassin struck. The dagger blade flashed down toward Ronan's back . . . and stopped dead an inch short of the target. His wrist had smacked into the palm of someone who had stepped from behind him, someone who moved even quicker than he. The hand that held his wrist in a steely grip was slim and elegant, and Karth turned and stared at the slight figure, hooded and cloaked as he was, but smaller, no more than five foot four. It raised one elegant hand and lowered the hood, and Karth found himself looking down into a pair of green female eyes, beautiful but deadly. 'You!' he hissed, and the fear was evident in his voice. The woman stared back at him unblinkingly.

'Hey, Muscles!' she said, digging Ronan in the ribs with a free finger, and the warrior turned round to find a dagger blade wavering mere inches from his back, and his would-be murderer struggling in the grip of a small and slender woman. He stared dumbfounded as she forced Karth's hand back until the dagger fell from his numbed fingers.

'Let me introduce you,' she smiled, without taking her eyes from Karth's face. 'This dungball is Karth, Master Assassin . . .' She broke off suddenly as a knife appeared in Karth's free hand, flashing towards her breast, but again it stopped short as her fingers closed around his wrist.

'Tut, tut,' she said. 'Naughty.' And then her hand clenched, there was the sound of several minor bones in Karth's wrist snapping, and he screamed with pain and dropped the knife.

Ronan had the unaccustomed feeling of not being in control of events. This chit of a girl had saved his life? In a fit of embarrassed anger he grabbed Karth by the hair and dragged his head back, with the intention of asking him a few questions. A loud crack like a whiplash echoed round the room as Karth's neck vertebrae snapped, and his legs buckled as he fell to the floor.

The woman raised her eyes to the heavens. 'Oh, nice going, Muscles,' she said. 'You've killed him. Now you can't find out who sent him.'

Ronan gawped at her like a dwarf ogling a seam of gold. Her slim, almost boyish figure was dressed in leather that was cut warrior-style and was the same tanned colour as her skin. Her dark brown hair was cut short, in elven fashion. She was young, no older than he, and yet despite her lightness of tone there was a tiredness and a world-weariness about her that made him feel about twelve years old.

'So you're Ronan,' she mused. 'I heard you were in town.'

He stared at her, and then realised that his mouth was hanging open and shut it hurriedly.

'I'm Tyson. The Champion of Welbug.' There was a glint of something that could have been laughter in her eyes, and then she turned away, shaking her head, and sauntered slowly over towards the spearboard.

Tarl emerged from under the table where he had taken refuge when the fight broke out. 'So that's Tyson,' he said. 'I'm impressed. Good job she was here, she saved your life!'

'All right, all right!' snapped Ronan. 'I know!'

The barman leant across and looked down at Karth. 'He's dead, is he?' he asked. 'Great!' He turned and called through the door to the kitchen. 'Wayne! Come and help me get this body into the fridge. Then nip down the mortuary and cancel tomorrow's order.' Ronan threw him a look of distaste, but Tarl was grinning.

'Typical orcs,' he said. 'Never waste a good body. Reminds me of when I went to see a mate of mine in court, back in Orcville. Sentenced him to death, they did.' He changed to a snarling impersonation of an orc judge. 'You will be taken from this place to a place of execution, where you will be lightly poached until

98

you are tender . . .' He paused, staring across to the spearboard alley. 'Hang on,' he said. 'Look!'

Tyson was standing on the throwing line, holding three spears. All round the tavern people were whispering, 'Tyson! It's Tyson!' Then as she hefted the first one the place fell silent. Every eye was on her. She looked across to Ronan and winked at him, and then her arm whipped forward, and the spear thudded into the double twenty. She paused, and suddenly the reverential silence was broken by one of the zombies.

'Huh!' he said, dismissively. 'Fluke! I've seen goats with a better action than that skinny bitch.'

Tyson stared at it like a cat gazing at a bird through a window, and Ronan suddenly realised that she hated the evil creature every bit as much as he did. And then her arm blurred once, twice, so fast that both remaining spears were in the air at the same time. The second one thudded into the double twenty beside the first, but the third one smashed into the loud-mouthed zombie's head, ripping it from the body, and pinning it to the wall behind. The zombie's hands went up and groped along its shoulders for a few seconds as though searching for the missing head, and then foul black liquid oozed from its neck and it crumpled tiredly to the floor. For a moment the room was totally silent, and then the organiser's voice rang out.

'One Undead and eighty!' he yelled, and the place erupted.

Ronan stared around the tavern in amazement. In every corner people were shouting, cheering, stamping, and chanting Tyson's name. Beside him Tarl was laughing delightedly and thumping the bar-top with his hand.

'She beat you,' he chuckled. 'She sodding well beat you! I've never in my life seen throwing like that!'

'She's simply the best,' grinned the barman. 'Better than all the rest!' And he started singing this catchy refrain to himself.

Ronan was feeling more than a little peeved. When it came to this sort of spectacle, it was normally he who was the centre of attention. He hadn't been bested at anything for a couple of years now, and yet in the space of five minutes he'd had his life saved and then been beaten at spearboard. And by a woman as well!

'She wouldn't beat me in a straight contest,' he heard himself saying.

'Oh, yes?' answered a soft voice behind him, and he turned to find Tyson standing grinning up at him. 'And what contest do you suggest? Arm-wrestling, perhaps?' She held her arm next to his and pulled back her sleeve. Ronan's biceps was about five times the size of hers. 'Come on then,' she continued. 'If that is your wish, let us begin.' And she sat down on a stool, rested her arm upright on the table, and gazed up at him with an amused gleam in her eyes.

'A contest!' The whisper raced round the tavern and everyone closed in, straining for a view of the table. Ronan suddenly realised that she was making him look like a total pranny. If he turned down her challenge everyone would think he was scared, but if he took her on, it would be so one-sided it would look ridiculous. He reminded himself that despite her looks, she was a warrior, and obviously a good one. The way she had dealt with Karth . . . and the way she had thrown those spears . . . he'd better take this seriously.

He sat down opposite her, positioned his arm, and clasped her hand. 'As you've chosen the method of contest,' she said, 'I would suggest it is fair for me to start it.' Ronan wasn't aware that he'd made any choice, but he wasn't going to argue. 'When I say ready . . . go . . . then we start,' she continued. 'Agreed?'

'Agreed.'

'OK then.' She wriggled herself into a comfortable position, and then looked into his eyes. And looked. And looked.

By the gods, thought Ronan, she's beautiful! Suddenly he was very aware of the feel of her hand in his, the touch of her breath on his face, the scent of her skin . . . He studied her face. Her huge green eyes seemed to be glowing, and she moistened her lips. Her breath was coming faster, and then she was slowly leaning forward towards him, nearer and nearer. Ronan's stomach suddenly seemed to be filled with a million butterflies as he realised that she was going to kiss him. Her free hand came up to caress his neck, her mouth was only an inch from his, and for an instant his heart seemed to stop. And then her lips parted as she breathed the words 'Readygo!' and her arm was slamming his down on to the table-top with such force that he was sent flying off his stool. Then she was standing over him, arm raised in triumph, and the place had erupted with so much cheering that the roof seemed in danger of coming off.

Ronan sat on the floor, horrified, with the bitter taste of defeat in his mouth. No, this wasn't defeat, this was humiliation! He stared round at the yelling, exultant crowd, then back at Tyson, and the realisation hit him. Klat, she was good! Skilled with weapons, faster than anyone he'd ever met, clever, cunning . . . the way she'd suckered him and led him along was beautiful! Even while the macho male side of his brain was desperately searching for excuses, the warrior side was lost in admiration. And what a leader! If she'd asked the people in the tavern to march with her into battle against an army of dragons, at that moment they'd have flocked to her banner! Even Tarl was cheering and applauding her. And then she was smiling down at him.

'I'm sorry about my little . . . subterfuge,' she said. 'But against a guy like you, what's a poor girl to do?' Suddenly she bent and kissed him on the cheek, and then she was striding to the door between the ranks of cheering people, grinning and slapping their outstretched hands as she went.

The barman walked over to Ronan and proffered his hand to help him up. 'Don't think that you've lost anyone's respect,' he said. 'Even to be challenged by Tyson is an honour in this town. None here would have done better.'

Ronan nodded his thanks, but absently. For he hadn't really heard. He was thinking hard. With all the background noise, he was certainly the only one in the room who had heard Tyson whisper something as she bent to kiss him. Just three little words. 'The Claw. Midnight.'

What the hell was she up to?

In the private quarters of his stronghold near Setel, Nekros received the news of Karth's failure with apparent equanimity. But the moment that the crystal in front of him darkened he swore violently and hurled a fireball across the room at a large vase in the corner. Unfortunately, the fireball missed by several feet and struck the old cleaning crone who was polishing his armour. There was a rather soggy explosion, and Nekros stared angrily at the resulting mess.

Typical! he thought. Klatting typical!

Nekros had never had much luck with magic from the day Shikara had managed to destroy her book of spells. The Torque of Vataan had given him some power, but not as much as he had expected, and his control was at best patchy. Sometimes the magic worked perfectly, but at others it was downright dangerous. There was that time when he had hurled a curse at a servant and missed. The spell had rebounded from the mirror straight at him, and Nekros had spent a hundred years as a very disgruntled statue standing in his own bedroom.

However, the combination of his magical abilities and his fighting skill had been enough to make him a force to be reckoned with. He'd had a pretty good time seeing the world, being evil, and generally scaring the crap out of people. But then he began to realise that there was so much more to do. It was pointless hiring himself out to evil leaders less talented than himself. He could do their job so much better.

Taking over the Tribe of Fallon had given him a power base, and for a satisfying couple of years they had terrorised the countryside, looting, burning and killing. But the problem was, cities controlled countries, and whenever they rolled up at a city, the people would just close the gates and fire insults and arrows at them from the walls. Strong though the Tribe were, they weren't an army.

But then, four years ago, his backers had contacted him. They were organised. They had money. They had plans. And they had Anthrax the Wizard. Slowly but surely he had followed their plans, until the Six Cities of Baq d'Or were ready to fall. Setel and Goblin City were theirs. Minas Welvair, Minas Tryk and Malvenis hung by a thread. Only Welbug and that Tyson woman had caused any problem. But their plans were too intricate, their plots were too clever. Within days she would be dead and Welbug would fall, and with it the whole of Baq d'Or. And then they could turn their attention to the other countries of Midworld . . .

Then suddenly, a couple of days ago, Anthrax had foretold the advent of this black warrior from nowhere, and warned that he could cause not only the destruction of all their plans, but the death of Nekros himself! Nekros had moved quickly, but the warrior had somehow stumbled past both attempts to remove him. Well, Ritta had better get it right next time. Both Tyson and the black warrior had better be dead within twenty-four hours, or Ritta would find he was re-decorating his bedroom ceiling with bits of his small intestine.

A more accurate fireball swept suddenly across the room, and the *kalaya* in the golden bird-cage exploded in a mass of feathers.

Nekros was feeling *really* pissed off.

At a quarter to midnight Ronan was striding through the darkened streets of Welbug with a drunken Tarl staggering along beside him. Every now and then he paused, ostensibly to stare into a shop window, but in reality to check that he was not being followed. Not that anyone would have had to keep them in sight to follow them, for Tarl kept bursting into fragments of song and could have been heard streets away.

'Take me back to Goblin City,' he bellowed, well off-key. 'Where the girls are really sh . . .' He was cut off as Ronan clasped a hand over his mouth, before pausing to look in another shop window. 'Mmmmmph,' he said, and Ronan relented and removed his hand.

'Just keep quiet. OK?'

'All right, all right! So you don't like good music!' Tarl gazed blearily through the window. It was full of the dirty black garments beloved of fashion-conscious female orcs. Over the window was the shop name: 'Eat 'em'. 'You thinking of buying yourself a new dress?' he giggled. Ronan glared at him.

'I'm making sure no one's after us,' he snarled. 'I've had enough of people trying to sneak up on me. I don't trust this Tyson. Trust no man, my dad warned me. Remember?'

'Oh, come on! If Tyson is a man, then my name's Beppo the Wonder Sheep!' Tarl paused, and then added, 'You know, if she is a man, I wouldn't mind a husband like her . . .'

Satisfied that they weren't being followed, Ronan dragged Tarl swiftly round the corner. He could be right, he thought. In vino veritas. She's not a man, so maybe I can trust her. Ah well, we'll soon find out.

The door of the Dragon's Claw opened before they could knock, and Ronan and Tarl slipped quietly inside. Behind them, Posner barred the door before motioning them through into the lounge.

All the candles of the magnificent chandelier had been snuffed out and the room was lit only by a couple of wall-torches. It was empty, save for Tyson, who was sitting at a table near the marble statue with a tankard of beer in front of her. As Posner slipped out through the door at the far end by the bar she rose to greet them.

'Thanks for coming,' she said, and extended her hand to Ronan. They shook warrior-fashion, each gripping the other's wrist, then she turned to Tarl. 'Help yourself,' she continued, indicating the bar. 'On the house. Whatever you want, and as much as you want.'

Tarl stared at her in disbelief. 'I think I love you,' he said, making his way unsteadily to the bar. 'This calls for a cocktail!'

Tarl had a thing about cocktails that probably dated back to his childhood. His old mum had loved them too. He could remember her mixing one of her specials every night. Equal measures of gin, gin, and gin, in a tall glass, and topped up with gin. Drain quickly, then beat the shit out of your little boy. Still, at least it had taught him how to roll with a punch. He winced at the memory, and grabbed a shaker and a bottle of brandy.

Tyson watched him with a tired smile, then turned back to Ronan. 'Right,' she said, 'take the weight off your brains.' Ronan sat down opposite her and eyed her with obvious suspicion as she took a mouthful of beer. 'We both have problems,' she went on. 'I have someone who is trying to take over the city. You have someone who is trying to kill you. They happen to be one and the same person.'

'Who?' asked Ronan.

'A guy called Nekros.'

Tyson leapt backwards from her seat and stood there, sword at the ready, as marble fragments showered round her. But Ronan remained in his chair, staring stupidly at the shattered remnants of the table, the spilt beer, and at his clenched fist, which had done so much damage.

'Er . . . sorry!' he muttered. 'I'm a bit, er, well, I get a bit worked up when I hear that name.'

Hesitantly, Ronan began to relate the story of his first meeting with Nekros, and as he did so Tyson watched him with a new respect. This appeared to be someone she could work with, all right. A dedicated warrior who was on the side of right, and who could smash a heavy marble table to pieces with one angry blow of his fist at the mention of a name he happened to dislike. He would make a great ally – and boy, could she do with an ally right now!

She listened as Ronan talked on, and her eyes opened wider as he told her of his father's apparition. 'That's the first hint of hope that we've had in ages,' she said. 'And they've screwed up badly over you. But I don't think you've any idea what you're taking on. Nekros has lieutenants in all the cities of the east, and they've been hard at work. Minas Welvair and Far Tibreth are crumbling from within, Setel and Goblin City have already fallen, yet people don't realise what's happening.

'These are guys who move with the times, you see. They're smart. These days, if you want to take over a city, you don't roll up at the head of an army and lay siege to the place. I mean, what's the use of that? You end up in control of a burnt-out shell with half the people dead and plague and famine ravaging the rest. That puts the punters off, and it's tourism that brings in the *tablons* in a place like Welbug.

'But these guys are clever. For four years, they've been up to all the tricks. Destabilisation . . . covert operations . . . terrorism . . . the odd assassination . . . and infiltration. Especially infiltration. They've got a powerful clique on the town city council, led by Ritta. He's a fat old toad, as sly as they come. But he was no match for my father.'

Tyson paused, visibly holding back tears, and Ronan suddenly realised that despite her light-hearted façade, she was under great strain. She took a shaky breath and continued.

'My father was the town Champion too, and the best warrior the east had ever seen. The people loved him. He carried them with him no matter what clever stroke Ritta tried to pull. Ritta was losing out, so he had my father killed. It was a knife in the back as he came home from a council meeting one dark night. They must have thought that with him gone the city would fall, leaderless, for he had no son to follow him. But they reckoned without me. Since I was a child he trained me, and trained me well. I was a match for the best that Ritta could send against me, and the people of Welbug trusted me. Yet each year we lose more ground, and they creep nearer to their goal. They've got their people in positions of power all over the city now and they're changing it, slowly but surely. They've even got control of the city council.

'Some months ago they passed a by-law granting orcs equal rights. Then last week they introduced an amendment to extend it to the Undead – zombies, wraiths, ghosts, werewolves. I thought we had a majority, but old Parbeard voted with them. Wouldn't look me in the eyes afterwards. They had some sort of hold over him, probably blackmail.

'You saw the result tonight. Ordinary, decent folk forced to rub shoulders with trash like those zombies. But the decent folk have started to leave. Those who remain are relying on me, but I won't be able to hold out more than a few days. Ritta is like a huge fat spider. His webs are everywhere.'

For a moment she paused, staring into space. A silence fell on the room, broken only by gentle hiccups coming from behind the bar. Then she sighed, and continued.

'He can't buy me, or frighten me out. And he's learned he can't discredit me. So he'll have me killed, as he did my father. I can feel them closing in . . .'

'Then they must be stopped,' said Ronan. He had listened to all this impassively, but inside his emotions were churning. To think that his enemy was behind such an audacious plan! And standing in his way was this female warrior, small and alone, but dangerous and determined . . . and brave . . . and beautiful. Ronan stared at her with something akin to awe. She smiled at him, and suddenly his heart started doing cartwheels round his chest.

'Two days ago,' she said, 'I heard a rumour that Nekros fears no man in all the world . . . except for a warrior called Ronan. And then, the word on the street was that you were on your way here. But you turned up on my very doorstep! Could be a trap, I thought, and so when you left here, I followed you and found you were being followed by someone else. Karth the Assassin! They must fear you greatly, to send him after you!'

She was gazing at him with outright admiration now, and Ronan felt his chest swelling with pride, almost as though someone was inflating him with a pump. He tried to look modest, failed abysmally, and ended up simpering horribly.

'Tell me where to find this Ritta,' he said. Tyson smiled tiredly, and shook her head.

'That won't work,' she answered. 'You'd just walk into another ambush. You've no idea how many fighting men he has in this town. And anyway, he's just a puppet.'

'Then I have to kill Nekros. But how do I find him?'

'I don't know,' she sighed dejectedly. 'No one knows his movements. Not even Ritta. But he's no ordinary warrior. He'd just swat you like a fly. Apparently the guy deals in magic, and you can't have a fair fight with someone who can turn you into a woodlouse and then step on you!'

'But there's got to be a way of stopping him!'

Tyson gave him a long, appraising look. 'There may be,' she said, 'although it could be too late for me. But there's a guy who wants to see you. A guy who seems to think that you can stop Nekros. The guy who passed the word to me that you were coming. The main problem is, I don't know if he can be trusted. I've never even met him, and I don't know anyone who has.'

'Who is he?' asked Ronan.

'He's a Wizard called Anthrax.'

Tarl had been having a seriously good time behind the bar. He had mixed himself an Elf's Pecker, a cocktail he normally couldn't afford (as it contained both Behan Champagne and Cydorian Brandy). Then he'd had another. And another. He'd done a bit of singing, while conducting himself with the cocktail. Then he'd stopped, when half of it had slopped out all over his shoes. And then he had begun to wonder what the others were doing, and whether they'd decided anything important, like what to drink, or which club to go on to, and so he'd focused his attention on them, and heard all this defeatist crap about Nekros and Ritta.

Indignantly, Tarl went to step out from behind the bar on to the floor, but missed it by quite a long way. 'Lishen,' he said, and then spent a while hauling himself upright. 'It'sh time to shtand up and be counted,' he continued, and immediately fell over again. Realising that he was going to have a bit of trouble doing two tricky things at once, such as standing upright and talking, he opted for lying on the floor while speaking. He felt he could just about manage that without having to hold on.

'I wash . . . was . . . talking to a guy in the Gizzard earlier,' he said. 'Reckoned he was a friend of yours, Tyson. Said his name was Oupase . . .' Ronan and Tyson listened with tolerant smiles as Tarl talked on, but after a while the smiles slipped away, to be replaced by frowns. Frowns of concentration. Because alcohol did strange things to Tarl. It gave him ideas. And some of those ideas were little belters.

TRAP

'Attack is the best form of defence, and surprise is the best form of attack.'

           Aragorn of Sunwood, Human General

'Kick them in the orbs, and run for it. Better still, get someone else to kick them in the orbs, while you pinch their drink . . .'

           Tarl of Welbug, Generally Human

In the room at the top of the tower, Ritta was sitting in front of the crystal ball, putting off the moment when he would have to report his failure. He'd been seriously contemplating sending all his men down to the Dragon's Claw in a last-ditch attempt to take out Tyson, but he didn't quite dare. His spies had reported that she had met with the black-skinned warrior last night, and a few days ago Nekros had given him one of those predictions of his.

'Together,' he'd said, 'they will destroy you!' Ritta wasn't sure what the two of them could do against all his men, but Nekros had an annoying habit of always being right. The trouble was, Nekros had also promised to destroy him if he made another cock-up. And when Nekros destroyed you, it was never in any pleasant, sorry-about-this-old-chap kind of way. It tended to be a nasty, painful, blood-and-guts-all-over-the-wall sort of destruction. Ritta's hand hovered nervously over the number buttons of the crystal, then fell back into his lap. It was no good, he'd . . .

'Master! Master!' An out-of-breath underling burst through the door and fell to the floor in a grovelling heap. 'The black warrior has left!'

'What?' yelled Ritta, leaping to his feet. The underling grovelled some more, looking as though he was trying to worm his way between the floor-boards.

'It's true, master!' he whined. 'He rode out from the East Gate mere minutes ago and took the Minas Tryk road!'

'What of his little piss-head friend? And Tyson? What of her?'

'His friend is in the Dragon's Gizzard, drinking enough for two! And Grimbal says Tyson hides within the Claw, and fears to show her face.'

Ritta paced furiously up and down, thinking hard. Another chance! He must seize it quickly! He glanced at the crystal ball. Use it to follow Ronan? No, the klatting thing kept breaking down. Men were more reliable. In a fever of excitement he began shouting orders at the terrified underling.

'I want five good men to follow him! No, make it ten! They are to keep their distance for today, but they must make sure he does not double back! And get someone next to the little piss-head. Someone with money to buy him drink and loosen his tongue. Then put men to watch the Claw, front and back! I must know of anyone who enters! And send word to Dagman and the other eight of the Council. They are to meet me here at noon!'

The underling bowed deeply, which isn't easy when you're prostrate on the floor, then fled. Ritta crossed to the single tall window, and looked out over the glittering roofs of the city.

'This time I've got you!' he muttered, and the thought of Tyson's bleeding body slumped at his feet gave him a soft shimmering of excitement across his stomach. 'You pathetic woman! You have no idea just how alone you are!'

In the Dragon's Gizzard, Tarl was enjoying himself. The bloke next to him kept insisting on buying him drinks and seemed to have a bottomless purse. Tarl hadn't bought a drink for hours. He drained his tankard, put it on the bar, and picked up the full one that had just been placed there.

'Friend?' he said. 'He's no friend of mine! Bloody warriors! They can drop you right in it, if you're not careful! He nearly got me killed the other day, by this band of orcs! I'm glad he's buggered off to Minas Tryk! What? Coming back? In a day or two, he said. Tyson? Nah, they didn't get on. Not at all. Well, he couldn't take being beaten by a woman, could he? Hm? Oh, same again, thanks. Very kind of you.'

*

Ronan reined in his horse and looked back along the road behind him. In the distance, the towers of Welbug sparkled in the early-afternoon sunshine. A little closer, a small cloud of dust marked the presence of pursuing horsemen.

He moved on. Ahead, the road dipped down to the right passing briefly through some woodland along the edge of the Great River. As soon as he had entered the cover of the trees Ronan spurred on his horse, emerging on the far side of the wood to find that the road ran past a small stone jetty stretching out into the river. It was hidden from the sight of anyone on the road behind. A boat was moored here and a familiar figure was waiting on the jetty.

Ronan rode up to him and dismounted. 'Yo, Posner!' he said. 'Everything OK?'

'Indeed, sir,' said Posner. 'Are they following you?'

'Yeah, but they're keeping their distance,' Ronan answered. He took off his cloak and handed it to Posner, who wrapped it about himself, and then swung up into the saddle. 'You sure you'll be OK?' Ronan asked him.

'No problem, sir. Tyson has many friends in Minas Tryk. I will be safe there.'

'Ride fast,' Ronan told him. 'And don't worry about Tyson. I'll look after her.'

Posner smiled pityingly at the warrior. 'Don't you worry about yourself, sir,' he replied. '*She'll* look after *you*.'

And with that he was gone, riding like the wind off up the road to Minas Tryk. Ronan smiled uncertainly. He wasn't used to being thought of as second-best to a woman. He turned to the boat whose owner was sitting waiting, oars poised. He was short but muscular, and had a face like a rusty man-trap. He grinned at Ronan as he stepped into the boat. Ronan grinned back.

'You're Oupase?' he asked. The ferryman nodded. 'OK, then,' said Ronan. 'Let's get this boat hidden.' Oupase bent his back and pulled on the oars and the boat edged out into the slow-flowing river, drifted along near the bank, and disappeared into the cover of some overhanging bushes.

Further back along the road to Welbug, the captain in charge of the force pursuing Ronan was relieved to see the cloaked figure on the mighty horse come galloping out of the woods as though the five Great Demons were after it. He'd been slightly worried when it had been hidden from view by the trees.

'Come on,' he yelled to his men. 'Keep that hobbit-fondler in sight!'

They spurred after him into the woods. Behind them, the ferry-boat broke unseen from the cover of some bushes and pulled rapidly downriver towards Welbug.

Ritta couldn't believe his luck. The black-skinned warrior had definitely gone – a rider had just come with the news that the captain and his men still had him in sight, half-way to Minas Tryk. And Tyson had been holed up in the Claw all day. The word from Grimbal was that the only callers for hours had been an early-evening wine delivery, which had been shortly followed by the little piss-head. No surprise there. Since late-afternoon Ritta's men had been in operation at either end of Rue Battue, warning off all potential customers except for those of his own choice.

Now it was late-evening. Ritta strolled up to the door of the Dragon's Claw, pausing to make sure his guards had closed in to prevent any rescue attempt that might be staged. He was feeling light-headed with anticipation. It was great to be in control again! At last he was about to be rid of Tyson. She would expect to be safe in her own establishment. Little did she know that he had suborned not only Grimbal but also her barman, and that apart from the little piss-head every single customer in the place was one of his own men!

He pushed open the door and entered. Inside Grimbal was at his post. Ritta smiled at him and glanced quickly around the room. Tyson was leaning at the bar, staring moodiliy into the bottom of a mug of beer. Her barman was polishing a glass and talking to Attali, one of the girls. The other girls were dancing attendance on nine male customers, all of whom were Ritta's men. The only other customer was the small piss-head, who was seated at a table near the marble statue of the warrior. He had twelve empty glasses in front of him, and was sipping a cocktail from a thirteenth and talking lovingly to a little brown donkey. The donkey had flowers in its mane.

Ritta grimaced. He had some fairly peculiar sexual tastes of his own but this was a bit much, even for his strong stomach. Momentarily, the donkey met his gaze and Ritta felt an inexplicable chill run down his spine. Although donkeys don't have the necessary equipment to go round pulling the legs off spiders, he got the impression that, could it have done so, this one would have adopted the practice with glee.

He shuddered and nodded to Grimbal, who barred the door. At this signal each of his men whispered something to the girl or girls he was talking to. Almost as one, the girls turned and headed for the door which led to the upstairs areas. They all looked a little surprised to find themselves part of a mass migration and some of them paused, but Ritta's men threw back their cloaks to reveal swords underneath. Frightened, the girls looked across to Tyson, but she just nodded wearily and they shuffled through the door and disappeared. The girl behind the bar went to follow them, but the barman grabbed her arm and pulled her closer to him, leering unpleasantly. One of Ritta's men locked the door, and they formed a threatening semi-circle around the female warrior as she stood by the bar.

Smiling, Ritta sauntered past the donkey, which was being drunkenly serenaded by the little piss-head, and pushed through his men until he stood in front of her. Not too close, though. She had her hand on her sword and he knew how dangerous she was. She stared at him with eyes like green flint and he felt a momentary frisson of fear. Quickly, he checked the men beside him. Good! Two of them had small arbalests trained on her, and the other seven had drawn swords. Even she would not dare to try anything.

Tyson leant back on the bar and smiled. 'OK, dragon-breath,' she drawled. 'What's all this in aid of?'

'My dear Tyson! I'm afraid it's that little matter of the unfortunate demise of a guest in our city. Killed by your own fair hand!'

'If you mean that foul zombie . . .'

'Foul or no, he has equal status accorded him by the Rights of the Recently Demised Act. And you have been tried and found guilty of murder. I therefore sentence you to . . .'

'You cannot sentence me! You have no right!'

'But my dear Tyson!' Ritta couldn't keep the enjoyment out of his voice. 'As a full Council member you can be tried by a decade of the Council and sentenced by the Chairman. Me.'

She threw out her hand and stabbed an accusing finger at two of his men. 'Gawulf and Sedgeling are but deputies!'

'Ah. I'm afraid not. Both have been automatically elevated to full Council status since the unfortunate deaths of their superiors, an hour ago.'

Suddenly it was very quiet in the room. Even the little piss-head had shut up. All the men were staring at Tyson hungrily. The barman ran his tongue over suddenly dry lips, then dragged the unwilling Attali hard against himself. As he slowly and lovingly drew his sword, Ritta ran his eyes over Tyson. Grak's blood! Under all that warrior gear she really had rather a good body. Maybe he should have her drugged . . . No, she was too dangerous. She would have to die. Ritta suddenly realised that the thought of killing her was giving him a warm glow in his loins, and that he was breathing heavily. Hm! This might be almost as much fun . . .

'And so,' he continued, 'in my capacity as Chairman of the Council of Welbug, I sentence you to death!'

As he took a step forward the girl behind the bar screamed. Ritta glanced at her in annoyance, and then stared. The barman was staggering backwards with a small and rather feminine dagger sticking out of his stomach. Klat! The bitch had stabbed him! Ritta met her gaze and was stunned to see the triumph in her eyes. And then suddenly he was frozen in place by a screeching braying sound that seemed to burst into the room from some foul netherworld, and all hell was let loose beside him. He turned and backed towards the bar, his mouth sagging open in disbelief.

To one side, three of his men lay on the floor with throats sliced open. Beside them stood the little piss-head, who was humming to himself as he emptied their purses, and Grimbal, who was wiping a jagged blood-stained knife on a rag. To the other side a man was sprawled on the floor with his head nearly severed, blood pumping in an ever-weakening fountain from his neck. His terrified neighbour was backing away, eyes fixed in horror on the donkey which was slowly stalking him, its muzzle soaked with gore. And in the centre, three more men lay at the feet of the marble statue, which seemed somehow to have come to life. As

Ritta watched in horror it scornfully parried the desperate lunges of his two remaining followers, before skewering one neatly with the spear and casually lopping off the head of the other. Ritta gazed in awe as it raised one hand and pulled off its helm to reveal the face of – the black-skinned warrior!

At that moment, he realised just how comprehensively he'd been stuffed. Grunting with rage and fear, he turned and slashed desperately with his sword at Tyson. She blocked his blows easily and then suddenly flicked a wrist, and his sword went flying over the bar. He just had enough time to hear her whisper, 'Welcome to hell, baby!' before there was an agonizing pain in his chest, and he looked down to see her sword buried up to the hilt between his ribs.

And that was the last thing he ever saw.

Tarl sat in a corner, watching the awe-struck townsmen as they dragged out the bodies. Apparently word of Ritta's plan had leaked out, and an irate mob had arrived in Rue Battue and dealt summarily with his outside guards before pounding at the door and demanding to know if Tyson was all right. Ronan had been upstairs washing off the marble-coloured make-up and the sight of just her and Tarl quietly sipping drinks with ten slaughtered councillors at their feet had stunned the mob to silence. Now word of what their champion had achieved was racing around from tavern to tavern. Her reputation and stature would be even more enhanced.

But that didn't concern Tarl. What did concern him was his own behaviour. For the past twenty-four hours, he'd been acting like some lame-brained hero out of one of the wilder Chronicles. Getting involved in fights against the odds, spreading rumours in pubs, thinking up plans . . . he'd nearly ruptured himself helping Ronan drag that klatting great statue upstairs! Admittedly, he had been pissed most of the time, but still! He could have been killed! He'd had loads of chances to slide quietly off, but he hadn't taken them. Tarl sighed. If this was what friendship did to you, the sooner he got out the better.

Tyson shut and barred the main door behind the last of the adulatory townsmen, and crossed over to Tarl. He looked up at her.

'I need help,' he said.

'You're telling me!'

'I'm serious. Tomorrow, when he leaves Welbug . . . he's expecting me to go with him, isn't he?'

Tyson nodded. Tarl winced. 'It wouldn't work,' he continued. 'I mean, he's on a quest! Danger, bloodshed, killing and maiming, hardship . . . It's all right for you two, you're trained warriors. It's your job. But on my papers, next to profession, it says "Full-time Coward". I mean, I'm supposed to be on holiday! All I want is a few laughs, a few beers, the odd girl – and believe me, I've known some really odd girls – and the occasional illicit substance. But if I'm still here in the morning, and he looks at me with those noble sodding eyes of his, and calls me his friend . . . well, that's it. Hero time. I'll be stuck with it.' He paused, and took a deep breath. 'I've got to leave. Tonight.'

'So what do you want from me?'

'Just . . . just don't tell him,' Tarl said wretchedly, 'and don't try to stop me.'

'OK,' said Tyson, smiling mirthlessly. 'Go tonight. But if you're still here in the morning and he wants you, then you're going with him.'

'No tricks, now!'

'If you stay, you stay of your own choice,' she said, looking at him out of huge, guileless green eyes.

She's up to something, he thought, and finished his drink.

Upstairs in the bathroom Ronan was also worried. Not about Welbug, or about his quest. Things had gone well today. It had been a tight fit in that wine-barrel, but he'd managed OK, and they'd smuggled him back into the Claw under the very noses of Ritta's lookouts. Then he'd had to be made up as the naked statue. Again, no problem. Standing stock-still for hours was basic warrior training, although he'd never before had to do it stark naked in a roomful of beautiful and provocative women. (Bits of him had been quite insistent about moving when Attali had sat in front of him, and he'd had to concentrate very hard on cold showers.)

Things would probably go well tomorrow, too. Tyson was going to smuggle him out of Welbug, to put Nekros's spies off the trail, and he felt sure that Anthrax the Wizard would be able to help him. No, the problem was tonight.

Firstly, he had a feeling that Tarl was planning to slip off quietly. He'd conceived an odd affection for the little guy and an even odder respect. He had an instinct for survival, could scent danger a mile off, came up with pretty mean plans, and knew how to have a seriously good time. Ronan didn't want to drag him off against his will, but he had been a great companion, and Ronan would miss him.

Secondly, Tyson had promised him and Tarl that they would spend the night with the women of their dreams as a gesture of thanks. A few hours previously, the idea of spending the night with Attali would have set him trembling with lust, but now, for some reason, he kept seeing Tyson's face. And her hair. And her hands. And her legs. He had spent a lot of time watching her while he posed as the statue, and he had felt nearly sick with hatred when Ritta had threatened her. Now, instead of his usual guilt at killing he was feeling a quiet satisfaction. He had seen the look on their faces. If they had hurt just one hair on her head . . .

Oh, Klat! He shook his head and stared at himself in the mirror. Come on, you big hero, he thought. All you have to do is go downstairs and ask her to . . . ask her if she'll . . . He stopped. His reflection had gone an unhealthy grey-brown colour. His hand began to shake, and his legs felt as though they were going to give way. At the thought of confessing his feelings to Tyson his heart started trying to do back-flips out through his mouth.

Ronan the Warrior, Vanquisher of Evil, Slayer of Thousands, was hopelessly in love.

Tarl walked quietly along the corridor towards his room. He knew that collecting his bag and getting out was a perfectly sensible thing to do, so why the hell did it make him feel like some nasty little insect scuttling under a stone? Maybe this was that guilt thing that people kept on about.

He'd nearly reached his room when a door opened and Ronan came out of the bathroom. He stopped, looking embarrassed, and Tarl quickly pasted a big cheesy grin on to his face.

'Hi!' he said. 'Nice and clean again?'

'Yeah,' answered Ronan. There was silence. The conversation

was tearing along like a horse with no legs going uphill. Ronan gave it a shove. 'So how's Puss?'

'Great! When I left him, he was standing in the kitchen with eyes like plates and his tongue hanging out. He's never seen a Steak Diane before, and Tyson's chef is cooking him ten of the things!' Tarl paused. He could feel his grin coming off in chunks. He rushed on. 'Well, can't stop. Got the girl of my dreams waiting in my room.'

'Yeah, me too.' Ronan didn't sound convincing.

'Good luck, Big Fella,' said Tarl, slapping Ronan on the shoulder. 'I'll see you around.' He turned away and walked up the passage to his room, wishing that the carpet on the floor was as deep-pile as the one downstairs. He could have hidden in that one.

Ronan watched him go, then turned to open the door to his room. Better get this over with. Maybe when he saw Attali lying there in bed, when he took her in his arms, maybe he could forget Tyson. Just for a few minutes. Maybe. He took a deep, hopeless breath, and marched in to meet his fate.

Tarl was in a hurry, stuffing his belongings into his back-pack as quickly as possible. He'd never had to turn a woman down before, especially one who looked like Serena, and so he hadn't dared to look at her, in case his resolve weakened. He was conscious of her there on the water-bed, but kept his eyes firmly on what he was doing.

'It's nothing personal,' he gabbled. 'But I've got this life I'd like to lead, and if I hang around here tonight, I might not have it much longer.' He strapped the pack closed and swung it on to his back. 'So thanks, but . . . no thanks!'

Confident now that he had the resolve to leave, he looked at her for the first time since he had entered, and saw – the woman of his dreams!

'Oh, no!' he said, sadly.

It was Serena. She was kneeling on the water-bed on all fours, with black rubber boots on both her legs and her arms. Over her back was draped an entire sheepskin, and on her head she wore a pair of curled sheep's-horns. She wriggled her rump and the little woolly tail swished back and forth. Then she looked at him with twinkling eyes.

'Baaa!' she said.

Tarl felt as though someone had kicked him in the stomach. His back-pack fell to the floor.

'Oh, yes!' he said, moving towards the bed as though drawn by a magnet. 'Oh, baby! Yes!'

Tarl was sunk, and he knew it.

ANTHRAX

*Travellers heading west from Welbug are advised to avoid
the Main Western Road, as it is believed that the Witch of
Southfork is operating in this area, and many travellers have
already been cursed or bewitched. Previous reports that the
root of the mandrake acts as a charm against her spells are
now known to be false, and travellers are advised to try an
alternative root . . .*

Welbug Weekly – Travel News

Tarl drifted slowly up from the depths of sleep. He was being
rocked by the gentle undulations of the water-bed and could feel
Serena's hot breath on his forehead. He sighed with contentment,
reaching one hand out to stroke her cheek.

Funny . . . it felt a little rough. And come to think of it, the
water-bed was a bit on the hard side, and the pillow was lumpy.
And he was freezing cold. He dragged one eye open, then the
other, and stared up in horror. Instead of Serena's beautiful face,
there was a foul upside-down vision with fang teeth, filthy skin,
and staring yellow eyes. It grinned at him and a miasma of foul
breath swept by. Tarl opened his mouth to yell, and a huge and
powerful hand was immediately clamped over it before he could
make a sound.

'Sh!' said Ronan from behind him, and then removed his hand.
Tarl hauled himself upright and stared round. He had been lying
flat out in the bottom of a boat, with his head on his back-pack.
Behind him sat Ronan and Puss, and in front of him was the
owner of the foul face – the ferryman, Oupase, who was rowing
them quietly along with cloth-wrapped oars. They were moving
quickly downriver, with a cold mist eddying round them and
hiding the shore from view. On the whole, thought Tarl, he'd
really rather have woken up next to Serena.

'What the hell's going on?' he hissed.

Ronan looked puzzled. 'Why are you whispering?' he asked.

Tarl gestured to the oars. 'We're slipping quietly out of Welbug in a boat with specially muffled oars, so I assumed . . .'

'They're not specially muffled,' growled Oupase. 'I always have them like this. You'd be surprised how many people with hangovers I have to ferry around. They appreciate the quiet.'

'Anyway,' said Ronan, 'we're miles away from Welbug now. We started before dawn.'

'You could have woken me,' said Tarl, grumpily.

The warrior seemed embarrassed. 'Well, you looked as though you needed the sleep, and Tyson said if you were still in your room it meant you definitely wanted to come, and I thought . . .'

'You thought I might have changed my mind.' Tarl peered longingly back through the mist, but all sight and sound of the city had vanished behind them. He sighed. 'Shame. I'd have liked to say goodbye to Serena.'

'She sent you a message,' said Ronan, smiling.

'Oh?' said Tarl, nonchalantly.

'Yeah. She said to say baa.'

Tarl could feel himself blushing. It was a pretty unaccustomed sensation. 'So, er, have a good night with Attali?' he asked, by way of distraction.

'No.'

Tarl looked up, surprised. The big warrior was looking embarrassed again.

'No? Why not?'

'Because it wasn't Attali.'

'Who was it?'

'Tyson.'

'You're joking!' Tarl studied his friend. He was staring into space with a particularly fierce expression on his face, but with a smile hovering around his lips. He looked like a deadly man-eating tiger thinking about his man-eating tigress.

Grak's blood! thought Tarl. He's in love! And he's got it bad. Mind you, I shouldn't be surprised. If ever a couple were made for each other! I bet they had a big row about who went on top . . .

Ronan grimaced horribly. 'I never realised,' he said, 'that a woman could be so . . . so . . .'

'Beautiful?' suggested Tarl. 'Cuddly? Sexy?'

'Deadly,' said Ronan. 'So lethal, so quick, so . . .'

'So anyway,' interrupted Tarl, 'what happened to Attali?'

'I don't know. I expected her to be in the bedroom, but it was Tyson who was waiting for me. She said if I went anywhere near Attali again, she'd slit my throat. She meant it, too!'

Tarl shivered inwardly. He wasn't keen on the idea of going to bed with lethal females. It reminded him of the revolting habits of some of the more unpleasant spiders that he'd read about, such as the Baq D'Orian Widowmaker, or the Black Teaser. Quickly, he shunted the conversation towards more prurient matters.

'So,' he leered, 'you screwed Tyson, eh? No wonder you look shagged out!'

Suddenly Tarl found himself dangling in mid-air with a large black fist clamped tightly about his throat. Ronan stared at him for a moment as though he'd just spat in his wine, but then looked a little shame-faced and put him down again.

'The reason that I didn't get a lot of sleep,' he said as Tarl gasped in air, 'was because it was too noisy. It sounded as though there was a flock of sheep going berserk in the next room.'

For the second time in a minute, Tarl could feel himself going bright red. He turned away from Ronan and watched Oupase, who was dipping the cloth-wrapped oars into the water, and pulling powerfully.

'So we've left the girls behind,' he said. 'And the city. And the pubs. And the food, and the wine, and the beer, and the gambling, and the shows, and the comfort, and the safety, and the fun, and the good times . . .'

His voice died away. There was a short silence that was at last broken by Ronan.

'I'm so glad you came along,' he said sourly, and then turned and stared sadly back towards Welbug as the boat swept on downriver through the mist.

Oupase held the ferry steady against the bank as the others disembarked. 'Head north, towards the Forest of Dreams,' he advised. 'They say the Wizard's house is just a few miles past the Trading Post.'

Tarl looked up, worriedly. 'They say?' he repeated. 'Don't you know anyone who's actually been there?'

Oupase shook his head. 'We have a saying in Welbug. "Never meddle in the affairs of Wizards. You can't trust the bastards an inch!"' And with that he pushed his boat off from the jetty, and began to row powerfully back upstream.

'Great,' said Tarl, as Ronan strode past him. 'Just what I like. A pre-breakfast yomp to a house of uncertain location, where some nut in a pointy hat and a long white beard is waiting to turn us into frogs.'

Puss looked at him scornfully. You could have it worse, it thought. You could have two sodding great back-packs strapped on top of you! And with a disdainful snort, it stalked off along the track after Ronan.

Back in Welbug, Tyson was having a busy morning. Although she was every bit as smitten by Ronan as he was by her, she wasn't the type to droop languidly around the house, pining for her true love. When she had Things To Do, she Did them. And that morning, she had a city to secure.

Within an hour of seeing Ronan safely away in the ferry she was at the head of a detachment of the City Guard, marching through the streets past cheering crowds on her way to arrest Ritta's confederates. But there didn't seem to be anyone left to arrest. The Sergeant of the Gate-guard told her that there had been a mass exodus at first light, with Southrons, Easterlings, orcs, and other unpleasant folk streaming through the gates and heading north. A heavily armed group of about twenty of Ritta's best men had headed off along the West Road, galloping furiously.

Ha! thought Tyson. I know who they're after. Well, tough, they'll never find him!

By the time she got to Ritta's house up in the merchant's quarter, half the city seemed to have joined them. There were stall-holders, builders, off-duty guards, all cheering and shouting and waving whatever weapons they could find. She paused on the steps leading up to the dead councilman's front door and gave them a few well-chosen words, ending with the suggestion that they should take the rest of the day off and celebrate with a few drinks. The crowd erupted and she turned away with a smile. Her father had taught her a thing or two about public relations.

Ritta's house was deserted but for a few slaves, who had

obviously feared and loathed the man and were overjoyed to be released. She searched the place thoroughly, but there was nothing of any use to be found. Someone had burned a mass of documents and parchments on the fire in the main hall before leaving. Tyson sifted carefully through the ashes but found nothing of value.

Shame, she thought as she climbed the stairs that led to the room at the top of the tower. If we'd moved as soon as Ritta was dead, we might have found a lot of useful stuff. But then she smiled to herself. What the hell! She'd had a great night with Ronan and she wouldn't have swapped that. Anyway, the guy was dead, they'd kicked Nekros's butt for him, and Welbug was safe.

She pushed open the door at the top of the stairs and found herself in a small square room. To one side, a curtain half hid a tall window that led on to a little balcony overlooking the city. In the centre of the room was a table, on which rested a smallish crystal ball.

She sat at the table and stared at the crystal, and was just wondering whether it could tell her anything when suddenly it began to glow with an eerie red light. As she watched, a dark and angry face appeared in its depths.

'Ritta!'

The voice that echoed eerily from the crystal was enough to send shivers down a dragon's spine, but Tyson was in no mood to be cowed. She realised that this must be Nekros, and that he hadn't yet heard the news. Excellent! Maybe she could learn something. She leaned forward.

'Unfortunately Ritta can't be here just now,' she purred. 'He's a little cut up about it.'

There was no change in the expression on Nekros's face but all of a sudden she was aware of a venomous hatred drifting out from the crystal and wrapping itself around her like the strands of a retiary.

'Ah! You must be Tyson. How nice to talk to you at last!' All of a sudden his voice was dripping with honey . . . but the sort of honey that would be made by deadly killer-bees in a very bad mood. 'I warned the stupid man that you and your warrior friend would cause trouble for him.'

'Not just for him. You can forget about Welbug. Start worrying about saving your own skin.'

Nekros laughed. It was the most unpleasant sound that Tyson had ever heard.

'Do you really think that the two of you can defeat me and the power that backs me? A woman, and a beardless youth fresh from Warrior School? Look! I have a special fate in store for you.'

The view in the crystal expanded, and Tyson could see that Nekros was holding a sword more than six feet long, jet-black and with a jagged edge. He began to sharpen it with a whet-stone and the grating screech of metal set her teeth on edge. She shivered, but affected disdain.

'Typical! You men and your swords. So impressed with size. Well, I've always found it's true what they say. Big sword, tiny dick.'

The metallic screeching stopped, and Nekros threw her a look of such malevolence that she found she was gripping the table edge white-knuckled.

'You cease to amuse me,' he growled. 'I think that the sooner I dispose of your large friend, the better.'

'Easier said than done!' said Tyson, confidently. She was getting the impression that things were swinging her way. She felt as though she was marching along life's highway with a song in her heart. At this point, fate slipped out behind her from a dark alley with a half-brick in its hand.

'It shouldn't be too hard,' laughed Nekros. 'He's on his way to see Anthrax, isn't he?'

Try as she might, Tyson couldn't keep the look of horror off her face and Nekros laughed delightedly.

'My dear girl,' he grinned, 'it was I who ordered Anthrax to invite him. Quite a lot of my men are riding that way at this very moment. But keep that crystal. When they bring him here, I'll let you have a last word with him. Or what's left of him.'

Tyson stared at Nekros, horrified. She felt as though a large and very angry horse wearing lead shoes had just kicked her in the stomach. At the sight of her face, he laughed out loud with glee.

'What, no snappy come-back?' he asked. 'Never mind. We can't all be at our best in the mornings. I'll give him your love, shall I?'

His visage vanished abruptly and the red glow faded, leaving the room as still and quiet as a morgue. And then Tyson was up and dashing down the stairs, yelling for someone to fetch her horse.

Welbug would just have to look after itself for a while. She had a man to save.

After the brilliant afternoon sunshine, the inside of the Trading Post was pleasantly cool. It was also very dark, and it took a while for Ronan's eyes to adjust. When they did so, he could see that they were in a large room that brought exacting new parameters to the word 'cluttered'. Wherever you looked, there were things piled on other things, next to things, under things, inside things, and with more things piled on top for good measure. Teetering mounds of just about everything under the sun climbed up the walls, covered the windows, and threatened to overwhelm the counter.

Behind this counter the owner of the Trading Post could just be seen. He was very tall and remarkably thin, and gave the impression that, long ago, an absent-minded torturer had strapped him to an automatic rack and then forgotten about him for two weeks. He looked as though if he fell asleep standing up, his body would just fold up like a concertina. His eyes gleamed happily behind circular eye-glasses as he peered excitedly at his potential customers over the top of, amongst other things, several pairs of hob-nailed troll boots, some swords, a stuffed *wiggat*, a complete collection of the works of Maxon the Small, an interesting sculpture made entirely from horse-shoes, a box of tinned apples in cider, an *alaxl* head mounted on a shield, and an old wheelbarrow with no wheel.

'Hi there!' he said. 'Hey! Nice back-packs! I'll give you thirty bronze *tablons* apiece for them!'

Ronan shook his head.

'Thirty-five, then. No? Well, how about that donkey? I'll give you two silver *tablons* for him.'

Again, Ronan shook his head. 'He's not for sale. Look, could you . . .'

'Well, two and a half then . . .' The trader's voice died away as the donkey bared its teeth in a most un-asinine snarl. 'Er . . . perhaps not.' His eyes alighted on Tarl. 'Ah, now how about your little slave here? I'll give you a gold *tablon* for him!'

Ronan's sword whirled viciously down on to the counter and

sliced the wheelbarrow clean in half. There was a moment's silence.

'Nice weapon. I'll give you five silver *tablons* for it . . .'

'LOOK!' Ronan's voice shook the Trading Post to its foundations and started several minor landslides among the stacks around the walls. 'We do NOT want to sell anything. And before you ask, we do NOT want to buy anything, either. We simply want to ask you if you can tell us where . . .'

'Well, if you don't want to trade, what the klatting hell are you doing here, then?' came an indignant interruption. 'This is a Trading Post. Where people trade. I am a trader. I trade for a living. My raison d'être is trading. Trading is what I do. If you want to do a nice bit of trade, then I'm your man. None better. But if you *don't* want to trade . . .'

'But we do!' said Tarl. He held up a skin of his home-made wine. 'We'll trade you this fine wine here, for some . . . information.'

'Now you're talking!' said the trader, excitedly. 'What do you want to know?'

'You've heard of Anthrax the Wizard?'

'Anthrax? 'Course I have! He often comes in here for supplies.' The trader indicated a shelf behind him, which was covered in tins and jars. Tarl peered at them. He could just make out a tin labelled 'Gourmet Fenny-snake Fillets' next to another one labelled 'Gatt and Boulder's Best Dog Tongues'.

'Can you tell us where he lives?'

'Certainly! Head north up the track for about two miles until you come to the House of Nolan, Father of Many Daughters. Turn left, and head west for half a mile until you come to the edge of the Forest of Dreams. Anthrax's house is about fifty paces inside the forest edge.'

'Thanks!' Tarl tossed him the wine-skin and turned to Ronan. 'Come on, we'd better move!'

Ronan hauled his sword out of the counter with difficulty, then threw the trader a dirty glance and followed his friend outside. He found Tarl peering worriedly along the road towards the east. In the far distance, he could just make out a small cloud of billowing dust.

'Oh, klat!' swore Tarl. 'Horsemen!'

They started to run.

*

Even carrying the back-pack that he'd taken from the donkey, Ronan could have kept up a fast loping pace for a lot further than two and a half miles. Puss, with just the other pack to carry, could have trotted happily along all day. But Tarl was a different matter. The nearest he ever got to strenuous exercise was running up a large tab in a wine-bar. And now he was close to exhaustion.

The horsemen too were tired, having ridden non-stop from Welbug. If it hadn't been for the trader, they would already have caught their quarry. When they stopped to ask him for news of Ronan he had insisted on bartering, and by the time they had struck a bargain Ronan and Tarl were half-way to the Wizard's house. But now they were closing fast. They could see their quarry ahead, at the forest edge, and were almost within bow-shot.

Tarl felt as though his chest would burst. There was a pain like a sword-thrust in his side and his legs seemed to have turned into wobbly pillars of agony. He clutched at the first tree he came to and leant against it, making strange gasping snorts, like a pig with asthma.

'Come on, Tarl!' yelled Ronan, from ahead. 'Just a few more yards! We must be near the Wizard's house!'

'Where?' gasped Tarl, in desperation. 'Look around you! There's no sign of a house anywhere!' Then an arrow stuck quivering in the tree above his head, and with a yelp of fright he staggered into the forest.

Ronan grabbed his arm and dragged him after the donkey, which was trotting purposefully further into the trees.

'It must be here somewhere!' he muttered, staring round wildly. 'If it's not, then we'll just have to fight!'

'Oh, come on!' yelled Tarl. 'They've got bows! We've had it! They'll just pick us off!'

As if to lend credence to his words, two more arrows whirred past them. A third hummed past Tarl's ear and thumped into Ronan's back-pack. They staggered blindly on for a few more paces with the triumphant yells of their pursuers ringing in their ears, and then all at once the trees and the very air ahead of them seemed to shimmer like a reflection on the surface of suddenly disturbed water. They burst through the shimmering air as though through a mirror, and in an instant, a house appeared out of nowhere in front of them, as solid and real as the arrow in Ronan's pack. Behind them, the sound of their pursuers vanished as though a door had closed.

As Tarl collapsed gasping to the ground beside the donkey, Ronan stared back the way they had come. He could see clearly beyond the confines of the forest, yet there wasn't even a trace of their hunters. They seemed to have vanished into thin air. He turned back, and studied the house in front of them.

It was a beautiful whitewashed cottage, with roses growing up the walls, birds singing happily in the eaves of the thatched roof, and butterflies floating like litter on the breeze amongst the profusion of flowers that clustered about the red-stone path leading to the front door. The whole place seemed to be bathed in sunshine, despite the fact that it was situated in the gloom of the forest and shaded by fifty feet high trees. It gave the impression that someone had scooped it up off a sun-covered hillside, complete with its surrounding light, and dumped it here.

Ronan helped the rapidly recovering Tarl to his feet, then gave the donkey a happy pat and strolled up the path. If this isn't a Wizard's house, he thought, then I don't know what is. He raised his fist and knocked heartily on the solid oak front door.

'Oi! What the frigging hell do you think you're playing at?' roared an adenoidal voice.

Ronan took a step back and looked around, surprised.

'You walk up here, cool as you please, and start thumping on people!' continued the voice. 'You're not on, pal! If I could move, I'd clock you one!'

Ronan stared round, baffled. Tarl moved next to him and whispered, 'I think it's the door! You must have upset it! I don't think it's used to being knocked on!'

Indeed, the door did seem to be quivering on its hinges with indignation. It suddenly yelled, 'Oi, Scotty! Did you see that?'

'Aye, I did,' boomed a voice from behind them. They turned to see a huge pine tree by the gate looming over them threateningly. 'See you, pal, don't you come throwing your weight around here!' continued the voice, and the tree lashed violently as though struck by a gale. A large dead branch crashed to the ground beside Tarl, showering the donkey with splinters.

Behind the pine, other trees were starting to sway ominously and there was a steady rising tide of aggrieved muttering. Ronan stood there indecisively, hand on the hilt of his sword, unsure what to do. He'd never been attacked by coniferous woodland before. Then Tarl pushed past him and stood in front of the door.

'Look, I apologise for my friend here,' he said, soothingly. 'It's just that where we come from, it's normal to knock on doors. Doors don't mind. And that way, people on the other side of the door know that someone wants to come through, and they come and open it. We're certainly not used to doors with an intelligence like yours!'

'Is that a fact?' said the door, mollified.

'Yeah,' said Tarl, and rested a friendly hand on the door. 'All we wanted to do was let Anthrax know we're here. We certainly didn't mean to cause offence.'

'Oh,' said the door. 'Well, er . . . look, I'm sorry if I flew off the handle a bit. I've had a rather trying time of late.' It lowered its voice confidentially. 'It's the windows, you know. We don't get on.' Then it raised its voice and spoke in a more businesslike manner. 'I'll just let the boss know you're here.'

There was a silence. Tarl and Ronan stood and waited. Behind them the trees seemed to be settling down. Then the door suddenly burst into life again.

'He won't be a moment,' it chirped. 'And in the meantime, here is some music for your enjoyment.'

A horrible tinny tune started to emanate from the door. It sounded as though someone was playing a toy xylophone in the bottom of an enormous oil-drum. Tarl winced, then stepped back and turned to Ronan.

'It's no good going at everything like a minotaur at a gate. Sometimes you need to use a little tact . . . a little persuasion . . .'

'I only knocked on the door!' said Ronan, indignantly.

'Yeah, and look at the result. It's a good job you've got me with you!'

'Now, you listen . . .' began Ronan, indignantly, but then the music stopped abruptly, the door swung open, and a man appeared.

Both Tarl and Ronan stared at him in amazement. He looked about twenty-five years old, was clean-shaven, and had a very neat haircut and a deep tan. He was wearing an exquisitely tailored suit, cut in a style that would have had Giorgio Armani or Jean Paul Gaultier literally weeping with jealousy. And in a world where the height of masculine chic was generally regarded as being jerkin, breeches, and leg-thongs, the effect can only be described as a knock-out. The only hint that here was a man who was involved in wizardry was his tie, which was covered in tiny magic wands, pentagons, pointed hats, and odd cabalistic symbols.

'Good afternoon,' he said politely, in an elegantly refined and rather plummy voice.

'Anthrax?' asked Ronan, doubtfully.

'I'm afraid so,' smiled the man. 'These childhood nicknames do tend to stick to one. I used to suffer from the most terrible acne, you see. My real name is Nigel, but if you're happy with it, you may call me Anthrax.'

'I am Ronan, Vanquisher of . . .'

'I know,' interrupted Anthrax. 'I've been expecting you.' He looked them both up and down. 'You seem a little . . . flushed.'

'That's because we've been chased most of the way here and nearly killed,' burst out Tarl. He gestured towards the edge of the forest. 'There's at least twenty of them, all on horses, with bows and swords . . .' His voice trailed off as he peered through the trees to the edge of the forest. There still wasn't a soul to be seen. 'Well, they were there a minute ago,' he finished uncertainly.

'I've arranged a minor temporal displacement,' Anthrax told him. 'They won't be here for several hours now. You'd better come in.' And with that he turned and disappeared inside the cottage, and Ronan, Tarl and the donkey followed him in.

The room in which they found themselves seemed far too large for the cottage. One wall was entirely taken up by a bookcase full of leather-bound tomes, in front of which was a circular library table and a number of comfortable leather chairs. Along a second wall was a wooden work-bench covered in glass jars, vials, beakers, and tubes. Above this was a glass-fronted wall-cupboard full of chemicals, and at one end was an alcove, screened off by a heavy curtain. The third wall was covered in posters, paintings, charts and wall-hangings from every world and time imaginable. There was a very rude piece of the Bayeaux Tapestry (which had been edited out in AD 1081), a wanted poster for Perkin Warbeck, Leonardo's third (and best) version of the Virgin of the Rocks, Leif Ericson's chart of the route to America, a letter from someone called Hitler to someone else called Chamberlain (undertaking to pull out of Poland within the next week), a poster for a film called *Reservoir Dogs*, and a glossy advertisement for Sunburst Startour Holidays ('We put the you in Universe').

'Please, make yourselves at home,' the Wizard began, and then the courteous smile faded from his face to be replaced by a frown as his gaze fell upon the donkey. 'Who brought that filthy animal in here?' he demanded.

I did, thought Puss. His name's Tarl. I'm sorry about the smell.

For a moment, Anthrax gazed at it, and then his face creased up and he roared with laughter. The donkey felt a feather-light touch caressing its mind, and stared at the Wizard suspiciously. Tarl and Ronan, who were not privy to the donkey's thoughts, just stared at him blankly.

'Oh, yes!' grinned Anthrax. 'I don't think your intellect should be confined to telepaths!'

He lifted a hand and muttered something. A little group of whirling sparks of light formed in front of him and drifted across to settle around the donkey's head. They floated there for a moment, then suddenly seemed to burst in a flare of light. The donkey blinked and wrinkled its nose as though about to sneeze.

'Here, that tickled!' it said.

Tarl stared at it incredulously. 'Where the hell did you learn to speak?' he asked, in amazement.

Puss looked at him pityingly. 'Night-school,' it replied. 'Where the hell do you think? I mean, here we are, standing in the workroom of the most powerful Wizard in Frundor, and wham! Suddenly I can talk. I don't suppose the answer could possibly be . . . magic? No, no! Surely not!'

Tarl shook his head in wonder. 'Well, bugger me!' he said.

'No thanks,' said Puss. 'I'm fed up, not hard up.' And it wandered across to a small hole in the skirting-board and stood there, sniffing delicately. It was feeling peckish and it thought it could smell mice.

It is only fair to warn readers who may be thinking of using a Spell of Animal Talking that such incantations can have both advantages and disadvantages. Here is an excerpt from *Old Raxie's Book of Charms for Children* (Second Edition. The first edition was withdrawn after an unfortunate transcription error resulting in the Exploding Hamsters outbreak):

Always be careful about which animals you confer the gift of speech upon. Donkeys or foxes can be most entertaining and witty . . . but cats are very sarcastic, horses moan incessantly, and sheep talk non-stop about grass. If you're happy with the idea of a three-hour monologue on the dietary advantages of rye-grass over couch-grass, then by all means, cast a Spell of Animal Talking on your favourite sheep. But don't say I didn't warn you!

Ronan had been staring round Anthrax's work-room with an increasing sense of awe. There was so much here that he didn't understand! He picked up an electric toothbrush from the work-bench and pressed the button on the side, then nearly dropped it in surprise when it started to hum busily. Like most other people in his world, Ronan had never heard of electricity. For a moment he peered closely at the vibrating head, wondering what the hell it was for, and then enlightenment hit him. He held it against his belt buckle, and grinned as it began to polish the metal.

'Amazing! Tarl, look at this magical buckle-polisher!' He stared at Anthrax, a little awe-struck. 'How do you produce such wonders?'

Anthrax gave a smug little smile. 'I don't suppose you're familiar with the theory of parallel universes?' he asked. Ronan looked at him blankly.

'He means,' said the donkey, 'that at every moment of choice, other realities split off from ours like fingers from a hand, so that every possibility is realised in one or another of these worlds.' It paused and looked sourly at Anthrax. 'It might even be conceivable that in one of them, a Wizard called Anthrax has actually offered some refreshment to his visitors.'

'Yes, yes!' said the wizard, impatiently, and clicked his fingers. A bale of hay materialised beside the donkey.

'Oh, great,' it said. 'Rabbit food. Thank you so much.'

'With the help of a little magic,' continued the tight-lipped Wizard, rather crossly, 'it is possible to send things through tiny worm-holes in space to these other universes. For example . . .'

He looked around for a suitable object, then opened a cage that was resting on top of the work-bench and extracted a large fat toad. He balanced this on his hand for a moment, muttered a low incantation, and stabbed a finger at it. The toad vanished with an audible pop and Tarl and Ronan gasped. The wizard kept his hand extended.

'And whenever you do that,' he said, 'you get something back.' He waited for a moment. There was another pop, and a smallish black book materialised and fell into his waiting hand. Ronan grabbed it and leafed through it in wonder.

'This must be a book of spells belonging to some powerful Wizard!' he said. 'Look! He's engraved his name in gold on the cover!'

'Could well be,' replied Anthrax. 'I wonder. Filofax . . . good name for a Wizard!' He took the book back from Ronan and bounced it up and down in his hand. 'You see, this is the problem. You're never sure what you're going to get back. It could be something obvious, like a cheese sandwich, or it could be something totally baffling.'

'Could . . . could a man travel to another world this way?' asked Ronan.

'Oh, yes. In fact my assistant, Van Damme, has already done so. He positively demanded that I send him. So I did. I do hope he's all right, wherever he is!' The Wizard sighed reflectively. 'In return, I got this bloke called Lucan. Absolutely charming chap, though a bit puzzled about what had happened. Gave me some pretty good tips about clothes . . .

'You see, one thing I have noticed about all this is that the item you get back always weighs exactly the same as the thing you send. I've actually postulated a little law about it.' The Wizard cleared his throat, then said rather self-consciously, 'For every action, there must be an equal and opposite reaction.' He paused, and then carried on a shade doubtfully, 'I'm pretty sure that I'm right. That is, unless I'm totally wrong. But then, I don't suppose it matters.'

*

Unfortunately, it did matter, rather a lot. For at that very moment in a parallel universe, a panicking sales representative was desperately trying to extract the telephone number of an extremely vital contact from a large, green, and rather puzzled toad. However, his failure to contact this client and arrange a meeting, the resulting collapse of a massive sales contract, and his subsequent dismissal, unemployment, and slide into alcoholism and vagrancy form no part of this narrative . . .

A while later, Tarl, Ronan and Anthrax were sitting at the table, finishing off the food and wine that the wizard had produced out of nowhere. The food was something called 'lasagne', the recipe for which had come through one of Anthrax's little worm-holes. Tarl thought it was one of the best things he'd ever eaten. He wasn't so sure about the wine, though. There wasn't even a single lump in it.

Anthrax had insisted on a policy of no business with dinner, so although the conversation had ranged far and wide (with the donkey taking a surprisingly knowledgeable rôle), the name of Nekros had not yet been mentioned. But now, as Anthrax pushed back the dishes and handed round some fat elfweed cigarettes, Ronan could wait no longer. Quickly he outlined the reasons for his quest, his father's warning, and all that he had learned from Tyson.

'So . . . is it true? Did you say that you could help me?' he asked. Anthrax sat back and studied him for a moment.

'Of course I can help you,' he said. 'Don't be fooled by my urbane sophistication. When it comes to the . . . Wiz Biz,' and here he drew imaginary inverted commas in the air with the first two fingers of each hand, 'I'm the best there is. Spells, charms, transformations, you want it, I got it. If you'd like proof, take a look at your little friend over there.'

He indicated Tarl, who was sitting back, wine-glass in one hand, spliff in the other, oblivious to everything. The Wizard muttered something and two little balls of light shot from his eyes, smashing into Tarl, who instantly turned into a very surprised-looking frog. It sat there for a few seconds, blinking, and then there was a brief flash, and Tarl was back in his normal form. He looked rather stunned and gazed at his cigarette in awe.

'What *is* this stuff?' he muttered. The Wizard turned back to Ronan.

'Anything is possible,' he smiled.

'Then tell me how to defeat Nekros!'

Anthrax crossed to the bookcase and took down a large volume that had the legend *Nav–Nyc* inscribed on the spine. He opened it and started leafing through, muttering to himself.

'Neck-ties . . . necrophilia . . . Nekros the Blue . . .'

'Nekros the Blue?' interrupted Ronan.

'A different Nekros. He was a very bad comedian. Absolutely awful. He died on stage – literally – at the Humiliation Club, in Goblin City. Apparently he was so bad that within ten minutes of the start of his act the audience had dismembered and eaten him. And that can't have been easy, as he weighed a good sixteen stone. Ah, there he is! Nekros the Black. Here. Know thine enemy.'

The Wizard handed the open book to Ronan, who began to read with difficulty. The pages were covered in neat, methodical writing, but they might as well have been in a foreign language. There were some words which he vaguely understood, such as syphilis, or misogynist, but there were many others that were way beyond him. What on earth was a sociopath? Nekros was, apparently, and he was also a paranoid schizophrenic, whatever that meant. Baffled, Ronan shook his head and looked at Anthrax, who was standing by the curtained-off alcove gazing thoughtfully into space.

'Well,' mused the Wizard, 'taking into account your father's message, I think we need an on-going double-stage precognatory diagnosis incorporating the infusion of a telekinetic hydrolyte and a transubstantiatory ergonomic locution.'

'Beg pardon?' said Ronan.

'Two predictions, a magic potion, and a Word of Power,' said the donkey, happily. It had just finished its fourth helping of lasagne.

'Yes, all right, smarty-pants!' snapped Anthrax, and pulled back the curtain.

In the alcove were what looked to Ronan like two vast metal boxes covered in buttons and flashing lights. Inside one, several reels of tape could be seen gently turning. Anthrax started pressing the buttons on it, and the box began to make a whirring sound. The reels started to whiz round, the lights flashed even faster, and a long stream of paper came churning out of a slot at the front. The Wizard scanned this paper, humming to himself.

Suddenly there was a loud 'click' and all the room lights went off. An eerie red glow began to emanate from a large glass ball about twice the size of a human head that was sitting on a small table beside the whirring box and was connected to it by a thick yellow cable.

'OK,' said Anthrax. 'Let's see what this chappie Nekros is up to at the moment.' Ronan and Tarl crept warily forward and stared into the depths of the glass ball in wonder.

Nekros was getting a little pissed off with this sword salesman. Normally he had very little to do with sales executives of any description, as actually buying items was not a thing he did very often. If, for example, his Tribe needed a hundred horses to mount a raid, the last thing he would have thought of doing would have been to go down to Big Mal's Used Horse Mart and pay through the nose for them. He found it easier, cheaper, and much more satisfying to drift in there unexpectedly one night with a few of his best men, give Big Mal a short back and insides with his sword, then stroll off with whatever horses he felt like.

However, he'd thought a sword salesman might be quite interesting, expecially one who was Sales Executive (South Frundor Region) for the Orcbane Sword Corporation, as Orcbane made some spectacularly brutal weapons. He was now beginning to realise that Interesting Sales Executives were up there with the White Dragon of Behan or the Lost Dwarfish Pub of Legend . . . they might exist, but nobody had actually ever found them. He was going to have no regrets whatsoever about following his backers' instructions.

Belladon, as with salesmen the world over, had no idea of what a bad effect he was having on his potential client. He had gone through his repertoire by the book. Treat the client like a long-lost friend, smile a lot, get in a couple of good (but smutty) gags, have a bit of a chat about horses (and impress him with how many miles-per-bale his was currently doing), pass on a useful tip about a short-cut across the Setel Downs that he'd found, and have a bit of a man-to-man about girls. Now, when the client would be thinking what a regular guy he was, would be the time to strike.

'But listen,' he said, 'I mustn't waste any more of your valuable time. Look, here's our latest catalogue. Keep it, leaf through it when you get a minute. If you've any questions, get in touch any time! But I'd just like you to have a look at this!' He grinned inwardly as he opened his case and took out a very short sword in a two-foot scabbard. This was the absolute latest in sword technology and it had never yet failed to captivate a warrior.

Nekros, who had been about to sneer openly at such a puny little weapon, stared in disbelief as Belladon took the sword from its scabbard and pressed an opal set into the pommel. With an audible hiss the blade smoothly extended itself into a six-foot broad-sword. Wordlessly, he reached out, took the weapon from Belladon, and hefted it in his hand. Beautiful! Light as a feather, perfectly balanced, yet deadly! And looks-wise, it was the most perfectly evil thing he had ever seen! Jet-black, with just a hint of silver tracery on the blade, and with rubies and garnets set into the pommel like pools of blood.

'It's the all-new Orcbane Retractable,' Belladon said, proudly. 'Otherwise known as the Traveller's Terminator. A really smooth piece of work!' And he was just starting to mention the sort of discount that might be possible on orders of fifty or more when Nekros sighed, leant forward, and gently but firmly slid the sword up to the hilt into Belladon's abdomen. The salesman's patter stopped abruptly and he stared down in horror at the blood that welled out round the hilt of the sword.

'See what I mean?' he gasped. 'It went in like a dream!' And then Nekros slid the sword out, the blood gushed, and Belladon fell to the floor. Nekros stared down at him and shook his head.

'No jury in the land would convict me,' he muttered to himself. Then he stooped and wiped the sword clean on Belladon's clothing, and marched to the door, shouting for his second-in-command.

Within seconds, Angnail had come sprinting up the stairs. 'Yes, lord?' he said.

'Have this body removed,' ordered Nekros, gesturing to the corpse. 'And pass the word to the Tribe. The east must wait. Our presence is vital if our forces in Port Raid are to succeed with their insurrection. We ride to join them in two days.'

Angnail turned and fled, and Nekros sat down, and began to examine his new sword.

The image in the glass ball faded and the red light died. Tarl and Ronan looked at each other.

'Well, he's a bundle of laughs,' said Tarl.

'So there's your first prediction,' said Anthrax, who was again scanning the computer print-out. 'In maybe six days, Nekros will have reached the lands of the west.'

'So should I seek him in Port Raid?' asked Ronan. Anthrax looked him in the eyes and smiled.

'You will know where to find him,' he said. 'You are involved in a cycle of vengeance. Just remember that a cycle is circular. Now, the second prediction. Your father's rhyme mentioned a dwarfish chart. The largest collection of charts and maps in the whole of Midworld is in the Chart Room of Albran's castle. That's all you need to know.'

'Albran?' asked Tarl.

'The King of the Wood-elves,' answered the Wizard, crossing to the second of the metal boxes. It was about six feet high and stood against the wall. 'Now for the potion. Erm, let's see.' He checked the print-out that he was holding, then started to press some of the buttons that stretched down the front of the box. 'Essence of batwing . . . toe of frog . . . lizard spleen . . . *wiggat* hair . . . anti-oxidants . . . flavour enhancer . . . preservatives . . . stabilisers . . . permitted colouring . . .' He turned to Ronan, with his finger poised over a button. 'Sugar?' he asked.

'Er, yes, please.'

'Sugar.' The Wizard's finger pressed home, and he stood back and waited. The box hummed into life and made various churning noises then stopped abruptly, and an aluminium can with a ring-pull top thudded into an alcove at the bottom of the box.

'Voilà!' said Anthrax. 'One magic potion. To be taken just before you come into contact with Nekros.'

Tarl picked the can out of the tray and studied the label suspiciously. 'Here,' he said. 'I wouldn't go drinking this, it's full of ingredients!' He pointed to a tiny patch of writing. 'Listen to this lot! Monosodium glutamate, vitamins B2, B6, D, ascorbic

139

acid, calcium propionate . . .'

As he spoke, the lights in the room dimmed slightly. His voice seemed to be taking on a deeper, more sonorous tone.

'Hydrogenated vegetable oils,' he continued. 'Sodium poly-phosphates, tartrazine, betacarotene . . .'

It was darker now. There was a distant roll of thunder. The air seemed to crackle and Tarl's voice swelled to fill the room.

'. . . emulsifier E471, E472(e), E475, and dextrose!'

There was a violent crash of lightning that seemed to lift the roof off the house, and for a moment everything went pitch-black. And then the lights came on again, the room was back to normal, and Tarl was standing by the vending machine with the can in his hand, panting as though he had just run another two-and-a-half miles. Anthrax took the can from him and handed it to Ronan, who shoved it into the pocket of his jerkin.

'Well, well!' he said to Tarl, smiling. 'You have the Power! Who would have thought it?'

'The what?' asked Tarl.

'The Power. It's latent, of course.'

'Here, who are you calling latent?'

'It turns up in the most surprising places! Heaven help us all if you ever discover how to use it. There is just the merest hint of a party animal about you. I have a feeling the Wizards' Convention would never be the same again. That is, if they let you in. Somehow, I can't imagine you in a tie.'

'What are you wittering on about?' asked the baffled Tarl.

'Oh, come now! You have definite magical ability and you know it. It's bound to have manifested itself in the past.'

Tarl thought back to some of the more frightening moments of his life. It had manifested itself then, too right it had. Whenever he was frightened out of his wits, Things Happened, and he seemed to have no control whatsoever over them.

'I haven't any Power,' he muttered. 'Things just . . . happen.'

'Of course they do! You haven't had any training. If I stuck you in the kitchen with a load of flour and butter and eggs and told you to make a cake, then unless someone had shown you how to do it, or given you a recipe book, you would just end up with a sticky mess.'

Tarl thought of the guy back in Orcville who had tried to mug him and had somehow got turned inside out. He'd been a sticky mess all right. He shook his head tiredly and poured himself another glass of wine.

'Forget it,' he mumbled. 'Just forget it.'

'You mentioned a Word of Power,' Ronan reminded the Wizard.

'Yes, of course,' Anthrax said, and then warned him, 'don't use it until you need it. Don't repeat it, or whisper it. Don't even think it. Just commit it to memory. There. Now, you've got all that you need to defeat Nekros. That will be, ooh, let's say, forty *tablons*, please.'

Ronan looked at him suspiciously. Forty *tablons* was the exact amount of money he had in his purse. As he handed it over, Tarl, who had been staring into the glass ball, spoke up.

'Here,' he said. 'Those are the guys who were chasing us. In fact, they still *are* chasing us! Look!'

Ronan stood beside him and peered once again into the depths of the glass ball. They could see the men on horse-back chasing two little figures and a donkey into the edge of the forest. As they watched, arrows shot silently towards the quarry, who staggered between the trees and suddenly vanished into thin air. Their pursuers, however, seemed unsurprised, but rode their horses slowly into the edge of the woods.

'Ah,' said Anthrax from behind them. 'Nekros's men, just in time to collect you.'

As the import of these words struck home, Ronan and Tarl turned as one and stared at the Wizard with horrified eyes.

'What?' gasped Tarl. 'But you've just told us how we're going to kill Nekros!'

'Oh, no . . . I'm sorry. I told you how you *could* kill him. That's what you asked me to do. Indeed, you might well have killed him – had I not already been paid by Nekros to find and hold you for him. Ah, no, I wouldn't try that, if I was you . . .'

At the realisation of the Wizard's duplicity, Ronan had instinctively grabbed his sword. Anthrax muttered something and gave a casual wave of the hand, and suddenly both Ronan and Tarl found themselves unable to move, or even speak.

'Master!' boomed the adenoidal tones of the front door. 'Visitors!'

'Ah,' said Anthrax. 'That will be Nekros's men now.'

*

Long, long ago, Anthrax had been an idealistic young magician full of the joys of spring. And then he met Naomi. She was a Princess – but one who was under a rather unfortunate enchantment at the time. Only someone with the Power could have recognised her for what she truly was. But when the teenage Wizard first stumbled across the frog with the long dark eyelashes sitting on a rock in the forest and crying to itself, he knew instantly that here was someone in dire need of a good magician. The Spell of Transubstantiation was a difficult one, but he had confidence in himself, and carried it out almost perfectly. Unfortunately, he made just one ever-so-slight mistake.

When the dust from the spell cleared and Anthrax saw the beautiful Princess with the long golden hair standing in front of him, he fell madly and passionately in love. To his surprise, she fell for him as well. They married, and at first were blissfully happy, but unlike most such cases, it was not to be for ever after. His mistake saw to that.

He could never work out quite what it was that he had done wrong, but for some reason, at times of high emotion or stress, Naomi would turn back into a frog. Not for long, just until she had calmed down a bit. And there was a slight frogginess that kept creeping into her personality as well. One time, they had gone to a very up-market restaurant for a meal. While he was studying the menu, Naomi went to the washroom. After twenty minutes, she still hadn't come back. Eventually, the worried Anthrax found her standing in the bin area outside the back door, watching the flies with a predatory gleam in her eye. Another worrying thing was her habit of trying to drag him off to the nearest muddy pond whenever she felt randy, although after a while he'd grown to quite like this one.

However, the biggest problem had been her personality. Frogs and Princesses don't have many things in common, but one thing they do frequently share is a complete lack of altruism. You don't get many frogs offering to carry your bags for you. Or many Princesses. So Naomi wasn't exactly the most selfless person in the whole world. In fact, after a couple of years, she had turned self-interest into an art form.

At first, Anthrax hadn't really noticed. One of the great advantages of being a Wizard is that you can get virtually anything you want at any time, and he'd rather enjoyed doing all these little things for his woman. But eventually, as she grew more and more demanding, and more and more short-tempered, the fun began to disappear. After a while, nothing he did seemed to please her any more. She didn't appear to love him, but unfortunately he still loved her, and despite all his magical powers, there was nothing he could do to change things. His life was totally miserable.

Then one day, he came home to find the house empty. He searched from room to room, but there was no sign of her. Then, as he was standing by the back door, wondering what had happened to her, he heard a familiar croaking. And there she was, in the pond in the back garden. Doing it with three male frogs. And not enchanted Princes, either. Just common-or-garden plain simple frogs. Naomi had started slumming it.

After that there was no going back. Anthrax had started divorce proceedings. He hadn't argued with any of her demands, hadn't quibbled. There was no point, as it was all simple enough for a Wizard to provide. He hadn't even argued over the maintenance order for several thousand tadpoles – which would have bankrupted a normal man – although he had a feeling that only a few hundred were his.

When the divorce was finalised, he had moved his whole house to a forest a long way away. And he had sworn that never again would he let his emotions sway him, never again would he give for the sake of giving. There would be no more Mister Nice Guy.

Since then, he prided himself on giving a plain, straight-forward, unemotional service. People paid him, and he did what they asked. Not necessarily what they wanted, just what they asked. For example, a man came to him with leprosy in both feet. He was quite a humble man and he begged Anthrax to help him. He said that if Anthrax couldn't completely cure him, he would understand, but that a fifty per cent improve-ment would be better than nothing. So Anthrax turned him into a mussel. When he complained, the wizard pointed out that he'd come to him with leprosy in both feet. Now he only had leprosy in one foot. That was a fifty per cent improvement, so what was his problem?

Whilst ostensibly providing a very effective service, Anthrax was taking his revenge on the world. It was cold, clinical, and totally amoral.

As Anthrax moved towards the front door, the donkey, which had been standing forgotten by the table, suddenly raised its head.

'Before you let those blokes in,' it said, 'can I ask you something?'

'By all means,' answered the Wizard.

'Why did you get Ronan to come here?'

'You know why. Nekros is paying me to capture him.'

'Bollocks!' snorted the donkey. 'You're probably the best Wizard in Midworld. You could have handed Ronan over to him anywhere, anyhow, any time. So why did it have to be here?'

Anthrax looked levelly at the donkey. 'I suppose I was curious.'

'You were tempted to let him get on with it, weren't you? You wouldn't mind at all if he finished Nekros off. You don't like the guy, do you? Under this cold man-of-the-world exterior, you're not at all happy about working for someone who pulls the legs off babies just to relieve the boredom.'

The Wizard was finding it a little unsettling being psychoanalysed by a small brown donkey, particularly when it was spot on in its analysis. He realised with some surprise that he was twiddling his thumbs, and frowned.

'All right, all right, I admit I've been rather peeved with the way he keeps throwing his orders around. Do this, do that . . . he really is very uncouth. It would be rather pleasant to put him firmly in his place!'

'So why don't you?'

'If you can see through me so clearly, then you'll know that I always keep my word. Even with a lout like Nekros.'

'What did you tell him you'd do?' asked the donkey, after a small pause.

'Erm . . . find Ronan, and hold him until Nekros's men got here.'

'Well, there you are then!' said the donkey. 'You've found him, and you've held him. Nekros's men have got here, so you've done what you promised. Now you can let him loose and then just sit back and enjoy watching Nekros get what he deserves.'

Ronan and Tarl had been listening to this conversation at first

144

with despair, but then with rising hope. As Anthrax paused and thought, both hardly dared to breathe.

'Do you know,' smiled the Wizard, after a moment, 'your logic is faultless!' And then he clapped his hands twice, there was another blinding flash, and Ronan and Tarl found themselves standing in a bright, misty, and rather eerie forest, surrounded by very surprised rabbits.

As the evening light was beginning to fade, an exhausted and very worried Tyson rode her horse into the edge of the wood. Although it was semi-dark, the Wizard's house still seemed to be bathed in sunlight. Tyson dismounted and stared at the scene before her. Scattered around in front of the house were twenty life-size stone statues of heavily armed men on horse-back. Stepping warily between them, she came to the garden path, and stopped. Basking in the sunshine on the doorstep was a small, oatmeal-coloured donkey, who was tucking in to a Four-Meats Pizza with obvious relish.

'Puss?' asked Tyson, doubtfully.

'You took your time getting here,' replied the donkey.

Tyson's jaw dropped open with surprise. 'You can talk!' she stammered.

'I don't see why everyone finds it so surprising,' muttered the donkey. 'Personally, I find it more difficult to understand how a creature with a brain as minuscule as Tarl ever manages to string together a coherent sentence.' It chewed on another mouthful, then added, 'I'd offer you some pizza, but it will all be gone in a minute.'

Tyson sat down beside the donkey, put an arm around its neck, and stared at the stone statues. 'So, those are Nekros's men, are they?' she asked.

'I think the phrase "were Nekros's men" would be more apt,' said the donkey, nodding. 'That Anthrax has quite a mean streak.'

'Then Ronan's all right? And Tarl?'

The donkey sighed mournfully and looked sadly at its empty plate. 'Well, it depends what you mean by all right,' it said. 'The Wizard has provided them with all the knowledge they need to beat Nekros and sent them on their way to the Forest of Dreams. On the other hand, it's just the two of them now. And how the hell are a pair of dip-sticks like those two going to manage without you or me to look after them?'

Tyson smiled. 'Then we'd better find a way of following them,' she said, and marched purposefully through the open door into the Wizard's house.

THE FOREST OF DREAMS

And so did Ronan find himself in the Forest of Dreams, one of the most insidious places in all Midworld. This fell place is the last relic of the Great Forest of primeval times. Those travellers who have emerged sane from its dark reaches have strange tales to tell – tales of huge tree-like creatures that stalk the forest glades, spiders the size of a house that have the foulest of personal habits, and gigantic yellow striped lizards that invite you home for tea and biscuits. The reason for these tales is simple – the Valdian Poppy.

This strange semi-intelligent plant, with its large, superbly flavoured root, is regarded as a great delicacy. In order to avoid being dug up and eaten, it has evolved an unusual and quite remarkable defence. When touched the plant emits a narcotic gas so powerful that any creature within twenty paces is instantly transported into a psychedelic dreamworld – hence the strange tales of walking trees and brightly coloured lizards.

Unfortunately for the Valdian Poppy, this clever strategy has one slight drawback. Its flower is so stunningly beautiful that the first thing anyone does in their blissed-out trance is to pluck it and place it in their hair. And so, although in the First Age it was semi-intelligent, by the Second Age the poppy had had its head ripped off so many times that its wits had become permanently scrambled, and it could hardly count up to three without getting confused.

The Pink Book of Ulay

The sudden transfer came as rather a shock to Ronan and Tarl. One minute, they had been standing immobilised in the Wizard's lounge, listening to him being comprehensively out-argued by a small brown donkey, then suddenly the house had vanished and they found themselves in the middle of yet another forest. They had been in a few depressing stretches of woodland recently but this one was just about the worst. The undergrowth consisted entirely of thorny brambles and stone-bushes. There wasn't a flower or a shrub or a blade of grass to be seen, and every tree seemed to be dying. Rotting logs and dead branches littered the forest floor. The only living things in sight were some clusters of unpleasant wart-covered brown toadstools that had erupted from a few of the fallen trees, and a group of emaciated rabbits that were vainly foraging amongst the rotting debris.

'Well, that was a lot of use,' said Tarl, sitting down gingerly on a moss-covered tree-stump. 'We travel all that way to see the greatest Wizard in Frundor, as somebody called him, and what do we come away with? A canful of ingredients and an incipient nervous breakdown! And we've lost Puss. Great!'

'No, we've done well!' insisted Ronan. 'We know I'll find Nekros within six days. And two of the things my father's rhyme mentioned have been explained. We've got the magic potion, and we'll find the dwarfish chart in the castle of King Albran.'

'Yeah, but what about the rest of the rhyme? "Sword of Myth shall Sing again" – what's all that about?'

'It must mean one of the Singing Swords of Legend. Our village story-teller used to sing of them. Like Akra, the Sword that Sings for the Glory of Battle, Vanda, the Sword that Sings as it Drinks the Blood of Enemies, and Linda, the Sword that Hums to Itself as it Does the Housework,' Ronan paused. 'Don't you know the Ancient Lays?'

'You mean like on Fridays in the Pink Centaur Club, when they used to have Grab-a-Granny night?'

'No, no! I mean the old folk-songs that were passed down from father to son!'

'Oh, them!' Tarl frowned, and started moodily to pull bits of moss off the tree-stump (thereby unintentionally rendering some thousands of small insects homeless. It's a cruel world). 'No, some bloke with a beard and a woolly pullover standing there with his finger in his ear, droning on about something that happened two hundred years ago, that's not my idea of good music. There's no danger to it. I like something that has a fair chance of permanently damaging an ear-drum.'

He was about to expound on his dislike of folk music when

Ronan shushed him. He seemed to be listening to something. Tarl followed suit. He could just make out a distant rhythmic noise which was slowly growing louder. It was the sound of marching feet.

'Oh, not again!' he breathed. 'Not more orcs!' Ronan beckoned silently and the two of them slipped into the dense cover provided by a stone-bush. Gradually, the noise increased as dozens of feet in perfect step grew nearer and nearer. The very floor of the forest shook, and the trees around them vibrated to the rhythm. Louder and louder it grew, until their ears rang and their teeth rattled. Ronan had never heard an army that marched in such perfect step together. Intrigued, he peered out between the leaves of the bush, and then stared in amazement as the feet hove into view.

They were owned by a twenty-feet-high millipede which was barging its way through the forest like a tank, crushing bushes and knocking down any trees that happened to be in its way. Its chitinous armour gleamed in the green light of the forest as its segments ebbed and flowed with peristaltic movement. Its antennae swayed and twirled in front of it, seeking the path of least resistance between the trees, and its jet-black eyes glittered malevolently. Suddenly it came to a halt, and the silence that fell on the forest seemed almost deafening. For a moment the warrior dared not breathe, as the antennae twirled towards him, sifting the air, searching for information. Then the black eyes of the giant creature met his, and the huge mouth opened.

'Afternoon,' it said. 'Nice day.'

Then it was moving again, crashing its way past the stone-bush like an earthquake. The feet seemed to be marching past for minutes, and then at last the millipede was gone, the sound of its passage diminishing until it was just a murmur, like a roll of distant thunder. The whole forest seemed to draw breath in relief.

Tarl opened his eyes and crawled tiredly out into the open. 'I've changed my mind. I think I'd like to go back to Welbug now, if it's all the same to you,' he said.

Ronan smiled. 'Look,' he said. 'We're perfectly safe. I mean, you've got to admit that as giant millipedes go, that one was a real softy.'

'Ha!' snorted Tarl. 'Safe? We're lost in the middle of a forest inhabited by invertebrates the size of a house! I for one do not want to be here when we stumble across a scorpion!'

'We're not lost. I reckon Anthrax has put us in the middle of the Forest of Dreams, right beside the Castle of the Wood-Elves. Listen!'

Once again, Tarl strained his ears. This time, he could hear the sound of a distant trumpet, muted and elegant.

'That's an elven horn,' said Ronan. 'Wood-elves are the kindest and most hospitable of folk. You are going to enjoy tonight!'

'Humph!' grunted Tarl. 'You'd better be right!' But as his friend set off towards the distant sound of the trumpet, he followed with a light heart, for he too had heard of the kindness of wood-elves and their legendary generosity. He'd also heard that they knew how to party.

The elven castle reminded Tarl very much of Welbug. From a distance it looked elegant and welcoming, with its soaring towers and slender turrets glittering in the evening light, and flags and banners fluttering in the breeze. Yet as they neared it they began to see signs of disrepair. One small tower had collapsed into the moat, a second had no tiles on its roof, and a third was leaning at a drunken angle, surrounded by scaffolding. Several windows had been untidily bricked up, and a large area of the front wall had been covered in cheap and nasty-looking stone cladding, which in places was coming away.

When they reached the drawbridge, they found that although lowered, it seemed to be stuck about four feet off the ground, and they had to scramble up on to it. As they walked across, they could see that some large holes had been repaired with ply-wood which had started to peel away. Underneath, the moat contained rather a lot of rubbish, including some broken scaffolding, a lot of empty cement sacks, and an old wheelbarrow.

The massive oak doors were shut. Ronan raised his fist and hammered on the small wicket set within them. 'Now you'll see some typical elvish hospitality,' he smiled to Tarl, and at these words the wicket door burst open and a horde of elven soldiers came pouring out, all waving swords and yelling abuse.

Ronan's reactions were quick. Drawing his sword, he defended himself desperately. Tarl's reactions were even quicker, and he had surrendered before an elf got near him. Despite their numbers the elves were limited by the narrowness of the drawbridge, and their small elven swords were no match for the massive broadsword that Ronan whirled about him. But when one of the elves held his sword to Tarl's throat Ronan was left with little option. Stifling a curse he threw down his weapon and was immediately overpowered.

'Bind the humans in chains and cast them into the lowest dungeon,' yelled the captain of the elven guards, and then he kicked Tarl in the stomach. 'Klatting builders!' he muttered.

Before Ronan or Tarl could so much as blink they were being man-handled through the gates and down a long stone stairway towards the depths of the castle. Tarl couldn't believe it.

'What is this effect you have on everybody?' he yelled back at Ronan, as they were hustled along a dark and chilly passage. One of the elves unlocked a door and Tarl found himself flying through the air towards the hard-looking floor of a sparse stone cell. So much for partying, he thought, and then his head connected with a flag-stone and he knew no more.

As far as Tarl was concerned, he might as well have been partying. The end result was the same – he woke up next morning with a mother of a headache. Groaning, he sat up, and was disappointed to find that it hadn't been some wild dream brought on by over-indulgence. He really was stuck in a gloomy stone-flagged cell lit only by a single flickering torch. In one corner, a small brown rabbit was scratching its nose. Ronan sat nearby, arms fettered, examining a large tray of food on the ground by the door.

'There you are,' he said. 'I told you elves looked after their guests. Check this lot out! Fresh bread, honey, cheeses, elf-cakes, fruit, a flagon of water, and a flagon of wine!'

'Great. And I suppose they're so concerned for our health that they have to lock us up in this dungeon for our own safety! Some hosts! I can't believe it! I mean, slinging us in here for no reason at all . . . that's not the elf justice that's famous the world over!'

'Yeah, well, it seems that . . .'

'Elves are legendary for their enlightened views,' cut in Tarl. 'Legendary! Do you know what happens to you in elven law if you commit adultery? You get stoned!'

Ronan was horrified. 'They throw stones at you? You're joking!'

'No, no, you get really stoned. Stoned out of your mind! You and your lover and the cuckolded partner are locked in a room with an endless supply of elfweed, and you're not allowed out until you've all come to some sort of amicable arrangement. I mean, that is so enlightened it's brilliant!' He paused, shook his head sadly, and then wished he hadn't, as it felt as though the top had come off. 'But slinging folks into dungeons for no reason at all, that's not like them,' he continued. Then a nasty thought struck him. 'Hey – you don't suppose Nekros has got at them, do you?'

Ronan had been patiently waiting to get a word in. 'No,' he said, 'that's not it. While you were out cold I had a bit of a chat with one of the guards. Apparently Albran has had a bad time at the hands of mortal men lately. I take it you noticed the state of the castle when we entered? Well, Albran decided it was time for a spot of renovation, but instead of using elven masons, he brought in this firm of human builders from Carn Betw. They were much cheaper, or something. The problem was, they were crap. They spent half their time sitting round playing cards and making disgusting suggestions to every elf maiden they saw. Then they knocked down some vital supporting walls and the north tower disappeared into the moat. They blocked off the wrong areas, put in doors that didn't fit, and generally made such a mess of the place that Albran refused to pay them any money until they put everything right. So they downed tools and are refusing to come back until Albran pays for the work done so far.'

Tarl winced. 'Yeah, that's pretty bad, but it's not our fault, right?'

'There's more. Feccatun, Albran's favourite daughter, ran off with one of the plasterers. He heard last week that she's pregnant. And then the final straw came two days ago. A couple of travellers called at the castle gates and despite everything, Albran took them in, threw a feast for them, and generally gave them the whole elven hospitality thing. But sometime in the middle of the night they disappeared. And the Elvenstone of Borachim disappeared with them!'

'The what?'

'The Elvenstone of Borachim. Some magic jewel or other that

Albran sets a high store upon. Apparently it's supposed to ensure luck for the royal household.'

'Sounds as though they're better off without it!' Tarl shuffled over to the tray and looked at the array of food and drink. He was starting to feel a little happier. 'So when they realise it's nothing to do with us, they'll let us go, right?' he asked, and helped himself to a couple of cakes.

'I wouldn't be too sure,' said Ronan, pessimistically. 'The guard reckons that although most ordinary elves would be pretty sympathetic to us, the royal family are really pissed off with humans.'

Tarl looked at him sourly. 'Well, anyway, this puts any idea of taking on Nekros out of the question,' he said through a mouthful of cake. 'And thank the gods for that! I mean,' he continued, warming to his theme, 'you're very good when it comes to slicing up orcs, or the average footpad, or other warriors. But the minute you step out of your league, you're screwed! Firstly, Tyson did you. Figuratively and literally. And then Anthrax. And now this gang of elves. What sort of a mess would Nekros have made of you, eh? Well, at least we don't have to worry about that. When Albran decides to let us out, let's just go straight back to Welbug and visit the girls again. We'll be safe enough with Tyson around.'

He paused, and broke off some bread and cheese. It had gone very quiet. He looked up to see Ronan staring at him with the expression of a little boy whose brand new cuddly puppy-dog has just bitten his hand off.

'Well, it needed saying!' he added, grumpily.

'Now, you listen here!' yelled the furious warrior. 'I would have had no trouble with those elves if you hadn't surrendered! We could easily have held them off. But no, not you, first sight of a sword and you're throwing down your own weapon quicker than a . . . than a . . . than something extremely quick,' he finished lamely.

'It's called using your brain. You want to try it sometime.'

'Here, who was it saved your life when those orcs appeared, eh?'

'Puss. Or hadn't you noticed the orc archer?'

'You ungrateful little . . .'

'You big boneheaded muscle-bound . . .'

'Rat-face!'

'Bollock-brain!'

'*Katimo!*'

With an expressionless face Tarl got up and hammered on the door.

'Hey!' he yelled. 'Guard! I want to be moved to a different cell. Preferably rat-infested. I'm not happy with the company in here!'

Behind him Ronan, Vanquisher of Evil and Slayer of Thousands, turned his back on his companion and sat staring sulkily at the wall.

After several hours of silence, Ronan was really beginning to get on Tarl's nerves. They're all the same, these warriors, he thought, as he carefully scratched another dirty limerick on to the wall of the cell with his belt-buckle. Bloody prima donnas! They have to bathe in admiration! Any criticism and we get the big sulks!

As it happened, Ronan wasn't sulking any more. Although Tarl's sudden outburst had hurt his ego, it had also made him think. And he'd been thinking hard for the past few hours. Ronan's big problem was that, since his second year in Warrior School, he'd had things all his own way. Everything in his world had been either black or white, evil or good. If things were good, you left them alone, and if evil, you took them on. And for the past three or four years, everything Ronan had taken on he had beaten. Outlaws and bandits, orcs, mountain-trolls, the odd rogue *lenkat*, whatever. He'd almost come to think of himself as invincible. Now all of a sudden he had been dragged back into the real world. He wasn't invincible at all. An assassin's blade or an orc arrow could easily kill him. A wizard could turn him into a frog with one hand tied behind his back.

And not everything was as black or white as he had grown up believing. Anthrax wasn't a particularly evil guy, yet he'd been prepared to sell them down the river to Nekros. And the wood-elves were basically good guys, yet they'd turned on him. As he'd already discovered, the major problem with being a Vanquisher of Evil is that moral aspect. You can't just cut loose with your sword whenever you feel like it. He wasn't going to be able to carve his way out of the elven castle in a sea of blood. A little more subtlety was called for. The problem was, sublety wasn't Ronan's long suit.

154

He'd also realised that he needed a bit more than brute strength to track down his enemy and kill him. He had always had this image in his mind of his own stern figure facing a terrified Nekros who, after a brief fight, would die screaming on the end of his sword. Now he knew that his enemy was a powerful figure at the heart of a vast organisation. Without help, Ronan stood about as much chance of killing him as that little brown rabbit in the corner did. He'd only been able to get as far as he had because people had helped. For the first time in his life, Ronan was appreciating the value of friends.

But the problem was that, although he needed to talk about this, he was finding it impossible. There was a wall of silence between them and Ronan had no idea how to go about breaking it. Warriors traditionally have a great deal of difficulty in putting a coherent sentence together, especially when it involves express-ing emotions. And while Ronan had a greater facility with words than most of his brethren, he still felt restricted by the macho nature of his calling. Warriors just don't say things like, 'Listen, guy, over the past few days I've really come to value your friendship. We've faced a few dangers together and you've come to mean a lot to me. I love you, guy, so just trust me, and everything will be cool!' Not unless they want to get a Reputa-tion. And so Ronan fretted, and wondered what to do.

It was probably just as well that Ronan didn't try to express his feelings. If he had done, Tarl would probably only have taken it the wrong way. He had heard about some of the things guys do in prison to help pass the time. Anyway, he was quite happy sulking and making up dirty limericks. He had just started on another particularly filthy one (about a young dwarf from Malvenis), when the door of the cell flew open and several elf soldiers marched in. Ignoring Tarl, they hauled Ronan roughly to his feet, bound his hands again, and marched him out through the door and off down the corridor. Tarl leapt up and tried to follow but the guard on the door stopped him.

'Hey,' yelled Tarl after the retreating elves. 'What about me? I want to come too!'

'No, you don't,' said the guard, gently but firmly restraining him. 'Believe me, you really don't.'

Tarl felt a sudden sinking feeling in the pit of his stomach.

'Why not?' he asked. 'Where are they taking him?'

The guard looked a little embarrassed. 'Well, it's the King,' he replied. 'He's announced a new edict. Humans are now a Proscribed Race. And your friend is being taken up to the King's Banquet, where he will be tried and sentenced as the representative of all men.'

'But he'll be all right, won't he? I mean, elven justice and all that . . .'

'He's a member of a Proscribed Race,' repeated the guard, shaking his head doubtfully. 'That means he has no rights, no entitlement to justice. This hasn't happened since the last Orc Wars. Any captured orcs used to be . . .' He stopped, and looked very uncomfortable.

'Used to be what?'

'Thrown unarmed into the Pit of Wolves!' The guard couldn't meet Tarl's shocked gaze. 'I'm sorry!' he said sympathetically, and then shut the door, leaving Tarl alone in the cell.

The elf soldiers marched Ronan purposefully along a short corridor, up some stairs, along another corridor, round a corner . . . and stopped dead. Their passage was barred by a new brick wall – and quite a shoddy-looking wall, at that. The sort of wall that might have been thrown together by a fairly crappy bricklayer who was in an extremely bad mood because he had just lost his entire week's wages to a couple of plasterers in a game of Cydorian Sweat. The captain of the soldiers kicked at it angrily, and threw a glance that could have killed at Ronan. They marched back down the corridor, up some more stairs, through a door, and down a passage that ended at another door. The captain flung this open, and found himself teetering on the brink of a hundred-foot drop straight down into the moat. Whatever bit of the castle had been here previously had now disappeared. With a snarl, he managed to haul himself back and slammed the door behind him.

'I hope they tear you to shreds,' he snapped at Ronan, before leading them all back along the passage and down another spiral staircase. This one led into a long room with exquisite oak panelling on the walls and an elegantly vaulted ceiling. It would have been quite beautiful if someone hadn't painted the panelling lime-green and stippled the ceiling. The captain stared around in horror. This was obviously the first time he had seen this particular piece of redecoration. He walked across to one of the new metal torch-holders which had been fixed slightly crookedly to the wall, and tried to straighten it. It came away in his hand. Cursing, he flung it at Ronan, then marched across the room and tugged at the door on the far side. It swung open to reveal a doorway that had been bricked up even more shoddily than the first passageway. Through the bricks it was possible to hear the sounds of distant revelry.

The elf captain began to tremble slightly, and his complexion turned from a healthy golden-brown tan to a choleric puce colour. He pointed a shaking finger at Ronan and for a moment his lips moved soundlessly. When he did manage to speak it was with a suppressed fury that made Ronan's blood run cold.

'Pick him up!' he hissed to the elf soldiers. 'Pick up that klatting human and break this wall down!'

Ronan found himself grabbed by many hands and lifted into the air. As they swung him back horizontally, the realisation of what they were about to do hit him, and he braced himself. The elves swung him forward like a living battering ram and his head smashed into the bricks blocking the doorway. Luckily, these had been put together so badly (and using such poor quality cement) that his head and shoulders burst through at the first attempt, and he was only semi-stunned. Kicking aside the debris, his guards dragged him through into the Great Hall and flung him to the floor. He lay there for a moment, shaking his aching head to clear it and looking round.

It was a vast place, over a hundred feet in length and packed with elves. Trestle tables ran the length of the room, and at one end, a larger table covered in an ornate cloth was raised on a dais. At this sat King Albran, his wife, Queen Silvana, and their family. All were laughing and feasting except for the King, who sat glowering in the midst of the frivolity. There was little sign of the ravages of the builders, save for a door twenty foot above ground level in the middle of one wall, and several buckets scattered around the floor to catch drips from a roof that now leaked quite badly. The strangest aspect of the scene was the fact that there must have been a couple of hundred rabbits in the room as well, skipping round the floor, hopping along tables, and stealing food. The elves seemed virtually unaware of them.

As Ronan was led into the room, an elven minstrel strummed his lute and began to sing. He was thin and weedy, with a strange haircut, and his whining voice was almost drowned in the general hubbub. Ronan was brought into the centre of the room to stand, arms bound, before the King, and the hum of conversation died away until the minstrel's voice was the only sound. He appeared to be singing about vegetables.

Albran flashed him an unpleasant look, then stood up and turned his attention to Ronan. But before he could say anything, Ronan spoke.

'Noble King,' he said, 'I came here in good faith, to seek your help. I am Ronan, Vanquisher of Evil, and I am on a quest to bring vengeance to Nekros the Black, adherent of the Five Great Demons, and slayer of my father. I seek only your advice and knowledge. I have learnt of the indignity you have suffered at the hands of uncouth builders and churlish guests, which I deeply regret, but as you know, it was none of my doing . . .'

'Nevertheless,' interrupted the King, 'you are a mortal man, and it was your race that did these things.' He glared again at the minstrel, who was warbling about how vegetables were his friends, and about how awful people were for eating them when they could be growing free in the sunlit glades of the forest, with their roots running barefoot through the fragrant soil. The King lifted a browsing rabbit out of a large bowl of mashed turnips. 'Oh, shut up, Morrisey!' he muttered impatiently, and flung the bowl at the minstrel. It bounced off his head with a resounding clang and the waif-like elf fell senseless to the floor. The King turned back to Ronan.

'You are the representative of your race. You must accept the allotted fate on their behalf!' Suddenly, he raised his voice and appealed to the assembled elves. 'How do you find this man?'

'Guilty!' yelled a young elf who was seated at the top table. From his facial resemblance to the King, Ronan thought he was probably one of his sons. His cry was taken up by elves all over the room.

'Guilty!' they yelled, a trifle uncertainly. 'Guilty!'

Ronan studied their faces. Some were genuinely angry, like

their King, but many seemed embarrassed and shame-faced. Still, it rather looked as though what the King wanted, he would get. Ronan sighed, and stared down at the floor. Oh-oh! he thought. He'd just noticed that he was standing on a large trap-door.

The King was surveying his people with a satisfied smile. 'And what is the fate reserved for a guilty member of a proscribed race?' he asked them.

'The Pit of Wolves!' came the answering cry. 'Cast him into the Pit of Wolves!'

The elves were beginning to get a little worked up now. Ronan didn't like this one bit. With an anxious look at the trap-door, he tested his bonds, but they were secure. He glanced sideways, to the guards who stood on either side, spears at the ready.

'The Pit of Wolves!' repeated the King, gleefully. The chant was taken up on all sides of the room, and the elves began to beat rhythmically on the tables with their fists. Ronan could sense the anger and expectation mounting. This was serious! He'd stand no chance against a pack of wolves with his hands tied. If he went for the guard on the left, who was trading glances with that elf maiden at the nearest table . . . he'd get his spear, and he could use that with bound hands. But to get out alive he was going to have to get a hostage . . . maybe the King's son . . . Klat! The King had his hands on that lever! Better do something quickly . . .

But before he could act Queen Silvana rose and lifted one hand commandingly. Silence fell upon the hall as the elves looked to their Queen expectantly, and Ronan watched her in awe. Like all elf women, she was tall and slender, with golden hair and eyes, and she seemed to radiate an aura of beauty and vitality. On her face, however, was the resigned look of a woman who realises only too well that her husband is acting like a complete prat.

'You cannot throw him to the wolves,' she said.

'Of course I can!' blustered her husband. 'I can do anything I like! I'm the King!'

'You cannot throw him to the wolves,' continued Silvana, patiently, 'because we haven't got any wolves. They all died years ago.'

'What? They can't have! I distinctly remember throwing all those orcs to them, oh, three or four years back . . .'

'That was fifty years ago.'

'Good grief! Was it?' The King rounded on his principal adviser, who was stood behind his chair. 'Why haven't they been replaced with stock from the wild?'

'You know damn' well why!' said the Queen. Her patience was beginning to wear a little thin. She started to mimic her husband. '"What can I do to help my people?" you said. "How can I make their lives safer?" you said. "I know," you said, "I'll get rid of all the dangerous animals. All the *lenkats*, the wolves, the bears, the *alaxls*. That will make the forest safe for my people," you said. But you didn't stop there. Oh, no! You had to hunt down every single predatory animal for miles around. Foxes, hawks, wild cats, everything! "It will be safe for my people's flocks," you said. I warned you! I told you what would happen if you started messing around with the ecological balance, but no, you had to go ahead.

'And now look at the result. There's been a population explosion of rabbits, deer and squirrels, because there's nothing left to keep their numbers down. All the forest trees are dying, because the herds of starving deer and the mobs of emaciated squirrels have stripped away every leaf and every last piece of bark that they can reach. And what about us? We have to import fruit and vegetables from vast distances, and why?' She paused and looked down in disgust at a sweet-looking rabbit that had lolloped along the table and was helping itself to the remnants on her plate. 'Because hordes of ravening rabbits eat everything that we try to grow.

'But that's not enough for you, oh no! Not content with wiping out half the species of the forest, now you want to start on any visitors we're lucky enough to get. Well, I for one have HAD ENOUGH!'

With that she stormed out of the door behind their table. The King was left blinking after her. There was a short silence, broken only by foot-shuffling and the odd embarrassed cough. The King turned to his adviser.

'Is that true?' he asked. 'Not even one wolf?'

'I'm afraid not, sire.'

'But isn't there a law or something about keeping the King's Wolf-pit stocked? I'm sure there is . . . how does it go? Blah, blah, blah . . . shall be replaced with the most savage creatures that can be found, blah, blah, blah . . .'

'That's right, sire, and we have done so,' said the advisor.

The King brightened instantly. 'Oh, good!' he said. 'What with?'

'A stoat, sire.'

'A stoat?' said the King, sadly.

'Yes, sire.'

'Just the one?'

'It's all we could find, sire.'

'Oh, well, it will have to do.' Albran turned back, and surveyed his expectant people. 'Throw him to . . . the stoat!' he yelled.

The elves took up the cry, but rather half-heartedly, as though well aware that this punishment lacked a certain something. 'The stoat!' they yelled. 'Throw him to the stoat!'

Without warning, the trap-door under Ronan's feet gave way and he hurtled downwards into the blackness below. He landed awkwardly on a stone-flagged floor, and lay there, winded, straining his eyes to see in the darkness. There was a very faint hissing sound, which raised the hairs on the back of his neck, and his arm muscles bulged as he fought to free himself from his bonds, to no avail.

After a while, his eyes grew accustomed to the gloom. He struggled into a sitting position and looked round. He was in a stone cell about twenty-foot square, with a door of iron bars set into one wall. Beyond this, a dank passage stretched away to a corner around which a faint glimmer of light showed. In one corner of the cell was a little pile of straw and there, on the straw, was the stoat.

It was a very old stoat, and patently unwell. It just lay there with its eyes shut, its flanks heaving, its breath coming in little hissing gasps. Occasionally it sneezed. It seemed to have no desire to try tearing Ronan limb from limb, and anyway, even at the peak of its powers and standing on tiptoe, it would only have reached up to his knee.

Ronan sighed and shook his head. He wasn't altogether sure that he shared Tarl's admiration for the legendary elven justice.

'And then he said, "I don't know whether to go for the pink or the brown!"' Tarl sat back with a grin on his face and waited for this punch-line to take effect. There was a long pause, then the elven guard's face creased up and he started to laugh, great hiccuping guffaws that echoed around the cell.

'Pink or brown!' he chuckled. 'Thash ver' ver' funny! Pink or brown!' Eventually his paroxysm of mirth died away and a look of puzzlement began to creep over his face like the tide creeping up a very steep beach. 'Er . . .' he said. 'Juss one thing. Wash thish, er, thish shnooker, when it'sh at home?' And he peered at Tarl blearily.

Tarl studied the guard's face. The lights are on, but there's no-one at home, he thought. One more drink ought to do it! He raised his mug. 'To snooker!' he said.

The guard raised his mug as though it weighed several hundred pounds. 'To shnooker!' he replied, and drained it in one gulp. And then his eyeballs rolled back in his head, and he fell to the floor in a heap and started to snore.

Tarl smiled, mentally patting himself on the back. The guard had been quite suspicious when Tarl had invited him into the cell for a drink, but had seemed quite reassured when Tarl offered him the flagon of water. Of course, he wasn't to know that Tarl had emptied the stash of salt that he carried into the water. Tarl hadn't been sure whether his home-made brine would have the same effect on an elf as sea-water, but after the guard's first sip, he'd realised it was going to work. And now, three mugs of brine later, the guard was as drunk as a *vart*, and out cold.

Carefully Tarl removed the large bunch of keys from the elf's belt, undid his fetters and crept to the door. He could hear no sound outside. Ever so gently, he pulled the door open, peered out – and found himself staring at the chest of the most regal and beautiful elven lady he had ever seen. He looked up, straight into a wondrous pair of golden eyes, and quickly pasted his cheesy grin into place.

'Hi!' he said, ingratiatingly. 'Care for a mug of water?'

Ronan had spent over an hour sitting on the floor, racking his brains for some sort of idea, and had just about admitted total defeat when he realised that the glimmer of light along the corridor was getting brighter. He stood up and crossed to the bars of the door. He couldn't hear any footsteps, but that didn't mean much, as elves were remarkably light on their feet, and so he stood and waited. Whatever his immediate fate was, things really couldn't get much worse.

A sudden blaze of light dazzled his eyes and he screwed them up against the glare. An elf carrying a flaming torch had come round the corner and was approaching the cell.

'Ronan?' The voice was soft and gentle, a little worried, and seemed somehow strangely familiar. Ronan cudgelled his memory, and then as the elf slotted the torch into a wall-holder near the door and the light flooded his face, everything clicked into place.

'Yo! Vosene!' Ronan grinned at the elven hairdresser as he fumbled with a bunch of keys. 'What brings you here?'

'Well, somebody had to do something!' answered the elf, a little irritably. There was a click as the key turned, and he swung open the door and drifted into the cell. 'And you're obviously incapable of looking after yourself. I mean, just look at the state of your hair!'

Ronan smiled inwardly and held out his fettered hands. The elf tutted. 'If you don't get to a good manicurist soon, your nails will be ruined! Ruined!' he said. Another key turned, and the chains fell to the floor.

'So what are you doing here?' Ronan asked, rubbing his wrists.

Vosene smiled proudly. 'I'm Queen Silvana's personal hair stylist,' he said. 'Well, I had to leave Port Raid. I mean the place is just going to the absolute dogs, dear. Southrons and orcs moving in, all sorts of strange laws being passed . . . an elf just wasn't safe out at night. Now, you come with me. We mustn't keep our Queenie waiting. She's expecting you.'

He led Ronan along the dank stone passage, past cellars and wine-stores, and through a labyrinth of little corridors, until at last he paused before a small wooden door. 'Through here,' he said, 'and up the stairs. Then along the passage to the left, and the fourth door is the Chart Room. You'll find Queenie in there!'

'Thanks, Vosene!' said Ronan, and slapped him on the back so hard he nearly knocked him over. 'I owe you one.'

The elf raised an arch eyebrow. 'I can hardly wait,' he replied. And then he patted Ronan's arm, and with a muttered 'Good luck, dear', was gone, gliding off down the passageway into the darkness.

*

The Chart Room was long and low-ceilinged, with wooden racks and shelves on all four walls holding pile upon pile of dust-covered parchments and scrolls. Cobwebs festooned the walls, and in the centre of the room was a single broad table. When Ronan gingerly pushed open the only door and peered in, he was amazed to find the Queen leaning over the table, poring over an ancient map, with Tarl at her side. She looked up and smiled at him, and he was almost overwhelmed by her beauty.

'Your Majesty,' he said, awed and bowing low.

Tarl winked at the Queen. 'I'm sorry about this, Silvie,' he said. 'The poor lad suffers from delusions of inadequacy.'

Ronan stared at him, appalled by this familiarity, but to his surprise the Queen didn't seem to mind.

'Please accept my humblest apologies,' she said. 'Our treatment of you has been shameful. I'm afraid my husband isn't himself.'

'No, no, it is quite understandable! What with your daughter, and those klat . . . er, those foul builders, and the Elvenstone . . .'

'Oh, we're not really worried about Feccatun,' smiled the Queen. 'She's run off with a nice boy, and it will be pleasant to have a grandchild. And as for the Elvenstone, well, that was no loss. I'll let you into a little secret.' She leaned forward, and spoke in lowered tones. 'It was paste! I had an imitation made some months ago, and then sold the original. You see, it was a horrible thing, really ugly, and of no use whatsoever. And with the castle needing so many repairs, I thought the money would come in useful. But then Albran has to try and cut corners by employing the biggest load of bandits in the west as builders. And now the castle is in a worse state than ever. That's what is really irking him. But it's his own fault. I'm afraid I've run out of sympathy.'

'So Silvie is making amends by helping us,' said Tarl. 'We've been looking at charts. Dwarfish charts. There's two of them. This one shows how to find some vast underground city in the mountains of the Dwarf Lands. The entrance is here, look, above the town of Carn Betw.' He pointed at the faded parchment that was laid out on the table.

'That must be Samoth,' said Ronan. 'The lost city of the dwarves, carved deep under the mountains from the living stone.

It is said that they abandoned it years ago.' He studied the map for a few moments, and his face creased into a frown. 'But I cannot see how this can help me in my quest,' he said.

'Ah,' said Tarl, unrolling a filthy, bewebbed scroll. 'But just look at this second chart. It's a large-scale map of Samoth, and look here, near the north end of the city, next to this cavern that's labelled the Bridge of Eldabad.'

'What is it?' asked Ronan, taking the scroll. He looked where Tarl was pointing, and his eyes blazed. 'The Cavern of the Singing Sword!' he gasped.

'So what do you reckon, hey?' asked Tarl, proudly. 'Have we struck gold, or have we struck gold?' All of a sudden, he was caught up in the excitement of the quest again. 'Where is this Carn Betw?' he asked, turning to the Elven Queen.

'It is built on an island downstream, outside the boundaries of the forest,' she replied. 'The River Betw flows through caves beneath the castle. There was much trade along the river between the town and castle . . . or there was in the days when we had things to trade. Now they send us wines, food, clothing, and in return we send them rabbit meat, rabbit fur, and live rabbits.' She sighed sadly.

At that moment, they heard the sound of distant trumpets, raised in an urgent, insistent call. The Queen rushed to the door with Ronan at her side and listened for a moment. In the distance they could hear the sound of many scampering feet. 'They have discovered your escape,' gasped the Queen. 'Quick, there is no time to waste! Follow me!'

With that she was gone, fleeing down the passage. Ronan followed her, and Tarl quickly rolled up both the charts, pocketed a small leather-bound book that had caught his eye, and scrambled after them.

Ronan was waiting in an archway at the end of the passage. 'Have you got the scrolls?' he yelled, urgently.

'No,' yelled back Tarl, 'it's just the way I'm walking!' Giggling hysterically to himself, he rushed past Ronan and charged up some stairs after Silvana. She was waiting for them at the top, holding open a thick oaken door.

'Straight down the passage and left at the end,' she told them. 'Through the door is a set of stairs that takes you right down to a postern gate on to the moat. Then head west. Quick! I'll lock this door behind you.'

The door clicked shut behind them. Ronan and Tarl sped down the corridor and round the corner – and found that the builders had struck again. The passageway was totally bricked up. Behind them distant shouts could be heard. Ronan jerked open the nearest door, found yet another set of stairs, and dashed up them with Tarl at his heels.

At the top they paused and eased open the door. It led into the Great Hall. The place was deserted save for a couple of hundred rabbits, which were polishing off the remains of the banquet, and for the elven minstrel Morrisey, who was sitting in a corner nursing a lump on his head the size of an apple. Quietly, gingerly, they picked their way through the overturned tables and spilt crockery towards a door on the other side. Then, when they were some ten paces short, the vast double doors at the far end of the Hall opened and the King strode in, followed by some thirty guards.

At first he was so busy issuing instructions that he didn't even notice his two escaped prisoners. But then Tarl discovered one of those immutable laws of nature. Whenever you desperately need to keep completely, totally silent, you are going to make the most God-awful racket. Although he could have sworn that he hardly moved a muscle, he somehow managed to knock over an entire table. For a moment, as plates, cups, bottles and rabbits cascaded to the floor, the elves stared at them in amazement, and then all hell broke loose.

Tarl stood rooted to the spot in horror as the elves charged at them, snarling with fury. Ronan grabbed him and leapt for the door. They burst through with arrows skipping and whizzing about them and slammed it shut. Dropping Tarl, Ronan thrust the bolt home, and then grabbed a heavy wooden table and wedged it against the stout oak door.

'That should hold them for a couple of minutes,' he panted. 'Let's get out of here.'

'How?' asked Tarl.

Ronan gazed round. They were standing in a large kitchen, which was remarkably well supplied with pots, pans, dishes, and implements of every description. Unfortunately, when it came to such things as windows and doors the room was woefully under-supplied. Apart from the door they had burst through, there wasn't one to be seen. They were stuck in a dead end.

Behind them there was a massive crash, and the oaken timbers creaked under the strain. The elves were beginning to hammer their way in.

In an expensively furnished room in a southern city, six smartly dressed men were discussing the progress of their strategy when a deferential underling hurried in and handed a message to the man at the head of the table. He scanned it expressionlessly and then cleared his throat gently. The others were instantly silent.

'Gentlemen,' he said, 'it would seem that we have another slight setback. Influenced by Tyson and the events in Welbug, the citizens of Minas Welvair have risen up. Apparently our people have had to flee for their lives. We have lost control of both cities.'

'Then should we not order Nekros to stay in the east?' asked one of the others.

'Without him and his tribe, the rising in Port Raid cannot succeed. He must be there in five days' time. The east will have to wait.'

'What does Anthrax advise?'

There was a slight pause. 'Acquisitions informs us that Anthrax has, for the moment, ah, withdrawn his services from our employ.'

'But without the Wizard we are half blind! No one else has such power!'

'We shall manage. Our plans are already made.'

'But what if Albran fails us?'

'He will not. The black warrior is trapped. Within minutes, he will be dead.'

In the kitchen Ronan was pacing round, examining everything, seeking some inspiration. Tarl had been helping him until he found a bottle of Balroger champagne, after which he had helped himself. Outside the door the elves had redoubled their efforts. The wood was beginning to splinter and was obviously about to give way.

Then Ronan noticed a hatchway that was set at floor level in one wall and was hidden behind a row of waste-bins. He pushed them to one side and hauled it open. Inside he could see a stone chute that disappeared downwards into darkness. Cold air wafted up, and he could just make out the sound of running water.

'Tarl,' he called. 'Look at this! It must be the waste disposal chute. I think it must go straight down into the River Betw.'

'So what use is a waste disposal chute? This bottle isn't empty yet.'

'It's a way out.'

Tarl shook his head. 'Sorry,' he said obstinately, 'but you're not getting me down there. I might hurt myself.'

Ronan ducked as an arrow whizzed through a hole in the oak door. 'It is just a slide,' he said. 'It may be dark, but it's nothing to be scared of!'

'Listen, I'm not scared! You're talking to a man who has been down the Suislide at the Welbug Summer Fair, and gone back for more. This is nothing!'

'So what's the problem?' asked Ronan.

Tarl looked a bit ashamed. 'I can't swim,' he muttered.

Ronan's eyes swept round the room and lit on a barrel that was standing nearby. 'In here!' he said, and dragged Tarl across to it by the arm. Tarl looked as though he was about to argue, but when Ronan took the top off, he peered inside and just nodded.

'OK,' he said, and climbed into the barrel clutching the bottle in one hand. Ronan thrust the elven charts in after him, hammered the lid into place with a wooden mallet that was hanging on the wall with other kitchen implements, and then trundled the barrel across to the chute.

As he did so the door burst open, and several armed elf soldiers tumbled into the room. Ronan gave the barrel a shove. It disappeared down the chute, and with a triumphant yell he hurled himself after it into the darkness.

THE DWARF LANDS

It is said that dwarves initially came unto the Western Lands during the First Age, led by three brothers. Each brother settled in a different place with his followers, who proclaimed him their King or, in the dwarf-tongue, their Tarse.

The first brother, Thrombin, settled in the High Mountains, and so was known as the Mountain Tarse. The second brother, Rennin, chose the banks of the Great River as his domain, and thus did his followers call him the River Tarse. The third brother, who was named Acetylcholin, was by a good head the smallest. He settled on the shores of the Western Sea, and thus did they call him the Shore Tarse . . .

The Pink Book of Ulay

Carn Betw. was originally a town built by men, but being situated where it was, it had become somewhat more cosmopolitan. Over the years, dwarves had moved in from the mountains that rise immediately to its west, as had elves from the Forest of Dreams to the east, and now the three races had lived here in harmony for so long that most of them thought of themselves not as dwarves, or elves, or men, but just as the people of Carn Betw.

The town was built on an island, where the River Betw widened and slowed, and many folk earned their living by fishing its deep, productive waters. Others crossed the waters each day to work the fertile small-holdings that lined the river banks, or to ride the mile or two to the many vineyards that covered the foothills of the mountains.

Late in the afternoon, a group of fishermen were mending their nets on the shore of the island, beneath the grey stone walls of the town. They were deep in conversation when one of them pointed a surprised finger at the river and cried, 'Look!'

A man was crawling from the water. A large, muscular man

with black skin and long dark pleats of hair that hung like drowned snakes about his shoulders. He was gasping for air and seemed nearly spent. But it was not he who so surprised the fishermen, it was the barrel to which he had been clinging in the water. For it was singing to itself.

The tallest of the fishermen made a sign in the air, to ward off the evil eye. ''Tis surely enchanted,' he exclaimed. 'A singing barrel! Whoever heard of such a thing!'

'My grand-sire spoke of wonders like this,' answered one of his friends. 'Have you not heard of the Chattering Boulder of Aethelbar, which poked fun at passers-by, and recited poetry backwards?'

He paused, as the barrel was getting rather loud. It was warbling a rather off-key ditty about an elven girl called Kailey, who liked it twelve times daily. Exhaustedly, the large man hauled himself upright and dragged the barrel on to the shore. Then he turned and called to the fishermen.

'I am Ronan,' he said. 'Please help me! I fear something has happened to my friend here!'

Most of the fishermen turned away, pretending not to have heard. A half-drowned warrior who claimed to be friends with a talking barrel was not the sort of person they wanted to get mixed up with. But one, an elf called Bewel, stood and walked down the shore to the water-line, where Ronan was vainly trying to prise the lid of the barrel off with his bare fingers.

'Let me,' said Bewel, and taking his knife from his belt, he inserted it between the lid and the barrel sides, and twisted it. There was creaking sound, the lid shot off, and a bedraggled and red-stained figure slowly straightened up from inside and stood smiling blearily at them. It was holding some sodden parchments to its chest.

'Tarl,' gasped Ronan, worriedly. 'Are you hurt?'

He reached out a hand, touched Tarl's arm, and looked at the red liquid on his fingers. Tarl followed his gaze.

'S'all right,' he slurred. 'S'only red wine. Th'barrel was a quarter full with red wine.'

Ronan sighed with relief. 'But why didn't you tell me?' he said. 'I could have emptied it!'

'Exactly! The wine was the only reason I got in the klatting barrel in the first place!' Tarl hiccuped gently, and a slow but happy smile spread across his face.

Bewel had been studying Ronan thoughtfully. 'Good Ronan,' he said, 'are you that Ronan of whom I have heard travellers from the north speak? The warrior who seeks out and destroys all that is evil?'

Ronan smiled. He was still young and inexperienced enough to get an immense buzz from being famous. 'I do what I can,' he said, trying (and totally failing) to sound cool and matter-of-fact.

'But you are tired and hungry, I will not weary you with questions now. My name is Bewel, and my father has a lodging-house in the town. You would be welcome to rest there tonight.'

'We have no money,' said Ronan. He was dead beat, and the thought of a comfortable bed with cool sheets was immensely appealing, but he'd discovered that honesty was the best policy. It saved a lot of bother in the long run . . . threats, law-suits, tears, climbing down knotted sheets, that sort of thing.

'You would be our guests. But you could repay me, if you wish, with your advice. There is a matter that bothers me and some of my friends. Tomorrow, on the Feast-day of Saint Ufmir when no man works, we meet to decide how best to solve this thing. The advice of a renowned warrior such as yourself would be of immense help!'

'You have a deal.' Ronan looked down at Tarl, who had slumped over the side of the barrel and had started to snore. 'Now, if you could help me with my friend here . . .'

Bewel beckoned to the other fishermen, who ambled interestedly across. They folded a net into a make-shift hammock, which four of them held between them, and then with Tarl slung in this like a large and drunken salmon, they led Ronan up the shore and through the gates of the town.

When Ronan woke next morning, the sun was already high in the sky. Its rays were streaming through the window of the tiny bedroom, warming the two scrolls that the warrior had spread out to dry on a little table the night before. He leapt out of bed and examined them worriedly. The wine stains were pretty bad, but some of the two charts could still be made out. On the whole, it could have been worse.

The door opened, and Tarl wandered in, chewing on a large piece of bread. His hair was totally unkempt and his complexion would have made a zombie look healthy, but by his own disturbing parameters he was looking quite well. Ronan shook his head. He was amazed at Tarl's tolerance for alcohol. He knew damn' well that if he'd drunk the best part of a quarter of a barrel of wine yesterday, right now his head would have been banging like an outhouse door.

'Look what I've got,' said Tarl, holding up the small leather-bound book that he'd 'liberated' from Albran's castle.

'What is it?' asked the warrior.

'*The Beginner's Guide to Magic*,' answered Tarl. 'I found it in the Chart Room. I thought I'd see if Anthrax was right. I mean, you've seen what happens sometimes. It would be pretty smart if I did have the Power and could control it!'

Ronan smiled. 'You'll have to read it later,' he said. 'Right now, we're due to meet Bewel. Come on!'

They hurried down the steep stairs, pausing to bid good morning to Bewel's mother, who was arranging flowers in a vase on the hall table. Outside, the narrow cobbled street was quiet, with just a few people sauntering along in the sunlight. To Tarl's surprise, everyone in sight appeared to be carrying a brightly coloured bucket.

'Good morning,' said Ronan to the first man they passed.

'Good morning to you, good sirs,' he replied, 'and a happy feast-day!' And lifting up his bucket, he poured a stream of thick, lumpy, white stuff all over Tarl.

The two friends stood there dumbfounded as the man strode off up the street, gaily whistling. Tarl grimaced as the glutinous gunge oozed down the inside of his shirt. 'What the . . .' he began, and then stopped as an elderly woman approached. She too was holding a gaudy bucket.

'Good morning to you,' she called to them. 'Am I right in thinking that you are strangers in our fair city?'

'That we are, lady,' replied Ronan.

'Then you must join us in our celebrations,' she carolled, and Tarl blinked as once again a bucket full of white gunge was emptied over his head. 'Happy feast-day, and may you enjoy your stay amongst us!' she bade them. Then she was trotting off up the street, leaving Tarl literally squirming with discomfort.

'Listen,' he said bitterly to Ronan. 'Don't talk to anyone. Don't smile at anyone. And if anyone comes near us, just punch their lights out before they can open their mouth. Old ladies, little kids, anyone! Got it?' And with that he turned and squelched off down the street, leaving a trail like a large and dispirited slug. Ronan followed, trying desperately not to laugh.

The Feast-day of Saint Ufmir the Unlucky at Carn Betw is surely one of the strangest and most curious of celebrations. *The Pink Book of Ulay* has this to say on the subject:

Born in Carn Betw, Ufmir the Unlucky was the first martyr of the Religious age. A deeply unlucky man for all of his short life, he was arrested one day for causing a breach of the peace after setting fire to a market stall by accidentally knocking over a paraffin lamp when a runaway oxen trod on his foot. On the day of his court case, however, he found himself on trial for heresy, when the presiding judge was given the wrong set of papers after an eagle had attacked the court usher in the gents' washroom, causing him to drop the files of the day's cases. Ufmir was unable to point out this mistake, having lost his voice after a mix-up in a tavern had presented him with neat Aqua Regis instead of his usual dry martini, and his defence lawyer had not yet arrived, having been mugged and savagely beaten on his way to court by a pack of renegade nuns. As a result, Ufmir was sentenced to death.

The mistake was, of course, discovered, and a reprieve was awaiting him at the appointed place of execution. Unfortunately, Ufmir never arrived there. He attempted to escape on the way, and while being pursued through the kitchens of Carn Betw's largest restaurant, tripped over the head chef's pet vart, and fell head-first into a large vat of freshly prepared mayonnaise. This would not have mattered, had it not been for the fact that an inexperienced commis-chef had turned on the wrong switch, and the mayonnaise had been steadily heating up, unnoticed for the past hour. When Ufmir fell into it, it was boiling – and seconds later, so was he.

All this would probably have gone unnoticed but for the strange events at his funeral. Large crowds of maimed and injured people had gathered to watch the funeral procession and make sure that Ufmir really was dead, and the streets were thronged. The hearse was unable to make progress, and so his pall-bearers decided to proceed on foot. Unluckily, all six had contracted Griffiths Syndrome, a highly infectious disease which afflicts the sufferer with temporary blindness when under stress. Unable to see clearly, they lost their way, stumbled along alleyways and through doors, and ended up blundering into a carpet warehouse. After barging around corridors and up staircases for half an hour they decided to stop for a rest, and thankfully lowered Ufmir's coffin on to a handy ledge. Unfortunately, this turned out to be a third-floor window-ledge. Ufmir and his coffin slid gracefully off and hurtled groundwards, landing with full force on the head of Lazlo the Lascivious, ruler of Carn Betw, and killing him stone dead.

As Lazlo was quite definitely the most hated ruler the town had ever known, the citizens were delighted, and an impromptu celebration broke out that lasted all day. Since then, Ufmir's memory has been venerated in the town by the Feast-day of Saint Ufmir, when they honour him by throwing large, gaily painted buckets of curdled mayonnaise over any stranger they meet.

Despite Tarl's instructions, he and Ronan were accosted three more times on their way to the tavern where they had arranged to meet Bewel. In each case, the person wished them a happy feast-day, took one look at Ronan, and emptied their bucket over Tarl. He couldn't say he really blamed them for picking him rather than the warrior, but even so, by the time they reached the tavern he was in such an ugly mood that the first person to speak to him was likely to have their head forcibly shoved inside their beer-glass.

Although Bewel had told Ronan that he hoped the meeting would be well attended and would last all morning, there were only two people sitting with him, an elf and a man. From their faces it looked as though the meeting hadn't been a great success, but Bewel leapt up with a glad cry when he saw them enter.

'Ronan! I am glad you came!' he said. 'These are my good friends, Megfal and Parvorchis.' The elf and the man smiled and nodded, and Bewel called across to the tavern-owner. 'Drongo, drinks all round, and a mayonnaise-brush for our friend here!' He grinned at Tarl. 'I see you've been joining in with the festivities.'

Tarl opened his mouth for a reply that would probably have been unprintable, but Ronan cut in hastily. 'How did your meeting go,' he asked, 'and how can I advise you?'

The elf's face fell again and he shook his head tiredly. 'We have a major problem in Carn Betw,' he said, 'but the townsfolk just ignore it. They hide their heads in the sand. But something must be done. You see, it's like this . . .'

For as long as anyone could remember, he told them, the dragon Philekazan had inhabited a system of caves high in the mountains to the north-west of Carn Betw. At first, his frequent visits to the town had caused no trouble. He was not a large dragon, being a mere twenty feet in length, and he was both young and friendly. In fact, he had been a positive boon as tourists had flocked to see him, bringing much wealth to the town. But more recently, as he matured, things had changed.

The dragon now came to the town about once a month for a night out. He would visit several taverns or wine-bars and then fly home. The trouble was, not only was he incredibly rich (for like all dragons, he had a vast hoard of treasure hidden in his lair), but he was also stunningly handsome and devastatingly charming. As a result, the young women of the town mobbed him, and every time he left, he took one of the prettiest with him. And no one would ever see her again.

'We have never found out what happens to these girls,' said Bewel. 'Are they all living in the caves, a happy community of dragon groupies? Or does he use them and cast them out, to roam the world in their disgrace? Are they alive, even? When last he was here, I confronted him, but no answer would he give. I have to say he is utterly charming, and yet there is a hint of the dissolute about him and I trust him not. This sad waste of our womenfolk must cease! But when we try to convince our neighbours that the dragon should be barred from the town, they refuse to listen. They are more interested in the money that he brings in than in the safety of our sisters. We must act, alone if needs be. But what should we do? You are a man of action. Advise us!'

The elf and his two friends were staring at Ronan with something akin to hero-worship, and he suddenly realised he was feeling hideously embarrassed. He cleared his throat and assumed what he hoped was a fierce, no-nonsense expression.

'If the dragon is harming these girls, then he is evil and deserves to die. So you must kill him.'

'But how do we find out? And what if he isn't?'

'Well . . . erm . . .' Once again Ronan was faced with a moral dilemma. Good guys don't kill dragons who might quite possibly have a perfectly reasonable excuse. You need proof that they've been up to no good before you lop their heads off.

Tarl had at last managed to remove most traces of rancid mayo from his clothing and was watching Ronan's discomfiture with enjoyment. Now he decided to lend a hand.

'It's easy,' he said. 'You want to know what the dragon is up to in his lair? Then go there. If the girls are all right, you'll find them. If they aren't, you may find a clue. And you can always just sit there and refuse to budge until he comes clean. Easy.'

To judge from the look on his face, Bewel found the idea of bearding the dragon in his own lair a little forbidding, and Ronan couldn't help but feel sorry for him.

'This is good advice,' he said. 'I would come with you, but I have my own quest and time is pressing. This very afternoon I must leave and seek a way into Samoth . . .' He paused, as Bewel was staring at him excitedly.

'Samoth?' the elf repeated. 'The ancient underground city of the dwarves? But I know the way! I can lead you! Fifteen years ago, I was with my father when he was the guide for a group of dwarves who wished to re-colonise it. They were led by Pectin of Unch Haven. The southern entrance is but two hours' ride from here.'

Ronan began to say how grateful he would be, but the excited elf gabbled on.

'And of course, then you will be able to help us. Because the caves inside the entrance to Samoth are the very caves where the dragon lives! You can show us how to deal with Philekazan, and then proceed with your quest. We will meet you at my father's house at noon. Come, Parvorchis, Megfal, we have much to do to be ready in time!'

He leapt up, and after shaking Ronan's hand several times with great exuberance and thanking him over and over again, he dashed out, accompanied by his two friends.

Ronan stared after them, feeling vaguely out-manoeuvred. Ah, well, the dragon shouldn't be too much of a problem, and he was still on course for his quest. He realised that Tarl was looking at him with disbelief and held up his hands defensively.

'All right. All right, I'm sorry about the dragon. But he doesn't sound too bad. And at least we don't seem to have people trying to kill us any more. We should be able to slip out of Carn Betw quietly. We'll be perfectly safe.'

Tarl didn't deign to reply, but merely sighed deeply and cast his eyes heavenwards. Orc ambushes, double-crossing wizards, nutty elven kings, and now a philandering dragon. This had to be some strange new usage of the word 'safe'.

When Nekros had been told of Ronan's escape from the castle of the wood-elves, he had lost his temper. This had resulted in him decapitating two of his men and trashing his bedroom. Now, as the Tribe prepared to ride west, he was sitting cross-legged in the fragments of his bed, trying to coax a crystal ball into working properly.

'So find him!' he yelled. The crystal fizzed and sputtered and the image faded for a moment. He thumped it hard and it flickered back into life. 'Find him, follow him and kill him! Use Bonaponere or Kaldis, they live in Carn Betw!' There was a loud buzzing sound. The air filled with a horrid burning stench, and then the crystal went dark. Swearing, Nekros threw it hard at the wall and stormed out, pausing only to lop off the head of another of his men.

I must stop doing that, he thought as he strode down the stairs. If I get much more bad news, I'll be arriving in Port Raid at the head of an army of seven.

Ronan and Bewel strode purposefully down the main street towards the Water Gate, with a reluctant Tarl slouching along behind them. Unfortunately, they weren't getting much of a chance to slip out unnoticed. Bewel and his two friends had organised a bit of a demonstration. There were quite a lot of young people waving banners that said things like 'Save our Sisters' and 'Dragons Out of Carn Betw', and a number of holiday revellers had joined them, thinking that it must be some sort of festive parade. And so, although you couldn't say that the whole town was giving them a rousing send-off, there were quite a few people cheering and emptying buckets of white gunge over each other. One or two even threw flowers into the road. It was almost a hero's farewell.

Yet Tarl didn't notice. For, as he slouched along in the rear, he had his nose buried in the *Beginner's Book of Spells*. And he was riveted. He had opened it an hour ago, to take his mind off the huge flock of dragon-sized butterflies that had taken up residence in his stomach, and he had been immediately captivated. There were spells for just about everything. Spells to improve beer, spells to defend yourself, spells to guarantee good luck at the gaming table, spells to attract women . . . it could have been written with him in mind! He decided he'd try an experiment.

His opportunity came at the Water Gate. The others had already passed through and boarded the swan-like elven-boat moored at the quay. As Tarl went to follow them, a sentry rudely shoved him backwards.

'Here, where do you think you're going?' he sneered at Tarl.

'It's all right,' called Bewel from the boat, 'he is the friend of the warrior here!'

'What?' said the sentry. 'This filthy little half-orc? Who'd have thought it!' Grudgingly, he lowered his halberd and let Tarl pass.

Right, mate, you've asked for it! thought Tarl. He could remember the words of the Spell of Mild Revenge that he'd just read, and so he muttered, 'May your innards liquefy and your bowels turn to water!' followed by the Word of Power that the book listed. Then he stared at the sentry expectantly. The sentry just stared blankly and stonily into space.

Huh! thought Tarl, disappointedly, as he followed the others into the boat. So much for having the Power!

He would have been much happier if he had known that the reason the sentry was staring blankly and stonily into space was because something unpleasant and extremely messy had just happened inside his underwear, and he was wondering what the hell the sergeant would do to him when he found out that he'd shit himself while on duty.

The first stages of their journey to the dragon's lair passed pleasantly enough. On disembarking from the boat, they found horses waiting for them at a riverside farm. As they rode north-west through rolling farmland and gently sloping vineyards they talked and sang. For Bewel this was a great adventure, and he listened open-mouthed in wonder as Ronan and Tarl told him stories of far-off places, of days spent tracking down rogue trolls in the Northern Mountains, or of nights spent literally dicing with death in the casinos of Orcville.

By the time they left the cultivated areas behind them, Tarl was in a rare good mood. Few things cheered him up more than a captive audience. He began to teach his companions all seventeen verses of 'Kailey', the song he'd been singing when they let him out of the barrel, and the sound of three young voices raised in ribald chorus echoed around the mountains. But then, as the path climbed even higher, and the green grass and pretty wildflowers gave way to barren, cracked rock and tumbled boulders, their voices fell away uncertainly.

After a while, Tarl reined in his horse to look at the view behind them. They were very high now, and although the mountains hemmed them in on three sides, to the east the land was spread out like a table-cloth below. Carn Betw looked like an ant-hill in the middle of the thin thread of silver that was the River Betw. Beyond it, the Forest of Pigeons spread out, separated from the Forest of Dreams in the distance by the strip of cultivated lands through which ran the Southern Highway. Sighing, he turned and urged his horse on after the others.

All at once, the narrow path breasted a rise in the ground, and led them into a shallow barren valley running from north-east to south-west. Through it an ancient road ran as straight as a die. It was cracked and broken, with tufts of *pata* grass growing through it, yet the craftsmanship and skill that had gone into its construction could still be plainly seen.

'This is the ancient road that ran from Unch Haven to Samoth,' said Bewel. 'We have not far to go now.' But when he urged his horse forwards it dug in its hooves and neighed skittishly.

'He scents the dragon,' said Ronan. His own mount was snorting nervously and the whites of its eyes were plain to see. 'We had best leave them here,' he continued, and dismounted.

They hobbled the horses, leaving them chewing unhappily at the clumps of *pata*, and carried on on foot. Although the valley began to slope steeply upwards, the even surface of the road made walking easy and they made good time. It was less than half an hour before the road led them around a spur of the mountain, and they found themselves looking up to the entrance of the dragon's cave.

It was plain to see that once this had been the gateway to some mighty underground city. The vast archway above was carved into beautiful designs, at the heart of which were the stylised shapes of the four tools of the dwarf; hammer, axe, chisel, and adze. All were inlaid with both light and dark marble, which glittered in the afternoon sun. At the sides of the entrance, huge hinges the size of a man were carved from the living stone, but of the doors there was no trace. They had been shattered into fragments by some arcane black mage-spell long ago, during the Siege of Samoth. Now, the gaping maw of the cave was open to the valley. A thin plume of smoke eddied out and a small trickle of water splashed over the rim, wetting the wide but graceful semi-circular steps that led down to the road.

Tarl looked up at the vast portal uneasily. He was suddenly aware that there was neither sight nor sound of any living creature in the valley save themselves. The silence was broken only by their footsteps and by the trickle of water. He turned to Bewel.

'Are you sure this dragon is friendly?' he asked. The elf nodded, but doubtfully. He seemed ill at ease. Only Ronan was unaffected by the air of menace that seemed to hang over them.

'Come on,' he said, 'it's only a dragon!' And climbing the steps he strode into the blackness, with the others following nervously behind.

Back down the ancient road, their horses were being examined by a couple of very unpleasant characters.

'The elf has left most of his gear,' said the first one. 'Looks like he'll be coming back. The other two must be heading through Samoth. Excellent! This will be easy. They won't know what hit them. Come on, Kaldis.'

And with that Bonaponere and Kaldis strode down the road in pursuit of Ronan and his friends.

Jeremy, the Beadle of Carn Betw, loved the Feast-day of Saint Ufmir. Every year, as soon as dawn had broken, he would be out stalking the streets with keen anticipation, bucket in hand, searching for strangers. But then, Jeremy was that type of person. Whenever he was about, people who smoked would find their pipes exploding, or emitting evil-smelling black fumes. Stink-bombs would go off, and folk would find themselves sitting on drawing-pins. Itching-powder would mysteriously appear in new shirts, and buckets of water would be propped on top of doors. And everyone who visited the latrines would have to check them out very, very carefully indeed. Jeremy just knew that he had a wonderful sense of humour and that people loved him for it. Unfortunately, everyone else just knew that he was a thorough-going pain in the arse and that they loathed him.

A couple of hours after Bewel and his friends had left, Jeremy was waiting near the town gates. It was a favourite place of his on Saint Ufmir's Day, as it meant he was always the first one to spot strangers entering the town. For the past half-hour, he had been thoroughly entertained by the sight of the Sergeant of the Guard berating one of the sentries, who had for some reason fouled his trousers. Jeremy was fascinated by this. What a neat trick, he thought, if you could get someone to foul their pants! He was just mulling over ways and means when he noticed that one of the other sentries was deep in conversation with a stranger. And, what was more, it was a young woman of about twenty or so! Perfect! Jeremy loved playing his little jokes on young women. Especially jokes that involved them getting soaked, so that their clothes clung to their slim young bodies . . . Eagerly, he watched as the stranger nodded her thanks to the sentry, and then began to walk up the hill into the town towards him. She was clad in brown leather leggings and jerkin, and had a sword at her side and a bow slung over her shoulder. She appeared to be talking to a scruffy brown donkey which ambled along beside her. Happily, Jeremy picked up his brimming bucket and advanced to meet them.

'OK, OK,' said Tyson to the donkey. 'You're right, Puss. They've set off already, so there's nothing we can do. So we'll grab a spot of lunch, and then follow the Wizard's advice and head off downstream.'

'Excuse me!' came a voice, and Tyson looked up. They were being approached by a man carrying a bucket. He was bearded, a little portly, and had an annoying smirk on his face. 'Am I right in thinking that you are a stranger in our city?' he continued.

Tyson nodded.

'Oh, good!' he grinned, and hefted his bucket.

'One drop of that stuff touches us and you're dead, pal!' said the donkey. Jeremy paused, and an incredulous look spread across his face.

'Hey, that's brilliant!' he gasped to Tyson. 'How do you do that? Ventriloquism? Or is it a trick donkey? That's it, right? It's a costume, with someone inside it!' And he bent down delightedly and began poking at Puss's head and neck.

'Er . . . I wouldn't do that if I was you,' said Tyson, a bit half-heartedly. Some unfailing instinct told her that this man deserved whatever he got.

'So it is a trick!' chortled Jeremy, delightedly. He carried on prying and poking for a few moments, but then suddenly he caught sight of the look in the donkey's eyes. For a brief instant his blood seemed to freeze in his veins, and then he leaped back, but too late! The donkey lashed out, its teeth sheared together, and Jeremy screamed and fell to his knees, hands clutching at his face, as blood flowed from the remnants of his nose. The donkey shook its head, and spat out the severed object.

'Ugh!' it said to Tyson. 'Let's find a bar quickly. I'd better wash my mouth out, who nose where that's been!' And chuckling to itself it ambled off up the hill with Tyson following behind.

'Guards!' screamed Jeremy the Beadle. 'Guards!'

One of the gate sentries came dashing up, sword in hand. 'What is it?' he asked.

'Those strangers assaulted me,' moaned the pain-stricken

Beadle. 'Look!' And he moved his hands away and showed the sentry the bloody mess where his nose had been.

'Serve you right, you bastard,' grinned the sentry, and wandered happily back to his post.

It was difficult to see anything inside the dragon's cave after the bright sunlight outside. When he had groped his way forward for about fifty paces Ronan struck flame, lit a couple of the torches that they had brought with them, and handed them to Tarl and Bewel. By the flickering light they could see that they were in a wide passage with small guard-rooms carved into the rock on either side. Slowly, the warrior led them forwards. After fifty more paces the walls suddenly fell away and they found themselves in a huge cavern. There was a mound of some kind in the centre. They walked forward, eyes straining to pierce the gloom that encroached around the rim of the torch-light. As they neared the mound their pace slowed, and as one they gasped with amazement.

It was a huge pile of treasure nearly ten feet high, a hoard of gold and silver, jewels and gemstones. Carvings and statues of jade and amber nestled next to swords whose hilts were bound about with a filigree of silver and platinum, and whose pommels and blades were studded and inlaid with rubies, sapphires and emeralds. Crowns, orbs and sceptres of long-dead kings and queens nestled in deep beds of gold coinage from every land in the world. Brooches, bracelets and tiaras studded with a thousand diamonds flashed and glittered in the light of the torches. It was a vast accumulation of wealth . . . more than a King's ransom, it was a world's. Even that legendary shopper Kahen the Spoilt, the Elven Princess of Behan, would have needed a few weeks to spend her way through this lot.

For what seemed like an age they stared in fascination at the wondrous sight, and then Tarl let out a slow sigh, leaned forward, and plucked a small statuette of the God Flak from the pile. It was of solid gold, with diamond eyes and sapphire warts, and by itself would have kept Tarl in Elf's Peckers for the rest of his life. He was just examining this and wondering if dragons played cards, when from the darkness to one side came the sound of someone elegantly clearing their throat. Tarl jumped guiltily and dropped the statuette, and all three turned and stared into the darkness beyond the light of the torches.

'Visitors! How absolutely charming!' said a deep and very cultured voice, then a sudden thirty-foot gout of flame shot across the cave first in one direction, and then in another, and two wall torches burst into flickering life. As their flames grew, they bathed in light the section of cave that was obviously the dragon's living quarters, and Ronan and Tarl had their first sight of the dragon Philekazan.

He was elegantly sprawled on a very long leather settee, with a giant economy size martini in one claw and a book by Jeffrey the Archer in another. There was a beautiful rug on the floor, and beside one wall was a bar that seemed to be liberally stocked with bottles of every description. Several man-sized chairs were carefully arranged in an arc opposite the settee.

'Do make yourselves at home,' drawled Philekazan, waving a languid claw at the chairs. 'Pour yourselves a drink if you wish. And then do feel free to tell me what brings you to my humble residence.' He flashed a charming gap-toothed smile at them and began to inspect one carefully manicured talon. Ronan was left with the feeling that here was a dragon who, could he have found them in size to fit, would have been totally at home in silk dressing-gown and cravat, and who, had he been able to wear a disreputable pencil-line moustache, would have done so with positive glee.

Ronan strode forward boldly, but Bewel followed rather more hesitantly and stood staring with his mouth agape. Ronan nudged him, and he pulled himself together with an effort.

'Good Philekazan,' he began, but the dragon interrupted him.

'Please,' he said, 'call me Phil.'

'Good Phil, then,' continued Bewel, 'we come on a matter which I have broached to you before. For some years you have been coming to our town, returning to your lair each time with one of our most beautiful young women. But now, we of Carn Betw are concerned for their safety. We feel that this cannot continue!'

The dragon looked at him and raised one golden eyebrow. 'My dear . . . Bewel, is it not? Let me assure you that all of these young women have accompanied me of their own free will.'

'Yes, yes! That much is well known,' admitted the young elf. 'But what is not so well known is what happens to them. Do they stay with you? If that is the case, where are they? Do they leave, and if so, where do they go?'

'Stay with me? My dear chap, I'm afraid I'm not the marrying kind!' smiled the dragon. He raised his glass and took a massive swallow of the martini. Ronan noticed that his claw was shaking slightly, and suddenly realised that the dragon was rather drunk. 'It's true,' Philekazan continued, 'that on occasion a young lady may accompany me back here for a night-cap, but they always leave by the next morning.'

'Why then do they not return to Carn Betw?'

'Who knows?' mused the dragon. 'Perhaps after a night with me they find such a small town of little interest any more. Perhaps they want to venture out into the wide world, to seek excitement, riches, romance. Perhaps they feel a need to live life to the full . . .'

'Perhaps they're not capable of returning,' came a flat, unhappy voice from over by the treasure hoard. 'Perhaps life is something they've run out of . . .'

Ronan and Bewel looked round to where Tarl was standing with bowed head and slumped shoulders. While they had been questioning the dragon, he had been prowling round the perimeters of the treasure. Now, he rather wished he hadn't. Wearily he raised his torch, and the light fell on something beyond the massive mound. A small sad heap of grey-white fragments that were charred with black. Human bones, broken and burned.

The others stared in horror, and Bewel turned on the dragon with flashing eyes. 'What means this?' he spat. But as they watched, the dragon slumped down in his seat. His golden scales seemed to lose their lustre, his wings drooped like tattered old curtains of lace and the muscles of his face sagged, making it seem lined and swollen. Suddenly, he looked tired and old, and very, very dissolute. A tear welled from the corner of his eye and splashed into his drink.

'I can't explain it,' he moaned desperately. 'It just started one evening, some years ago. This lovely young girl had come home with me. We'd had quite a lot to drink, and we both felt rather peckish, as you do. You know how it is. She suggested flying out for a pizza, but I looked at her, so young and beautiful, and I thought, My goodness, I could just eat you all up. And I did. Every last bit.

'Of course, I was horrified when I woke up next morning and remembered what I had done! I didn't go near the town for months. But then one day I felt I had to have some company. So, I flew down, had a few drinks, and ended up coming home with another wonderful young lady. And the same thing happened again . . .

'And now I'm hooked! I want to stop, but I can't! I really do feel like the most absolute bounder . . .' The dragon paused, and took another gulp at his drink. More tears were welling out now, and his mighty chest was heaving convulsively. Suddenly a look of horror crossed his face and he slapped one claw across his mouth.

'Oh, no!' he gasped. 'Hiccups! Look out!' But never having seen a singultous dragon before his visitors failed to take any evasive action and just stared at him, puzzled. For a moment he sat there, seemingly frozen, and then he gave a loud hiccup and a jet of flame shot out of his mouth, just missing Bewel.

The dragon looked mortified. 'I'm so sorry,' he muttered. 'I can't help it! I say, look out!'

Ronan and Bewel, forewarned, leapt for cover as Philekazan hiccuped again. This time, however, the dragon tilted his head back and the gout of flame shot thirty feet into the air and incinerated a small colony of bats which had been hanging from the roof bitching ultrasonically to each other about all the noise below.

Ronan glanced quickly round the room and then, as the dragon's chest contracted a third time, he leapt past him and grabbed the large soda-syphon that was standing on the bar. As the dragon turned to him with a look of mute apology in his eyes and opened his mouth for another hiccup, Ronan fired a jet of soda-water straight into his jaws. The hiccup was stifled by a paraoxysm of choking coughs.

Eventually, the spluttering dragon managed to draw breath. 'Thank you,' he said gratefully and rather damply. 'You've put my fire out. That's the only thing that helps when I get an attack like that.' Then he turned to Bewel. 'I really am most terribly sorry. I honestly couldn't help it. It's because of just this sort of thing that we dragons always live in stone caves miles from anywhere. I mean, you can't very well live in a nice house in the centre of town if every time you burp, you incinerate your next-door neighbour and burn down half the city!'

He gave his three visitors a sad, rather watery smile, but Ronan for one was not to be placated. The dragon had obviously killed several innocent young girls, and although he was rather more well spoken and chatty than the average bad guy, in Ronan's book this put him firmly on the evil side of things. Ronan drew the sword that Bewel's father had lent him and advanced on the creature.

'Dragon,' he thundered, 'this can't go on! How many more deaths will you cause?'

The dragon slid off the sofa and backed away, his great claws outstretched in supplication. 'Look, I'm most awfully sorry . . . I really couldn't help it, you know . . . I probably won't do it again, I reckon I can kick the habit, given a bit of support . . . No, please . . .'

But Ronan advanced inexorably until he had Philekazan backed up against the wall. He hefted the sword in his hand and stared fiercely up at him, and then realised the major problem inherent in being a six-foot human who wants to decapitate a twenty-foot dragon. He desperately needed a step-ladder.

'Listen, guy, I'm going to have to cut off your head.'

'I realise that.'

'But I can't reach it.'

'Shame.'

'You wouldn't care to bend down?'

'Do I look stupid?'

There was a pause while Ronan tried to think what to do.

'Look, I can quite easily slice open your stomach, you know. The end effect is the same.'

'Oh, tut!' The dragon looked disappointed. 'And what would the tabloids make of that? Savage warrior disembowels innocent dragon . . . fire-breathing lizard dies in agony with his guts all over the floor . . . How heroic. Not going to look too good at the next Warrior-School reunion, is it?'

'Oh, come on, guy! After what you did to those innocent girls? Have you no shame? Just look at that sad pile of bones over there!

What are their poor parents going to say?'

There was another pause. The dragon's lower lip quivered, and great tears welled up once more in its eyes and splashed to the floor, soaking Ronan's shoes.

'You're right,' he whispered. 'I know you're right. I deserve to die. Oh, God, how did it come to this? How did I sink so low?'

The dragon began to rock backwards and forwards, thumping his head against the rock wall behind him. And then he swallowed, and leaned his great head forward until the tip of his jaw was just touching the ground in front of Ronan's feet.

'Come on, then,' he said. 'Let's get it over with.'

Ronan swung his sword back over his head and picked a spot just behind the dragon's ears. His great muscles bunched as he tensed himself. And then he paused. And paused some more.

'Look, maybe you really couldn't help it,' he heard himself saying.

'What!' came an outraged roar from Bewel, who was quivering with indignation. 'After all that he's done, you want to let him off?'

Ronan held out his sword. 'If you want him dead, you kill him.'

The elf looked from the sword to the dragon, and then back to the sword again. He shook his head tiredly. The dragon looked up at them with moist, heavy-lidded eyes.

'You'd be doing me a favour, you know.' Somehow neither Ronan nor Bewel could meet his gaze. 'Oh well, I suppose there's only one way out for a dragon of honour. And that's what I used to be, not so very long ago.' He paused for a moment in thought, and then stood up and tiredly unfurled his wings. 'I am going to go for a little fly out over the Western Ocean. I may be gone some time.'

Ronan looked at the dragon with a new respect. One of the many stories he had read as a child told of the great dragon Atropos who, heart-broken at the death of his life-long companion, flew out across the ocean towards the west until his mighty wings tired and he could fly no more, and he plummeted to his death. He watched sadly as Philekazan looked round his home for one last time with an expression of utter wretchedness on his face. Then the dragon began to trudge towards the exit of the cave. Ronan went to move forward, but Bewel laid a restraining hand on his arm.

'It is for the best,' he whispered.

The dragon looked back over his shoulder. 'Do please divide my hoard between you,' he said, 'and give some of it to the families of the girls I... well... you know.' Ronan raised a hand in acknowledgement.

At the rear of the cave, Tarl was in a bit of a moral dilemma. He thought he might have a solution that would satisfy everyone, but if he kept his mouth closed the dragon would fly off to his death and he would suddenly be the part-owner of a massive hoard of treasure, which would give him enough money to buy the whole of Welbug if he wished. The Tarl of ten days ago would only have opened his mouth to say 'Goodbye' and would have been happily shovelling jewels into his back-pack. But this was a newer, finer Tarl.

'Hold on,' he heard himself saying, 'don't you think you're over-reacting a bit?'

The dragon paused and looked at him hopelessly and Bewel threw him an extremely dirty look. Tarl stumbled on regardless.

'Look, wanting to bite a pretty girl is no sin. I mean, we've all done that.' He looked at the shocked expressions on his companions' faces and hastily reassessed. 'Well, some of us have. But when you've got a four-foot mouth lined with needle-sharp teeth, accidents can happen. One thing leads to another, and before you know it... What I'm saying is, this has happened before.' He shrugged, trying to assume a man-of-the-world air, then added hurriedly, 'Not to me! But I've lived amongst orcs and trolls. I mean, you know what they eat! But they're not all happy about it. Some of them want to settle down in normal human towns, or decide that eating people is morally wrong. I came across a few self-help groups in Orcville. Why don't you join one of them?'

'Self-help groups?' snuffled Philekazan.

'Yeah. They've worked wonders for all sorts of creatures who were used to a diet of man-flesh. There's GAME – Goblins Against Man-Eating – although they're a bit extreme. And there's SOD'EM – Sentient Organisms Don't Eat Men. Apparently they're really supportive.'

The dragon looked hopefully across to Bewel, who thought for a moment, then sat down in one of the chairs.

'Tell us a bit more about them,' said the elf.

*

As twilight fell over the River Dagen, many miles to the east, nothing broke the quiet of the evening save for the rushing of the water and the plaintive call of a homeless and egg-less *pakas* that was emigrating north in an attempt to find a place where it could safely build a nest without having it shaken down. And then there came a noise like distant thunder from the north-east. Quiet at first, and then louder and louder, until it could be recognised for what it was, the sound of hundreds of hooves galloping across the plain.

They burst upon the river at the point where the Great East Road forded it and galloped through without pausing, dark horses with darker riders urging them on. And then they were gone, a wave of doom that faded into the encroaching night until the sound of their passing had vanished.

The Tribe of Fallon were riding into the west.

Ronan tugged the massive sword out from the treasure mound and swung it experimentally. It was well balanced and sharp. 'This will do,' he said. 'I only need it until I find the Cavern of the Singing Sword.'

'It is yours,' said the dragon. 'And take what treasure you wish.' He was lying contentedly back on his couch, martini in claw, and opposite him sat Bewel. The two of them had spent a couple of hours amicably discussing Tarl's idea. It had been decided that Philekazan would go off to join SOD'EM in Orcville until he had kicked his habit and that Bewel would go with him to lend support. An unlikely friendship seemed to be blossoming between the dragon and the elf, and they had discovered that they had a surprising amount of things in common (for example, both loved trashy literature, although Philekazan was a fan of Jeffrey the Archer, while Bewel admitted a fondness for Jilly the Cooper and her steamy stories about the sexual adventures of barrel-making folk).

Ronan smiled. 'Thanks,' he said, 'but we will just take what we need to buy food, lodging, and wine.'

'For the whole of Welbug,' added Tarl, under his breath. He was carefully wrapping several small but extremely valuable items in his unwashed underwear, where few people would be brave or foolish enough to look, and stowing them in his pack.

Ronan slung the sword around his neck, then picked up the bundle of unlit torches and tucked them under his arm. Although night was falling outside, he wanted to press on and make an attempt at finding a part of the underground city that he could locate on the chart, the southern part of which (including the dragon's cavern) was wine-stained and illegible. He turned to the dragon.

'You have heard nothing from Pectin and his dwarves since they passed through?' he asked.

'Not a dicky-bird,' answered the dragon. 'I haven't been that way myself. There's an old rock-fall a few hundred paces in and the gap that is left is far too small for a dragon. A roving orc did pop its head out a couple of months ago, but when it saw me it shrieked, made an awful mess of its clothes, and fled back whence it came.'

'Ah, well, we had better tread quietly,' said Ronan. 'Goodbye!' And taking Tarl's pack and slinging it on his back, he raised a lighted torch and paced towards the rear of the cave.

'Good luck,' said Bewel and Philekazan together.

'Thanks,' muttered Tarl. 'I think we're going to need it!' He staggered after Ronan, a little weighed down by the weapons he had chosen from the treasure hoard. There were two swords, a couple of daggers, a spear, a small mace, a long gold pointed thing (which, had he but known it, was part of a barbecue-set belonging to an ancient Cydorian king), two bows, a quiver of arrows, and a shield.

With orcs ahead, Tarl was taking no chances.

The passage-way ran straight ahead to the north. It was twenty feet wide and nearly as high, with a flat and even floor. On either side, passages and rooms were carved into the stone of the mountain, but after Tarl and Ronan had walked about a quarter of a mile, these became less and less frequent, eventually ceasing altogether. Now there was just the single wide road pointing like an arrow to the north. The air was dry and stale, and little clouds of dust eddied about their feet as they strode on for mile upon mile. The road never once deviated, never rose or fell, just burrowed through the heart of the mountain, dark and silent save for the padding of their feet and the flickering of their torches.

After they had been walking for an hour they stopped, and Tarl thankfully took a drink from his flask. His throat was parched, his nose was clogged with dust, and he had one of those tickles that never quite turns into a sneeze but just sits around and torments you.

Ronan studied the chart and tried vainly to decipher the wine-stained representation of the southern parts of Samoth.

'Are you sure we're going the right way?' Tarl whispered. 'I thought this was supposed to be an underground city.'

'It is,' came the reply. 'Or rather, it will be. As far as I can make out, this is just the road that leads to it. The rooms round Philekazan's cave are the remains of the fort guarding the South Gate. By my calculations, we have another two hours' march before we reach Samoth itself.'

After a brief rest, they rose and trudged on. Tarl started to sing but the tunnel seemed to magnify his words, sending them echoing ahead, and he soon stopped. There might be orcs in front of them, and not the semi-civilised city-dwelling types that he was familiar with, but the real subterranean sharp-fanged raw-flesh-eating horrors of his nightmares. And not just orcs either. There were other creatures that embraced the dark and shrank from light, creatures upon which it was best not to dwell. Tarl swallowed and tried to tip-toe as quietly as possible.

Ronan's calculations were pretty accurate, and it was a shade over two hours later that they came again upon side-passages and rooms. The first one they found appeared to be a guard-room. It was hewn out of the rock on the left of the passage and had several steps leading up to it. A solid oak door hung askew from one rusty hinge, with numerous slashes and rents in the wood. The blade of an axe was still embedded in one of these, and on the floor of the room they found a broken sword-blade and a dented and battered helm. Ronan picked this up and stared at it for a moment. It was so battered and misshapen that it could almost have been one of his father's. A wave of loneliness swept over him, but for the first time in his life his thoughts returned not to the home of his youth, but to a comfortable bed in Welbug, and to the slender arms and loving eyes of the deadliest warrior he had met in years. He dragged his thoughts back to the present.

'We had best stay here tonight,' he said. Tarl sank gratefully and noisily to the floor in a welter of weaponry. They shared some wine, bread, and dried meat, and chatted aimlessly for a while. Then as he peered sleepily at the chart, Ronan heaved the door closed and wedged it shut with one of his swords. The last thing Tarl heard before he drifted off was what seemed to be the sound of distant drums.

Hey, he thought, someone's having a party. And then he was asleep.

To their surprise, Philekazan and Bewel got on like a house on fire. They swapped stories, had several large drinks, and laughed and sang for a while, and so it was quite late by the time they fell asleep and the two shadowy figures of Kaldis and Bonaponere were able to creep round the hoard and slip past the rock-fall towards Samoth.

Ronan and Tarl awoke stiff and cold. They shared some more bread for their breakfast, and then Ronan dragged open the door. Faint light was entering the passage outside through small holes in the arched ceiling, holes that must have been bored all the way up to the mountain's side, hundreds of feet above. It was just light enough to see, so they extinguished their torches and continued on their way.

It was obvious that they were now entering the underground city. Not only were there frequent side-passages, with signs written in the runic alphabet of the dwarves, but there were many doors and windows opening on to the road they followed. In places it widened out into vast underground squares and piazzas, with elegant pillars that tapered to a distant roof, and colonnaded walkways of marble and stone that shone with a ghostly glitter in the faint light seeping down from far above. At first there was little sign of life, but then the detritus of past residents began to appear. A cast-off shoe, a broken spear, a battered and many-holed bucket, and a few empty bottles.

At the point where the road left what appeared to be an old market-place, Ronan paused, struck fire, and in its flickering light tried vainly to locate their position on the map. Tarl lit a torch, and prowled around the edge of the market, looking into some of the abandoned shops that lined it.

'It's no use,' muttered Ronan, shaking his head. 'I can't tell where we are. And this city has several levels! I don't even know which one we are on!'

He peered at the chart and sighed in frustration. He had left Warrior School convinced that he was ready for any eventuality. His course had included most things likely to be of use to a warrior such as Weapons Training, Survival, Languages, Chivalry, and even the Physiology of Intelligent Races. (For example, it is useful to know that it is a sheer waste of time kneeing a troll in the groin, as they have no testicles. None of their own, that is, although many trolls like to wear earrings or other items made from the testicles of other, unluckier, folk.) However, his course had signally failed to include a section on Deciphering Ancient Charts Which Small Piss-head Friends Have Soaked In Red Wine.

'Ronan?' Tarl's voice was low, but the note of urgency and fear in it was plain to hear. Quickly, Ronan bundled up the chart, and crossed to where his friend was standing peering nervously down a side-passage. It was quite narrow, running for ten paces before bending sharply to the left. At this point four steps rose gently to an open door, and on either side of this door windows hewn into the rock stared blindly out. Slumped on these steps surrounded by old bottles and broken crockery, were the mummified remains of a dwarf.

Ronan took the torch and crept silently forward, followed by Tarl. When they reached the bend they could see that the passage turned into a staircase, which led precipitately downwards into darkness, and from this darkness came a rank and foetid smell. They turned, stepped over the remains of the dwarf, and climbed the steps to the open door. Inside, they found themselves in the vestibule of a house. Slowly, sadly, they explored.

Each room was the same. The floor was covered in broken glass, fragmented crockery, shattered mugs, and discarded clothing, and dried encrustations of food were splashed across the walls and ceilings. There was litter and dust everywhere, and in one upstairs room they found the remains of three more dwarves. One was clutching a largish leather-bound book in his bony hand.

Respectfully, Ronan took the book and opened it. Inside, the pages were filled by a neat and tidy elven script.

'What does it say? Can you read it?' asked Tarl.

Ronan nodded sadly. '"This diary belongs to Wain, the son of Dayne,"' he read aloud. '"If this book should dare to roam, box its ears and send it home."' He turned more pages. They were brittle and dry and stained with what looked like wine. Someone appeared to have been sick over them at least once, but they were still legible, and Ronan scanned them with a growing sadness.

'We seem to have found the last remains of the dwarves' brave expedition,' he said, after a while. 'Alas! I fear their end was brutal! Listen to this!' He turned some more pages and began to read aloud once more. '"Yesterday we heard the drums throbbing in the depths, and then orcs came in many hundreds, inviting us to join them in a party. At first, our leader Pectin refused, but the drums were rousing and the orcs insistent, and so did we weaken and accept. We lost Thyasin almost at once! He was but inches from the bass speaker when the music started, and both his ear-drums shattered."'

Tarl winced, and Ronan turned the page. 'There's more,' he said. '"For four days now has the party raged. We cannot go on like this! We lost Basalt when he drunkenly took on the bouncer, a giant stone-troll the like of which I have never before seen, nor ever hope to see again. Alas for Basalt! His dress was casual, and he wore not a tie. I fear his end was swift. Old Rian was the next to go. We dragged him senseless from the dance-floor, but we could not revive him. We had told him he was too old to break-dance, but alas! he would not heed us. Then yesterday we lost Ptyalin and Pepsin. Orcs bet them that they could not cross the Bridge of Eldabad by walking on their hands. Oh woe, for they had drunk so much that both fell laughing to their deaths in the abyss. Then Trypsin perished when his liver went, and our hope went with him. For many an orc had he drunk under the table, yet if he could not survive this fell party, what hope was there for the rest of us. And late last night, we found Kerosin floating face-down in a vat of ale."'

Ronan turned more pages. Something unpleasant had stuck two of them together, and he prised them gently apart. 'More days have passed,' he said. 'See how the hand-writing has deteriorated. In places it is almost illegible. Only the gods know how much they had drunk by then. Listen!' He began to read again. '"This fell catering will be the death of us! The bacteria in the water took Oen, and the seafood vol-au-vents have done for Pectin and for Dene. They cannot have been fresh! They cannot have been fresh!

'"And this morning we lost brave Endocrin. He died of sheer embarrassment when we told him what he did with his helm last night at the party. Now there are just seven of us left. We have managed to creep away, but sleep is nigh impossible for the noise. The drums! The drums in the depths! And now the orcs are at our door! They have invited us back to their infernal party!"'

Ronan's voice was low, no more than a whisper, as he turned the final page. 'It ends in this scrawl, here. "We are trapped! We have no excuses left! We cannot get out of it! We cannot get out of it!" There is no more.'

He closed the book and laid it gently by the bony hand that had held it for so long, and then bowed his head and stood in respectful silence. Tarl waited quietly, thinking of the massive and terrible party that had wiped out the colony. And then all at once, there came a slow and rhythmic pounding, echoing through the windows from the black stair-well beyond. Tarl and Ronan stared in horror at each other.

'Drums!' gasped Ronan. 'Drums from the depths!'

Suddenly the pounding beat was matched and underscored by a rapid rhythmic throbbing. 'Bum-ba-bum-ba-bum-ba-bum-bum', it went, and the very stone of the walls seemed to reverberate to the rhythm.

'Klat!' swore Tarl. 'A bass guitar! The music is starting again!'

Gasping, the two of them dashed out of the house. Ronan ran for the market-place, tripping and sliding over the broken bottles in the corridor, but the pulsating beat welling up from the depths below seemed to grab at Tarl and drag him towards the stairs. Unwillingly, his feet began to shuffle in jerky little steps in time with the music and his breath came sharply and quickly. He closed his eyes, and a pale sheen of sweat stood out on his face.

'Party,' he gasped, as though enchanted, 'got to party!' His feet reached the top of the stairs, and the foul orc stench that drifted up from below hit him like a physical blow and made his head spin. And then he was staggering down into the darkness below.

As the first rays of the rising sun hit her face, Tyson was instantly

196

awake. She stretched to ease the stiffness caused by the hard ground then sat up and threw off her dew-covered blanket. Nearby, the last embers of the previous night's campfire were still smouldering, and she threw on a handful of dry sticks and blew gently on them until the fire burst into life.

Puss ambled up from beside the river with a decapitated wild duck hanging from its jaws. It found hunting pathetically easy in these fertile areas. The local birds were used to donkeys that hung around munching grass all day, and so when one wandered up and stood beside them, they weren't expecting it to bite their heads off.

'You could be happily lying in a comfortable bed back in Welbug, you know,' it told her.

'No. I love all this.' Tyson gestured to the tenuous mist that wafted gently across the surface of the river, the graceful willow trees that lined its banks, and the myriad birds that were singing their hearts out in the branches. 'There's the feeling I get when I look to the west . . .' She paused. Somewhere she thought she heard a guitar chord.

Puss looked at her, head on one side. 'You're a bit of an old hippy at heart, aren't you?' it said.

She smiled and looked up at the mountains that towered above them on the other side of the river.

'I hope Ronan and Tarl are all right,' she murmured.

Ronan swore viciously as he hurtled down the stairwell after Tarl. At first it was pitch-black and he stumbled and nearly lost his footing. But then a faint reddish light began to creep up from below. After a while the stairs turned sharply, and the right-hand wall gave way to a precipitous drop. Ronan could now see that the staircase was clinging to the wall of a vast cavern. The floor far below was cracked and pitted with fissures that glowed a fiery red, from which tongues of flame licked and played. It was packed tight with orcs, jostling, yelling, singing and fighting. Every now and then, one would be forced over the lip of a fissure by the crowd, and would fall screaming, only to disappear in a sudden brief flash of orange flame. Heavy, thumping music pounded from a dozen orc mage-decks in a deafening wall of sound. Acrid smoke curled up, and the body odour and mass halitosis of five thousand orcs arose in a mephitic cloud.

Ronan could see Tarl further down the stairs, stumbling onwards as if in a daze. He leaped after him, taking the steps five at a time. As he neared him, the orcs at the foot of the stairs caught sight of them and started yelling and gesturing, waving mugs of their foul sweet black wine invitingly. They were the savage mountain-orcs of nightmare, tall menacing *Uttuks* and squat but powerful *Kulashaks*, and Ronan knew that if his friend reached the foot of the stairs he was lost.

Throwing caution to the wind he threw himself down the stairs. To his relief Tarl had stopped and was staring blankly at the orcs below as they yelled obscene suggestions to him in their harsh, guttural tongue. Catching him up he grabbed Tarl by the arm, and yelling, 'Sorry, we're just nipping out for a bottle! We won't be long!' dragged him through a roughly hewn archway and along a dark, claustrophobic corridor. Tarl stumbled and nearly fell and Ronan, seeing the glazed blank look in his eyes, grabbed him by the arms and shook him.

'Stop your ears with this,' he yelled, handing Tarl two strips of cloth torn from his shirt. He had already blocked his own with other strips. Dazedly, Tarl jammed the wads of material in place while Ronan quickly lit another torch. By its light he could see that they were at a crossroads. Three of the tunnels had a cloying, unpleasant feel about them, but the fourth sloped upwards, and cool air wafted from it. Ronan dragged Tarl into it and hustled him along as fast as he could, away from the hypnotic beat. Faster and still faster they ran, and as they ran Tarl slowly emerged from his trance, shaking his head as if to rid it of the persistent rhythm that echoed down the corridor behind them.

After a while, Tarl could run no further. He felt as though he had covered several leagues, although it was probably no more than a mile, and he collapsed against the wall. Ronan turned, and seeing him slumped there, ran back. He paused, sword in hand, and listened carefully, but the music was distant now and could hardly be heard above Tarl's laboured breathing. There was no sound of any pursuit. Gently, he helped his friend to rise and supported him as he limped on down the road.

They stopped after a further half-mile, when the music had completely faded away. The tunnel had been sloping gently upwards for a while now and had increased in both width and height, and although they had passed several intersecting corridors, there had been no large caverns or rooms.

Tarl sat down on a long low slab of carved stone that looked like a doorstep and leant against the wall. He waited patiently while Ronan opened the pack and handed him a loaf of dry bread and their last water-bottle.

'Thanks,' said Tarl. 'That was a bit too close for comfort! For a moment there, I thought I was going to end up like those dwarves!'

'I've heard of orcs and their foul parties,' said Ronan, 'but never have I heard of such a one as that!'

'Oh, they used to tell some tales back in Orcville,' answered Tarl. 'City-orcs aren't so bad, but mountain-orcs are another story.' He tore a chunk of bread off the loaf and handed it back to Ronan. 'I wonder where we are,' he added.

'I can tell you exactly where we are,' muttered Ronan, who was now staring at the map. 'We're lost.'

Tarl unstoppered the water-bottle and sniffed at it disparagingly. 'By the gods, I'm thirsty!' he said, and at that very instant there was a loud 'crack' from the wall behind him that echoed along the passage. Tarl jumped, and looked round.

'Here,' he said. 'Where did that come from?' For in the wall above the step-like stone, the outline of two vast doors had appeared. He stood aside and allowed Ronan to examine them, but no matter what the warrior did, he could not get the doors to open. It was as though someone had painted the hair-thin outlines on solid rock. Eventually he tried thumping them in frustration with his fist, but that just hurt.

Tarl watched sympathetically for a while, then raised the water-bottle and sipped. He grimaced. He didn't think he'd ever get used to the taste.

'I could do with a real drink,' he said. As if these words were a signal, the hair-thin crack slowly but smoothly widened, and the two massive stone doors gently swung open to reveal a room beyond. For a moment the two travellers stared, and then lifting their torches they stepped inside.

It had clearly been a tavern long ago, although they could tell from the undisturbed layer of dust on everything that no one had been here for years. There were marble-topped tables with beautiful wrought-iron legs, and elegant but inviting chairs plumply upholstered with leather. Along one side of the room was a spearboard alley, and on the other side ran a lane for skittles. There were also tables for shove-*tablon* and for bar-bastard. The floor was tessellated in strangely restful patterns, and on the walls were framed posters and cartoons, nearly all of which were either interesting or humorous. The bar itself ran the full length of the far wall and seemed somehow to beckon. It was of carved stone and was one with the floor, with an iron foot-rest running along its base.

It was probably the most wonderful room that Tarl had ever entered. He couldn't have said why it was wonderful, any more than he could have said why he found certain faces beautiful. It was just a combination of unremarkable and separate features which, when viewed as a whole, suddenly came together as something special. The place seemed almost to speak to him, seemed to promise that here you would find friends, here you could talk, or laugh, or read, or do whatever you felt like, and do it with a mug of the best beer in the world at your elbow.

He walked slowly forward, almost in a dream, and leant on the bar. Most of it would have been a fraction too low for him, having been designed with the comfort of dwarves in mind, but a small section was higher, for the benefit of the occasional human visitor like himself, and as soon as he leant there, it felt as though his body had merged with the bar. He could have stood there all night. He looked up, and his eyes fell upon a carved sign above the bar. It said simply, 'The Stonemason's Arms'.

'I don't believe it!' he whispered reverently, half to himself, half to Ronan. 'We've only gone and found the Lost Dwarfish Pub of Legend!'

The Pink Book of Ulay has a tendency to exaggeration. At times, it makes books such as *The Autobiography of Tarl, the Hero of Welbug,* or *A Loser's Guide to Marriage (and how to survive it)* by Maxon the Small, seem positively sober and well balanced. However, on the subject of the Lost Dwarfish Pub of Legend, it is, if popular folk-law is to be believed, completely accurate . . .

*

Ah! The Stonemason's Arms! The Stonemason's Arms!
Where never was a man served out of turn, yet never did he
have to wait for serving! Where never did the landlord call
you 'squire' or 'chief', but always by your first and given
name! Where never was the customer short-changed, nor
was his change left lying in pools of beer upon the counter
top! Where never was the toilet blocked, hot water absent,
and the cold tap wont to soak your pants with gouts of
freezing water! Where always was there soap to wash your
hands, and fluffy towels as well! Where strangers told you
interesting tales, and never was a boring story heard! Where
never did the ale taste sour or fizzy, and yet was it always
fair and justly priced! And such ale! Such beers! Rangvald's
Mild, or Mithril Stout, or Gobbo's Pearly Light! Never shall
we see their kind again . . .

Rumours that the editor of *The Pink Book of Ulay* received a
life-time of free drinking in the Stonemason's Arms as a result of
the above passage are no doubt false. In the interests of fairness we
did attempt to contact him, but were unable to do so. His
secretary informed us that he has been continuously as pissed as a
vart for the past eighteen years.

Ronan spread the wine-stained chart out on the bar, and excitedly
traced along it with his finger. There were only four or five inns
shown on it, and all were fairly close to the Cavern of the Singing
Sword! Surely he could work out where they were now! He turned
to Tarl, but it was clear that he wasn't interested. He had gone
behind the bar and was gently stroking the fittings with the
expression of someone who has stumbled upon paradise.

In fact, for Tarl the word 'paradise' was pretty close to the truth.
If at any time in the recent past he had been asked to devote his
life to some sort of holy or noble quest searching for some lost or
fabled object, it is almost certain that he would have ignored
Grails and all such pointless objects, and settled upon a Quest for
the Lost Dwarfish Pub. And now, before he had even contem-
plated such a quest, he had completed it! He wandered slowly
along behind the bar, dazedly reading the legendary names of
ancient ales, and then stopped at one of the taps. Spleenwort's

Ichor Ale! Wow! Stories of the deadly effects of that brew had been passed down from father to son for generations! Old Spleenwort the Brewer had taken the formula to the grave with him, which was probably just as well considering the huge numbers of people the brew itself had taken to the grave. What was the old saying? 'One and you're anybody's, two and you're everybody's, three and you're just a body.' What a shame he'd never be able to taste the brew!

Smiling, he idly played with the tap. There was a hiss of air, and a dark brown liquid started to trickle forth. Tarl stared, unbelieving, then snatched a dusty mug from under the bar and filled it.

By the Five Great Demons! he thought. This place has been abandoned for hundreds of years and yet the beer still pours! In a way it was rather a pity. He would have loved to have sipped it, just so he could tell people that he'd actually sampled a pint of Spleenwort's Ichor, but the ale would have turned to vinegar after all this time. Tasting it would be rather like seeing an old but famous ex-champion warrior hacking his way round in the lower reaches of some non-league tournament, a pathetic shadow of his former self. Gingerly, he sniffed it. It seemed to smell OK, and so, gritting his teeth and hardly daring to hope, he raised the mug to his lips and sipped.

And immediately spat it out. Sadly, it tasted like a mixture of concentrated acetic acid, cabbage water, and fresh orc-dung. Tarl was strongly reminded of a pint of Whitebeard's Flagon that he'd once been rash enough to drink. He sighed and wandered along to Ronan, who was still poring over the chart.

The warrior hadn't got too far as he still couldn't work out which of several taverns was the Stonemason's Arms.

'The problem is,' he explained, 'they aren't named on the map. Look! Tavern.' He stabbed at the chart with a finger, by way of illustration, then pointed again an inch away. 'Tavern. And here, look. Tavern. There's too many of them!'

Tarl looked at the chart, and said, 'That's where we are. That one, there.'

Ronan peered at where Tarl's finger was pointing. 'How do you know?' he asked. 'It just says "the tavern".'

'Not the tavern,' said Tarl. 'THE tavern. Change of emphasis. It has to be that one, it's the only one with a "the" in front of it. I've been to loads of inns and taverns in my life, and believe me, this is THE tavern!'

Ronan stared at the chart again with a new excitement. 'If you're right,' he said, 'then we're almost there! We just go down two levels, cross the Bridge of Eldabad, and that's it!' Hastily, he folded the chart and stuffed it into the pack, and then picking up his torch he strode to the doors. Regretfully, Tarl followed him, but as the warrior was about to stride off down the main passageway he caught him by the arm.

'Listen,' he said, indicating the massive stone doors standing invitingly open. 'We can't leave it like this! You know what orcs and trolls are like! One good party and the place would be ruined! It needs to be preserved! One day, it should be opened to the people, as a sort of museum! A shrine, even! I know folk who would walk a hundred miles just to see it!'

Ronan shrugged, then got hold of one of the doors and pulled. Again, nothing he did could budge it.

Tarl gestured for him to stop. 'Look,' he said, frowning, 'I reckon those doors opened when I said the magic words, "I could do with a drink", right?'

'Yeah, I guess so,' replied Ronan.

'OK, then, surely there must be some equivalent phrase that will shut them!'

Ronan considered this and nodded. Tarl sank into thought for a few moments, and then suddenly he smiled. 'Goodnight, all!' he called, and the doors swung silently together, closing so tightly that it was impossible to find even the faintest of cracks to mark where they had been. Expecting some word of praise, he turned back to the warrior, but Ronan was already striding off down the passage. Sadly, Tarl caressed the stone wall.

'I'll be back,' he murmured reverently to the invisible doors. 'Just trust me. I'll be back. And one day, you'll open again.' And then he was scampering after Ronan.

The warrior was setting a fierce pace and it was all Tarl could do to keep up. Reaching the first junction, he turned right, strode down a narrow dark corridor, and then ducked through an opening. A spiral staircase led downwards and he followed it, taking the stairs two or three at a time in his haste, with Tarl struggling to keep up. His heart was beating rapidly and he felt a massive surge of anticipation, for suddenly he felt as though he was almost there.

Since seeing the vision of his father eight or nine days before, he had been searching for the three items mentioned in the rhyme. Two he had attained, and the third one, the Sword of Myth, was within reach. Excitement filled him at the thought of successfully completing his quest and he laughed aloud with pleasure. All at once the tunnels no longer seemed claustrophobic and threatening, but oddly cheerful and welcoming.

Reaching the base of the staircase he emerged into a large cavern and stopped dead. The walls around him were sparkling with a strange greenish glow and the air seemed charged. The floor was split into two by a seemingly bottomless ravine, in which the sound of rushing water could be heard far, far below. The thirty feet wide gap was bridged by a graceful arch of stone barely one foot wide. There was no other way across.

'Here,' gasped Tarl breathlessly as he staggered into the cavern. 'What's the hurry?'

Ronan looked at him with interest. Tarl's hair was standing on end and a thousand tiny points of light were scurrying up and down his body like ants. The air around him was crackling and popping like fire-crackers heard from half a mile away. He stared at the rock bridge with horror.

'I'm not crossing that!' he exclaimed, and as he flung out one hand and pointed, the little beads of light rushed along his arms, merged, and exploded from his finger-tips as one big fireball which whooshed across the cavern, missing the bridge by inches and blowing a big chunk out of the stone edge of the ravine.

There was a silence broken only by the distant sound of rock fragments plunging into water far below then Tarl clicked his fingers.

'Got it!' He looked round at the green-glowing walls. 'We must be in the middle of a seam of mage-stone! I'd better get out of here before I explode!'

Ronan threw him a look of fury. 'You nearly blew up the bridge, you pranny!' he yelled, shaking the chart in Tarl's face. 'This is the Bridge of Eldabad, according to the chart. And do you know what is just on the other side? The Cavern of the Singing Sword, that's what!' And so saying, he dashed across the narrow rock bridge without hesitating.

Tarl stared in horror. He found this habit of rushing head-long into danger highly questionable. Personally, if he had to die (and he was hoping to find some way of avoiding this) he would prefer to die at an advanced old age in bed. Hopefully someone else's bed. Then he realised that more of the whirling points of light were collecting about the extremities of his body and that a strange orange glow was emanating from his groin.

'Klat! I'd better get out of here!' he muttered, and screwing his face up into an ugly snarl of determination he dashed across the bridge. Cold air seemed to well up from the depths of the abyss and a wave of vertigo swept over him, then he was across and rushing after Ronan.

The cavern narrowed into a wide passageway which Ronan was striding along impatiently. Tarl dashed after him and managed to catch him just before he came to a T-junction.

'Ronan!' he hissed. 'Klat, guy, slow down a minute!'

The warrior stopped. 'What is it?' he snapped impatiently.

'Look,' replied Tarl. 'That was the Bridge of Eldabad back there, right? And we know from the dwarf's diary that orcs have been round these parts.'

'So what?'

'So orcs aren't going to miss out on some marvellous sword that is just lying around in a cave, are they? Either they've found it and stolen it, or else it must be . . . protected.'

The impatience on Ronan's face died away, to be replaced by a thoughtful look. 'How do you mean, protected?'

'I don't know.' Tarl shrugged, and gestured very, very carefully at the glowing green walls. 'Magic, or something like that. I mean, we are in the middle of a seam of mage-stone. If we are seriously discussing a sword with vocal capabilities, then this is major league enchantment we're dealing with.' He paused and shrugged. 'I've got a feeling that there's something unpleasant round the corner, that's all.'

Ronan looked at him thoughtfully. He'd learned to trust his friend's judgement by now. Tarl had turned scenting danger into an art form. On the other hand . . .

'Bollocks to that!' he scoffed, and drawing his sword he strode round the corner and found himself fighting desperately for his very life.

Bonaponere was sitting on a piece of broken column in a massive hall carved out of the living rock, waiting for Kaldis to return from scouting ahead, when a group of twelve orcs came swaggering in. For a moment they paused and stared, then their leader drew his barbed knife and fingered its point lovingly.

'Well, boys,' he snarled, 'looks like this is our lucky day. Let's have some fun.'

Bonaponere returned their gaze coolly and for a moment they faltered. Then Kaldis emerged from an archway behind them, axe in hand. As they turned to face him he blurred into motion. For a few seconds screams echoed around the lofty columns of the hall, and then Kaldis stood alone in the middle of a mass of quivering flesh and spouting blood. He smiled with satisfaction and licked his axe-blade clean.

'I like this place,' he said to Bonaponere. 'It's fun!'

'Any sign of the black warrior?'

'His trail goes down into the orc caves.'

'Then we'll wait at the north gates. Who knows? We might find some other travellers to . . . enjoy. Come on.'

The fearsome warrior was huge, at least a head taller than Ronan, and his skin was jet black. He was wearing only voluminous silk shalwar, and his thick arms and massive bare chest were so powerfully muscled that he made Ronan look as though he had been pining and refusing food for several weeks. His shaven head gleamed in the eerie light, and his enormous scimitar whirled in front of him almost too fast for the eye to follow. Only by using every last vestige of his skill and concentration could Ronan keep him at bay.

The floor of the passage was littered with the proof of his fighting prowess – dozens of broken and crumpled bodies in various stages of decomposition. Severed skulls lay amongst the bodies like discarded, misshapen footballs. Behind the huge warrior was an arched doorway through which pulsed an eerie blue light. With the shining green of the mage-stone in the passage walls it gave the strange impression that they were fighting under water.

Ronan's mind was rapidly calculating and evaluating, and was trying not to panic, but the last lightning-fast swipe of the scimitar had nearly got through.

He's good, you don't kill all those people by luck, there must be nearly a hundred bodies, there's loose skulls everywhere, he favours head shots, he's got firm ground underfoot, we're treading on corpses, better give ground, lure him out a bit, he can be the one tripping over dead bodies, klat! that was close, gods, he's so fast, the best I've ever faced, KLAT!

The huge warrior smiled coldly, secure in the knowledge that he had the advantage. 'All who dare to challenge the Guardian of the Sword have died!' he sneered, in a voice so deep it would have made Paul Robeson sound squeaky.

'Oh, yeah? Well, you can stick your sword up your ass and swivel, *katimo*!' gasped Ronan, as he readied himself for the murderous assault he knew was about to come.

The Guardian stared at him myopically for a moment with surprise etched on his massive face, all thoughts of attack forgotten.

'Klat! It's one of the brothers!' he said in amazement. 'Yo! My man! Gimme five!' He held out a hand palm upwards, and Ronan rather dazedly slapped it and then turned his own hand over to receive the answering slap. 'Am I glad to see you,' continued the Guardian. 'You know how long I've been stuck down here in this goddam cavern? Five hundred years! That's why I didn't recognise you at first. My eyes ain't what they used to be! Do you know how much decent company I've had in all that time? I'll tell you. None! Zilch! The big zero! Though there's been plenty of uncool white guys trying to take the Sword off me. First there were all the stocky guys with the beards and axes. Then there were the smelly little guys with the nasty personal habits. And not one of them bothered to pass the time of day. All they ever said was, "Gimme the sword, gimme the sword"! But hey, what's . . .' He stopped dead and his expression hardened. 'Shoot!' he said. 'Here comes another of those nasty little mothers now! Pardon me, but this will only take a moment.'

Raising his wicked-looking scimitar he started to prowl forwards. Ronan turned and saw that he had his eyes fixed on Tarl, who had decided that, as the Guardian had taken a liking to

Ronan, it was safe to come out of hiding and join them. From the look on his face, he was regretting that decision. Quickly, Ronan caught the Guardian by the arm.

'He's with me,' he said.

The Guardian looked surprised. 'Are you joking?' he asked doubtfully. Ronan shook his head. 'That's cool,' said the Guardian, lowering his sword. Tarl nearly collapsed with relief, and long crackling arcs of orange light started shooting out from his body.

The Guardian watched him with interest. 'Hey! Righteous, man!' he grinned.

'So how did you get to be the Guardian of the Sword?' Ronan asked him.

'I answered an advert in the Situations Vacant column of the *Ilex Times*. It said: "Smart warrior wanted. Must be self-motivated and able to work unsupervised. Steady work with long-term prospects. Uniform provided." Uniform? Ha! Look at these pants!' He looked enviously at Ronan's stylishly cut warrior leather gear and laughed bitterly. 'I reckon that guy Nekros suckered me good and proper!'

'Nekros?'

'Yeah, that's right. He's the guy that placed the Sword down here.'

Ronan and Tarl looked at each other. 'That makes Nekros at least five hundred years old,' said Tarl. 'I told you there was enchantment about.'

'And he's got something to do with the Sword,' replied Ronan, thoughtfully. 'You don't hide a magical sword in a place like this with a guard to look after it unless you want to keep it well away from people. Nekros must be worried about it for some reason. This has got to be the Sword that my father mentioned!'

The Guardian was looking from one to the other, puzzled. 'You know this guy Nekros?' he asked.

'You could say that,' muttered Ronan. He frowned, and one hand crept up to fondle the ragged teddy-bear head that still hung at his chest. 'He slaughtered my tribe and my father. I'm looking for vengeance and I need the Sword that you guard.'

Am embarrassed look crept across the face of the Guardian. 'Aw, shoot!' he said wistfully. 'I'd love to give you the mother, but

Nekros put a powerful enchantment on me. If I let it go, something real nasty is gonna happen! I just can't do it.'

Ronan nodded slowly. He'd been rather afraid that this might be the case. 'Then I guess we have to fight.'

'I guess,' agreed the Guardian sadly.

'No, wait!' interjected Tarl, stepping between the two of them. 'How long did Nekros tell you to guard the thing for?'

The Guardian thought for a moment. 'I don't know,' he said. 'He was kinda vague. He just said my job was to guard it.'

'So if the Sword isn't here any more, then your job's finished, and you could go home, right?'

'I guess so,' said the Guardian, a little doubtfully.

'And what instructions did Nekros give you?' continued Tarl. 'I mean, exactly what words did he use?'

There was a silence as the Guardian tried to remember the events of five hundred years previously. 'Well,' he said hesitantly, 'he said that I must let no one and nothing enter the Cavern of the Singing Sword. If anyone tried to do so, I must kill them.'

'Well, there you are then. We won't enter. We'll just wait here while you go in, fetch the Sword, and bring it out to us. Then your job is over and you can get the hell out of here!'

The Guardian considered this. He was obviously tempted but still looked doubtful. Tarl put one hand on his shoulder (which meant standing on tip-toe), and lowered his voice.

'Look,' he said beguilingly, 'we know this Nekros. He's never going to come back. You could be stuck down here forever. And you should see the world outside these days. Take Welbug. There are restaurants, wine-bars, taverns, casinos. And there's a little place we know called the Dragon's Claw . . .'

His voice faded away. The Guardian looked at him, intrigued. 'What's so special about this Dragon's Claw?' he asked. Tarl smiled.

'The women!' he said. There was a pause.

'The women?' said the Guardian, and in those two words could be heard the total loneliness of a life spent standing guard on your own in a cavern under a mountain in the middle of nowhere.

'Beautiful women,' continued Tarl. 'And we're very matey with the boss. If you go to the Dragon's Claw and say Ronan sent you, they will take you in, and they will look after you, nurture you, cosset you. They will do anything you want. And I mean absolutely anything. Believe me, I know.'

The Guardian stared at him for a moment and Tarl could see the hope burgeoning in his eyes. 'OK,' he said. 'You want a sword, you got a sword!' Once again he and Ronan slapped hands, then he disappeared through the doorway.

Ronan and Tarl peered after him. Inside was a vast, high-roofed cavern which was bathed in an eerie blue light that seemed to come from nowhere. An odd pulsating tune could be heard that sounded like an invisible mellotron playing a very long way away. Had they come from any one of a number of parallel worlds, Tarl and Ronan might instantly have thought 'Pink Floyd'. And there, hanging from a golden hook set into the far wall, was the Sword. The Guardian stood in front of it. For a moment he hesitated, then he raised one hand and lifted it down, wincing as he did so. It was obvious that he half expected something to happen to him, but nothing did, and so he grabbed the scabbard that had been hanging beside the Sword, and hurried across the cavern and out through the archway.

'Here it is!' he said, and handed the Sword to Ronan. The warrior hefted it in his hand. It was plain and unornamented, and rather smaller than the massive weapons he was used to, but it seemed to glow and pulse with some inner light. He suddenly realised that the distant music seemed to be coming from deep within it.

'Hey, it's singing!' he exclaimed.

'Huh!' said Tarl, unimpressed. 'Dinosaur music!'

At this, the Sword suddenly went quiet. Ronan looked at it, a little worried. He had the distinct impression it was sulking.

'Listen,' continued Tarl. 'You've got the Sword, now let's get the hell out of here!'

'Yeah,' said the Guardian, looking round a trifle nervously, 'before something nasty happens!'

Ronan smiled at him, and then brandished the Sword above his head in a fit of exhilaration. 'Nothing will stop me now,' he cried, and his voice echoed along the corridor. 'Nekros, your doom approaches!' And then he slid the Sword into its scabbard, tossed the one from the dragon hoard carelessly through the archway of the cavern and strode off down the passage. The Guardian followed and Tarl, still gently giving off sparks, brought up the rear.

They had little difficulty in deciphering the chart for this area as it was relatively unaffected by wine-stains, and after climbing several staircases they found themselves marching along a broad stone passageway. It was obviously a road that was in occasional use as it was littered with discarded or broken items, and there were frequent unpleasant and distinctly smelly signs of the recent passage of orcs. However, Ronan was in no mood to feel in the slightest bit threatened by a bunch of degenerate and cannibalistic party-goers and strode boldly on. The Sword was for the most part silent now, although occasionally it seemed to be muttering grumpily to itself.

They continued for a mile or so then the passage bent to the right and they could see daylight ahead. They rounded a bend, and there in front of them was an open doorway. Tarl might have stopped and exclaimed in admiration at the skill with which long-dead dwarf stone-masons had carved the magnificent archway above this, the northern entrance to the city of Samoth. But he had other things on his mind. He was suddenly almost overwhelmed by a burst of claustrophobia and started to run. For most of his life, daylight had been something he liked to see fading as he got up and had breakfast before heading off to a party, but now, after the best part of two days in gloomy underground caverns, it seemed achingly attractive. He burst through the doorway ahead of the other two and stopped right on the edge of a precipitous drop, blinking in the bright sunshine and staring in wonder at the view that was spread out before him.

He was standing on a flat stone balcony hewn out of the cliff. To one side, a steep flight of steps wound tortuously down the side of the mountain. In front of him in the vale below he could see the River Betw winding its way westwards, and beyond it, soft green pastureland rolled away to the north. In the very distance, he could just make out the snow-covered peaks of the Northern Mountains, and far away to the west, a distant shimmering blue marked the position of the sea. He sighed at the sheer beauty of it all, and then sat down with his legs dangling over the edge. Ronan walked up beside him, and stood staring into the distance, a small smile hovering on his lips. Behind them, the Guardian stood blinking in the unfamiliar daylight.

'Well, you've got all the things your father said you'd need. You just haven't got this Nekros,' said Tarl.

'I know where to find him,' said Ronan, softly.

'You do?'

'Yeah. Remember what Anthrax said to me about a cycle being circular?'

Tarl nodded. 'I thought he was just talking a load of bollocks.'

'No, he spoke the truth.' Ronan pointed at the distant pasture-land. 'Over there, no more than a day's march away, is a quiet little land called Tak, and in Tak was the small village where this all began. The village where I grew up. When I reach there, I've gone full circle. That's what the Wizard meant. That is where I will find Nekros the Black.'

Tarl looked out over the verdant scenery laid out below them like a map. He found it depressing, all this countryside. He ached for a nice smoky casino in the middle of a noisy great city. All at once he knew in his heart that it was time his path left Ronan's. He looked up at the big warrior, who was standing gazing at the view with a dreamy smile on his face. How the hell was he going to break the news?

Then, from somewhere down the mountain, came the scream of a terrified woman.

Ronan dashed down the winding stone steps that curved round the side of the mountain then skidded to a halt. Cowering on the ground in front of him was a beautiful young woman, and towering above her with axe upraised was a snarling cave-troll. Without a moment's hesitation Ronan drew the Singing Sword and leapt to her defence, but seconds later he found that he was almost wishing he hadn't bothered. The troll went straight on to the attack, its axe whirling lethally, and for the second time in an hour Ronan found himself faced by a phenomenally good opponent.

However, it had never fought anyone as skilled as Ronan before and seemed surprised when he managed to ward off its attack. For a moment it stared at the Sword, which was literally humming with excitement, and then it lunged forward again. But Ronan defended calmly, almost contentedly, for he had spotted a flaw.

Three times the axe-blade whirled at his head, only to be deflected at the last second. Then, as it came at him a fourth time, Ronan struck, slicing upwards with the Sword. The axe whizzed past his head with a severed troll hand still clinging on to it, and then he struck again backhanded, and the Sword sliced cleanly through the troll's neck.

The young woman watched incredulously as the troll's body toppled forward and its head bounced off down the mountainside, and then she picked herself off the ground and flung herself sobbing into Ronan's arms. Awkwardly he stroked her flaxen hair, trying to soothe her. She looked up into his face and smiled, and he was struck almost dumb by her beauty. He felt her arms begin to encircle him, and then something whizzed past his shoulder, and he gasped in horror as a throwing-knife thudded home into her eye-socket. She gave a little gasp, then the colour drained from her face and she fell limply from his arms.

Swearing, he spun round, and was stunned to see Tarl still crouched in the follow-through of his throw, with the Guardian standing behind him. Uncomprehendingly he watched as his friend straightened up, walked down the steps, and jerked his knife free.

'You pranny!' yelled Tarl. 'What do you think you're playing at?' With his foot he kicked loose the needle-thin assassin's blade that was still held in the dead woman's hand. Ronan felt a chill like a small icicle melting run down his spine. The tip was stained dark with poison!

'That's Kaldis,' Tarl continued, gesturing at the troll, 'and this rather pretty young girl is Bonaponere. I saw them once, up in Orcville. They're two of the top hit-men around. Or they were. Always worked as a team.'

He stooped and wiped his knife clean on the grass. He was feeling angry. He'd played quite a lot of *skeels* during his life, but that eye-shot had probably been the best throw he'd ever done and he hadn't even had a bet on it.

'Thick as two short planks[1], you are,' he snapped at Ronan. 'Hugging a snake like her! What the hell is Tyson going to say?'

[1] Very thick (as opposed to 'thick as two short Plancks', which means not in the slightest bit thick, in fact, quite frighteningly intelligent. The Planck twins were a pair of Dwarves from Ilex who made incredible strides in the field of quantum mechanics).

Ronan blanched. This time the chill down his spine felt as though an entire glacier had melted. Tarl looked at him and shook his head.

'It's painfully obvious that without me around you're about as much use as a glass of milk at an orc party. Come on, we've got to get you to a show-down.'

And without waiting to see if Ronan or the Guardian were following, Tarl set off down the stone steps towards the distant lands below.

VENGEANCE

*The tiny land of Tak, although virtually unknown outside
Frundor, had until recently one main claim to fame. It was
the scene of the Great Baylene Disaster, early in the Second
Age. Baylene were, at that time, the world's most famous
musical group, and their decision to stage an open-air
concert in Tak one midsummer day resulted in the largest
festival crowd the world had ever seen. The concert was
spectacular, with lights, fireworks, and numerous other
special effects, but the highlight of the show was to have
been during their final song, when eleven Golden Dragons
from the Eastern Wastes had been booked to perform an
aerobatic act. This was reputedly the most incredible sight
of the Age, with the massive dragons diving, rolling and
swooping in perfect formation low over the heads of the
crowd, their golden scales and jewelled wings glittering and
shining like a million tiny suns. Unfortunately, someone
had forgotten to ask the dragons specifically not to breathe
flame (which they habitually did when excited), and as a
result, the largest outdoor concert in history became the
largest mass cremation . . .*

The Pink Book of Ulay

The Tribe of Fallon were camped on the bank of the River Menea,
in northern Frundor, awaiting a decision. The huge dark horses
cropped at the sparse grass, while their riders bustled about
impatiently, occasionally casting a wary eye at the black tent that
was pitched in the centre of the camp. They were impatient
because they knew they would be hanging around here until their
leader had come to some sort of a decision. They were wary
because they knew that to help him come to a decision he was
messing around with his magic again, and that invariably meant
he would be in a foul mood for the rest of the day. And when

Nekros was in a foul mood, people suffered.

There was a sudden flash of light and a very small explosion from the direction of the tent, followed by the sound of Nekros's voice raised in loud and fervent cursing. Wisps of grey smoke began to eddy out through the tent flaps. The men of the tribe looked fearfully at each other, and a couple of the horses whinnied nervously. As usual, it sounded as though things were not going well on the magic front.

Inside the tent, Nekros was staring frustratedly at the small round crystal ball which sat on a little table in front of him. Beside it was a dish in which a burning wick floated in aromatic oil. In one hand he was holding a notebook which contained large numbers of spells and charms, all written in his small and rather untidy handwriting. In the other, he was holding a vial of grey powder, which he had just sprinkled over the flame. His face was blackened, smoke was slowly wafting from his hair, and his beard looked slightly singed around the edges. He turned his eyes to the notebook, and peered at it again. Klat! Why couldn't he write neatly? He always found it difficult to read his own spells. He could have sworn that word was nitre! He peered at the crabby script. Maybe it was nacre . . . Cursing again, he hurled the book from him in a fury. It was definitely one of those days.

When Nekros had met and tricked the witch Shikara all those years ago he had been of the opinion that magic was easy. All you needed was the Power and a spell-book. With his savage fighting ability, his charisma, his evil intelligence, and now his magical powers, he expected to be ruling the world pretty damn' quickly. Yet here he was, five hundred years later, and he still hadn't made it. And all because this magic lark wasn't as straight-forward as he'd thought.

True, he had enough basic powers to run rings around the average non-magical warrior. But when it came to the more complex stuff, things were different. It was a bit like cooking. Some people can take a strange recipe, bang about in the kitchen for a bit, and produce a perfect meal. Others can practise the same damn' recipe for weeks, yet it still turns out tasting like a plate of orc-dung half the time. You either have the aptitude or you haven't. And when it came to magic, Nekros didn't. Sometimes the tricky stuff worked, to be sure. Sometimes he could rap out a spell and everything would work perfectly. But other times, it just went totally wrong.

Recently, it hadn't mattered too much. The backers had contacted him, providing organisation and planning, and had brought in Anthrax. Then the Wizard had warned him about the threat offered by the black warrior who sported a teddy-bear head at his chest. For some reason this reminded Nekros of something, but he couldn't quite pin it down. The guy had duly turned up out of nowhere and looked like being a real pain in the backside. Firstly Welbug had slipped from Nekros's grasp, and then Anthrax had calmly mentioned that this lone warrior presented a threat to his very life! And every time Nekros thought he'd trapped him, the guy slithered out from his clutches. And now, for some reason, Anthrax had gone incommunicado. Nekros had thought it wouldn't matter, as he had the power to make his own predictions, but now, just when he dearly wanted to see a mere twenty-four hours ahead, his powers were playing him up again.

Scowling, he racked his brains to try and work out what he'd done wrong, and deciding to have one last go at contacting the Wizard he grabbed the crystal ball in both hands and muttered another incantation. To his surprise, this time it appeared to work. There was the faint humming noise that meant his crystal was linking itself to another, then it went dark and an opaque mist began to grow inside it, swirling and eddying until it seemed to fill the crystal. The mist vanished, to be replaced by the face of an old woman.

'Malvenis 371,' she said.

'What?' said Nekros, a little taken aback.

'I said Malvenis 371. Who is this please?'

'Er . . . Nekros the Black.'

'What?' screeched the woman. 'Did you say the necklace is back?'

'No! Nekros! Nekros the Black! Look, get me Anthrax!'

'What hand-bags?'

Nekros stared crossly at the image, puzzled. This couldn't be Anthrax's number after all. Maybe he'd connected to the oracle, instead of linking with the Wizard. 'Listen,' he yelled, 'I need a prediction!'

'A free what?' The old lady looked totally baffled. Nekros sighed. It was just his luck to get an oracle who was as deaf as a post.

'A forecast!' he yelled. The old woman looked affronted.

'There's no need to shout,' she said. 'And anyway, this is a cake-shop, not a betting-office. Good-day!'

The crystal ball went blank again and Nekros covered his eyes with one hand and silently counted to ten. Then he stood up, retrieved the book from where it lay, and thumbed through it until he came to the Spell of Precognition section. Hmm. Perhaps that did say nacre after all. He wrenched open a wooden chest that sat on the ground by the table, replaced the vial of nitre, and took out a small bottle of powdered oyster-shell. He muttered the incantation again and sprinkled some of the powder over the burning flame. There was a loud bang and a flare of indigo smoke. When it had cleared, Nekros found that the burning flame had turned into a bunch of freesias. His face darkened in rage, and he was just about to storm off in search of a neck to sever when there was a ringing tone from the crystal ball, and Anthrax's face suddenly appeared inside it.

'Ah, Nekros, my dear chap!' beamed the Wizard's image. 'Sorry I haven't been in touch. Been up to here with things. You know how it is.'

Nekros grunted, mentally counting to ten. Whenever he heard the Wizard's smug, middle-class, patronising tones he found that he was seized with an almost irresistible urge to smash a sword straight through the middle of the crystal ball.

'Well, now,' continued the image of the Wizard. 'I have new orders for you from our backers. They want you to send some men down to the River Betw ferry this afternoon. And then, tomorrow, they want you to stop off at a little village in Tak . . .'

Anthrax sat back as the crystal ball faded and Nekros's ugly face disappeared. For a few moments he toyed with the gold token in his right hand. One side of the token held the letters DCGP, and the other had a stylised pair of hand-restraints. Then he stood up.

'May the best man win,' he murmured, and went off to pack.

The filthy old ferryman poled his battered little boat up to the jetty and flung the mooring-rope over a wooden bollard with unerring aim. Ronan and the Guardian, who had been deep in conversation about weapons, stood up, and Ronan stirred the sleeping Tarl with his foot. Grumbling, Tarl dragged himself up and followed the other two on to the jetty, where they stood looking round.

In front of them was a group of wooden shacks which were leaning drunkenly against each other seeming in imminent danger of collapsing. A couple of moth-eaten dogs were snarling warnings at each other in the middle of the dusty track, but there was no other sign of life and, apart from the distant call of a *pakas* which had got extremely lost and was beginning to sound rather cross, there was no other sound. Ronan and the Guardian began to walk along the track, but Tarl paused. The hairs on the back of his neck were rising again. Something was wrong. He turned and saw that the ferryman had cast off from the jetty, and was heading towards the other bank as quickly as possible, occasionally casting frightened glances back over his shoulder. Something was most definitely wrong.

Tarl turned back and stared at the tumble-down buildings ahead of them. They seemed to be deserted. Everything was still. Too still.

'Ronan!' he called. The warrior heard the nervous edge to his voice, stopped, and looked back inquiringly. At that moment Tarl saw a flash of movement at two of the windows. 'Ambush!' he yelled, and dived for cover. Ronan, with his experience of Tarl's in-built threatometer, threw himself behind a large rock without looking round, but the Guardian stood rooted to the spot for a couple of seconds. Black-shafted arrows whizzed about him, but luckily for him they had been aimed at Ronan, and by the time the ambushers had altered their aim and loosed a second flight, he had joined Ronan behind the rock.

'What's going on?' he asked in an aggrieved tone as Tarl came wriggling through the dust to join them.

'Oh, it's just that Ronan here is a really popular guy,' said Tarl. 'Wherever he goes, people want to give him things. Arrows. Knives. Swords. Fetters. Poison. That sort of thing. You soon get used to it.'

Ronan peered round the rock and gestured to Tarl. 'Give me the

219

bow,' he ordered. There was an awkward silence and Ronan ducked back and stared at Tarl, who was giving him one of his wide range of cheesy grins. It was a particularly ingratiating one, which was a sure sign of bad news. Ronan sighed sadly.

'You haven't got it, have you?' he said.

'Well, I thought that once we'd left Samoth, we were safe,' gabbled Tarl. 'I mean, I'd been carrying all that stuff for miles, I just thought I could lighten my load a bit. I did keep my dagger, though!'

'Oh, great!' snarled Ronan. 'Pass it here. I'll chuck it at them, and maybe with a lucky shot I might kill all fifteen of them!'

He sat back and thought for a moment or two, and then drew the Sword from his scabbard. It was pulsing with a faint light, and began to make an eerie keening sound that set their teeth on edge.

'Of course! The Sword!' cried Tarl. 'It's magical! Couldn't it sort of fly through the air like an angel of death and maybe kill all the . . . erm . . .' His voice died away into an embarrassed mumble. Ronan and the Guardian were looking at him pityingly.

'Get real, guy,' said the Guardian.

Tarl pretended to look for something in his pack. 'Klatting Sword,' he mumbled in embarrassment. 'It's no klatting use at all!' The Sword immediately stopped its keening and muttered something. Tarl wasn't sure, but he thought the second word sounded like 'off'.

'You reckon there's fifteen of them?' asked the Guardian.

'About that, from what I can see,' answered Ronan.

'Better make it twenty,' said the Guardian, who was staring out over the river. Ronan saw that the ferry-boat was now heading towards them, and crouched behind the ferryman were five black-clad warriors, armed to the teeth. He peered round the rock again, urgently scanning their surroundings and looking for an escape route. The occasional arrow was still winging its way past and Ronan knew that trying to run for it would be tantamount to suicide.

'Er, shouldn't we do something?' asked Tarl, who was now beginning to get a little nervous. Ronan peered up the track past the decrepit wooden buildings for a few seconds, and then stared steadily at his friend.

'Yes,' he said. 'Surrender.' And to Tarl's horror, he thrust the

Sword into his scabbard, threw it out into the open, then raised his hands, and walked out after it. Tarl and the Guardian stared blankly at each other, and then the Guardian shrugged and stood up. Tarl waited for a few more seconds, just to see if anyone was likely to fill surrendering people full of arrows, and when the Guardian remained upright and unhurt he stood up himself and waited apprehensively.

The door of one of the shacks opened, and a black-clad warrior strolled insolently out. Ronan recognised him as the one who, five years before, had forced the odious Prior Onion from his lair. What was his name? Angnail, that was it. Nekros's second-in-command. Well, well, well. It would be a pleasure to kill him.

Angnail stood smirking at Ronan while his men swarmed out of the shacks and took up their positions, five to one side with bows ready to fire, the others lined up behind him, swords in hand. At the river's edge, the five remaining men clambered out of the ferry. Ronan and his two companions were surrounded.

Angnail swaggered forward and raised his sword until the tip was resting at Ronan's chest. Ronan gazed at him steadily, without flinching. Angnail's eyes fastened on the bear head at Ronan's chest and he smiled scornfully. 'Say night-night to teddy,' he mocked, and raised the point of his sword until it was resting under Ronan's chin.

Tarl couldn't bear to watch. He was feeling horribly sick. It looked as though these guys took no prisoners! He couldn't believe it, after they had come so far! Was this how they were all fated to die, butchered in the wild by the Tribe of Fallon? Were they to be slaughtered off-hand, with no witnesses save for the frail old peasant woman who was limping down the track towards them with her moth-eaten donkey? He stared hopelessly at these two pathetic creatures, praying that they would realise the danger they were stumbling into.

The donkey stared back at him and winked.

Tarl's heart gave a lurch. It couldn't be! But there was only one donkey who looked that knackered, and the old peasant woman might be limping, but when you looked closely she didn't seem all that frail . . . Puss and Tyson! No wonder Ronan had surrendered with such a confident smile on his face! But he'd mistimed it! Angnail wasn't going to mess about, and they were too far away to help. Ronan only had seconds left . . .

'Hey, do you know what we've found?' Tarl suddenly found himself babbling. 'Up in those mountains behind us? A dragon's hoard!'

There was a sudden silence as every eye turned to look at him. 'I'm not joking,' he rushed on. 'You wouldn't believe how much loot is there! Just take a look at this!' He lowered one hand to the dagger at his belt, and became painfully aware that five arrows were instantly pointing directly at his heart. Slowly, so as not to nudge anyone's trigger finger, he lifted the dagger from its scabbard and held it up. The solid gold handle gleamed dully and the silver tracery and inlaid jewels flashed in the afternoon sun. The men all stared at the weapon with avarice, and for a brief moment you could have heard a pin drop.

Then all at once the silence was shattered by a maniacal and unearthly braying. Tarl thought that Puss must have been practising. Not only did its horrible bray chill the blood, but somehow it had added a sort of demonic quality that froze the muscles, too. For an instant the tribesmen were all rooted to the spot. Out of the corner of his eye Tarl saw Tyson snatching a bow from within the folds of her tattered disguise, and Puss seemed to turn into a small brown thunderbolt streaking towards the foe. Beside him, Ronan stooped to grab the Sword, jerking it free from the scabbard, and as it came loose it blazed with light, emitting a keening wail that was even more chilling than the donkey's foul racket. Then he was swinging it in a vicious backhand cut at Angnail's throat.

Yammering with fear, Angnail leapt backwards and the sword hissed past a hair's breadth away from his neck. He turned to run, yelling at his bowmen to shoot, but the words froze on his lips. Three of them were lying there with arrows sticking out of their eye-sockets, and as he watched, the old peasant woman calmly put another arrow straight into the mouth of a fourth, who fell backwards with a horrible choking scream. The fifth had managed to notch an arrow to his bow and was drawing the string back when the dragon-hoard dagger whirled through the air and thumped home in his neck.

The rest of Angnail's men were faring no better. He watched in dismay as the black warrior attacked them, his triumphantly wailing sword dismembering or disembowelling five men in as many seconds. Behind them, a small brown whirlwind with teeth like knives and eyes like windows on hell was ham-stringing others with vicious slashes of its powerful little jaws. At the riverside, the five from the boat were being cut to bloody ribbons by the whirling scimitar of the other warrior. Wherever he looked his men were screaming and dying in a welter of spouting blood and flayed flesh.

Three of them broke and ran, and Angnail, who had been Nekros's lieutenant more for his sly cunning than for any valour or fighting skill, ran with them. To his horror the old woman brought them down with carefully placed arrows, but then she threw down her bow and drew a tooth-pick of a sword. Under the rags he could now see that she was really quite young, a mere slip of a girl. Excellent! She was out of arrows and none of the others had a bow. All he needed to do was hack her down and run to the horses hidden behind the shacks and he'd be away. They'd never catch him!

Grinning mirthlessly, he slashed at the girl, but just as his blade was about to slice home she seemed to shimmer, and somehow his sword was deflected. And then there was a shrieking pain in his guts that felt as though someone had poured red-hot lava straight into his stomach. Staring down, he saw that her sword was plunged deep into his midriff, and he looked up unbelievingly to meet the gaze of a pair of flinty green eyes. His vision faded, and as the day turned suddenly to night he heard a soft whisper.

'No one threatens my man. Welcome to hell, baby!'

Tyson tugged her sword free and watched dispassionately as Angnail's lifeless body toppled forward. Stooping, she wiped the blade clean on his clothing, and then she turned and found Ronan walking towards her, a silly grin on his face. Her heart did a funny little skip inside her.

'Hiya, Muscles,' she said. 'Miss me?' She lifted one hand, brushed a couple of dreadlocks back from his face, and gently stroked his cheek with the back of her fingers. Ronan put one arm around her, pulled her to him, and held her against his chest. In his other hand, the blood-stained Sword was pulsing faintly and humming softly to itself in a satisfied tone.

Tarl was watching the two of them with a soppy smile when he realised that something was rubbing against his leg and looking down he saw that the donkey was nuzzling against him. 'Hey, Puss!' he said, scratching it behind its ears. 'Was I glad to see you! I thought we'd had it!' The donkey closed its eyes blissfully and revelled in the scratching for a moment. Then it wrinkled its nose delicately, and looked up at Tarl.

'Here,' it said, 'when are you going to realise that, just because you're on the road, it doesn't mean that you shouldn't take a bath every once in a while? Or is it some new after-shave you've found? Old Socks for Men? Eau de Iferous, perhaps?'

Tarl stared at it. 'I'm glad you can talk,' he said dryly. 'Remind me to thank Anthrax, won't you?'

The donkey smiled to itself and rubbed its blood-stained muzzle happily against his legs. Like both Tarl and Ronan, Puss was beginning to appreciate the value of friends.

Three hours later Ronan, Tyson, and Tarl were sitting around a camp-fire passing a wine-skin back and forth, while Puss lay on his side nearby. The Guardian had already left, clutching a gold token with DCGP on one side and an image of a pair of hand-restraints on the other. It was a Dragon's Claw Gold Pass, valid for one year, presented to him by a grateful Tyson. The Guardian was jogging along the Welbug road as fast as his legs would carry him, with a song in his heart and a warm but urgent glow in his loins.

Tarl gazed up at the stars and savoured the wine. No lumps at all, Ah, well, never mind.

'What's puzzling me,' he said after a while, 'is how you knew where we'd be?'

'Anthrax,' answered Tyson. 'He said you'd be in danger. We followed you to Carn Betw, but we missed you by half an hour, so we took a boat downstream and waited.'

'I wouldn't trust that Wizard an inch,' muttered Tarl.

'Oh, he was as good as gold,' said the donkey. 'Mind you, Tyson had something he wanted.'

There was a brief silence. Ronan had gone very still. Tyson looked at him with a mischievous grin on her lips. 'It was only a Gold Pass,' she laughed. 'When I told him about Takuma, our muddy pond specialist, he couldn't do enough for us!'

'The dirty old warlock!' said Tarl.

'He deserves it,' said Tyson. 'He's set Nekros up for us. Now it's up to you and Ronan.'

'Me?'

'Yeah. You've got the Power. Anthrax said so.'

'No, I haven't! Well, maybe. OK, I might have. But I can't control it!'

'The book will show you how.'

'What book?'

'The book of spells that you stole from the castle of the wood-elves. Anthrax said we won't succeed without that.'

Tarl looked a little shifty. Things were coming to a pretty pass if you couldn't borrow a book without some klatting Wizard grassing on you to all your mates.

'Oh, that thing!' he muttered. 'It's crap. I tried to curse a sentry at Carn Betw. No effect at all.'

'Don't you believe it!' scoffed Puss. 'If it was the Water Gate sentry, it worked OK! He'd made a right mess of his trousers. Smelt worse than you do!'

'You're joking!' exclaimed the astonished Tarl. 'You mean, I can really do it?'

'Too right,' said Tyson, 'and tomorrow you're going to find out just how powerful you are!'

Tarl studied her laughing face, and then grabbed the wine-sack and took a long swallow. He had an awful feeling he wasn't going to enjoy the next day one little bit.

The village stood waiting, as it had always stood, a tiny corner of a tiny land. Much had changed since Ronan left. The village hall had finally conceded defeat to gravity, and was just a pile of rotting timber. The well looked decidedly ill. Many of the huts had collapsed. And yet some still stood, and one or two new ones had been built. Those folk who had successfully fled from the Tribe of Fallon had painfully put their lives back together again. The village still lived, but only just.

Ronan and his companions had been walking for three hours when they finally came to the village, and for most of the time Ronan and Tyson hadn't been talking. They had started by discussing their strategy, but then had come a major disagreement. Tyson wanted to be in at the kill beside her man, but Ronan was worried by Anthrax's predictions. The Wizard had told him that he could prevail against Nekros, but no mention had been made of Tyson. Anything might happen. For instance, she might get killed. And so he flatly refused to have her come anywhere near his enemy.

Tyson was stalking along the road wearing an expression that would have frozen lava. Behind her, Ronan was looking like a six year old who has just been sent to bed for giving his dinner to the cat. Behind them, Tarl was half embarrassed by the row and half scared crapless by what lay ahead. Only the donkey seemed happy, and that was mainly because it was fairly confident of getting a good square meal out of the forthcoming encounter.

But when Ronan finally breasted a low rise and saw the huts of the village ahead of him, the argument was suddenly forgotten. He could feel a pricking at the back of his eyes, and he had a lump in his throat. Suddenly, he was scared to go on. Not because of Nekros, but because of the memories that crowded into his mind. Long summer days playing among the huts with the other village children. Cold winter nights huddled by the warmth of the fire as his mother read to him. Those searing days in the smithy at his father's side, learning to forge weapons. And, most painful of all, the night when the Tribe of Fallon had torn apart his life.

Seeing the expression on his face, Tyson relented. Now he was looking like a six year old standing in the middle of a busy street who has just realised that his parents have disappeared. She gave his arm a squeeze of encouragement and Tarl stopped on his other side and offered him the wine-sack. Ronan shook his head. But then he remembered his father's image in the eerie blue flame of the camp-fire. Now, after five long years, he was only hours away from a revenge as sweet as honey. Suddenly he couldn't bear to wait. With a new determination he strode forward, and the others followed him.

At first as they entered the village it appeared deserted. They paced slowly up the main street past the tumble-down huts and cottages, all of which seemed in desperate need of repair. There wasn't a sound to be heard, not even a *pakas*. And then an old man came tottering out of one of the huts and nervously approached them. Tarl thought he'd never seen anyone so thin. His legs looked as though you could make fire by rubbing them together, and his arms were even skinnier. Tarl had seen healthier-looking skeletons. He was about to make some comment when he realised that Ronan was staring in awe at this vision, almost as though he had seen a ghost.

The old man staggered up to them and stopped. 'Greetings, noble strangers,' he said in a voice that was surprisingly strong. 'Welcome to our village. My name is Palin. If there is any way I can be of help to you . . .' His voice died away as he became aware of Ronan's rapt gaze, and he looked a little uncomfortable. 'Well, almost any way . . .' he muttered.

'Old Palin!' gasped Ronan. 'The last time I saw you, you were pinned to the ground by an arrow! I thought you were dead!'

'Pinned to the ground? Here, you're not one of them pillaging bastards, are you?'

Ronan shook his head, and smiled. 'I'm Ronan,' he said. 'I've come home.'

The old man looked at him unbelievingly, and then a slow smile crossed his face. 'Young Ronan,' he said. 'By all the gods, it is you!' He seized Ronan's hand and pumped it rapidly up and down. He was so frail that to Ronan it felt a bit like shaking hands with a piece of origami. 'Just look at you,' continued Palin. 'Your father always said you'd make a warrior, but we never really believed him.' He turned to the others. 'He was such a skinny boy, you see. And weak! Just the effort of picking up a sword used to give him a nose-bleed! Why, I can remember one day . . .'

As the old man related his story, Ronan felt like cringing. Why was it, he wondered (like so many people before him), that when you brought a girl home for the first time, people had to start relating embarrassing stories about your childhood? If he tells the one about the day my potty shattered, he thought, and where they put the stitches, I shall have to leave.

But luckily the old man suddenly stopped and struck himself on the forehead with one hand. 'Listen to me,' he cried, 'wittering on about the past when you have travelled so far to visit us! Come, rest awhile in my hut and tell me what has been happening to you!'

As he led them across to one of the largest and least decrepit huts, Tyson grinned at Ronan. 'So you weren't always such a hunk, eh?' she said.

'I'll bet it was no different for you when you were young,' said Ronan, a little uncomfortably. 'I'll bet you were all pretty frocks, pony-tails and freckles!'

'Don't you believe it,' she answered. 'I was the son my father never had, remember. Even when I was in my cot, I had a morning star instead of a rattle.' She smiled up at him, and gave his arm a squeeze as they entered the hut.

The interior gave an impression of roominess, mainly because there was nothing inside it except a couple of shelves and, in one corner, a malodorous blanket. The donkey took one sniff, wrinkled its nose in disgust, and walked out again. Old Palin fussed about, taking some cracked mugs from a shelf and filling them with a sludge-brown liquid that he claimed was fresh water. Then he picked up a jar and offered it round. It held a number of pieces of straw, all about six inches long.

'Cheese straw, anyone?' he asked.

Tyson stared. It was just straw, plain and simple.

'They're a bit light on the cheese,' said Old Palin. 'You have to use your imagination. Would you prefer a Twiglet?'

He produced another jar, which contained a few bits of twig. Some of them still had leaves attached to them. Tyson took one and looked at it, horrified.

'You actually eat these?' she asked in disbelief.

'Not personally,' replied Old Palin. 'I can't chew them up any more.' He grinned at them, and they saw that he only had the one tooth, which sat glowering in the centre of his lower gum like a moss-covered tombstone. 'Occasionally I try and suck the goodness out of one. When I've got something to celebrate, like. But these are for visitors. Well, we heard a rumour someone was on their way. Mind you, we thought it was another of them marauding tribes. That's why the village is empty. They've all fled to the mountains for safety. They left me here to greet the marauders when they arrive. To shake their leader's hand, and that.'

'What good would that do?'

'Well, I've got leprosy, you see. They were rather hoping I might pass it on.'

Ronan looked at the old man, then got up and walked to the door. He stood there looking out for a moment, and then turned back.

'You are going to have visitors,' he said. 'The Tribe of Fallon. They'll be here soon. But don't worry. We're here to help you.'

'The Tribe of Fallon, you say. How many of them?'

'About seventy.'

Old Palin looked at Tyson, then at Tarl, who had seated himself on the blanket and was busily finishing off the contents of the wine-sack. At that moment Puss the donkey wandered in again. Palin met its gaze and visibly blanched.

'And you have a woman, a piss-head, and a small brown donkey?' The old man paused for a moment. 'Fine. Well, if you want me, I shall be up in the mountains. Good luck.'

With that he shot out of the door as though all the demons in hell were after him. Ronan watched him disappear up the road at a rate surprising for one so frail, and Tyson joined him and linked her arm through his.

'OK, Muscles,' she said, and all of a sudden he could hear the apprehension in her voice. 'It's you, me and the Dead-beat Brothers here against seventy savage tribesmen. We'd better get ready.'

Ronan could feel the butterflies starting up in his stomach. He took a deep breath. He'd been confidently planning this moment for the last five years, but all of a sudden the odds didn't look too good. No. That was wrong.

They looked klatting awful.

Nekros was beginning to feel a little uneasy. He stood up in his stirrups and gazed across the rolling plains to the south. Nothing. Where the hell had Angnail got to? Presumably he was still waiting to ambush the black warrior at the Carn Betw ferry. But according to Anthrax, the guy was supposed to turn up there yesterday. So what had delayed him? Ah! Kaldis and Bonaponere must have caught up with him! Excellent! Yes, that would be it. It was a pity he couldn't find out for sure.

Over the past few years Nekros had been operating at the hub of a communications network the like of which Midworld had never before seen, with agents in every town and city connected to him by Anthrax's crystal balls. Now all of a sudden he was stuck out in the wilds of Frundor without the faintest idea what was going on elsewhere. His own crystal ball had steadfastly refused to work properly ever since Anthrax's last message. Every time he tried to operate it, it just flashed up the words 'Normal service will be resumed as soon as possible' in flowing Gothic script. He scowled at the heavy velvet bag hanging from his saddle in which it rested. He hated being cut off.

The phrase 'cut off' had unpleasant connotations for the rest of his tribe as well, but for different reasons. Their leader had become decidedly stroppy in the past week or two, ever since his plans had started going wrong, and a number of the tribe had had their heads cut off just because they had been handy when Nekros had flown into a rage. Originally, they had followed him mainly because his sorcery granted them a greatly extended life-span, but now, if you happened to be in the wrong place at the wrong time, your life (and your body) was likely to be abruptly truncated, and the first faint murmurings of disquiet could be heard amongst the men.

Nekros frowned and shifted restlessly on his horse. He had a feeling that something was wrong. It wasn't like Anthrax to be out in his predictions, and the latest instructions that the Wizard had given him were a little puzzling. Take out some obscure little village, well yes, fair enough. His backers presumably had their reasons. But why had they told him to ride into the village with no more than twelve men? Presumably they knew what they were doing. But he didn't like it, didn't like it at all.

Abruptly he shook his head, annoyed with himself. He was turning into a right old woman. The village hadn't been built which could harm him and twelve of his best men! But still, things had been going wrong lately . . . He swung round and hurled out his orders. Six bowmen and six swordsmen to ride with him, the rest of the tribe to remain here and follow them in ten minutes. Then feeling distinctly un-macho, he spurred his horse and galloped off, followed by his twelve chosen men.

In Palin's hut, Ronan was watching Tarl, who was sitting cross-legged upon the floor breathing hard, with a sheen of sweat upon his face. A small fire was burning in front of him, and he held the book of spells open in one hand and Tyson's blood-stained sword in the other. On the fire rested a small copper dish on which was a hank of Angnail's greasy scalp which Tyson had cut from him in readiness. A faint smell of singeing hair began to pervade the air, and Tarl leant forward and began to mutter the words.

The remaining members of the Tribe of Fallon waited to follow their leader. Some were milling about aimlessly on their horses, others had dismounted and were talking furiously. A rumour had swept through them that Angnail had seized his chance and had deserted, taking his men with him to search for richer and easier pickings down south.

Suddenly, their horses began to skitter nervously as a figure appeared hovering in the air above them. It appeared to be a normal man clad all in black. He was hooded, and his head was bowed so that they could not see his features, yet there was an air of menace about him. Despite the fact that they were sixty strong, some of the Tribe shivered. Then the figure threw back his hood and they could see that it was Angnail. His face was clearly visible and yet they could see through him, as though his flesh had no substance. His eyes were red and burned like coals, and when he raised one hand to point back where they had come from it was the fleshless hand of a skeleton. He opened his grinning mouth and spoke.

'Look, lads, if I was you I wouldn't bother going on. It's not really safe. Why don't you just nip off home . . .'

Suddenly his voice cut off with a yelp, and he was jerked backwards and disappeared with an audible pop.

The tribesmen gaped, and looked at each other in wonder. What the hell was going on?

Tarl was sweating heavily now. The hair on the copper plate was smoking and shrivelling, and fumes filled the hut. Angrily he spat out a few words and the wraith of Angnail materialised in front of him, seeming to dwarf him. He scowled furiously up at it.

'What the hell are you playing at?' he demanded.

The wraith seemed embarrassed.

'Well, really,' it blustered, 'making me scare the crap out of my own tribe! That's a real bastard's trick, that is! I haven't been dead five minutes, and already you're calling my spirit up! Do this, do that! I mean, I haven't even found out what it's like being dead yet!'

'Scare them?' asked Tarl in disbelief. 'Scare them? You couldn't frighten a four-day-old kitten! I've been to bed with more frightening things than you!'

'Look, I've never done this before, and . . .'

'Listen, chummy,' interrupted Tarl, nonchalantly twirling the Sword, 'I've got the weapon that took your life, I've got a lock of your hair, and I've got the Power. This means that as far as you are concerned, what I say goes. Now if you don't want to spend the next five eons haunting some miserable ruined cottage in the middle of the Nevacom Plains you'd better get on with it. Comprenez?'

The wraith seemed to go even paler, if that was possible, and looked quite sick. 'All right, all right! Keep your hair on!' it muttered, and then abruptly disappeared.

The tribesmen were all discussing what Angnail's visitation might portend when he suddenly reappeared above them. This time, however, he was about fifty feet high, and when he spoke his voice seemed to echo up from the depths of hell itself.

'Go back!' he wailed. 'All who enter the village will die! Go back whence we came!'

And then the waxen flesh of his face seemed to melt, vanishing like lard upon a hot stove until just the skull was left. His eyes burned like fire, and his tongueless mouth opened wide, and white clouds of vapour billowed forth, freezing whatever they touched. And then he screamed, the sound of a mortal soul in hellish torment.

'Go back!'

Suddenly the air was filled with foul wraiths and phantoms that soared and screamed and swooped and dived, grabbing for the tribesmen with skeletal hands as they struggled to control their rearing, terror-stricken horses. The putrid stench of rotten flesh made them gag and retch, and their ears rang with the clamour of demonic laughter and the screams of tortured souls.

As one man they turned their horses to the east and fled, their pace not slowing until they reached the banks of the River Menea. And in every man's head was the same thought. Sod this for a game of soldiers. And sod Nekros. I'm going home!

*

Angnail's wraith re-materialised inside the hut with a smug smile on what was left of its face.

'Brilliant!' it enthused. 'You should have seen 'em! They won't stop running until . . .'

'Yeah, you can bugger off now,' muttered Tarl, tipping the remnants of charred hair into the fire.

'You might at least say thank you,' complained the wraith, as it vanished in a flare of flame.

Tarl sighed heavily and began to struggle to his feet. His legs felt like rubber. Ronan was just helping him up when Tyson put her head through the door.

'They're here!' she said. 'Thirteen of them. It's show-time, folks!'

She disappeared, and Tarl clapped Ronan tiredly on the arm. 'Right, Nekros is all yours,' he said. 'Leave the rest to us. Oh, and don't forget the potion.' And then he followed Tyson out, leaving Ronan standing nervously alone in the hut.

They dismounted and tied their horses to the remnants of a fence, and then leaving two men to guard them Nekros led the other ten along the muddy track that was the main street of the village. It was deserted, and not a sound could be heard. The place seemed familiar, and Nekros was just beginning to wonder what on earth they were doing there when the silence was broken by a discordant off-key braying.

Peering at them from behind a ramshackle hut was a shabby brown donkey. One of the bowmen fired an arrow at it but the donkey ducked, then stared scornfully at them and redoubled its efforts.

'Karl, Velham, deal with that . . . noise,' ordered Nekros, and the two swordsmen drew their swords and walked purposefully after the donkey, which hastily withdrew round the corner. Smiling in anticipation they followed, while Nekros led the rest of his men towards the centre of the village.

The donkey had retreated to the next hut along. Karl gestured to the right. 'You go that way,' he said to Velham. 'I'll go this. We'll trap it.'

Velham nodded and strode to the opposite corner of the hut. As he walked round to the back he heard a small whimper that was cut off abruptly by a quick crunching noise. 'Klat!' he thought. 'Too late!' Shame. You couldn't mistake the distinctive sound made by something slicing through bone, and he had been looking forward to carving up that donkey. Still, maybe it wasn't dead yet. He jogged round the corner and screeched to a halt.

There on the ground right in front of him was Karl, with his sword arm sheared off at the elbow and his throat bitten clean through. And standing over him was the donkey, with blood all over its muzzle and something unpleasantly pink and stringy hanging out of its mouth. It looked up at Velham and its eyes seemed to blaze, and then it was leaping for his throat.

Velham opened his mouth and screamed.

Brogan stroked his horse and wished, not for the first time, that he had been picked to go with Angnail. He was damn' sure that the guy had buggered off south with his men. Angnail had the right ideas. He'd never been in favour of this raiding of poverty-stricken villages. He went for loot, gold and silver. That was the way to do it, by Brogan's reckoning. He wasn't as keen as some of his fellows on all this killing, and was quite relieved to have been made one of the horses' guards.

A sudden scream tore the air, and then died away in a horrid bubbling gurgle. Brogan stared towards the village. Sounded like the guys were at it again. He turned to say something to Haglad, the other guard, but was surprised to see he was draped over the fence, as though asleep. Klat! There was an arrow in his neck! Brogan opened his mouth to yell a warning to the others, and Tyson's second arrow went straight between his lips and burst through the back of his throat, killing him instantly.

Tyson wriggled out from the shadows of a collapsed hut and smiled to herself. Four down, eight to go. And then it would be up to Ronan.

Nekros had sent three of his men to search the eastern end of the village, and three to the west. He was standing in the deserted village square with the other two when the scream rang out. That in itself wouldn't have alarmed him, as screams of agony were fairly commonplace wherever his men went. But he was sure he had heard the soft twang of a bow shortly afterwards, and it sounded lighter than the bows his men carried.

Better be careful! Cautiously, he searched his memory for the words of a Spell of Searching, but as he muttered it he became aware that there was another magic force nearby. A very amateurish and shaky force, to be sure, but strong enough to resist his spell. He reached up and gently touched the Torque about his neck as if for reassurance.

What the hell was going on?

Tarl sat cross-legged on the open ground in front of a large but empty pig-sty at the eastern edge of the village. In front of him was the copper dish, which now contained a violet powder. In his left hand he held a jug of pig's blood poised over the powder. In his right hand he held the book. His lips were moving as he practised the words that he had to say, and his chest was moving under the impetus of a heart that was beating so rapidly that it threatened to burst through his rib-cage.

Three men came into view at the end of the street. As soon as they saw him one lifted a bow, but a second stopped him with an unpleasant smile and drew his sword. Apparently Tarl was harmless enough to provide them with some entertainment.

As they strode towards him Tarl thought he was going to be sick with fear. What if he screwed it up? The impulse to scramble to his feet and run was almost overpowering, but somehow he fought it down. Then with trembling hand he poured the pig's blood on to the powder and spoke the words.

Rogarth was highly pissed off with this village. He and his two companions had searched virtually the whole of the western side but hadn't found a single peasant, and Rogarth had a very low boredom threshold. Moodily he swung his viciously barbed sword, relishing the hissing sound it made as its razor-sharp edge cut through the air. If he didn't find someone to lacerate soon he was going to have to pick a fight with one of the other two . . .

And then the slight figure of a young woman stepped out from a doorway. Rogarth couldn't believe his eyes. This was something out of his dreams! She was slender, pretty, and was holding a sword. Oh, yes! True, she was about twenty or so, which was several years older than he liked them, but still, she was going to be an absolute joy to carve up. Licking his lips, Rogarth motioned to the other two to stay back. She was his! He took one pace forwards, and then something cannoned into his legs from the back, and the most god-awful screaming horrible pain tore through both of his calves . . .

Tyson glided past the ham-strung Rogarth, leaving him to Puss's tender mercies, and attacked the other two. They were both rooted to the spot by the sheer surprise of the donkey's attack and she was able to kill the first one with a single thrust. The second man made a quick recovery and was a skilled swordsman, but even so it was only seconds before she was able to open his throat with a neat backhand cut. She was surprised to find that Puss hadn't dispatched the ham-strung man but was standing there watching his death throes with evident enjoyment. She grimaced and finished him quickly with a single thrust.

'You're getting to be as bad as they are,' she admonished the donkey.

It looked at her steadily. 'You really wouldn't have liked his thoughts,' it said. 'Very unpleasant. He should have had more respect.'

She returned its stare, and suddenly she could have sworn that Puss was embarrassed. It shuffled its hooves and turned away.

'Well,' it mumbled, 'I'd better go and make sure that bollock-brain hasn't turned himself into a cabbage.' And with that it was trotting rapidly towards the other end of the village in search of Tarl.

Ronan stood in the large empty hut grasping the hilt of the Sword. He was a little worried. He'd taken it out of the scabbard a few times since the previous day's fight at the ferry, and each time it had behaved rather oddly. Triumphant singing and chanting had been interspersed with funereal dirges, strange crooning, and a lot of indecipherable muttering. Sometimes it would suddenly clam up, and once it seemed to be sobbing desperately. Ronan was beginning to think it was a bit deranged, and he'd discovered that the one thing which really saps your confidence is going into battle with a Singing Sword that is two arrows short of a quiver.

Taking a deep breath he drew it out, and was relieved to see that it was gleaming brightly and emitting a steady eager humming. As he watched the brightness increased and the humming grew louder and more eager. Nekros must be close!

Ronan pulled Anthrax's potion from his pocket and jerked the ring-pull loose. It opened with a light 'pop', and liquid foamed out all over his hands. Quickly he raised the can to his lips and drained the contents. It tasted foul and he could feel it foaming and bubbling all the way down to his stomach.

He strode to the door and peered out. There, stalking warily down the street outside with two of his tribesmen was his mortal enemy!

With rapidly beating heart and heavily frothing stomach Ronan waited for his moment.

Puss trotted round the corner and sighed with relief. There was Tarl, most definitely alive to judge by the energetic way he was throwing up the contents of his stomach. Puss trotted across and, carefully avoiding the unpleasant bits, nuzzled his side.

After a short while Tarl straightened up and wiped his mouth with the back of his hand. Then he gave Puss a shaky pat.

'So it worked then,' said the donkey, impressed despite himself.

'Yeah,' said Tarl proudly. 'It worked. I can actually do it. Transformations 'R' Us.'

And the two of them gazed at the pig-sty where three large and very pink pigs dressed in black warrior gear were happily arguing over who should get the muddy patch.

Nekros had just decided that maybe the village was deserted after all when there was a brief clash of swords and a loud and bubbly burp behind him. He swung round just in time to see one of his men falling with a dagger in his chest, while the second sagged to the ground clutching his stomach, blood welling between his fingers. And there, disappearing through the door of a nearby hut, was the black-skinned warrior.

So he was still alive! Klat! Angnail must have fouled up, and so must Kaldis and Bonaponere. Anthrax was right – the man was trouble. But now he was trapped in that hut.

Nekros opened his mouth and shouted for his men. His harsh voice rang round the streets and houses of the village but was met with silence. Not a creature moved, not a soul stirred. He waited, but it was as though his tribe had vanished from the face of the earth.

But Nekros wasn't particularly worried. Two of his best men had been ambushed and killed, another ten had vanished, the rest of the tribe were late, and he was apparently on his own against a warrior who the best wizard in the land had predicted might kill him. But he was confident. He knew how good a swordsman he was. The man wasn't yet born who could beat him in a straight fight, and although his magical powers might be a little on the shaky side he was good enough to hold his own with anyone but a high-class wizard.

Quickly he cast a Field of Force about himself. It was a bit of a shaky one, but it was strong enough to deflect any non-magical weapon. He could feel the other magical presence hovering at the eastern end of the village. It had an odd greenish tinge that gave an impression of nausea, and it felt decidedly unthreatening at the moment. Excellent! It was just him against the young upstart in the hut.

Sword in hand, Nekros strode confidently towards the door.

Tarl, Tyson and Puss stood miserably beside the remains of the well, listening to the ringing sword-blows that echoed round the village. When the first clashes had sounded they had felt full of confidence, but as the fight dragged on and on, sounding more and more ferocious, they had grown very worried. All three desperately wanted to go running to help Ronan, but all three had promised him that they would keep well out of Nekros's way. After all, Anthrax had forecast that Ronan could kill the guy, so they wouldn't really be needed.

Now they could hear the grunts and gasps of the two warriors. Ronan sounded desperate, and close to exhaustion. Tyson could stand it no longer.

'I've got to find out what's happening!' she muttered, and drew her sword, but Tarl caught her arm.

'That's no good,' he told her. 'There's a Field of Force around Nekros. Your weapons can't harm him!'

'We've got to do something!'

'Yeah, but it's going to need magic.' Tarl paused. 'Klat!' he continued, unhappily. 'It's gonna have to be me, isn't it?'

When Nekros had walked through the door of the hut the black warrior had been standing waiting for him, looking all proud and noble. You could just tell that he was waiting to make some trite little speech about good triumphing over evil, but Nekros hadn't stood around and waited. He had casually slammed a Mind-sting at him. This was his favourite spell, and the one he was best at. It had never failed him, but this time it just bounced off with no effect. The kid was protected! Apprehensively, he Probed and was relieved to find that it was a Shield Spell, a very strong one, but proof only against sorcery. The young warrior had no magical defence against weapons. Nekros snorted to himself with amusement. The fool was obviously hoping to best him in a straight fight! Well, he had a shock coming, then! Without warning, he attacked.

Ronan had been expecting Nekros to do a little of the taunting that he had used against his father. He hadn't expected the guy to storm straight in, sword in hand, and go for him like a bat out of hell. And not a plain ordinary bat out of hell either, but a blood-crazed, homicidal one with psychopathic tendencies. He had only just got the Sword up in time to prevent himself being sliced in half.

But as their two weapons clashed together for the first time the Sword had blazed with light and wailed vengefully. Nekros had stood rooted to the spot, an expression of absolute horror on his face, and Ronan had realised that Anthrax had put him on to a real winner. Now for the Word of Power . . .

It was then he realised that he had totally, utterly and completely forgotten the Word.

For several seconds Nekros had stood rooted to the spot. How, by all things evil, had Ronan managed to get his hands on the Sword? No, it couldn't be the same one! He had hidden it in the deepest darkest place he could find, surrounded by the strongest magic of which he was capable! Realisation had hit him like a torrent of ice-cold water. Anthrax! The Shield Spell had his stamp all over it. Suddenly the extent of the Wizard's duplicity was clear to him, and Nekros swore to himself that if he managed to get out of this alive, he would slice that *vart* of a sorcerer into a million pieces. *If* he got out alive.

Then he realised that things weren't as bad as he had thought. The kid was standing there with his mouth gaping open, but the only sounds that had emerged were several rather bubbly burps. He had the Sword but he obviously didn't know what to do with it, and he was looking about as happy as a fish with hydrophobia. Nekros still had a chance! He felt like a man whose doctor has just diagnosed cancer and then seconds later has said: 'Only kidding!' If he could just kill Ronan quickly . . .

Ronan didn't know how he managed to keep Nekros's blade away. Paralysing blows rained in from all sides at a speed he had never before encountered and with a strength that threatened to cleave straight through the Sword. His mind didn't have time to think. He was fighting purely by instinct. Somehow he managed to deflect every blow, but he was driven backwards, and he had no chance of going on the attack. It was all he could do to defend himself. Then he stumbled and fell. Nekros struck as quickly as a snake, and Ronan desperately threw the Sword up in front of his face. His enemy's blade smashed into the weapon with all of his evil strength behind it, finishing up within an inch of Ronan's forehead.

'Ha!' yelled Nekros, triumphantly.

'Klat!' swore Ronan, fearfully.

'Ouch!' yelped the Sword, painfully.

And then Ronan had scrambled to his feet and was backing away, cudgelling his brain for the Word. But try as he might it would not come to mind. Slowly, confidently, Nekros followed him, feinting once or twice and testing his defence like a cat toying with a mouse. Then he attacked again.

Gasping and grunting with the effort, Ronan defended. He knew without a shadow of doubt that Nekros was stronger, faster and more skilful. Already his arm was aching with the effort of wielding the Sword, his lungs were labouring to draw enough breath, and the sweat was running down his face and stinging his eyes. He blinked it away, then flung up the Sword, gasping as another awesome blow nearly knocked it clean out of his hands.

Nekros was driving him backwards again, and now his back was against the wall and there was nowhere left to go. Four huge blows came powering in at him, yet somehow he managed to deflect each one. But when the fifth one hammered at him his tired muscles could not react in time and he was a fraction slow. He managed to deflect it, but not enough, and a vicious pain stabbed through his left-hand side. Looking down, he saw the blood oozing from a deep cut under his ribs.

Nekros gave him a look of grudging respect. The kid was good! Any other warrior he had fought would have been lying dead with his blood seeping into the floor by now. But Nekros knew the fight was nearly over. He could see the despair in the young warrior's eyes. With a lazy smile he readied himself for the final assault, drew his sword back, and found that he was suddenly standing in a bed of nettles five feet deep.

When Tarl had peered nervously through the door of the hut he had seen instantly that Ronan was nearly spent. He had to do something effective, and do it quickly. He riffled through the book and blindly flung the first half-way suitable spell he could find at Nekros. Unfortunately, he got the words a bit wrong, and instead of a bed of flaming coals appearing under the guy's feet and consuming him, it was a bed of stinging nettles.

However, it was enough to distract Nekros. Seeing Tarl in the doorway he cursed and flung a Mind-sting at him. Somehow Tarl managed to conjure up a deflection, and the Mind-sting ricocheted upwards and hit a spider in the roof-thatch, giving it the worst headache in the whole of arachnid history. Nekros was about to follow it up with a Lightning Ball when Ronan slashed blindly at him with the Sword. The Force Field was strong enough to stop the blow but Nekros lost his concentration at the vital second, and a half-inch diameter ball of rather soggy lightning fizzled out from his finger-tips and nose-dived sadly into the ground.

Ronan backed away, keeping his eyes firmly fixed on his enemy. 'The Word!' he yelled to Tarl. 'I've forgotten the klatting Word!'

Tarl stared at him blankly. 'Don't look at me,' he yelled back. 'I never knew what it was.'

He ducked as Nekros fired a more effective lightning ball at him, but the evil warrior's aim was way off and it blasted harmlessly through the wall of the hut eight foot away, leaving a smoking hole. Then Ronan went on the attack, and Tarl began leafing desperately through the book, searching for a way of helping his friend.

Although the odds were now two against one, Nekros wasn't unduly worried. His Force Field Spell was shaky, but strong enough to prevent Ronan from hurting him. True, with the distraction of that little gimp slinging his second-rate spells at him he would find it harder to break through the kid's defence, but it was only a matter of time. And as for the gimp, Nekros could feel the shakiness of his magical power. He might be able to produce spells that would be irritating, but none that could damage him. Yes, perhaps it might be best to ignore the little gimp altogether and concentrate on killing Ronan. Let him do his worst!

Unwisely, Nekros went ahead with this plan and attacked Ronan yet again. Over the next few minutes he was to discover just how irritating Tarl's magic could be.

Deciding that a lot of very quick and easy spells might be better than something overpowering (which would probably only come shooting straight back at him redoubled in force), Tarl turned to the beginner's section of the book and went to work with a will. One moment Nekros was ferociously pressing home his attack, the next moment a bunch of flowers appeared from nowhere and hurtled into his face, and a large fish hit him on the back of the head. Then he discovered he suddenly had his own personal rain-cloud. After a few moments this disappeared and a very, very small forest fire started up in his beard, and then three large bright-red toadstools erupted out of his groin like volcanoes, exploding in a cloud of spores that started him sneezing helplessly. Next, a flock of tiny bright blue birds began orbiting his head, chirruping loudly, and then in the space of ten seconds he contracted mild forms of measles, chicken pox, whooping cough, and swine vesicular disease.

Even though these distractions made it very difficult for him to concentrate on his swordplay, Ronan was by now exhausted, and Nekros twice got past his guard. Unfortunately, on the first occasion, a coal scuttle materialised over his head, blinding him just as he was about to deliver the coup de grâce, and on the second his sword turned momentarily into a five-foot loofah which smacked wetly but harmlessly against Ronan's neck.

He did manage to fire off several spells in return, but although any one of them would have splattered Tarl into charred fragments, had it connected, Nekros was having one of his off-days and just couldn't quite get it right. For some reason, everything was going off at a ninety-degree angle to where he was aiming it.

However, after several minutes it was becoming obvious that, annoying as they were, the two of them could do him no real damage. Nekros decided that it really was time to stop messing about. All he needed was to concentrate on one massive spell that would blow the little gimp apart. He paused, and runnels of black light began seeping out from his nostrils and mouth, gelling into an unedifying sphere of darkness that whirled about his head.

Tarl stared, impressed despite himself. This was potent stuff! And then he suddenly realised that he had about a fifth of a second to find a device against the black mage-spell that was about to be blasted at him. In one rapid movement he screamed, ducked, and fired off the only spell he could think of.

Tyson and Puss watched anxiously as a massive black fireball exploded through the roof of the hut and rocketed up to the sky.

'Right,' said the donkey. 'My turn.'

It trotted purposefully up to the doorway and peered through. The place looked as though it had been lived in for months by a family of *varts*. There were gaping holes in the roof, walls, and even the floor. Steaming yellow goo was plastered all over one wall. The floor was littered with strange items, including dead nettles, bunches of flowers, and several large fish. At one end of the hut icicles were hanging from the rafters, and at the other end a glowing orange ball of flame was bumbling aimlessly along the top of the wall.

To one side, Ronan was leaning on the Sword and panting as though he had just run thirty miles. He was soaked with sweat and streaked with dirt, and a wound in his left-hand side was bleeding badly. Next to him stood Tarl. He was panting as well, and his face wore the haunted wild-eyed look of someone who has reached the end of their tether. Opposite them stood the furious Nekros, who looked if anything even worse. His clothes were singed and burnt, his hair had turned a strange yellow colour, his face was covered in boils, and he seemed to have developed an outsize pair of female breasts.

'You're taking your time,' called the donkey to Ronan.

'He's forgotten the klatting Word of Power!' yelled Tarl.

'Good job I'm here, then,' said the donkey, calmly. 'It's "Shikara", if that's of any help.'

Nekros threw it a look of horrified disbelief, but before he could fling himself back into the attack, Ronan had brandished the Sword aloft, gasping, 'Shikara! Shikara!'

For a second, nothing happened, and then the Sword blazed as though it had turned to flame. It seemed to leap from Ronan's hand, burying itself point-first in the ground between the two warriors. For a moment it stood there quivering, and its keening wail turned into a triumphant chant of victory. And then it shimmered and seemed swiftly to expand, growing, widening, changing before their disbelieving eyes, until in its place there stood a woman, beautiful but terrible in her anger, with long cascades of auburn hair and eyes that flashed a furious fire. Ronan and Tarl stared at her, awe-struck, but Nekros was backing away from her with a look of abject terror on his face.

'Shikara!' he whispered.

'Nekros,' she purred. 'How nice to see you again. After all this time!'

'I . . . I can explain,' he stammered, still backing away.

'Oh, sure,' she laughed, mirthlessly. 'I bet! You betrayed me, Nekros. Used me, then played me false. I've spent five hundred years imprisoned in that sword. Five. Hundred. Years.' Power seemed to emanate from every pore in her body and the air crackled with static. Her voice took on an evil, malignant tone. 'Nekros,' she hissed, 'you . . . are . . . a . . . RAT!'

And before their horrified eyes, Nekros dwindled and shrank. Sleek hairs sprouted from his skin and a naked ugly tail emerged thrashing from the base of his spine. His deep-voiced pleading turned gradually shriller and shriller, until it was no more than a pitiful squeak, and then he was simply a small and insignificant brown rat grovelling at their feet.

Shikara turned to Ronan. 'Kill him!' she ordered. But as Ronan looked down at the sad creature that had been his mortal enemy

244

and the slayer of his father, he felt only pity. He shook his head.

And then the donkey came trotting across. Placing one hoof on the rat it reached down, and Ronan winced as its teeth nipped lethally together. Then it lifted its head and began slowly chewing.

'Ugh!' said Tarl, with feeling. The donkey stopped chewing and looked at him. The rat's tail was hanging out of one side of its mouth like a piece of spaghetti.

'Look,' it said, 'I'm starving! OK?' And chewing hard, it walked out of the hut door, looking for a bit of privacy.

Shikara turned to Ronan. 'Hey,' she said, in a voice like honey dripping off toast, 'I like your ass!'

'He's called Puss,' replied the warrior. 'And he's not mine. He's a friend.'

'I'm not talking about the donkey,' she said, and Ronan realised that she was staring at his rear with a predatory and hungry look. He stirred uneasily, and then winced as a shaft of pain shot through his side.

Shikara noticed the blood seeping slowly from the wound, and stretched out one hand as if to touch it. 'Poor boy!' she said, with a lazy smile. 'Never mind, I can soon take your mind off that!'

Ronan began to shake his head, but Shikara was not the sort of person who was prepared to have her first flirtation in five hundred years end in rejection. For a moment she scowled and then her eyes flashed light, and suddenly he was staring at her with a totally blank expression, his mouth hanging loosely open.

'As I said, I've been stuck in that sword for five hundred years,' she purred, 'And that's a long time to go without love!' She began to stroke Ronan's chest with a proprietorial air. And that, of course, was the moment that Tyson chose to walk into the hut.

In an expensively furnished room in a southern city, the six smartly dressed men had been watching an image of the scenes in the hut. As Puss swallowed the last sad remnants of Nekros, five of the men began noisily arguing. The sixth stabbed out some numbers on the dial of the crystal ball that stood on the table in front of him, and then held up his hand for silence. Instantly, the others were quiet.

'Acquisitions, please,' he said to the female face that appeared in the crystal. Then he turned to the other five enquiringly. 'Comments, anyone?' he asked.

'Nekros is dead!' one of the others burst out. 'And without him, our whole strategy is in ruins! There's no one else who has his capabilities!'

'But there is,' said the first man, before speaking into the crystal. 'Acquisitions? I want Shikara. Priority one. What? No, she's re-emerged. And she is exactly what we need. Far more suitable than Nekros. Get her for me.'

Tyson was staring at Shikara like an emperor staring at a courtier he has just caught pissing behind the imperial throne.

'Just what exactly do you think you are doing?' she asked, in a voice coated in permafrost.

Shikara was still stroking Ronan's chest as he stared blankly ahead. 'I'd hate to see a body like this wasted on someone who didn't appreciate it,' she smiled.

Tyson's knuckles whitened on the hilt of her sword, but Tarl laid a restraining hand on her arm. Now that he was going with the Power instead of resisting it he was getting quite receptive, and he could feel a massive magical force about this woman, much bigger than Nekros had possessed. He was well aware that she could blast them both apart with one hand tied behind her back if she chose.

'Now, you just hold on a minute!' he began, and then stopped as Shikara turned to stare at him. He had only seen a look like that on someone's face once in his whole life. It had been in Goblin City, when he had been playing cards with a group of orcs. The stakes had got quite high during one hand, and there was a small fortune in the pot. Only he and a large mountain-orc were left in. The mountain-orc had triumphantly laid down his three aces, only for Tarl to cover them with his flush of hearts. As he had scooped up the money, happily burbling away about people who ought to learn to play the game, Tarl had looked up and seen this very same look in the orc's eyes. Then, as now, it meant, 'If you say one more word, my friend, even a tiny, harmless word like "but" or "oh", you will die immediately in a particularly horrible way. Comprenez?'

Desperately, he tried to think of something clever and cunning

246

to do, but then Shikara threw a condescendingly smug smile at Tyson.

'I think this hunk deserves someone a bit more feminine for a change, don't you, darling!' she drawled, giving Ronan another caress.

'Get your fat hands off him!' Tyson snarled, but before she could do anything there was a blinding flash, and both Shikara and Ronan had vanished.

Tyson gaped uncomprehendingly as the air rushed in to fill the gap where they had been with a little 'pop'. Then her face set like stone. For a moment Tarl wasn't sure whether she was going to burst into tears or cut his head off. To his relief, she did neither, but just slumped to the floor with despair written in every line of her body.

'The bastard!' she muttered.

'It wasn't Ronan's fault,' Tarl said forcefully. 'That bitch put a spell on him. I mean, you could see that! Honestly, the guy's crazy about you! But he was wounded. He just had no resistance left!'

But he couldn't seem to get through to her. She just sat there, slumped dejectedly against the wall. If ever a sculptor had wanted to carve a statue called 'Abject Misery', she would have made the perfect model.

Tarl squatted down, grabbed her by her shoulders and shook her violently to and fro until her eyes at last focused on him, and he had her attention again.

'Listen!' he yelled. 'He loves you! But he's no match for some spell-casting vamp like her! He needs our help! If you want him back, then we've got to go and fight for him!'

And so they did.

But that's another story.

APPENDIX 1 – GLOSSARY

ALAXL – A large and very fierce semi-intelligent lizard that inhabits the forests of the more tropical regions of Midworld. They are savage killers, but as they have a brain the size of a walnut located half-way down their spine they are also remarkably stupid. If you tell an attacking *alaxl* that you are not really a defenceless human but a thirty-foot dragon who could eat them for breakfast, it will be at least three hours before they realise that there is just a chance you might be lying.

APATODONS – Massive elephant-like creatures found throughout Iduin. Their unusual behaviour is caused by three factors: their highly gregarious nature, their remarkable stupidity, and their appalling memory. Apatodons spend a vast amount of time wandering around looking for other *apatodons* to be with, but they can never quite remember what kind of creature they actually are, or how they are supposed to behave. They have a habit of latching on to the first thing they come across and copying it, in the firm belief that this is probably what they should be doing, and this can make them very dangerous. Should you come across one in a forest standing stock still, convinced that it is a tree or a rock or something, there is of course little danger. However, many people have drowned after their boat has been capsized by the wash from an *apatodon* that is vainly trying to follow its fellow salmon upstream, and in the mountainous regions of Southern Iduin the final sound heard by many an unfortunate traveller is the baffled trumpeting of a plummeting *apatodon* that is desperately trying to work out why it isn't gliding gently away from the cliff with all the other eagles.

BAR-BASTARD – A tavern game that rather resembles billiards for six people. The aim is to do horrible things to your opponents' balls and generally to humiliate and upset them. This is not a good game to play with friends if you want to keep them. It is definitely not a good game to play with enemies, unless you want your cue to be forcibly jammed into an unpleasant part of your anatomy. If you feel you must play, we recommend that you wear a full suit of armour and have an excellent lawyer with you at all times.

BAQ D'ORIAN WIDOWMAKER, BLACK TEASER — see SPIDERS.

CAVE-TROLLS — Eight foot of rock-hard muscle, with brains to match, cave-trolls are horribly violent and bad-tempered creatures that get into fights at the drop of a hat. However, when extremely drunk they often end up staggering about being nice to people and hugging them. This is a great embarrassment to their friends. Should you ever get kissed by a drunken *cave-troll*, his companions will probably come across and apologise profusely for his behaviour before kicking the crap out of you.

FESTA — A long, creeper-like vine that grows in forests, where it is found in large numbers hanging from trees like long green ropes. It is used as an aid to locomotion by many arboreal-dwelling creatures, especially monkeys. Unfortunately for these monkeys the Giant Monkey-Eating Spider has, over the years, evolved a tongue that is long, green, extremely sticky, and virtually indistinguishable from a festa vine. These loathsome arachnids tend to hang around in the tree-tops with open mouth and tongue hanging down to the forest floor, waiting for dinner to climb aboard. Anyone who is naive enough to think of Nature as being rather sweet and wonderful should try discussing this viewpoint with any of the squealing, terrified monkeys they see being hauled rapidly upwards past them through the branches toward the gaping maw of the spider above.

FLAK — Minor Behanian deity, with the body of a man and the head of a wart-hog. Unsurprisingly, he was a little pissed off about his looks, and spent the whole of his existence in a foul mood. Flak is the God of Temper Tantrums.

KALADION — A musical instrument, rather like a cross between bagpipes and an accordion. It looks extremely difficult to play well, but this is misleading as it is in fact impossible. The sound produced has been likened to a tom-cat being put through a mincer. Good *kaladion* players are hard to find, as anyone attempting to play in public normally gets a sword through the chest from the nearest enraged music-lover.

KAHEN THE SPOILT — An elven princess, Kahen once spent the entire Gross National Product of her father's kingdom on clothes and shoes in one afternoon during a state visit to Cydor. A month later, she persuaded her father to declare war on Cydor when a shop in Ilex refused to replace a pair of *wiggat*-skin high-heeled sling-backs after one of the heels had come off. The War of Kahen's Heel nearly bankrupted both countries and ended in the Shoe Riots of '74, when an irate populace burned down every shoe-shop and lynched every shoe-salesman that they could find. In some parts of Cydor it is still an indictable offence to be found in possession of a cobbler's last, or of one of those sloping metal stools on which you rest your feet to try on shoes, and calling someone a 'shoe salesman' is asking for a punch in the face.

KALAYA — A cage-bird popular throughout Midworld, and also known as the Brown-nosed Creeper. The *kalaya* is a small flightless bird normally found in urban gardens. As a defence against humans it has evolved a quite extraordinary birdsong that sounds remarkably like human speech and is most attractive to the sort of humans who might otherwise enjoy killing little birds. For example, its dawn song sounds exactly like 'Hey, you're-an-incredibly-handsome-guy, you-know-that?', whilst its warning cry is: 'Gee, just-look-at-those-muscles, I-bet-all-the-girls just-eat-out-of-your-hand!' Its evening song is almost unprintable, but includes phrases such as: 'Wow, yeah, do-it-to-me big-boy!' The *kalaya* is an incredibly popular pet with the more macho (and lonely) sort of male.

KATIMO — A large mammal native to Iduin, the *katimo* has ugly wrinkled skin and sparse curly ginger hair, and looks like nothing so much as a giant scrotum on legs. The male of the species has an extremely small, almost non-existent, penis, and is a very shy animal, hiding in remote mountain areas where it is less likely to be laughed at. '*Katimo*' has become a word of derision used by the dark-skinned southern folk for those who they suspect may lack genitalia.

KLAT – An extremely rude orchish swear-word which, on account of the current obscenity laws, we are not allowed to translate.

LENKAT – A huge predatory mammal with sleek greasy hair and row upon row of gleaming, grinning teeth. It is often used as a particularly vicious form of game-show host.

MAGE-DECK – A magical device of orcish origin which can turn a drum kit or a double-bass into a device which is capable of demolishing town walls by sound-waves alone. Like most orcish magic, *mage-decks* were developed as a way of spicing up their parties, and orcs reckon they haven't had a really good time unless at least one eardrum has been permanently damaged by the sound-system.

MULAMPOS – A meat dish made with remarkably hot spices from the Southlands. It is the only dish that is required by law to carry a government health warning when included on menus. Travellers who are tempted to try it are warned to stay extremely close to good toilet facilities for the next forty-eight hours, and would be well advised to alert their next-of-kin.

PAKAS – A huge carnivorous bird. To quote from the *Pink Book of Ulay*:

> The Pakas of the Forests of Frundor was a huge and loathsome bird that settled in this region during the First Age. Great terror did they cause, for many were the size of dragons, and they did feed upon the flesh of Men, serving them up with wedges of giant lemons from the Gardens of Delmonte. Heavy were their depredations, and men were forced to flee, forsaking their homes, until none still dwelt here. Then did these fell birds resort to feeding on whatever foul or putrid flesh they could find, and their lemon wedges

availed them naught . . .

By the Second Age, few now remained, and these were
mere shadows of the former birds, being less in size. Yet still
their eggs remained enormous, and thus were they known as
Pakas, from their cry 'Pa! Kas!', which in the Ancient
Tongue means 'God! That hurt!' Yet on occasion did a bird
like that of yore appear. Such a one was the bird which
terrorised the city of Minas Welvair in the east. Many folk
did it devour, before the warrior Drax the Strange sliced off
its head. It nested in the huge green bay-tree that grew
outside the city walls, and thus was it known to the folk of
Minas Welvair as the Green Bay Pakas . . .

Also an insult. If someone calls you *'pakas-breath'*, you can
safely assume that they are not over-enamoured with your oral
hygiene.

PATA — Dry, thorny grass that grows in desert conditions. It is
about as edible as barbed wire, but is only half as nourishing.

SEVENTH DAY HEDONISTS — A religious order dedicated to the
observance of the rule 'Six days shalt thou keep holy, and on the
seventh day shalt thou party!' In more modern times the six days
are usually taken up with getting rid of the hang-over. The order
can easily be recognised by their distinctive hooded robes of
lime-green with orange swirls, and can often be found on city
street-corners, begging for Alka-seltzers.

SKEELS — A form of spearboard played with throwing-knives.
Also known in some areas as 'fat-bastard', a reference to those
who play the game. Porgo Lardbelly, the all-time champion of
Minas Tryk, was so obese that the only way he could enter and
leave his favourite tavern was by being rolled through the door
sideways. He was frequently employed as the bouncer there, and
would deal with persistent trouble-makers by leaning gently
against them until they were dead.

SPIDERS — Readers are advised to consult the pages of a reference
work such as Maxon the Small's *Vita Horribilorum* (available

from Succubi Publications (Ilex) Ltd, price 15 tablons), from which this extract is taken.

Whereas after making love the thoughts of most of us would turn to pizza, it is a sad fact that in many species of spider the female likes nothing better than to polish off her own partner after (and sometimes during) sexual congress.

Take, for example, the Black Teaser, a spider found in the Southern Cydorian Desert. The female, which is quite large, with long shapely legs and soft black hair, lures the mates of other Black Teasers to her web, has sex with them, and then instantly devours them. In the meantime her own mate, a somewhat smaller and more insignificant spider, scuttles about the place muttering unhappily to himself, cleaning and tidying the web, doing the shopping, and making endless cups of tea for the female. After several years of this, however, he frequently snaps, and chases off after the first other female he sees, where, of course, he ends his life happily but abruptly as a post-coital snack.

There is a lesson in this for all of us.

Maxon the Small, it should be noted, had a particularly unhappy married life, and students of ecology should take his musings on the sex-lives of Midworld fauna with a large pinch of Tibrethian salt.

STONE-BUSH — A dense shrubby plant that grows to a height of six feet or so. Its fruit are probably the most luscious things in the whole world to look upon, having a soft velvety skin of an enticing golden-orange colour that seems to promise the taste sensation of a life-time. Unfortunately, underneath this skin the fruit has the consistency of concrete (hence the name of the shrub), and those poor unfortunates who have never seen the fruit before and have been taken in by its appearance are guaranteed to lose a few teeth. Indeed, poor and unscrupulous orthodontists have been known to sneak round town in the dead of night sowing stone-bush seeds, in the sure knowledge that when the shrubs grow and fruit next year business is bound to improve.

TABLONS — The unit of currency throughout Midworld. The

rather odd system of 59 bronze *tablons* to a silver one, and 17 silver *tablons* to a gold, was devised by a group of young, thrusting merchant bankers from Far Tibreth. They devised such a complex system so that the less intelligent folk of the world could be more easily short-changed. This was a phenomenally successful ploy, and they all got very rich, married incredibly beautiful (but rather vacuous) women, and had lots of none-too-bright children.

However, when these children reached maturity and took over the family businesses, they found that the financial system their fathers had devised was a little tricky to understand, and they were all taken for a rather expensive ride by the children of the less intelligent folk, who had grown up street-smart and canny. Thus every generation or so, the rich banking families were forced to change places with the less well-off. This phenomenon was known to everyone except merchant bankers as 'A jolly good thing, too!'

TABOGHEE BUSH — A frequently cultivated shrub with dense masses of white, gorgeously scented flowers. The *taboghee* is native to the remote island of Scawdror, which is famed for its unusual flora. The island has evolved without bees (or indeed insect life of any kind), and so the indigenous plants have been forced to rely on other creatures to pollinate them. The *taboghee* had evolved flowers with the most gorgeous, almost orgasmic, scent, and humans are unable to pass near them without burying their noses in the flowers and breathing in this perfume. The pollen is thus transported from plant to plant on the nasal hairs of humans. It is easy to identify someone who has been sniffing the plant by the large clump of greenish pollen hanging down – hence the common expression: 'you've got Taboghee up your nose.'

TRANN — Another minor Behanian deity, Trann is the Goddess of Lost Causes, and is most frequently invoked by those who are really deep in the mire. Interestingly, the prefix 'tran' seems to share this lost cause connotation in most other worlds. Examples in our own language include transit lounges (where luggage is lost with monotonous regularity), Public Transport (especially British Rail), and Tranmere Rovers.

VART – Large rodent with a strong predilection for alcohol. When sober, and alone, a *vart* is as mild-mannered and inoffensive as anything. However, *varts* are usually found in large groups late at night when, after vast quantities of drinks, they roam the hedge-rows singing, yelling, and making raucous and frequently obscene suggestions to innocent rabbits. They are slovenly by nature, and their burrows are usually full of empty tins, trays of half-finished take-away *mulampos*, dirty washing, and soiled nappies. They make appalling parents, frequently forgetting about their young for days at a time, and there have been numerous sad cases of newly born *varts* found lying unattended in their own squalor. Hence the old Midworldian saying, 'You smell like a week-old *vart*!'

WIGGAT – A small furry animal so rare that even *it* doesn't believe that it exists. *Wiggats* can occasionally be seen sitting on tree branches in the more inaccessible parts of the forest with worried frowns on their faces, undergoing acute identity crises. Should you be lucky enough to see a *wiggat* in the wild, do avoid making loud noises or sudden moves, as they are nervous little creatures, and any sudden shock can often result in them bursting into tears.

APPENDIX 2 – ELVES

There are two branches of the elven race commonly found in Midworld; the wood-elves, *Homo Viridis Galadrialis*, and the high elves, *Homo Viridis Cannabinus*. As their name suggests, wood-elves are much more at home in the countryside. They love forests, and frequently build their houses in trees. High elves, on the other hand, are city folk as a rule. Faced with having to climb a tree, they would probably fall out of it and lie there giggling (hence the expression 'out of his tree').

For information on elven physiology and behaviour, the definitive text is generally regarded to be *Elfwatching*, by Morris the Bald. We would like to thank Succubi Publications (Ilex) Ltd for permission to quote the following extract concerning elves and the sea:

Much has been written in other chronicles about the almost magnetic attraction the sea has for elves – but never before has the true reason for this attraction been set down. The elven race, although visually similar in many ways to Homo sapiens, has a quite distinct physiology, and their metabolism is surprisingly different. For example, they are able to break alcohol down rapidly by means of an enzyme secreted by their pancreas, which combines with it to form a skin pigment similar to melanin. Thus elves are able to drink a skinful of ale at a party without turning a hair, and wake up next day with no after-effects at all, save for a pretty cool tan. Salt-water, however, is a different kettle of fish. The chloride radical acts as a very powerful stimulant, and its presence in the bloodstream leads to the formation of a large number of toxins. In other words, salt-water gets an elf as pissed as a vart, and leaves him with the mother of all hangovers next day. Even a sea breeze is enough to leave him giggling helplessly after ten minutes.

For most elves, this is no problem. They are an inland race and tend to keep away from the sea, apart from the more extreme social occasions such as stag-nights or teenage parties. But for the unfortunate few who become addicted to brine, there is little that can be done.

Elfwatching contains many other fascinating insights into various aspects of elven behaviour, including aggression (chapter 4), food (chapter 7), and sex (chapters 2, 3, 5, 6, 8, 9, 11–17, and 19). It is available from all good scriptoria, priced 9 *tablons*.

APPENDIX 3 – ORCS

Orcs, or *Homo neanderthalis ebrius*, are around five and a half feet high, with bandy legs and hunched backs, dark grey skins, clawed hands, yellow slits for eyes, and green fang-like teeth. Their life-style is summed up by their motto: 'Born to fight, live to party, dying for a drink'. In fact their whole life is based around having a good time and getting as drunk as possible. Orcish, a harsh, guttural language that sounds like a chain-saw coughing up phlegm, has twenty-nine different words for a hangover. These range from *graznik* (a dull headache which disappears after half an hour) to *kushganazg* (those room-spinning stomach-emptying head-down-the-latrine jobs that last all day).

Generations of orcs have consumed so much alcohol that it has become a natural part of their body chemistry. Their cells are full to bursting with it, and as a result their chromosomes are so pissed that they couldn't tell a gamete from a gynaecologist or a zygote from a zebra. Thus they are genetically unstable, and mutations such as stripy skin, horns, or extra limbs often occur.

Orc drinking sprees are legendary. Orcs do not have stag-nights. They have stag-months, where they go on a town-crawl spending three days drinking continuously in each town. This love of a good bender has spread into all facets of their behaviour. For example, the orcish equivalent of the human general or the dwarf warleader is the *Uzmak-kchan* which means, when literally translated, 'party-giver'. The reason for this can be traced back several hundred years. In those days, the mountain-orcs used to party for several months continuously until the booze ran out. Then, led by the giver of the party, they would all come surging out from their filthy lairs under the mountains, march off to the nearest town that was likely to have a good supply of booze, and lay siege to it. When the town fell[1], they would continue the party

---

[1] Which never took long. The defenders would find it almost impossible to sleep at night as the noise coming from the partying orcs outside the city walls was indescribable. They would normally give in after four or five days just to get a decent night's rest.

inside the town walls until the booze ran out again, and then they would march off to the next town. A popular hero still is the legendary party-giver Gaz the Tall, who in AD 785[1] led his followers on a ten-month binge that devastated every major city in Baq d'Or. It was at this time that Welbug changed its name to Temperance City and banned all alcoholic beverages. However, Gaz the Tall still laid siege and, when the city fell, all supplies of grapes, wheat, barley, potatoes, apples and elderflowers were impounded. The city's name was changed again by the orcs to Home-brew-ville and for weeks the city hummed and gurgled with the sounds and smells of a thousand illicit stills and back-street breweries. Yeast was changing hands at thirty *tablons* an ounce, and innocent folk were murdered for their isinglass finings. This year came to be known in the Orcish calendar as the Year of the Living Dangerously, for many an orc was laid low by a dodgy pint.

For those interested in learning more concerning orcs, further information will be available in Morris the Bald's thoroughly researched new book, *Orcwatching*, which will be published next year when Morris has finally recovered from the hangover.

---

[1] AD – After Drinkies.